The Enchanting Nanny

K. Sterling

To Gabriel

Love and happy reading!

K. Sterling

For Roshni, Reese Ryan, and Leigh Carron. This series wouldn't be possible without your amazing support, inspiration, and friendship.

And my deepest gratitude to Melissa. She's carried me over the finish line again, and I am blessed to count her as a friend.

Finally, for my editor, Charles Griemsman. Thank you for helping me shine and making every book fun and feel like a dream come true.

The Enchanting Nanny

by K. Sterling

Illustrations by @Irisartss

The Enchanting Nanny Playlist

Be My Baby	The Ronettes
Fell In Love With A Girl	The White Stripes
If I Could Ride A Bike	Park Bird, Chevy
Strawberry Blond	Mitski
Cosmic Love	Florence + The Machine
Holocene	Bon Iver
Pretty Girl	Clairo
The First Taste	Fiona Apple
The Rain (Supa Dupa Fly)	Missy Elliot
Marceline	Willow
We'll Never Have Sex	Leith Ross
Kingston	Faye Webster
Cry To Me	Solomon Burke
Crush	Jennifer Paige

Content Warnings

Dear reader,

This love story is meant to be *fun* and filled with the promise of summer. But a few moments might be triggering for some readers. There are very brief discussions of the loss of a spouse and a child due to an accident, cancer, and death of a parent. Please take care because no reader should ever be harmed in the making of a book.

Love and happy reading,
    K. Sterling

Chapter One

Agnes Cameron had many nice things. Born into one of the wealthiest families in America, she'd been pampered and pandered to before she could speak her first words. But Agnes hadn't had many *good* things in her life.

Yet.

Her name was June and she was so much better than good. *Everything* changed for Agnes the day they met.

Agnes's eyes had dried out from staring at The Killian House's front door as she waited in the foyer. After months of forms, interviews, classes, and home visits, Agnes had been approved to adopt June. A social worker was due at noon with her, but it seemed surreal, having finally reached such a *big* moment. Agnes could barely believe that she'd been deemed competent enough or worthy of being anyone's mother, let alone a child as clever and as special as June.

"You're not getting cold feet, are you?" her brother, Walker, whispered from behind her. They were waiting, along with Walker's husband, Fin, and their triplets, Amelia, Beatrice, and

Charlotte. The Killian House's butler, Pierce, and the house-keeping staff had also gathered. The foyer was filled with excited whispers as everyone waited to welcome the newest Cameron.

Agnes shook her head and snorted. "Not at all. I've been ready for months, but all the home visits and interviews... You saw how long all of that took. I'm just shocked that it's finally over," she said, earning a sigh from Walker.

"I told you we could have found a faster, more private way to go about this."

Agnes turned and cut her eyes at him. "And I told you, I want to do this right and find a child from *this* city who's been waiting for a home."

Plus, it didn't seem fair to Agnes to cut the line when there were so many parents out there who deserved a child more. And she didn't want an infant or a toddler with mysterious origins. She wouldn't be able to live with herself if she found out she'd stolen someone's child or that her child's mother had been a victim of human trafficking. There were just too many awful possibilities and Agnes had a strong aversion to the unknown, in general.

Instead, Agnes had followed the rules for once, trusting the foster care system and remaining as emotionally detached as possible until she was certain it was truly happening. Agnes understood that as a Cameron there wouldn't have been any barriers with a private adoption thanks to her wealth and privilege. But she assumed the foster care system had hurdles for good reasons.

She had passed, though, with the understanding that Agnes and June would be living at The Killian House temporarily until their new home on East 63rd Street was completed. Many of the approved renovations were underway, but Agnes had put a number of major design decisions on hold until she knew *who* her child was.

Agnes had had a beautiful glimpse of June during their first meeting. Mary Wilson's foster home had looked like all the other rowhouses on the street, but it might have been the loudest house in Harlem. Not loud in an aggressive or disturbing way, though. Pop music had blared from an upstairs window with someone banging on a piano's keys in one of the front rooms. A trio of young boys with neon water guns chased each other around the side of the house.

The occasional laugh or shout had come from the backyard or inside, adding to the buzzing, hive-like energy. It was far from the orderly calm of The Killian House, yet Agnes was drawn to the warmth and the tight little community she sensed behind the faded front door as she climbed the stoop.

"We keep things pretty relaxed and casual around here, as you can see," Mary had informed Agnes as she was given a tour of the downstairs common rooms. "Most of the kids are out back, including June, but they're playing *Just Dance* upstairs if you're in the mood to work up a sweat."

"I think I'll start out back," Agnes said quietly, earning a nod from Mary. Agnes had already selected June for possible adoption, and Mary had suggested that it would be best if their first meeting was informal. She explained that there would be less pressure and June would act naturally if the kids all assumed Agnes was there to check on Mary or to observe conditions inside the house.

"The kids are used to social workers or doctors and students dropping in for visits," Mary said. "Take your time and give me a shout if you have any questions."

Agnes ducked her head. "Thanks, I will," she said, then made her way down the hall to the back door. She heard more laughter from the backyard and was smiling as she eased the door open and leaned around it to get a look. The narrow yard was littered with balls and there was a chunky plastic slide and a set of swings. Half a dozen children ranging from older toddlers to a young boy Agnes assumed was eleven or twelve were playing in the yard.

But Agnes's gaze caught on the little girl sitting on the back steps. She was wearing overalls and hugged a notebook as she watched the other children. Agnes cleared her throat softly and carefully sat down next to her.

"Hi. I'm Agnes. You look like you know what's going on around here," she said, earning a quick nod from the girl. Her sleek black hair had been cut into an adorable bob that swung around her jaw. She had warm, tawny-colored skin and Agnes was momentarily trapped in her big brown eyes. They were quick and bright as the girl sized Agnes up. She must have decided that Agnes was safe because she scooted closer after taking a quick look around.

"My name is June. I've been here almost as long as Josiah and I can always tell who's getting a home when new parents come to visit."

"You can?" Agnes asked and the girl offered her a much firmer nod.

"I've been right the last four times." June's neck stretched while she searched the yard, then pointed at a tiny Black girl by the swings. She was wearing a pink shirtdress and matching leggings and her hair was braided with little pink ribbons. "That's Joy. She's the youngest, but she can already read and she's easy, she never gives Ms. Mary any trouble."

"I see..." Agnes's brows jumped. Joy looked like she was only three or four. "What about you?" She asked, but June's lips twisted before she shook her head.

"I can read high school books and I *never* get in trouble, but I'm too old now. I'm eight."

Agnes stifled a groan and covered it with a thoughtful hum. They were sharing an unguarded moment because June didn't think Agnes was a prospective parent. "Is that so?"

"Yeah. People usually want a baby boy or a little girl who's close to a baby, but not as much work as a baby. I'm small, but I'm already eight so I'll probably stick around and help Ms. Mary until I'm old enough to go out on my own."

"Oh?" Agnes had to blink back tears. "And what do you think you'd like to do once you're old enough to go out on your own?"

"I'm gonna be a foster mom like Ms. Mary so more kids like me can have a home and I want to read books."

"That's—" Agnes's voice caught and she coughed, her heart aching over June's selflessness. "For a living? Or as a hobby?"

That earned another shrug and June's face scrunched. "I haven't decided yet, but I can read really fast and reading's my favorite thing in the world."

"I think it might be mine too... Or art," Agnes murmured, her eyes narrowing as she thought back through her recent reads. Unfortunately, Agnes couldn't think of any that might interest June. "I've been reading a lot of memoirs lately myself."

"I read those sometimes. I like fantasy and mythology."

"Oh! Me too!"

"Have you read *Percy Jackson*?" June asked excitedly, forgetting the other kids in the yard as she turned and focused all her attention on Agnes. Her brown eyes grew brighter and glittered with excitement. Agnes had clearly found the key to this particular child's heart. And it was thrilling for Agnes to have found it so quickly and easily. She wasn't feigning her own excitement as she leaned in closer.

Agnes shook her head. "No, is it any good?"

"It's a whole series! There are seven books and I have all of them. You can borrow *The Lightning Thief*. I'll go get it!" June said abruptly, then scrambled to her feet. Agnes rose and leaned against the railing as she watched the girl race back into the house.

"Okay... I'll wait here."

"Slow down, June! Where's the fire?" Mary asked as she joined Agnes on the back stoop. She was shaking her head and laughing. "That girl... Let me guess, she wants to show you a book."

"*The Lightning Thief.* She's loaning it to me," Agnes supplied and Mary looked impressed.

"She must like you. That book is June's most prized possession." She gave Agnes a loaded look, then checked to make sure no one was in listening distance. "You make sure she gets it back if you leave here with it. Or else I'm going to have to hunt you down." She teased.

"You feel free to hunt me down if you need anything at all, Ms. Wilson," Agnes said as she opened her pocketbook and took out a card. She'd have her assistant send a contractor over to see to anything that needed repairing or replacing. Agnes was ready to die for Mary Wilson and vowed that Mary and her kids would want for nothing from now on. "And I've made up my mind. I don't need another visit. I'd like to tell June and see if she'd like to be my daughter. If you think she's ready," she added quietly and hopefully.

"Oh. I've known this was coming for a few weeks, but it still feels fast!" Mary looked slightly dazed. "And you're sure that June..." Her voice trailed off and Mary's eyes shimmered as she looked back toward the stairs.

"Why? Is there something—?" Agnes began but Mary shook her head quickly.

"No. She's a *wonderful* child and I couldn't be happier." Mary's lip quivered and she had pushed out a hard, shaking breath. "I'm just going to miss her so damn much!" She had whispered, then had sworn at herself as she had fanned her watering eyes. "It's the most amazing feeling, seeing one of these kiddos find a *good* home. And I've wanted this so badly for June. She's a brilliant child and she's always making me laugh. I just love her so much and I'm really going to miss her."

"I can tell that she's special and I promise, there's nothing I won't do to give June the best life possible." Agnes had given Mary's hand a squeeze, hoping to reassure her. "You're always welcome to check on June whenever you're missing her."

Mary's smile widened and she laughed softly. "You're a lot nicer and more...normal than I was expecting when I heard you were coming and saw the limo," she admitted with an apologetic cringe. "And I can tell that June's going to be happy with you. I wasn't expecting you to make up your mind so quickly, but I think you two are going to fit really well together. June's smart and the good kind of sassy, and so are you from all I've heard and seen here."

"Thank you," Agnes replied. "I think so too. I'm not one to dither once I've made up my mind, but I don't think I've ever fallen in love with anyone this quickly."

June stole Agnes's heart again when she raced back into the kitchen with a bundle of books. "I brought all seven in case you really like *The Lightning Thief.* You look like you might be too busy to come back for a while and I didn't want you to have to wait." She huffed breathlessly and rose on her toes as she handed the stack of dog-eared books to Agnes. "You *have to* promise to bring them back because they're my favorites."

Mary and Agnes traded watery smiles.

"What if you kept them and we read them together?" Agnes asked as she bent and tipped back June's face so she could see her eyes. "Because I was hoping you'd like to come and live with me."

"I didn't know you were here for one of us," June said to Agnes, then looked up at Mary. "Can I go live with this lady?"

"Do you think you'd like that?" Mary asked and June nodded as her big brown eyes swung back to Agnes.

"She's nice and she seems like she has a lot of books."

A laugh burst from Agnes. "I have so many books and you're going to help me collect more. Our new home is almost ready and we're going to fill it with books."

"Really?" June whispered as her eyes grew even bigger.

"Really," Agnes vowed. She didn't want to overwhelm

June, but Agnes would buy her any and every book her heart desired.

June gasped and spun to Mary. "I'm getting a home and there's gonna be books!"

"And a mommy!" Mary added.

"A mommy?" June repeated, her features going slack as she blinked up at Agnes. "You want to be my mommy?"

"Of course!" Agnes nodded, too overcome to articulate how deeply she wanted to be the one to love and protect June. It felt like a privilege to be entrusted with any child, but June had become precious to Agnes in just a handful of moments. "I'd be honored to be your mother if you think you'd like that. It might be just you and me because I haven't found a grownup I want to share my life with," Agnes warned. "But I have a lovely brother and three little nieces who are just a bit older than you who can't wait to welcome you to the family."

"I would like that a lot," June said, sniffling hard as tears filled her eyes.

"*Good.*" Agnes straightened and offered June her hand. "Because I can't think of anything that would make me happier than to be your mommy."

They still had to wait and it had taken almost a week before the final paperwork was signed and June was legally Agnes's daughter. All the hurdles had been worth it, though, and June was on her way. She was utterly perfect and Agnes vowed she'd do whatever it took to give June a perfect life.

Agnes wanted to squeal, she was so *excited*. Instead of piggybacking and cherry-picking from the best parts of Walker's life, she was finally creating her own family. She wasn't sure if she would ever be ready or if she even deserved something that good, but Walker and Fin had been a wake-up call for Agnes.

Watching her widowed brother get a second chance at happily ever after with his nanny proved that it wasn't too late to find happiness. Walker had come back from the death of his beloved Connor and saved his family just before turning fifty. Agnes was nearly fifty-two and had lived a charmed life, not counting a few romantic stumbles. She figured it was time she grew up and got her act together as well.

And she could see the writing on the wall. Walker and the triplets had been the *only* good things in Agnes's life and they were moving on. She could still glom onto their happiness by lurking at The Killian House until the girls went off to college. But they would need her less and less until Agnes was just Walker's clingy, eccentric spinster sister.

She shuddered and gagged at the thought. Agnes Cameron would not be pitied and she would not become the butt of New York society's jokes. If anything, Agnes hoped to be feared and avoided like Muriel Hormsby. The old dragon had been a thorn in many an eligible bachelor's side lately and she certainly knew how to dress the part. The last time they had crossed paths was at a fundraising gala. Muriel was wearing a gorgeous peacock-patterned velvet cloak and turban ensemble, complete with feathers and dripping with emeralds.

Agnes wasn't quite ready for turbans and canes, and she wanted her existence to be meaningful and *useful* in a real and tangible way. People knew of her reputation, obviously. The Walker and Agnes Cameron Foundation was mentioned as a sponsor at the beginning of numerous PBS productions. Her art sold well, but she never knew if it was any good or if people bought it just because *her* name was on it. One of her paintings or sculptures was a sound investment because the value could double or triple if she did something truly messy or died in a scandalous or grueling manner. But that was it and all she'd ever be known for or mean to anyone other than Walker and the girls.

That was about to change, and Agnes was determined to get this right. She hadn't waited until she was in her fifties to be a mother just to make childish mistakes. And she hadn't come all this way to find out she was just like her mother—selfish and empty.

There was a soft knock at the door and Agnes's heartbeat matched the soft, swift click of the butler's soles on the marble as Pierce hurried to get the door. He opened it and she held her breath, craning her neck to listen as Pierce murmured softly.

He spun back to the foyer, causing Agnes to jump. "Miss Penny Tucker," he announced as he opened the door wider and waved her in.

"Oh." Agnes's racing heart lurched to a halt as the feral-looking younger woman stepped over the threshold. Agnes blinked, stunned and confused to find herself face-to-face with a former fling.

Penny's flame-colored hair hung in Pippi Longstocking braids and she was wearing voluminous overall...shorts? Agnes wasn't sure what she'd call the oversized garment. It was a melange of denims that had once been a pair of men's overalls. The legs were cut off just below the knees, and there were several patches; most of the pockets had been replaced with what Agnes could only describe as "tablecloth florals." Penny was known for her hippie-punk-pixie aesthetic and her current ensemble did not disappoint. She had paired her curious overalls with a white tank top, tall rainbow socks, and black Converse.

"Surprise!" Walker said, sliding an arm around Agnes's shoulders and giving her a squeeze. "I know you discussed hiring a nanny with Reid, but I told him to send his best and to let me take care of the bill for the first year. Consider it a belated Mother's Day gift."

Agnes was both moved at his thoughtfulness and *mortified.* "Oh!" It was still all she was capable of. Walker's brother-in-law, Reid Marshall, ran the now prestigious Marshall Agency and his nannies were in very high demand throughout the city. But of all the nannies in Manhattan, why did Reid have to send the only one Agnes had banged? *Twice.* "Thank you! That's..."

"Is something wrong?" Walker asked innocently, but Agnes caught the wicked glint in his eyes and saw his lips tilt in a subtle, knowing smile.

"No! Why would anything be wrong?" Agnes laughed despite her rising panic. The best day of her life had just taken an unexpected and possibly catastrophic turn.

Chapter Two

This. Is. It.

It has to be.

Penny crossed her fingers behind her back as she stood on the threshold of The Killian House, enduring Agnes Cameron's shocked stare. After almost two years of being Reid's emergency/substitute nanny and caring for the children of high-profile visitors, Penny was ready to meet *her* family. But fate was having one heck of a laugh at her expense.

She had hoped for an opportunity to bond with her clients and help a family grow. Unfortunately, Penny had already bonded with Agnes Cameron. In the biblical sense.

Penny was a bit baffled as to *how* she'd ended up in such a pickle as well. The morning had started off with a summons to Briarwood Terrace for what Reid had promised would be the job of a lifetime. But matters took a concerning turn when Reid had informed her that she was headed to The Killian House.

"The Killian House?" Penny had frowned and scratched her head in confusion. Little did she know, fate was about to kick her in the shorts. "Did Fin quit?" She'd asked, and had received a wry chuckle from Reid.

"No, he did not quit. This isn't for the triplets. Walker's sister, Agnes, has adopted a child and she arrives today," he had added. He watched Penny over the rim of his cup as he sipped.

"Oh." She stared back at him, lips pursed and brain locked.

"You've met Agnes Cameron before, haven't you? She was at Fin and Walker's wedding and Walker brought her to Penn and Morris's commitment ceremony," he had said helpfully.

"Yes!" Penny nodded. "Agnes!" Her brain was still locked but Penny thought she could feel something leaking out of her ear.

"So you remember her?"

"Mm-hmm." She continued to nod. Reid's brow furrowed and his roommate, Gavin, frowned at her over his paper while Dash's head tilted like a curious puppy.

"You okay?" Dash had asked and tossed her an apple. A fellow nanny, Dash had also been Penny's lifelong best friend and became her roommate after her brother moved in with his husband, Morris. Dash had a naturally nurturing nature and his love language was hot beverages and hugs, but Penny didn't drink tea or coffee.

"Yup!" Penny had taken a big bite out of the apple and shrugged. *Why wouldn't I be okay?* She asked wordlessly and smiled serenely as she chewed.

But Penny had been anything but serene and had suspected that she was the opposite of okay. She had to play it cool, though. Penny trusted these men with her life and loved them like they were her brothers, but they'd start circling if they smelled blood in the water. They would attack and she'd never hear the end of it if they found out about her and Agnes Cameron.

Penny couldn't help it, though. Something happened to her

every time she laid eyes on the obscenely sexy older woman. Penny melted, went weak in the knees, felt butterflies, got dizzy, heard violins... *The works.* Penny couldn't think straight and she couldn't keep her hands to herself whenever they were close. And she knew exactly what Reid would do if he knew.

First, he'd tell her brother. Then, Penn and his co-conspirators would put their heads together and plot against *her.* Which would be humiliating because neither Penny nor Agnes were looking for romance when they hooked up at Fin and Walker's wedding. Or at Penn and Morris's commitment ceremony. But they would be unbearable if she told them about her and Agnes and then they would go ballistic when she explained that there was nothing between them but wild, unbridled lust.

So she had stalled. "I wasn't aware that Agnes was adopting..."

Reid hummed into his coffee. "She started looking into it after Fin and Walker got married. You know how long these things can take."

"I'm surprised she didn't pull some strings," Penny mused out loud, earning a humph from Gavin.

"Walker said she wants to do everything right and that she's going to raise her child *here.* And he says it's important to Agnes that her child is from this city and is someone who's been waiting for a home," he explained.

"I think that's great," Penny had stated sincerely. Their past aside, it was a wonderful decision on Agnes's part and Penny was thrilled for an opportunity to help a *new* family. "Does she know you're sending me?" She had asked, keeping her tone light and nonchalant.

Reid squinted at the window and shrugged. "I told Walker you were the obvious choice. Dash is still in training. Cyrus and Alicia could do it, but you already know the Camerons and you're great at connecting with older kids. They're a lot harder to impress than toddlers, especially if they've had a rough time in the past with adults."

"They just want to know that someone's listening and that they're safe," Penny said, earning a solemn sigh from Reid.

"Exactly. Walker says that Agnes has picked the best doctors and schools and she's found the perfect home. She bought a place over on East 63rd, but it won't be ready for a few more weeks so they're staying at The Killian House. Agnes has thought of everything, but she needs a nanny who can help provide the intangible things this child will need to feel safe and loved."

"I'm in," Penny said adamantly. She had been confident that she could set aside her attraction to Agnes and was ready to roll up her sleeves and get to work. And she had assumed and reasoned that Agnes had come to a similar conclusion or else she would have requested someone else.

"I knew you'd be on board," Reid had replied and winked at Penny. "She's done a lot of research and Walker says she's ready, but she just needs some training wheels."

"I'm gonna adopt a bunch of kids," Dash said with a determined nod. He snuck a cautious, hopeful glance at Gavin.

Gavin snorted behind his paper. "Better someone decent like you than some celebrity who's in it for clout or good PR."

Dash relaxed and brightened. "Right? I feel terrible for some of the kids we take care of, but the Camerons seem like really cool people," he said and Reid hummed in agreement.

"We'd be out of business if the city was full of perfect parents. All I can do is give our families the best nanny that suits their unique needs. And hopefully, I can match them with a nanny who plays off the parents' strengths and balances their weaknesses. That way, *everyone* wins, especially the children." He crossed his arms over his chest as he reclined and Reid smiled at Dash and then at Penny. "The Camerons are a *great* family and they're my family now too. That's why I'm allowed to admit that Agnes is going to be a handful as well," he said with an apologetic wince for Penny. "But I'm hoping the two of you will be like peas in a pod and balance each other out."

That had made Penny laugh. "You might be asking for trouble. We could be like the posh and punk Thelma and Louise," she teased. She already knew how dangerous a handful of Agnes could be. Reid might have second thoughts if he knew what she was thinking so Penny tossed her apple into the trash and planted her hands on her hips confidently. "I can handle Agnes Cameron."

"I know you can," Reid said, then waved and dismissed her.

This time, Penny felt different when she squared up to The Killian House, made a wish, and climbed the imposing front steps. She'd had a premonition—a warm rush of certainty and satisfaction—that *this* was the day she had manifested and meditated on for countless hours. The crystals in her pocket had clicked together as she ran up the steps, comforting and reassuring her.

Clear and rose quartz, green aventurine, amethyst, and obsidian to boost her intuition, open her heart, and attract prosperity. She'd set her intentions and carved a sigil into an orange candle before burning it. They were on the third crescent day of the new cycle and Penny had pulled both the Ace of Pentacles and the Sun when she drew her cards for the morning, meaning that an important opportunity was hers for the taking and that this was a time for optimism and *growth*.

Growth. That was Penny's whole purpose in life. She wanted to cover the world in growing things and help families grow strong and healthy too. Most importantly, *she* wanted to grow.

That meant starting over fresh with Agnes and proving she could leave the past behind and bring her A-game. Penny had been attempting to muster said A-game and put on her bravest face before ringing the bell when the front door opened. The Camerons' perfectly dour butler had stared at her for a moment, then glanced behind Penny expectantly.

"May I help you?"

Penny was used to being confused for a lost or malicious teenager and confronted in finer establishments while in the course of her work. But The Killian House was a Gilded Era palace and the Camerons were *old* money. Her nerve buckled when she caught a peek at all the glowing white marble and crystal behind the slight, yet impervious-looking older man. He remained silent and still like an obelisk as he waited and Penny could see Fin with the Camerons, all in a line at the foot of the stairs, like deities in a Manhattan temple.

"Howdy! I'm Penny Tucker." She waved and smiled cheerfully. "Reid Marshall sent me. I'm the new nanny."

The butler blinked and there was a faint twitch at the corner of his lips. "Excellent. Just a moment," he said, turning to announce her. "Miss Penny Tucker."

He waved her in and Penny gulped loudly as she stepped over the threshold. "Golly! I can't believe Fin lives here now," she whispered in awe, taking in the massive curved staircase and the twinkling crystal chandelier overhead. It had to be as big as a bus.

"My name is Pierce and I'm the butler here. Please let me know if there's ever anything I can do to make your time here at The Killian House more comfortable."

"Okay..." Penny slid him a bemused look before glancing back at the ceiling.

"May I take your bag, ma'am?" He asked in a low murmur.

Penny shook her head, still mesmerized by the crystals in the chandelier and the way the light fractured around them, creating rainbow halos on the ceiling. "Just call me Penny, please, and you can take my arm before you can take my bag. My whole life's in here," she said, distracted and hugging it protectively.

"I'd rather not, *ma'am*. And you may keep the bag, I have all the appendages I need, thank you," the butler replied dryly, just as Fin hurried forward to greet her.

"Hey, Penny!" he said, opening his arms wide and gathering her into a hug. "I am *so* excited. We've been about to explode, we're all so happy about the newest little Cameron. But then I heard that Reid was sending you and I knew *everything* would be amazing."

"Isn't this great?" Penny squealed as she squeezed his neck, then kissed his cheek loudly. "I've always wanted to work with you and there's a little kiddo out there who's about to get a really awesome home."

"I know!" Fin set her down and fanned his eyes. "This feels like one of the best days ever and you're like the cherry on top."

"So you knew about this?" Agnes said to Fin accusatively as she joined them. She turned and hitched a brow at Penny.

"I've known for about..." Penny raised her wrist to check her grandfather's watch. "Half an hour. How long have you known?" She asked him suspiciously.

Fin coughed and flapped his hand awkwardly. "Why get hung up on the little details? *June* is going to be here at any moment and isn't that so exciting?" He smiled widely, clearly in on whatever scheme Walker and Reid had hatched.

"June?" Penny asked Agnes rapturously. She couldn't strangle Fin in front of his husband, the triplets, Agnes, and the entire Killian House staff so Penny focused on the positives. "Isn't that a *perfect* name? I think that might be my favorite month and I've always wanted a little girl named June." This was a wonderful opportunity for Penny to *grow* and she was about to witness something truly good and beautiful for Agnes and *June*.

The softest, loveliest laugh burst from Agnes and her eyes misted over as she nodded. "Yes! June! She's so—" A big tear rolled down her cheek and Penny could see and feel the joy radiating from Agnes. "That's my little girl and I'm so excited." Her hand was shaking as she swept the tear from her face.

Penny swung back to Fin. "Can we have a moment?" She asked, tipping her head toward Agnes.

"Right! You two probably need to catch up!" Fin gave them both a thumbs up as he backed away, then went to join his husband and the triplets.

"There's an understatement," Penny muttered, shaking her head at Fin before casting Agnes an apologetic grimace. "This is a lot for you, isn't it?"

That earned a weak smile from Agnes. "Thank you for noticing," she said, clearing her throat and taking a quick glance over her shoulder at Fin and her brother. "I don't think they *know*, but they know something," she whispered.

Penny hissed and nodded. "I think you might be right. Are you okay?"

"Me?" Agnes swatted dismissively, but Penny noted that her hand was still shaking. "Of course!"

"Would it be better if we came clean and told them to send someone else?" she suggested hesitantly. Penny *hated* the idea. Not as much as she hated seeing Agnes ambushed and over-whelmed when she should be celebrating one of the best moments of her life. Penny knew Walker had meant well and was probably hoping for another fairytale romance like his and Fin's, but that's not where Agnes's and Penny's heads had been at when they hooked up. And it was safe to assume that Agnes had very different priorities at the moment.

"I think it might be better..." Agnes said slowly, then wrinkled her nose. "But I'd honestly rather run down Fifth Avenue barefoot and naked than tell Walker about our...history. He's already convinced I've slept with damn near everyone in Manhattan."

"Ouch," Penny whispered. "I'd like to avoid Reid and my brother finding out as well," she admitted absently. She was imagining Agnes naked and running down Fifth Avenue.

"So, it's agreed? We never breathe a word about this to *them?*" Agnes asked conspiratorially and held out her hand.

"Agreed," Penny said, all too ready to aid Agnes in her battle against her brother. "And you're sure you'll be okay with..." She widened her eyes suggestively and there was still a tremor in Agnes's voice and hand as she waved Penny off.

"Of course! All that matters is that Reid thinks you're the best nanny for our new family. I trust his judgment and I'll trust you if *you're* sure. I understand if our past—"

"No!" Penny shook her head quickly and reached for Agnes's shoulders. "I am so thrilled for you and I think you're doing a beautiful thing, Aggie. I would be honored to work with you and June."

Agnes let out a relieved breath. "Wonderful! I can do this if you can," she said quietly, her gaze flicking impatiently to the door.

"Sure. No sweat," Penny insisted, despite the fact that she was sweating beneath her tank top and overalls.

She was still picturing Agnes naked. And Penny had that spinning, breathless feeling she always got when she was close to Agnes. It had hit Penny like a truck the first time they were introduced at Fin and Walker's wedding in the Camerons' Sagaponack compound.

"Wow! You're even more stunning up close. Wanna dance?" Penny had asked with a giggle as she stood on her tiptoes and brushed Agnes's cheek with her lips. Agnes was statuesque and so elegant. Penny was sure the older woman would laugh and send her on her way.

"Thank you, yes, and it's nice to meet you..." Agnes had replied, casting a confused glance at her brother.

Penny had snatched Agnes's hand and hurried to an open spot by the band before she changed her mind. They had loosely wound their arms around each other and there was nothing provocative about the bouncing sway of their bodies as they danced to "Your Song." But Penny had been enthralled as Agnes danced and casually sipped from her champagne. Penny wished she'd held onto her glass as the garden became stifling and the night turned sultry. Which was bizarre because it had been a cool and breezy evening until she'd been introduced to Agnes.

"So... Penny. Is that short for Penelope?" Agnes had asked, checking Penny out from the corner of her eye. She must have liked what she saw because she eased closer, her thigh parting Penny's.

A calculating smile tugged at Penny's lips. She was certainly game if Agnes was. "Depends on who you ask. My brother was born nine months after my parents spent a rainy weekend stuck in a tent in the Allegheny National Forest in Pennsylvania. My maternal grandmother's name was Penelope. But I was the result of a romantic anniversary trip to London and Liverpool so my birth certificate says Penelope Lane Tucker. Penny Lane, for short."

"How...appropriate." Agnes snorted, shaking her head. "Though somewhat tawdry, naming one's children after where they were conceived," she observed.

"Doesn't Agnes mean pure and chaste?" Penny countered and winked at Agnes.

A surprised laugh burst from her. "I promise you, I am neither of those things."

"I've heard," Penny replied with a wry grin. Her free hand had made its way under Agnes's coat and she'd spread her fingers between her shoulder blades. Agnes's skin was even softer than her pink silk camisole. "What if—after the song was over—I snuck into the house to use the restroom?" Warmth spread up Penny's neck and she was blushing as her fingers trailed down Agnes's spine. She was being incredibly bold, but Agnes seemed to like it. Penny recalled Agnes's rebellious reputation and wasn't all that surprised that she'd be up for a little fun.

"You don't waste time, do you?"

"Do you want to slow down and see if we're soulmates first?" Penny asked, raising her brows at Agnes, daring her.

Agnes let out a defiant, contrary snort that made Penny's pulse gallop just a little bit faster. "What if you met me in the study instead? There's a line to use the bathroom and I gave Fin my room to use for the day. But no one needs the study. Not that I've given much thought to where I'd get laid if the opportunity presented itself," she clarified.

"Oh, of course not," Penny agreed soberly. "Where might I find this study?" Penny purred, dragging her finger under the waistband of Agnes's trousers. Penny was achingly curious to know how someone as fine and elegant as Agnes tasted.

"Go through the kitchen and take a right down the back hallway. It's the last door on the left. I'll check in with the caterer and fetch us another bottle of champagne. Then I'll meet you there."

"Sounds like a plan," Penny agreed, then slipped out of Agnes's arms so she could take a turn around the garden with Riley Fitzgerald, Fin's best man and one of her closest friends.

Penny was sitting on the desk when Agnes reached the study ten minutes later. Penny kicked off her shoes and untied the straps of her dress while Agnes locked the door, then bared her breasts, luring Agnes closer before she came to her senses. Never in a thousand years would Penny have expected *the* Agnes Cameron to say yes to a dance, let alone a quickie in the study.

With dinky ol' Penny Tucker? Ha!

"Are you always this fast?" Agnes asked as she poured and handed Penny a glass.

She hummed thoughtfully while she sipped. "We only have so much time and I know what sorts of games I'd rather play tonight." Penny strummed a nipple, inviting Agnes to touch and taste.

And Agnes had tasted. She started with Penny's lips, kissing her senseless before licking the freckles on her shoulder and the bee tattoo buzzing along her collarbone. She teased Penny's nipples until she whimpered and squirmed, then dropped to her knees and feasted. Penny held onto the desk and Agnes's head as the study spun around them. All traces of refined aloofness were gone as Agnes devoured Penny, her tongue and lips lapping and suckling. She was demanding as her fingers filled Penny with slick, twisting thrusts. Penny encouraged her with mindless moans, panting and begging for more.

She whispered naughty orders in the dark and writhed against Agnes's face until she came *twice*. When she could trust her legs, Penny slid off the desk and unzipped Agnes's pants. She bent her over, determined to give as good as she got, slapping Agnes on the ass. "That's a good girl," she declared huskily. "I've never felt anything as fine as you," Penny said, her fingers skating down Agnes's thighs and sliding her panties and trousers off.

"Don't you dare treat me like I'm delicate," Agnes scolded, challenging and taunting Penny.

And just like that, the study turned into an inferno. Penny

smirked and nipped at an asscheek while sliding three fingers deep into Agnes and grinding with her knuckle.

"How about that?"

Agnes swallowed a yelp and nodded frantically. "Good. Don't stop."

"Not unless you tell me to," Penny purred, tilting her head and dragging her tongue along the cleft of Agnes's ass. Penny breathed her in; Agnes smelled elegant and expensive like the inside of a fancy silk-lined purse.

"Penny."

That firmly impatient tone struck Penny's nerves like a match, making them flare with anticipation and setting her alight. "Yes, ma'am," she murmured, then swiftly pulled Agnes's hips back.

"Oh!" Agnes grabbed the desk and there was another strained yelp when Penny's tongue dragged over her hole.

Now, Penny adored women of all ages, but older women pushed all her buttons because they tended to be more assertive and rarely wasted time. It was a heady combination of emotional maturity, understanding their bodies, and the lack of fucks or the ability to give a damn that comes with age and experience.

But Agnes wasn't your common cougar or garden-variety MILF, she was an atomic bomb. She was pure, scorching heat and insatiable need as she swore and writhed against Penny's tongue, begging for more. Penny crooned softly and told Agnes that she was so, so naughty as she fingered her, winding her up and making her even more desperate. She was so wet and bucked against Penny's hand when she reached around and found Agnes's clit.

She came with a muffled sob, growing even more luminous and dewy in Penny's hands. Agnes turned shakily, intending to pull Penny up and into her arms. But Penny hadn't had enough and wanted the slick sweetness coating the inside of Agnes's thighs.

"Stay there," she ordered, lifting Agnes's left leg and diving back in. Penny bathed her thighs with long, lazy licks before savoring her tender, quivering lips. She was succulent and silky at her core and Penny was drunk on the taste, smell, and feel of Agnes as she feasted. Nothing had ever felt or tasted as soft; Agnes was luscious like a ripe sun-warmed melon.

"Penny!" Her name was a tight squeak and goosebumps covered Agnes's skin.

"Mmmm..." Penny agreed drowsily. She was so turned on, she'd probably come again if she bumped against the desk, but Penny was content as she grinned up at Agnes.

"What if we—?" Agnes started and they jumped when they heard a soft tap at the door before Reid murmured something about the band and the last song.

"Stay right here!" Agnes pleaded while shimmying back into her pantsuit. "I won't be more than fifteen minutes."

"Okay!" Penny said, laughing as she shooed Agnes out the door.

She had meant to wait because Penny had wanted to know what Agnes had been about to suggest. But she had hastily scribbled a note thanking Agnes for a lovely time and had climbed out the window after someone else had knocked on the door and called for the key.

"No sweat," Penny repeated, giving herself a mental slap and returning to the present. She couldn't bring her A-game if she was fixated on Agnes's A. Or her T. Or her P... Penny forced her eyes to Agnes's, avoiding her phenomenal tits and holding up a thumb. *I think I might be in trouble.* "No sweat at all!"

Chapter Three

Agnes didn't have long to absorb the shock of Penny's appearance at The Killian House before Pierce announced June's arrival. The world stopped for Agnes and she momentarily forgot about the potential mess she had made with Penny and their pact as June tiptoed into the foyer. She looked so small and wary as she hugged a shoebox in her arms, wearing a dingy red backpack and hiding behind a social worker. He passed Pierce a woefully small duffle bag before giving June an encouraging nudge.

"Everything's gonna be great!" He said, backing away but watching June closely.

"June! Sweetheart!" Agnes held out a hand, hoping June still trusted her.

"Agnes!" The little girl brightened and ran to Agnes, the contents of the shoebox rattling and jangling as she tucked it under an arm. June was shaking as she tightly clasped Agnes's hand. "I thought you said we were going to live in a house," June said, her voice wavering. The little girl's deep brown eyes were huge and unblinking as she stared up at Agnes.

"I... Yes? This is my brother's house and we're just staying here until *our* place is ready." Agnes slid Penny a confused look. She winced and crouched next to June.

"Hey, June! My name's Penny and I'm new here too. I was kind of nervous at first, but everyone's super cool here. Even Pierce. He's the butler and he has to act all stiff and proper, but he's actually really nice. He'll hook you up with anything you want if you tell him we're friends." She gave June a cocky wink and held out her fist so she could bump it. "And the Camerons are an awesome family. You're gonna have a blast."

"Okay," June said shakily, hesitantly bumping Penny's fist back. She swallowed loudly and looked at Agnes. "What if they don't like me?" She whispered.

Agnes took June's hand firmly in hers and sneered. "Then I'll fight them. But you don't have to worry about that here. Ever," Agnes stated. "Walker and the girls are ecstatic and they're dying to meet you. And I'm sure the entire household will go out of their way to make you feel at home."

"But what if they don't? I didn't have a good family or someplace nice to live before, that's why I went to stay with Ms. Mary," June said in a soft rush.

"I want you to listen to me," Agnes ordered gently and lowered so they were eye-to-eye. "You. Are. A. Cameron. Now. Your Uncle Walker is my best friend in the whole world and we won't judge you based on who your family was or where you're from. That would make us hypocrites because our parents are *terrible* people. You'll have to meet them, eventually, but don't worry. They're too old to do anything but bore us to death. And you'll only have to meet them a few times a year and just for a few minutes." Agnes gestured dismissively. They couldn't care less about Agnes. She could have adopted a troupe of circus performers, for all their parents cared. Walker had always mattered *most*. And that the family's finances were strong and the houses were being managed well. Walker had all of that well in hand so Agnes was free to do as she pleased as long as she showed her face in Connecticut for birthdays and holidays. "You and I are a family now and they're our family too," she added with a toss of her head at Walker, Fin, and the girls. "That means they *have* to love us." She smirked at June, receiving a wobbly smile in return.

"Okay. If you're sure. It's a really big house."

"It is," Agnes agreed as she rose and considered it, then raised a shoulder. "But we only have to go up two flights of stairs to get to our rooms and you can ignore the rest of it. There's a lovely nursery with all kinds of toys and art supplies and a very impressive library," she said with a wiggle of her brows.

June gasped. "It has a library?"

"I think you'll enjoy the selection in the nursery more—for now—but I know your uncle Walker will be happy to share his library with you. The Killian House is our home too. Uncle Walker's in charge of it and everything is technically his, but you and I are Camerons. This is our family home and Walker will always want us to feel welcome here," she explained simply. Because that was the end of it, as far as Agnes and Walker were concerned.

As Agnes had predicted, Walker was overjoyed and the girls were ready with hugs and a hundred questions apiece for June. They wanted to know June's favorite foods, colors, books, games... The social worker quietly excused himself after reminding Agnes and June that he was just a call away and that he'd see them in a month for a check-in.

Penny retreated to the sidelines with Fin, quietly observing and offering encouraging smiles. It was hard for Agnes to take her eyes off June, but Penny kept pulling Agnes's attention to that quieter corner of the foyer. The two nannies had their heads together and Agnes noticed that they seemed concerned, but she also couldn't tear her eyes away from *Penny*.

She had been enchanting in Sagaponack and at Penn and Morris Mosby's commitment ceremony, dressed up in what must have been borrowed gowns. Because *this* Penny was captivating in an entirely different way. She was also astute as she engaged with the triplets and attempted to draw June in. But June drew closer and closer to Agnes until she was almost hiding behind her.

Penny sprang into action, capturing everyone's attention as she swept forward and efficiently gathered up the triplets. "Alright, ladies! Let's give June a moment to catch her breath," Penny said, gently tugging one of Charlotte's ringlets so she'd unwind her arms from around June's neck. "Fin and I would like the three of you to run up to the nursery and find those cards you made for June. We'll be right up behind you."

"Come on!" Amelia called as she snatched Beatrice's hand. "Let's put June's name on her art cubby so she knows where her stuff goes!"

The triplets loudly clamored up the stairs and Charlotte paused to wave back at June. "I'll miss you and I'll see you soon!" She called before she was towed around the corner, making the adults laugh and groan adoringly.

"I told you they'd like you!" Agnes said as she hugged June against her side. But the little girl was shaking.

Penny smiled warmly and held out her hand. "You're doing great! Want to walk with me so we can get to know each other? I'll be your nanny and I'm here *just* for you," she said cheerfully. But June was alarmed as she looked up at Agnes.

"Are you leaving me? I thought you were going to be my new mom."

"No, no, no!" Penny shushed gently as she bent and booped June's nose, effectively pausing the little girl's panic. June jumped and blinked at Penny curiously. "Agnes isn't going anywhere, June bug. I'm here to be part of Team June and Agnes is our captain. My job is to help you and Agnes have fun and make this big, big change as easy for *you* as we can. Because we all understand that this is *a lot* to adjust to and we're all here to help. Okay?"

June nodded quickly, hanging on every word and clearly enchanted by Penny as well. "This looks like a castle," she confided shakily.

"Let's see if you feel better once you've seen the nursery. It's not made for grownups like all of this down here," Penny said and beckoned June as she headed up the stairs.

"Are you coming too?" June asked Agnes.

"You heard Penny. I'm the captain of Team June. I'm sticking by your side until you're sick of me."

"Okay." June grabbed onto Agnes's hand, linking the three of them, and nodded. "I'm ready."

Agnes lowered and kissed June's hand, then brushed the hair away from her eyes. "Oh, sweetheart. I know this is all scary and new, but I promise that you'll get used to it soon. When you're ready, we'll go exploring and we'll snoop around every inch of this place. You'll see just how boring it really is."

Walker chuckled in agreement. "You're allowed to snoop *anywhere* you wish and I want you to let us know if the triplets get too pushy or if they try to make you an accomplice to something illegal," he added with a teasing wag of his finger. "I'm so glad you're here, June. You should consider The Killian House your home."

"Yes, sir," June said, then curtsied.

A loud laugh burst from Agnes and she clapped a hand over her mouth. "He's just your old uncle Walker. Don't bow to him or he'll think he's important."

There were several snorts and giggles and Fin was turning

red as he bit into a knuckle. Walker stuck his tongue out at Agnes, then straightened his tie. "Not that old. I'm needed on a call soon so I'll leave you to it." He offered everyone a bow and welcomed June once more before taking himself off to his study.

"Let's check out the nursery!" Agnes said, and they followed Penny and Fin upstairs. The girls were ready and waiting with handmade cards introducing themselves and welcoming June to the family.

"We wanted to make it easy for you so you don't have to remember everything right away," Beatrice explained proudly. Each of the girls had shared important personal stats like favorite colors, foods, songs, cartoons... And a questionnaire and a crayon were provided so June could give them a comprehensive list of her favorite things.

"We can help you fill it out over here!" Amelia had June by the hand and was leading her to their reading corner.

Penny and Fin traded grimaces before he cleared his throat. "Hey, Agnes," he said quietly. "Why don't you let me keep an eye on things in here while you and Penny do some brainstorming." His head swung toward the nursery door and he raised his brows suggestively.

Agnes frowned and craned her neck, becoming more concerned and wary by the moment. Had she missed something?

Already?

"What are we brainstorming about?"

"Just a quick chat!" Penny suggested brightly and looped her arm around Agnes's.

"I'll be right back, June." Agnes waved as she was led from the room and noticed that June's shoulders were pulled practically up to her ears as her gaze followed Agnes out the door. "What is it?" Agnes asked, her tone brisk with impatience, once she and Penny reached the hallway. "I'm trying to help June acclimate and she needs me."

"She does," Penny agreed and nodded quickly. "You two are off to a great start, but our little girl is having a tough time." She waved back at the nursery and around them.

"What do you mean," Agnes asked nervously. "What did I miss? June has *everything* a little girl could possibly want here."

Penny winced hard, tilting her head. "Does she though?"

"What did we miss?" Agnes looked around the hall and leaned to see down the stairs. "I'm sure Pierce can—"

"It's nothing like that, Aggie!" Penny laughed softly as she caught Agnes's cheek and turned it.

"No one calls me that but Walker," Agnes said, hitching a brow at Penny.

"Oh? I shouldn't, then?" She asked and Agnes's lips pursed again. It seemed churlish, given their past encounters. And Agnes kind of liked hearing her childhood nickname coming from Penny's lips.

"Just don't overdo it."

"Gotcha!" Penny gave a playful salute and a wink before growing serious again. "June doesn't need pretty clothes or more toys or books right now. She needs some space! The triplets are obviously over the moon and they're being angels. But June's got that deer-in-the-headlights look because she doesn't understand where she is and what's going on yet and they're asking her a hundred questions. It's too much!" Penny explained, grasping Agnes's hand and giving it a reassuring squeeze. "Let's have everyone else take a step back while *you* show June around her new home for the next...?"

Agnes's cheeks puffed out as she recalled her last meeting with the East 63rd Street designer and the architect and considered the list she was mentally compiling for June's floor and bedroom. "It might be...at least a month," she guessed, and Penny cringed as she turned back to the nursery.

"Okay..."

"What?" Agnes demanded as she searched Penny's face. "I can't imagine a more comfortable place for us while our new home is under construction."

"Comfortable?" Penny stared at Agnes, looking mystified for a moment before shaking her head. "That goes without saying. I'm worried that this is overwhelming her and that June's going to have too much competition."

Agnes's head pulled back. "Competition?"

Penny gestured at the girls, who were framed by the doorway. The triplets were hopping and babbling excitedly at June, each vying for her attention. Agnes didn't get why that was a problem until Fin told the triplets to find their favorite book to show June. Amelia and Beatrice raced to the bookshelf and argued over who could show off their newest books while Charlotte pulled out a cowboy hat and a trampoline, making everyone laugh. Each girl was showing off or acting up while June held onto her shoebox and silently took in the chaos around her.

"Alright," Agnes said loudly as she headed into the fray to rescue June. "I think it's time for me to take June upstairs so she can see her room."

"Can we come too?" Amelia asked as Charlotte possessively looped an arm around June's. The triplets grew louder and more excited as they decided who would show June what.

Agnes shook her head, then held up a finger when the triplets began to protest. "Imagine how you'd feel if you were in a big, new, scary place and all these new people were talking to you and asking you a bunch of questions," she said gently. Amelia always responded better when she understood *why* if she was told no.

Her eyes widened as she nodded and her sisters suddenly grew calmer and retreated, giving June more room. "We should stay here," Amelia agreed and gave June a tiny wave as Agnes led her from the room. "Sorry if we were too much, but we're happy you're here!"

"I really like them!" June whispered up at Agnes as they made their way to the gallery. "They're very pretty, but they talk really fast and all at the same time."

The triplets did have a unique language and Agnes often got dizzy when they got excited. They would finish each other's sentences and speak in triplicate. Or they'd chatter in incomplete bits of jumbled phrases because they didn't need to articulate full thoughts to understand each other.

"You'll get used to it and you can tell them to pipe down or slow down if they get to be too much. I promise, we tell them to zip it all the time. And they know they're little monsters, but they're loving little monsters and they mean well," Agnes said while they climbed the stairs. "This is where we'll stay when we're here," she said as they reached the third floor.

"This is all for us?" June asked, still clinging to Agnes's side as she leaned and looked around the smaller foyer. The sitting room and lounge were decorated in powder blue and light gray.

"This is *just for us* and your room is through here." Agnes guided June to the room on the left and opened the door. She had chosen light gray upholstery and bedding three months earlier, when she had had the old office turned into a room fit for a child who was eight to sixteen years old. "I didn't know what color you'd want. I figured we could add as much pink, or blue, or...purple as you want once you had a chance to see the space."

June shrugged and looked down at her shoebox. "I've never had my own room or got to pick what color I wanted. But I can put all my stuff in here?" She asked as she opened it and held the box up so Agnes could see the contents. There were a few small figurines, trading cards, a rather dingy and ratty purple bow on a hair clip, plastic rings that Agnes suspected had once been adorned with candy... Agnes understood that these were June's most-valued possessions. "My *Percy Jackson* books are in my backpack if you want to read *The Lightning Thief.*" She hitched her thumb over her shoulder, making Agnes's heart hurt. Aside from the duffle bag the social worker had left, that was all June possessed in the world before she arrived at The Killian House.

"I'd love to read with you after we find a place for all your things."

It didn't take long to put away the clothes and books in June's bags. The contents of her shoebox were spread among the various shelves, drawers, and cubbies, making the room look more sparse, somehow.

"We should go shopping tomorrow!" Agnes suggested and glanced at June hopefully. The little girl shrugged again and went to sit on the bed. The mattresses were wide and the bed was tall so June had to stand on her tiptoes and pull herself up by grabbing hold of the duvet. Agnes followed and made a note to have Pierce find some steps or a stool for her. "I'd like to get out—just the two of us—and see what kind of trouble we can get into together," she said, remembering Penny's suggestions. This time, June smiled as she gave the mattress a test bounce. Agnes felt that smile deep in her chest. She held onto the bed's post because her feet felt like they weren't touching the ground. "Do you like it?" She asked hoarsely and coughed to hide the emotion.

"This is the biggest bed I've ever sat on but I like it!" June said, looking genuinely pleased and relaxed for the first time since her arrival. She crawled to the bedside table and retrieved her cherished copy of *The Lightning Thief* and Agnes went to sit next to her.

"Ready to start now?" Agnes asked as she propped the pillows up behind June. She nodded, patting the spot next to her. The small gesture touched Agnes deeply and she was humbled as she sat next to her daughter and cautiously slid an arm around her. June leaned into Agnes and gave her shoulders a little wiggle, then opened the book.

"Percy has to go to a scary new place and meet new friends who help him, too."

"Really?" Agnes asked and humphed thoughtfully when June nodded. "But he's happy that he gets to go?"

"Not really. He finds out he's a demigod and he has to go all the way to Montauk," June explained.

"Montauk?" Agnes squinted thoughtfully and nodded. "I knew a man from Montauk who thought he was a demigod."

June giggled and snuggled closer. "You're funny, Agnes."

"Thank you," Agnes said with a bow of her head. "I think you're funny too." She craned her neck and carefully kissed June's hair. She heard June's contented sigh and there was another burst of joy in Agnes's chest. "Why don't you get us started," she whispered, not trusting her voice.

That made June cheer and it wasn't long before they were both caught up in the story. June read until she grew drowsy and eventually nodded off. Agnes slipped the book from her grasp and was happy to have the time to hold June and simply stare at her. She was grateful to Penny for hitting pause and changing the course of their afternoon before June was shocked into her shell. Suddenly, Agnes craved June's peace and happiness more than her own and would do anything to give her both.

As if she'd heard Agnes's thoughts, Penny tapped softly on the door and leaned in. "How's it going?" She whispered.

"Wonderful," Agnes said sincerely. She pressed one more kiss to June's hair, then eased her onto the pillow as she got up.

Penny was waiting in the sitting room, a wide smile across her face. "I am very impressed with you, ma'am."

"Me? Why? I didn't— What?" Agnes blurted awkwardly. She laughed and waved as if nothing out of the ordinary had occurred. "It's just... You know," she mumbled.

"I do," Penny said, then turned as Pierce arrived pushing a cart with covered dishes. "We thought the two of you might like to dine up here and watch a movie tonight."

"Brilliant!" Agnes went to peek as dinner was efficiently arranged on the coffee table. The macaroni and cheese, chicken fingers, and miniature cherry-covered cheesecakes all looked delicious and Agnes clutched her stomach when it growled loudly. "I haven't eaten all day. I was too nervous," she confided and checked the bedroom. "June's been asleep for over an hour and should wake up soon if that didn't do it."

"I'll give her a nudge before I go. I've got *Percy Jackson* cued up for the two of you," Penny said, pointing as Pierce used the remote to lower the screen for the projector.

"You're leaving?" Agnes asked, hoping she didn't sound too disappointed.

"Yeah. It's almost seven o'clock and I plan to be back bright and early. But remember, I'm just a call away," Penny said as she checked the men's watch dangling from her wrist. "Fin's here if you have any urgent questions, but I'm sure you'll be fine. After the movie, let her take a shower and put on some comfy pj's and she'll fall asleep after another chapter or two. I'll be here when the two of you wake up and we'll be ready for another amazing day." She threw her arms around Agnes and squeezed tight. "I'm so proud of you, Aggie! And I know we're going to have so much fun!"

"I'm sure you're right," Agnes said as she patted Penny's

back. She ignored the tickle in her stomach and how *happy* Penny's praise made her. "I'll see you in the morning, then."

Penny tiptoed into June's room and gently woke her before scooping her into a hug and kissing her cheek loudly. "Today will be one of my very favorites because I got to meet you, my June bug. I can't wait to see you in the morning."

"I can't wait to see you too!" June was bouncing on her knees on the bed, animated and getting chattier by the moment. "Agnes says we're going out. Just the two of us!"

"Oh, my goodness! That's gonna be so awesome," Penny predicted, then gave June another boop on the nose before she skipped back to Agnes and captured her hands. "And remember what I said: I'm *proud* of you, Aggie. And we're going to have tons of fun." She popped up onto her toes and pressed a quick kiss to Agnes's cheek, then skipped out of the sitting room.

"Yay. Fun..." Agnes murmured as she stared after Penny. She gave herself *one* moment to imagine what that could mean, then forced those very impure thoughts to the back of her brain. She was a mother now and she had more important things to think about than fooling around with the nanny. Again.

Chapter Four

It didn't seem possible, but Agnes had only gotten hotter.

"Rats!" Penny muttered, then bent at the waist, picking up the rumpled coffee cup she'd kicked for four blocks and tossed it in a trash can. She had a feeling she might be in trouble as she stomped up her stoop. "Who knew she had an inner mama bear? Or that I'd be so into that?" She was still baffled as she unlocked the front door.

"Hey, Penny Lane, how was your day?" Dash sang from the living room. He was usually the first one home in the evening and that was how he always greeted her.

"Brilliant." She hung her bag on the hook and hesitated. Aside from one *minor*...complication, the day had been downright brilliant. Penny smiled as she spun and went to join Dash. "Oh! What are we making?" She asked, excited at the array of brightly colored construction paper shapes. Dash was on his knees on the other side of the coffee table and cutting a piece of orange paper into the shape of a flowerpot if Penny's guess was correct.

"They put me in charge of the kids' summer reading display at the library!" He declared proudly.

"Lucky!" Penny whispered, then cheered when Dash pointed at the open bottle of wine on the end table. An empty mug was also waiting, and Penny hummed in approval at the sketch under Dash's elbow while she poured. He was indeed planning a garden-themed display with vines and potted plants. Dash had photocopied and craftily cut out colorful book covers to use along with the construction paper to create petals, leaves, clouds, a sun... "How cool!"

"Thanks! But don't keep me in suspense. How was your first day at The Killian House?"

"I told you it was brilliant." She shrugged and lowered to the floor next to him. "June is eight, and she's an angel. And she's *smart* smart! She knows more math than I do!"

"You already told me that." He gave her a pointed look. "How many times did you text me?"

"And I can tell you as many times as I want," Penny said imperiously. "She's the most special little girl in the whole city and I get to hang out with her *every day!*" She made a triumphant sound and sipped. "We already felt like best friends by the time I left and I can tell that we're going to be friends forever. This is it, Dash."

There wasn't a doubt in her mind that fate had meant for Penny and June to find each other. It wasn't fair to say that June was shy. She was quiet and it took her a moment to open up—which wasn't all that hard to understand, honestly—but June was a highly observant and intelligent little girl. She was also warm and kind once she knew it was safe to trust someone.

"I'm so happy for June. And Agnes," he added, reaching for one of the glue sticks scattered across the coffee table. "How was *that*?" He asked while coating the back of his paper pot.

"Fine!" Penny said as she swiped the scissors off the table.

She went to work on the petals Dash had traced on a piece of pink paper. "We took a moment to catch up before June arrived and I spent most of the afternoon with Fin and his girls. The house and the triplets and all those new people were a little bit of a shock for June so I thought she could use some quiet, one-on-one time with Agnes."

"Good call," Dash said as he nodded. "I've never been inside, but I get a little nervous whenever I walk by The Killian House and imagine ringing the doorbell and asking if Fin's home."

"You should, though! He'd be so happy to see you, and Walker is so much cooler than you'd expect. He was so great with June! They all were!"

She gushed about the Camerons for several minutes, then stopped and asked herself why she was babbling about her über wealthy bosses. She rarely talked about her clients because she rarely had anything nice to say.

"Any developments with Gavin?" Her voice rose hopefully. It was so easy to change the subject and distract Dash. All she had to do was bring up Gavin and he got google-eyed and dreamy.

"Nothing interesting to report, but I feel like we're on the verge of a development," he said as he held up two sets of crossed fingers.

"I've always admired your determination, Dash."

"I asked him again—if he'd be interested in getting coffee sometime."

"Really? What did he say?"

Dash cleared his throat and stiffened his posture. "'I doubt it,'" he replied in a dry rumble. He sounded just like Gavin and Penny groaned as she hugged his arm, but Dash slid her a sly grin. "'I doubt it.' isn't the same as 'No.' and it's a lot better than 'Absolutely not!' Which is what he said the first few times I asked him. I'm taking it as a sign of progress!"

"Gavin doesn't stand a chance," she predicted as she beamed at Dash. He looked just like you'd expect someone named Dash to look. He was tall and strapping and had the finely chiseled face of an Adonis, but the pure, loyal heart of a golden retriever. "Why Gavin, though?" She whispered. "Don't get me wrong, I love him with all of my heart. I just wonder why *you're* so sure about Gavin." He'd been pining over Gavin for at least a year but Penny knew of several mutuals who were madly in love with Dash—both guys and girls. He had options, but Dash was patiently chipping away at Gavin's resistance, one cup of tea at a time.

He sighed dreamily as he stared at the wall and slathered glue on the back of a pink petal, oblivious to Penny's amused smirk. "He's so...uptight and cranky, right? But I caught him swearing in the kitchen because he couldn't find his favorite cup once. He didn't know I was there and he yanked open the fridge and slammed it—the way you do when you don't actually want anything, you just want to slam something that won't make a lot of noise. He was so *hot*, Penny!" He whispered excitedly as he leaned toward her. Penny blinked at the table, utterly dismayed. She couldn't imagine Gavin raising his voice or losing his temper.

"That's...weird."

"No. It was seriously hot. I'm pretty sure it had nothing to do with his teacup because he'd been extra cranky all day. But I started to wonder what he's *really* like when he loses control and I couldn't stop after that. I kept imagining him naked and sweaty and swearing and that's kind of all I think about now when I..." He cleared his throat suggestively.

"I see!" Penny couldn't, really, because she rarely thought about naked men. She couldn't even imagine Gavin without a crisply ironed shirt and a tie. But the idea of Gavin doing anything as common and undignified as some good old-fashioned sweaty shagging was almost absurd.

"Yeah... I've done my best to keep tabs on his teacup and make sure he never runs out of tea or his special sugar because it's kind of like foreplay. Or as close as I can get to foreplay without being creepy."

"What?" Penny laughed. "That's so—!" She waved her hand in front of her face. "There's a solid tea-bagging joke in there."

Dash sighed again and shrugged. "I don't mind waiting. It's nice to really know the person you're in love with before you get wrapped up in all the physical stuff. Like, I know he's a *good* person and he's super loyal to his friends. He's everything I'd want in a partner and I think I could make him really happy."

"Of course you could!" Penny snorted defiantly on his behalf. She couldn't imagine anyone better than Dash and doubted that anyone could take better care of Gavin. They were so perfectly suited because Dash *wanted* a husband and a home to care for and Gavin was happiest when he was at home, warming his feet by the fire, reading his paper, and drinking his tea. Both were suited to domestic bliss and Penny wished Gavin would open his eyes and see what was right in front of him.

Dash continued to ramble about all the kids he and Gavin were going to adopt while Penny's mind wandered. To Agnes.

Before arriving at The Killian House, she could have told you where Agnes was ticklish and that she liked to play rough, but Penny was realizing that she didn't know a single thing about the woman herself. And she was beginning to suspect that Agnes's wild and rebellious reputation and much of the gossip were just the tip of a rather fascinating iceberg.

She wasn't anywhere close to the aloof and selfish socialite

Penny was expecting. In fact, Agnes had been warm with the triplets and so happily in the palm of June's little hand, Penny found herself swooning as the older woman revealed her softer and more vulnerable side.

Penny understood that this was *real* for Agnes. She truly wanted her own family and was building it on her own terms. That fierce willfulness was what had initially sparked Penny's curiosity and drew her to Agnes. Now, Agnes was beginning an important new chapter of her life with that same willful determination and Penny wanted to be a part of it.

Which meant that she had to prove that she could separate the Agnes of their fast flings from the woman and mother she was becoming. That was going to be tricky for Penny because Agnes's bold confidence was just as alluring as her easy elegance and magnetic charm. Penny suspected that motherhood would only emphasize Agnes's best qualities and make her even more irresistible.

She was the most graceful woman Penny had ever seen. Agnes didn't walk, she floated, and she was lighter than air when they danced. Penny had never seen a woman move the way Agnes Cameron did. She carried herself like a ballerina, never rushing or stumbling, but gliding from conquest to conquest. And her skin was as soft and as smooth as silk and she practically glowed, she was so radiantly flawless. Penny trembled whenever their eyes met and her nerves went completely haywire when she was close to Agnes.

It was a deep, internal tremble that caused her hands to shake and sweat and made her tummy do somersaults. Penny had never felt anything like it and was already bracing herself for their next encounter. She had to be all business and stay on her A-game or else she'd make a fool of herself in front of Fin and the rest of the Camerons.

Penny reminded herself that a couple of quick shags were

very minor in the grand scheme of things, especially to a woman like Agnes Cameron. Agnes had most likely moved on —Penny certainly had—and had set their past encounters aside for the sake of her child. In a way, it was an honor to know that Agnes still valued her experience and trusted Penny's reputation enough to hire her.

Because Penny's behavior at their brothers' weddings was certainly...questionable. But Penny didn't believe she had a choice at the time. One didn't pass up an opportunity to dance with *the* Agnes Cameron and Penny had to shoot her shot while she had a chance.

She gave her head a slight nod, pretending to listen as Dash went through a brief synopsis of each book that was going on his summer reading board. She was still stunned that any of it had happened. Their second encounter had been even more of a magical surprise and Penny suppressed a shiver as she remembered how ethereal Agnes had looked at Penn and Morris's reception.

Agnes's name was on the guest list and Penny thought she was prepared. But it was like the Fourth of July—minus the patriotism and fireworks-induced animal trauma—when she laid eyes on Agnes again. Penny was dazzled and breathless, but also giddy. Her nerves fizzed and flared and Penny swallowed a gasp when their hands touched.

How could she not, when Agnes looked so magical? She had worn a sleek, sharp pantsuit to Fin and Walker's wedding. But Agnes had turned up in the Merchant's House Museum's Secret Garden in just a wisp of silver that clung to her willowy curves. The back was open and the silk draped provocatively low. Agnes looked like a goddess, with her pale gray hair pulled up into a loose bun.

Oh, and the way she smelled! Penny wanted to sniff every luxurious inch of Agnes and bury her face in her hair. And other places. But Penny played it as cool as she could while they chatted and danced. Which lasted for about half a song before Penny invited Agnes for a tryst in the small upstairs bathroom. It was just for the wedding party so there was little chance of being interrupted since everyone was in the garden celebrating. Shockingly, Agnes had accepted *again* and Penny was determined to make the most of her second chance of a lifetime.

"Are you sure you wouldn't prefer my suite at the Baccarat and a king-size bed?" Agnes had murmured when Penny spirited her upstairs and into the bathroom. The older woman's perfectly pointed nose had wrinkled and Penny couldn't stop herself from kissing it.

"I'm sure!" Penny whispered, locking the bathroom door behind her.

She never knew how to act at places like the Baccarat and any attraction Agnes felt toward Penny would probably fizzle right up once they got to talking. Agnes would realize that Penny was the opposite of sophisticated and had only cleaned herself up for Fin and Penn. There were very few people worth putting on a dress for, in Penny's estimation, and Agnes had managed to be present at both of their weddings. Penny laughed as she imagined scurrying through the lobby of the five-star hotel the next morning. They'd probably call security if they caught her in the halls.

"In fact, I do my best work in tight spaces," she purred against Agnes's lips and backed her through the narrow room and up against the pedestal sink. Penny traced the cleft of Agnes's ass through the thin silk and thrilled at her startled gasp.

"I remember," Agnes breathed, cupping Penny's face and kissing her hungrily. Her throaty moans encouraged Penny as she slipped the spaghetti straps over Agnes's shoulders. The gown slid down her legs and pooled at Agnes's feet, leaving her in nothing but a pair of kitten heels and earrings.

"Goodness, you're the loveliest creature I've ever laid eyes on," Penny said, unable to hide the quiver in her voice or her awe as she tugged the straps at her shoulders, letting her own dress drop to the floor.

"Come here." A hand curled around Penny's jaw and she was lost as Agnes pulled her closer and pecked at her lips. "I think you're pure magic, Penny Tucker."

A delighted giggle burst from Penny. "Do you?" It *felt* like magic when Agnes nodded and traced her cheek.

"I'm under your spell."

They kissed and there were sparks and more goosebumps as their hands wandered. Penny did regret that there wasn't a bed or a decent-sized sofa so they could get really wild and writhe and grind against each other, but her heart was racing and an ecstatic laugh swelled in her chest. It wasn't nerves, though. Penny was just so excited and *happy* to have another taste of Agnes and to get to hear her come again.

Penny chanted words of awe and teased Agnes with naughty suggestions as she kissed her gracefully long neck and sucked on her shoulder. Penny whimpered adoringly as her hands glided down Agnes's back, over her ass, and skimmed her thighs. She smiled at the tattoo on Agnes's ribs, just under her left breast.

A-B-C

"What's that for?" Penny whispered against Agnes's skin.

"Amelia, Beatrice and Charlotte. My girls. I mean, Walker's girls." She licked her lips and shook her head. Penny loved that Agnes was so flustered. "They used my eggs and...they're my girls."

Penny kissed the dime-sized letters, then sank to her knees. She raised Agnes's thigh so she could rest her foot on the toilet seat. "That's beautiful." She panted the words against Agnes's mound, making her shiver. She pulled in a deep breath and groaned ecstatically as she opened wide and lapped at the delicate folds of Agnes's pussy.

"Mm-hmm!" Agnes hummed. It came out as a high squeak as her hands clutched at the sink and Penny's head. "Christ, Penny!" She began to shake when Penny curled her tongue into Agnes's core, seeking every luscious drop. Her thumb was slick with saliva as it swirled over Agnes's clit, winding around and around as Penny drilled with her tongue. Agnes came with a strangled sob, a hot, wet rush coating Penny's lips and chin.

Everything about Agnes was so fine and graceful, like drinking from a crystal flute and eating on bone china. She was refined and composed, even when she gasped and swore. Penny would always feel like an outcast in a five-star hotel because she was from a different world than Agnes. But for a handful of moments, Penny could have a handful of elegant, ethereal Agnes and that was an experience she would never forget. She'd gotten what she came for and Penny knew she could get off a thousand times on the way Agnes had squeaked her name.

That wasn't enough for Agnes, though. She grabbed Penny's hair, yanking her to her feet and backing her into the wall. Penny was already *there,* but her eyes rolled back when Agnes bit into her neck. Then, she slid Penny's panties to the side, her fingers urgent and demanding. They swept along Penny's folds, quickly parting them and pressing deep. Her fingers curled and Penny rose on her toes as Agnes's palm ground against her clit.

Penny would have screamed like a siren if Agnes hadn't captured her lips for a soul-stealing kiss that left her breathless and shaking for entirely different reasons. "Wow!" Penny hung onto Agnes's shoulders, blinking dazedly. It wasn't the kind of kiss that closed a show and Penny was rethinking her decision to decline Agnes's invitation to the Baccarat. "Maybe we could—"

There was a swift tap at the door. "Penny? Are you in there?" Reid whispered loudly. "The photographer's looking for everyone for family photos."

"I'll be right there," she answered, shooting Agnes an apologetic grimace.

Reid coughed softly. "Hurry. Penn's made it *very* clear that he's ready to leave. He's had a lot to drink and I'm not sure if we can trust him to behave for much longer."

"I'm on my way," Penny had said firmly, hoping Reid would get the hint and give her a moment.

"Go!" Agnes whispered, laughing as she lowered and scooped up Penny's dress. She helped Penny into it and found her shoes. Then, Agnes gave Penny a quick kiss before pushing her out of the bathroom. "I know what Reid's like when he's in charge of a reception and we can't keep the grooms waiting."

"Thanks!" Penny giggled and stole another kiss. She waved as she skipped down the stairs, but Penny regretted her hasty exit before she reached the bottom. She risked a glance at the bathroom, wondering if she should race back up and give Agnes her number "just in case." Penny's nerves got the better of her, though.

An inner voice that Penny seldom heard had whispered that Agnes would never give someone like *her* a chance and that she'd be making a fool of herself. "I'm coming!" Penny had called when Penn had spotted her and yelled for her to hurry up.

"Maybe I was wrong..." Penny mused, returning to the present.

"Wrong?" Dash asked and frowned at the glue stick in Penny's hand. "That's getting dry. Are you okay?"

Penny made a dismissive sound as she passed it to him.

"Yup! Just thinking about how wrong I was about Agnes. She was funny and kind and she wants to be a decent parent. Like her brother, Walker."

"That's so great," Dash said, then gasped excitedly. "Maybe she'll fall in love with her nanny like her brother, too." He wiggled his eyebrows at Penny.

"Hush!" She looked at the sticky petal in her hand before smacking it onto his forehead. It looked like a chicken's comb and she cackled.

"Oh, yeah?" Dash slapped a book cover onto her cheek. "Now Agnes can really check you out!"

"That's it," Penny rolled her eyes as she peeled it off and got up, taking her wine with her. "I've got an early morning. I'll finish this in the shower."

"Sweet dreams," he called after her. "About Agnes, probably," he added, earning a scowl from Penny before she stomped up the stairs.

"I will not dream about Agnes!" She stated on her way to the bathroom. *I might think about her while I'm in the shower, though.*

Chapter Five

Their first evening had gone just as smoothly as Penny had predicted. June was delighted to watch *Percy Jackson & the Olympians: The Lightning Thief*, even though she claimed it wasn't even close to as good as the book. From the few chapters they'd read, Agnes was inclined to agree, but she had still enjoyed the movie and her dinner on the sitting room floor with June. They stayed up until almost 11:00, giggling over their cheesecakes and glasses of chocolate milk until June let out a loud yawn and declared it "the best day ever."

Agnes had cried as she waited outside the bathroom door, holding a new teddy bear for June. It had been her best day ever, too, and tucking June in and kissing her goodnight had been a dream come true. Agnes knew Penny deserved half the credit. The quirky young nanny was right: the day had been an emotional rollercoaster for Agnes as well. She was elated and grateful to see that chapter of their adoption journey come to an end at one moment, then wallowing in mortification the next. The last thing she'd expected was to be confronted by a one-, or rather two-night stand in front of her brother, his family, and Pierce.

Penny was a lot more than a one-night stand.

Agnes snorted at the canopy over her bed. It was an even larger blue and gray version of June's and Agnes wondered if her bed was unusually big. June seemed to think it was huge when she explored their suite and Agnes's room.

How big is Penny's bed?

Agnes scolded herself for having a one-track mind and worried that she'd already stumbled with Penn Tucker's little sister. The modicum of common sense that existed within Agnes had screamed that fooling around with Penny was a bad idea. Walker's friends and *all* of Reid Marshall's nannies should have been off-limits, but Agnes couldn't resist the frisky nymph. Penny was utterly captivating and refreshingly direct, stunning Agnes and leaving her reeling after each encounter.

Fool me once...

Agnes blamed their first encounter on the champagne, the romantic wedding fumes, and Penny for being irresistible. She had looked like a luscious treat, waiting to be unwrapped and tasted as they flirted under the stars and string lights. Penny's long ginger waves had been arranged into a messy bun and she was wearing a gauzy pink baby doll dress. She'd tied a simple pink ribbon around her neck, letting the ends dangle along her nape. Penny's luminous skin was decorated with the wonders of summer. Tattooed bees buzzed around the flowers, mushrooms, and strawberries that trailed down her limbs and across her back.

She had seduced Agnes. Penny had pounced first and there wasn't a coy bone in that girl's body. Being pursued by someone as vibrant and enchanting as Penny had gone right to Agnes's head.

And Penny came out swinging as soon as Walker introduced them. "Wow! You're even more stunning up close." She held onto Agnes's hand and stood on her tiptoes. "Wanna dance?" Penny asked with a giggle as she kissed Agnes's cheek.

"Thank you, yes, and it's nice to meet you..."

She had swept Agnes right off her feet while they were dancing, flirting and teasing before they snuck away to meet in the study. Penny had thoroughly enthralled Agnes, then slipped out the window. Agnes was left reeling and holding a hastily written note.

Thank you for a magical evening.

That was it.

Agnes had told herself it wasn't a big deal or as good as her memory made it out to be. She had no reason whatsoever to expect a call or a text—they hadn't even mentioned exchanging numbers or seeing each other ever again—but she had secretly hoped Penny might track her down through Walker.

That hadn't happened and Agnes had moved on a few weekends later, but she'd still thought of Penny in the quiet moments of the night. She was usually touching herself or using a toy at the time and afterward, Agnes would wonder why Penny never called and what would have happened if she had.

But Penny was even lovelier than Agnes remembered when they met almost two years later at Penn Tucker and Morris

Mosby's commitment ceremony. Of course, Agnes had jumped at the chance to attend with Walker. What better way to prove that Penn's sister hadn't made much of an impression and that it hadn't been that big of a deal? But Agnes got cold feet as soon as they arrived and Penny was just a few yards away. There was a tickle of nervous excitement and Agnes felt flushed every time their eyes met.

It was hard to look at anyone but Penny. Her pale blue beaded flapper dress floated around her thighs, *almost* too short to be decent and offering a tantalizing view of her entire back and tattoos. She looked like everything that was *good* about summer and Agnes knew she tasted like tart berries and morning dew. Agnes was actually trembling as Walker steered them closer to the cake so they could join Penny and the grooms.

"Agnes, this is *the* legendary Morris Mosby," Walker drawled as he gave Morris's shoulder a familiar squeeze. Agnes had heard that Morris had become a regular visitor at The Killian House. Apparently, Reid had asked if Walker could look after Morris's investment portfolio after the death of his twin sister.

"I am a huge fan!" Agnes shamelessly raved about her favorite albums before Walker dragged her away.

"And you remember Pennsylvania and his little sister, Penny."

"Of course," Agnes replied coolly as she kissed Penn's cheek. "Congratulations! I'm so happy for you, Penn."

"Thanks, and thank you for coming!"

"Are you kidding? This is the most exclusive event of the season," Agnes said.

"You've met Penny Lane, right?" Penn asked and Agnes smiled and nodded.

"I have." She offered her hand casually but was pulled into a hug.

"It's so amazing to see you again!" Penny kissed each of Agnes's cheeks, then leaned back. "And you look *amazing*. Wanna dance?"

"Thank you. I..." Agnes blinked at her, feeling disoriented. She was almost inclined to believe she'd imagined their last encounter, Penny was so unaware and unaffected as she smiled expectantly at Agnes. "Sure."

Agnes experienced deja vu when Penny hooked their arms and towed Agnes away so they'd have more space and a little privacy. "What's it like being the loveliest and the most elegant, every time you walk into a room?" Penny asked with a sigh, making Agnes chuckle.

"I'm sure I wouldn't know. So... How have you been?"

"Wonderful," Penny said simply and was content to sing along with the music and wreak havoc on Agnes's nerves. Agnes had chosen a simple silver silk sheath dress and had worn her hair up because the forecast had promised a warm evening, but she got chills as Penny's fingers glided down her spine. "Wanna sneak away again? There's a bathroom upstairs just for the wedding party and it looks like everyone's out here," she added, her neck craning as she perused the garden.

That's it?

Agnes was even more confused. No apologies or explanations. Not even an awkward excuse.

But she'd snuck away with Penny for an incredibly hot quickie in the bathroom anyway.

She couldn't shake the feeling that Penny *could be* her soulmate, but once again, they didn't exchange numbers or promises to stay in touch. Agnes spent the next few weeks kicking herself for letting Penny slip through her fingers again.

Why hadn't *she* asked if she could call or if they could get together for drinks or dinner?

I should have said something to Walker, she'd admitted to herself, then immediately dismissed the idea. He wouldn't be able to resist teasing her and playing matchmaker, and he certainly owed her, after the way she had meddled when he was fighting his feelings for Fin. She worried that he'd already caught on to her and set her up with Penny as the nanny in an attempt to settle the score. "No..." She glared at the canopy defiantly. "I'll ride it out. He might not know and Penny's clearly over it. I can be too."

She nodded and pulled the covers up to her chin. There was a soft tap on the door before it cracked open. "Agnes?" A tiny voice called.

Agnes sat up and leaned toward the foot of her bed. "June? Is that you, sweetheart?" She called and June's head peeked around the door.

"I've never been by myself like this before and I can't sleep."

"I'm so sorry! Would you sleep better here with me?" Agnes asked, throwing back the covers and patting the bed next to her.

June hesitated for just a moment, then hurried around the footboard and onto the bed. "I got scared and then I forgot which door was yours and I got *really* scared!"

"You poor thing," Agnes said, lying on her side. June did the same, easing back gingerly and remaining rigid until Agnes pulled the covers around them and hugged June against her chest. June slowly exhaled as she gradually sank into Agnes's embrace, then sighed and snuggled closer. Agnes bit down on her lips, afraid she'd laugh or cry and spook June. But it felt like magic to Agnes, holding June and knowing *she'd* made her feel safe and happy. "Tell me what scared you and we'll have Pierce fix it immediately," she vowed.

There was a soft titter from June and she shook her head. "It's a really pretty room but I've never slept by myself before and it's really quiet here," she whispered, as if she was afraid someone would hear them. "I'm worried that Uncle Walker and Fin and the triplets will change their mind and they won't want me here anymore," June said, her neck stretching around so she could see Agnes's face.

She whispered June's name and kissed her temple. "I told you, that won't happen. I've done just about every rotten thing you can imagine and the worst Walker's ever done was threaten to send me to a convent."

That made June giggle. The sound made Agnes's eyes water and her nose burn, it was so beautiful. "He's really nice. Do you think the girls will want to borrow any of my books? I don't have any other toys or pretty things I can share with them."

"You will soon, sweetheart. But they don't care. They're just so excited to have a new cousin to play with and chase around this old place."

"I can't wait to see Penny tomorrow."

"Really?" Agnes leaned back and raised a brow at her.

"I think she's awesome! Penny said she's going to teach me how to do yoga. And she said she'd see if we can go fishing with her dad in Hoboken. I've always wanted to go fishing!"

"That does sound like a lot of fun," Agnes agreed. "I'm fond of yoga myself so I'll join you and I love being on the water," she added.

"Are you a good swimmer? I took some lessons and I'm okay, but it was always really loud and crowded when we went to the pool and I'd get nervous."

"I'm a very strong swimmer and I'm sure Penny is too,"

Agnes said, and June's hum of agreement turned into a yawn. That was another magical victory so Agnes decided to keep sharing. "I was proficient in many sports. Mostly because my mother and the other society snobs said it was unladylike when I was a young girl. I swam, rowed, rode horses, played soccer, sailed, and even did a little mountain climbing. I almost played field hockey for Columbia, but I went to school for art instead."

"That's still really cool," June said, yawning again. "I'm good at jump roping and I used to swing a lot when we'd go to the playground. Ms. Mary's son, Anthony, was teaching me how to play basketball," she said and sounded sad.

"We can visit him and Mary whenever you want."

"Really?" June perked up momentarily.

"Of course. I think Mary is a wonderful woman and her home felt like a special place. I'd like to go back. Maybe you can come up with some ideas for how we can make things even better for them there."

June wiggled around so she was facing Agnes. "I'd love that! Can we send them lots of those big paper rolls for art? We liked to draw *a lot*. And lots of crayons!" She added, getting louder as her excitement grew.

"All the crayons they could ever need," Agnes said, shushing softly. "But we're going to think bigger and give my assistant a serious list. Maybe we can think about it before we head out tomorrow." She made her voice softer and slower as she stroked June's hair. It was working and June made a drowsy, contented sound as she hugged Agnes's middle and burrowed into her.

"I keep thinking this has to be a dream because you're exactly the kind of mom I would have wished for."

"You're my dream girl, June. I didn't give a lot of thought to what my perfect daughter would be like, but every time I learn something new about you, I feel like you were made for me and I was made for you."

"I feel that way too, Agnes. Everything else here is kind of scary, but I don't mind when I'm with you."

"Then, we'll stick together. I'll always, always, always protect you and we're going to go on lots of adventures and collect so many books."

"Should I...should I call you Agnes or do you want me to call you Mom?"

"I... Oh. Well..." Agnes had devolved to hoarse croaks. "I'd like it if you called me Mom, but only if you want to. And you can also call me Agnes. Both work," she babbled.

"Both, but mostly Mom?"

"That sounds perfect, sweetheart." She whispered the words into June's hair, so grateful to Walker for pushing her to follow this wild idea to the end. She'd almost given up several times, but he had promised that her child was out there waiting, and he'd been so right.

Penny drifted back into Agnes's thoughts. It wasn't surprising that June had taken to the vivacious younger woman so quickly. Penny was warm and intuitive and had immediately tuned into June's needs to the exclusion of all others.

She was *nothing* like Camilla. Agnes had thought their old nanny was warm and affectionate—she'd been the *only* source of warmth and affection in Agnes's and Walker's childhoods—but Camilla had still maintained more traditional boundaries. She'd wipe their cheek with her handkerchief or smooth the hair away from their eyes and there was the occasional hug after a bad dream or a scuffed knee. But Penny bombarded Agnes's senses, showering her and June with affection. Everyone was treated to spontaneous hugs, high fives, or a kiss on the cheek, but Penny had been the most generous with June and Agnes and automatically gravitated to their side. She loved everyone and had plenty of laughter and smiles to share, but there was no doubting that Penny was *solely* there for June and Agnes. They were her absolute priority and to Agnes, that felt like a blessing.

And as Penny had predicted, June had recovered from her shock and the two were already bonding. There was no telling what was going through Penny's head when she agreed to come on as June's nanny, but Agnes was already profoundly grateful. And she was optimistic. If she could work this much magic in an evening, what could Penny do in a few months or a year?

Initially, her brother's intentions may have been misguided, yet he'd found June the perfect nanny when he thrust Penny back into Agnes's life. It had felt like a catastrophe at first, but now the unconventional young woman was ready to shape Agnes into the mother June deserved.

If Agnes could behave herself and keep her head out of her nanny's pants.

Overalls, Agnes reminded herself, smiling as she drifted off to sleep with June.

Chapter Six

Penny was focused and ready with her A-game when she faced The Killian House the next morning. She had her favorite amethyst and a black tourmaline heart stone in her pocket to combat the mild flutter of anxiety she'd woken with. She'd tried yoga and a big bowl of oatmeal with blueberries, but it had lingered. Penny told herself it was just the anticipation of seeing June again and getting her hands dirty with her new family.

It had nothing to do with Agnes.

Nope. Not one little bit!

She crossed her fingers and interlocked her thumbs, said a quick prayer, then used her outstretched pinkie to give the buzzer a "lucky" push. The door was thrown open a few seconds later and Penny received a low "Ma'am," as Pierce bowed and waved her in.

Penny couldn't help but pull her shoulders back and straighten her spine. "Good morning, Pierce," she replied with a graceful nod.

She was doing her best impression of Agnes, hoping to

impress Pierce. As Agnes's nanny, Penny wasn't technically part of The Killian House's staff, but she still wanted the starchy older butler's approval. Penny had worked for enough wealthy people to understand that the butler ran the ship in any household and the fastest way to drown was to get on his bad side. But Pierce was much more than your average butler. Penny had heard enough from Fin to know that Walker respected his butler implicitly and that Pierce was the house's heartbeat.

"Ms. Cameron is still in bed. As is Miss June," he informed her softly. "Breakfast is being prepared and they'll be dining upstairs, instead of in the dining room with the rest of the family. You may wait in the kitchen if you like. There are beverages and pastries if you're hungry or we can send another plate up with Ms. Cameron's and Miss June's," he said quietly and quickly.

Penny's lips twisted as she considered. "I already ate and I'd hate to be in the way," she began, then turned as Fin rushed down the stairs.

"Thanks, Pierce! I can take it from here," he said, opening his arms wide and scooping Penny into a hug. "Good morning! It's so great to have another early riser in the house."

"Eek! Good morning!" Penny squealed as she squeezed his neck, then kissed his cheek. "How did last night go? I didn't hear a peep out of Agnes or June after I left."

"So great!" Fin set her down and fanned his eyes. "You have to see this." They shared more gleeful hugs and giddy squeals as Fin grabbed Penny's hand and pulled her up the stairs to the third floor. They were silent as they hurried through the sitting room on their tiptoes. "Hang onto your pigtails," he whispered, then eased Agnes's bedroom door open.

A breathless "Oh!" huffed from Penny and she clutched her chest.

Agnes was curled protectively around June and the little girl looked so peaceful and content. Her hands were tucked under her cheek and a faint smile curved her lips. But it was the way Agnes cradled her child, with her nose nestled in June's hair, that nearly knocked Penny off her feet. She looked like she couldn't get enough of June and that she truly cherished her. And June could feel it too.

Penny hadn't realized she was crying until Fin passed her a Kleenex. "Let's go!" He whispered and gave the strap of her overalls a tug. She followed, blowing her nose once they returned to the sitting room.

"I think that might have been the sweetest thing I've ever seen," she said, receiving a jerky nod from Fin as he brushed away a tear of his own.

"I keep these on me at all times now," he explained as he tucked a pack of tissues into the pocket of his cardigan. "I've wanted this so badly for Agnes, but it's even better than I ever imagined."

"Who knew Agnes Cameron had it in her?" Penny chuckled, but Fin's brow furrowed.

"Um... Just about anyone who knows Agnes," he said and snorted when he caught Penny's surprised expression. "There is no limit to what Agnes would do for the people she loves. Like, *none*. She'd burn down Manhattan for Walker or bust me out of prison if I got into trouble. And she's *lived* for the triplets since the day they were born."

Penny remembered Agnes's A-B-C tattoo and dabbed at the corner of her eyes. "I had no idea. Everyone says she's a wrecking ball and doesn't give a damn, that she does whatever the hell she wants."

That got a good laugh out of Fin. "Chaos, thy name is Agnes. There's no telling what she'll do next because she can be wildly impractical, but you can bet that she's gonna look hot while she's doing it. And she's all or nothing. Agnes never does anything halfway."

The other empty bedroom was proof of Agnes's thoughtfulness and her complete commitment to June. Penny had expected an adult suite that had been haphazardly stocked with toys, but it was clearly a child's room. The bedding was similar to the triplets', but in a soft shade of gray. The furniture was upholstered in coordinating gray velvet, but the pieces were smaller—for an older child or a teen. There was a gauzy tent in the corner filled with oversized pillows and string lights glowed invitingly, making it an ideal spot for reading, decompressing, or meditating. A wall of bookshelves was ready to be filled with books, teddy bears, puzzles, craft supplies... And a telescope was set up in front of one of the windows. It was a clean slate and Penny imagined *any* child would be thrilled to move in and make it their own.

Fin put an arm around Penny. "Walker says the triplets love Agnes because she's even more chaotic than they are, but she's just great with the girls and they love her. They know they're safe and that they're the center of her world when they're together and that's why I knew she was going to be an amazing mom. I have concerns about June and the triplets, though," he said under his breath, gesturing for Penny to follow as he shoved his hands into the pockets of his corduroys and headed for the stairs. He was the same old Fin Penny had known for almost twenty years and she was glad that marrying Walker and moving into The Killian House hadn't changed him.

"I'm already worried that June's going to have to compete for Agnes's attention," Penny said and Fin hummed in agreement.

"You noticed too." He sounded pleased and guided her around the stairs when they reached the foyer on the main floor. "The triplets won't mean to do it because they *want* to be the best cousins ever, but Agnes has always been very hands-on and showers them with affection. June needs 100% of that right now. I'm just not sure if Agnes or the triplets are capable of stepping back from each other and maintaining a little distance."

"Agnes will try," Penny guessed, then shook her head. "We might need a backup plan if this goes the way you're expecting."

"That's what I was thinking so I thought I'd give you a heads-up."

They chatted about options in the kitchen and Fin asked the cook to add sprinkles to the triplets' pancakes because they had crushed their last math test. "They're little geniuses! Their tutor says he's never met kids that smart before!" He boasted. Fin was fizzing with pride as he requested whipped cream and *more* sprinkles. "I can't wait for him to meet June. She's so clever and such a pistol once she opens up."

"She really is. I can see why Agnes fell head over heels for our little June bug," Penny said.

"Me too. And Agnes is *the best* and you're going to love her once you get used to some of the Camerons'...foibles," he said with a sheepish wince. "They honestly can't help how they were raised and they don't mean it when they sound like rich snobs, I swear."

"Fin!" Penny giggled as she looked around the kitchen, but he just waved it off.

"I'm telling you, you're going to have so much fun with the Camerons and you'll fall in love with Agnes," he predicted.

"Maybe," Penny replied with a breezy smile. "Let's see how today goes. Agnes won't love *me* if I tell her this won't work," she said, quickly changing the subject because falling in love with Agnes Cameron was the last thing Penny wanted to do.

The pancakes on Agnes's and June's plates were less festive because Penny thought they'd prefer their breakfasts more low-key. She picked at their fruit salads while they munched on bacon and discussed their plans for the day. Agnes was taking June out for some shopping and lunch while Penny stayed behind and helped Fin distract the triplets.

As they had expected, the triplets were obviously disappointed when they weren't able to join June and Agnes for their outing. They did their best not to pout because Fin explained that June needed some time to bond with Agnes and that she was still in a little shock. But they must have asked when June and Agnes would return a hundred times between the three of them. And the triplets stampeded to the nursery door when June and Agnes reappeared a few hours after lunch.

"Where did you go?"

"What did you buy?"

"Did you get ice cream?" This from Beatrice, of course.

June looked flustered again, clinging to Agnes's side and answering in timid mumbles.

"She's trying," Fin whispered to Penny, pointing at Agnes.

She had an arm around June but she was using the other to comfort Charlotte because Beatrice had scolded her for asking *too many* questions. "It's fine, Charlie! June found lots of books and some fun board games to play with you later."

"Yikes," Penny whispered back at Fin and shook her head. "I don't know if the novelty is going to wear off fast enough for the triplets or if June can cope with this much attention. And she shouldn't have to compete for Agnes's attention right now, either," she added, earning an emphatic head shake from Fin.

"This won't do. You need to talk to Agnes."

"No sweat," Penny said, holding up her thumb. Even though she had begun to sweat and was rubbing the heart stone in her pocket for all it was worth.

But her solution was simple and ingenious and Penny loved it more and more by the minute. She had a feeling Agnes would need convincing because Penny's plan was...a little extreme. And she'd be testing Agnes's limits and her boundaries. She was also putting Agnes's trust to the test.

To Penny, it was a no-brainer because she was a whole-hearted believer in the power of nature to heal, inspire, and soothe. Especially for less fortunate children like June who rarely got an opportunity to leave the city. Penny also had a feeling that getting Agnes outside of her comfort zone and away from her assistant and servants would help her focus and bond better with June.

"Hey, Agnes," Fin had distracted Charlotte and Beatrice by asking them to clear off the art table while Amelia called for snacks. "I think Penny wants to have a quick word," he said, then asked June if she wanted to see where he hid the best stickers.

"I already know where this is headed," Agnes said when she joined Penny in the hall. Her eyes were still on June, though.

Penny crossed her fingers behind her back for luck. "I bet you don't and I'm hoping you can keep an open mind."

"Try me," Agnes said, sounding wary.

"We need to help June find some high ground," she started, causing Agnes to gasp.

"I know the triplets are coming on strong, but they'll settle down. They're just overjoyed to have a new cousin to play with," she said defensively.

"I know!" Penny held up her hands and shushed gently. "They're being the sweetest and I'm so proud of them," she stated firmly. Then her gaze hardened. "But right now, *our* little girl is very overwhelmed. She feels like an outsider and she's having to compete for your attention."

"I was afraid of that, but I had hoped the triplets would settle down after a day or two." Agnes turned and peeked around the door. June had wrapped herself into a tight ball, her arms around her knees, and her huge eyes swung between the triplets and around the nursery. "I was so sure this would feel like a dream come true, but she looks terrified."

"It's too much," Penny whispered as she watched from around Agnes's shoulder. "She doesn't see all the new books and art supplies. *Yet.* Right now, she sees three pretty princesses who dress and talk and think alike and she's in *their* castle. And you and the triplets already share a deep bond. June's already seeing it and worried if you'll love her as much as them and if they'll resent her for taking you away. That could create some tension and make June's transition more difficult."

"But our girls would never!" Agnes insisted quietly. "They can be vicious little pranksters, but we've all been excited about this for months and they've promised to love June and make her feel welcomed."

Penny gathered Agnes's hands and gave them a reassuring squeeze. "Of course! They have the *best* intentions." She waited until their eyes locked and leaned closer until their foreheads and noses nearly touched, demanding Agnes's focus and wordlessly asking for her trust. "Amelia, Bea, and Charlotte are being the best cousins ever. But June's not ready for this. She needs to be the center of attention for a while and she needs time to feel secure in her relationship with *you*, first. And you need the freedom to give June your undivided attention. You might try, but you *can't* hold back with the triplets and I don't want to make you choose."

"Okay... What do you suggest?" Agnes had leaned back and crossed her arms over her chest.

"I was thinking we could get out of the city until your new place is ready."

"Oh. That's fine. We'll go to the cottage." Agnes turned and waved. "Pierce?"

"Wait!" Penny caught Agnes's hand. "That's not what I had in mind," she said, glancing at their hands and wincing, then looking toward the stairs as Pierce appeared. "Never mind!" Penny told him and smiled at Agnes. They were still holding hands and Agnes was blinking at Penny curiously. "That twelve-bedroom colonial palace in Sagaponack is breathtaking, but it *is not* a cottage," Penny informed her.

"What's wrong with my cottage?" This time, Agnes sounded truly offended but then Penny felt a rush of sadness and loneliness from her. Agnes's eyelids fluttered as she pulled in a steadying breath.

"I'm so sorry," Penny whispered and cradled Agnes's cheek. "I bet they were really special, whoever you're missing."

Agnes's jaw fell as a large teardrop formed on her eyelashes and dropped onto the carpet between them "How did you...?"

"Pisces sun with Cancer moon *and* Cancer rising," Penny explained with a solemn nod.

Agnes stared back at Penny. "I don't know what that means."

Penny smiled and shrugged, used to the blank looks or eye rolls whenever she explained that she could feel other people's moods and sense when the people she loved the most were close. "It means I have an extra antenna. It's easy for me to tune in and pick up someone's emotional wavelength. I can practically hear Penn's thoughts and I know when he's close by. I can't explain it. It's like knowing there's a plate of warm cookies in the room when he's around. And I'll always follow my heart."

"I see... I know I'm a Scorpio, but I've never really cared enough about astrology to learn more," Agnes admitted. "The cottage has always been our hideout. The three of us would head there whenever we needed a getaway."

"The three of us?" Penny parroted gently.

"Me and Walker and Connor—Walker's first husband."

"You were close?"

Agnes nodded and chuckled. "Like the Three Stooges, but Connor was the normie and Walker was the uptight one."

"I'm so sorry for your loss," Penny said as her hands glided up and down Agnes's arms, soothing and comforting her.

"It was worse for Walker. Connor was his entire world. He was so *lonely* before Fin came to rescue him and the girls."

"I'm glad fate brought them together. Fin's one of my closest friends and it makes my heart so happy to see how much love he has in his life now."

"That's how I feel about Walker," Agnes said, easing out of Penny's embrace and retreating to the doorjamb. She rested her cheek against it and watched as Fin distracted the triplets with an impromptu dance lesson, allowing June a chance to retreat to a bean bag chair on the edge of what was now the "dance rug." June was clearly more comfortable as a spectator and the triplets were having fun entertaining her while Fin taught them a dance he had learned from TikTok. "I don't see why the cottage won't work until East 63rd is ready. The cottage might bore June to tears, but it's not *that* bad. I have a room ready for her there too."

Penny leaned against the opposite jamb. "It's a beautiful place, but it's too big and she'll feel lonely there."

"Lonely? The staff at the cottage is small and lovely. I adore Camilla. She's my Pierce and was more of a mother growing up than the black hole that birthed me."

"Oh, dear."

"I was fine. We were both fine because we had Camilla," Agnes said with a bored swat. "She's eighty-two now and retired ages ago, but she was our nanny. Walker moved her to the guest house and put her in charge of the cottage when we went off to school. She still lives there and I spend most of the holidays with her."

"I bet Camilla is an angel," Penny said sincerely, but her nose wrinkled. "It isn't exactly a *normal* environment for a child, though, and it'll be easier for June to hide there."

"Hide?"

Penny nodded. "How much is just one of the dining chairs worth?"

Agnes gestured dismissively. "I couldn't care less."

"June will. She's still afraid to touch something she isn't supposed to and she'll want to hide if she breaks a plate or spills juice on the furniture. Let's go someplace where the furniture's already got stains and been patched up. Let's go someplace small and out of the way so we have to bump into each other and *bond*."

"What did you have in mind?" Agnes asked suspiciously.

"I've got a cabin up in the Catskills!" Penny sang and cheered excitedly. "June bug will love it. The closest she's ever been to nature is Central Park but she'll be able to run amuck and climb trees up at my cabin. And think of all the bugs and birds and little furry things we'll get to play with!"

Her giddy delight seemed to set off warning sirens for Agnes. "Hold on. What kind of cabin are we talking about?" She asked, leaning back and looking around like she might call for help again.

"Okay." Penny turned Agnes and held onto her shoulders. "It's a perfectly decent camping cabin by most people's standards. But it's probably fairer to call it glamping, by yours."

"Hmmm... That sounds ominous. Is there running water?"

"Yes!" Penny spluttered and swatted Agnes's arm. "It used to just be the pump in the kitchen, but Dad and Penn added a bathroom with running water and a water heater when I was six."

"Dear Lord," Agnes murmured.

"It'll be great! We can jump in Cherry Lake whenever we want and there's no one out there but my aunt Mabel and my uncle Silas. She was actually my mom's aunt and he's technically my cousin because he's Mabel's son, but we always called him Uncle Silas or just Silas," Penny babbled, then caught herself. "They have a little farm next door. The cabin was left to my mom and they took care of it for us until we were old enough to look after it ourselves."

"I see." Agnes frowned and fidgeted with the hem of her cardigan.

Penny could feel the *no* rising in Agnes. "It's not as isolated as it used to be but it's still quiet on our corner of the lake and the area's stayed pretty private," she added.

Agnes sucked in a breath. "That means it's hard to get to and extremely primitive. It would be a spa or a resort if it had decent road access," she translated, making Penny smirk.

"It's a little...cozy, but it's heaven, I promise."

"Does it have air conditioning?" Agnes asked and Penny snorted.

"Why would we need it? The high might get up to seventy-five or *maybe* eighty once or twice this summer. The weather's perfect for sleeping with the windows open and listening to the katydids and peepers."

"Penny, I'm not sure if—"

"Do you trust me?" Penny asked, cutting Agnes off.

"For the most part."

Penny's finger shot up. "Hold on. You *have to* be able to trust me. I'm caring for your child."

Agnes waved dismissively. "I know I can trust you with June. Even if I didn't know you, I know Reid and Fin and I've met your brother a few times. I trust their judgment if they tell me you're the best nanny for June. I'm just not sure if I trust your...standards when it comes to accommodations," she said with an apologetic smile, earning a serious "Hmm" from Penny.

"That's a super fair point and I'm not gonna lie: it's pretty rustic and there will be ticks."

Agnes jumped and shook her head. "Oh, God. No."

"Don't worry! There're ways to scare most critters away without dipping ourselves in chemicals. And I'll be happy to help you check for ticks at bedtime," Penny whispered and gave Agnes a playful poke.

"Umm... Okay." Agnes turned back to the nursery and stared at the girls.

"Okay!" Penny clapped and danced a little jig. She wasn't sure *why* she'd offered to check Agnes for ticks, but Penny waited for *that* fantasy to finish playing out before bracing her hands on her hips. "Pack your bags, Agnes Cameron. You're headed to the Catskills for a month of family fun and bonding in the country," she announced like a gameshow host. She had a feeling she was playing herself by inviting Agnes Cameron to the cabin because there'd be no hiding how uncouth and unsuitable Penny was. But... "I'll bet every carroty hair on my head that June's going to love it."

Agnes winced at Penny. "You're absolutely sure she'll love it?"

"I promise, this will be good for both of you. But more than anything, June is going to have a blast." It was an easy promise for Penny to make. She couldn't think of any place better for a child to play and explore. She couldn't think of any place better in the world and couldn't wait to share it with Agnes and June.

"Alright..." Agnes was watching June. "I guess I can't say no if this will be good for June and make her happy. I'm in."

Chapter Seven

Agnes had to admit, Penny was right again: June was ecstatic about the trip to the cabin. Especially when she learned that it would be *just* the three of them. With Penny's great-aunt Mabel and her uncle Silas close by to make sure they had everything they needed.

June said she felt bad, leaving the triplets behind, but they planned to be penpals and call over FaceTime whenever they had a strong connection. Penny warned that phone reception was seriously patchy and only good in a few spots and strongest on the end of the dock. That was alarming, but Agnes's assistant, Melinda, had promised to hold down the fort in her absence.

"Do you think the triplets would want to borrow some of my *Percy Jackson* books while we're gone?" June asked just before she nodded off later that night.

Agnes made a shushing noise and kissed June's hair. "We're still reading them and Walker ordered a set. We're leaving early in the morning, but you and your cousins can FaceTime and talk about what kinds of books they like when we're at the cabin. If Penny isn't dragging us to the Bermuda Triangle," Agnes said, making June giggle. The sound made Agnes's tummy flip. Agnes thought it might be her new favorite thing in the world.

"I can't wait to see Penny's cabin."

"Really?" Agnes leaned back and raised a brow at her. "I promise, you can tell me if you're scared about this trip. I will not be disappointed. We could always try the cottage if you'd prefer something a little more comfortable and...modern."

Her hopes were dashed when June shook her head. "I think it's gonna be awesome! Penny said my room is like having my own treehouse and I've always wanted to go up in a treehouse."

"That does sound lovely," Agnes whispered softly. She brushed her fingers through June's hair and felt the last of the tension leave the girl's frame as she melted against Agnes.

Lovely?

What had she done? Agnes had been a mother for a little more than twenty-four hours and she was already making questionable decisions. And why? Because the new nanny was unfathomably gorgeous and had Agnes in the palm of her hand.

Agnes reminded herself that Fin had given his complete approval, insisting that this would be "a rad adventure" and just what June and Agnes needed. He also endorsed Penny as a camp leader and nature expert, calling her their Plant Nerd Supreme. Fin said he had only heard tales and seen pictures of the Tuckers' cabin in Cherrytown, but he promised they were headed to paradise.

Alone in paradise with June and Penny for a month?

That's when they had to return for their check-in with June's social worker, and by then the contractors and the interior designer would have the place on East 63rd ready. It would also give June two weeks to get settled there before school started. According to Penny, there was nothing else for Agnes and June to do but meet her in front of The Killian House at 7:00 the next morning. Agnes had requested that her car be ready and they were packed, but she was still having second thoughts.

She said she'd do anything to make the transition easier for June and their new family, but this was testing her limits. Agnes was naturally athletic and enjoyed most sports, and she was happiest when she was on, in, or near the water, but the rest of nature? She had an aversion to most insects—ticks in particular—and panicked if *anything* got in her hair. Sweating made her extremely irritable and she couldn't eat or sleep if she was hot and her body was sticky.

But she would be alone with June and Penny for a month and Agnes did like the thought of that. And she *had to* try if Penny thought she could transform Agnes into a decent parent and help June feel more secure.

Packing with June had been an unexpected treat for Agnes. The little girl was over the moon when she found out they were going to a cabin in the woods and that there would be fishingand lots of "critters."

Agnes wasn't looking forward to the critters but had resolved to make the best of it and stay positive for June. This was just the sort of thing Agnes's mother would have scoffed at. It was also the sort of adventure that Agnes and Walker had dreamt of and longed for as children. They had made blanket forts at the cottage and pretended they were camping in the woods or living in a treehouse in the jungle. Agnes would be brave for her inner eight-year-old and to show June that she wasn't a prissy stick in the mud.

If Agnes could survive the Catskills and resist temptation. Which would be right in arm's reach, from the sound of things. Agnes wasn't seriously claustrophobic, but she was prone to restlessness and felt particularly so in smaller spaces after more than a few minutes. How would she cope with spending every day with Penny in such close quarters? And June would be there to witness Agnes's humiliation because there was no way she wouldn't stare and get tongue-tied. She wouldn't be able to go more than a few days without making an ass out of herself over Penny.

Despite the fact that she was heading out into the tick-infested unknown to live in a cramped and rustic cabin with June and her ultimate crush, Agnes was still grateful to Penny for putting their past aside and giving her another chance. Agnes decided she'd treat the summer like a parenting boot camp and would put herself in Penny's capable hands.

Penny's *clever* hands. They had wound Agnes up when they were alone at the cottage and The Merchant's House, but to see them in action while she was tying June's shoelace and braiding a section of hair that kept falling into her little girl's face...

For the love of—!

Why did Agnes have to think about Penny's hands? They were rougher—scarred, the fingers tipped with little callouses. Did she play an instrument or was that from an art or a craft? Being an artist, Agnes was captivated by Penny's colorful botanical tattoos, the faint blues, greens, and pinks staining her nibbled cuticles, and her rainbow punk ensemble. Penny was vibrant in a way that people in Agnes's world shied away from and turned their noses up at. That drew Agnes to Penny even more. And made Agnes desire her more.

Agnes wanted to prove she could be vivacious and fun because she didn't want to let June down. But there was also the novel desire to be noticed by a very cute girl that Agnes hadn't experienced since she was in her late teens and early twenties. It had been a very long time since Agnes had felt giddy and wanted to turn someone's head the way she wanted to turn Penny's.

And so few people had the ability to truly impress Agnes these days. Penny had been eye-catching and Agnes had blamed her irresistibility on too much champagne before, but seeing Penny "in the wild" and doing what she did best had only made her more enthralling. She wasn't just a natural with children, she spoke their language and understood how their little brains processed the world and the grownups around them.

Seeing Penny and Fin conferring as they observed and diagnosed in the nursery had afforded Agnes a chance to see a new side to both of them. Their combined expertise in an area that many of the city's wealthiest and most powerful figures frequently failed was humbling to Agnes. These were far more than high-paid babysitters. Fin and Penny had been trained by Reid Marshall to be childcare oracles who could save hapless parents from themselves and repair struggling families.

That was god-tier in Agnes's book because many of the skills that Penny and Fin possessed couldn't be learned from a manual or by watching a mentor. They had finely honed instincts and natural charm that children and adults alike were drawn to. Both had a heady and beguiling combination of charisma and quick wit that was uniquely effective, and Agnes felt blessed to have befriended them, and for Penny's willingness to help.

It behooved Agnes to repay Penny—and overlook their past indiscretions—with trust and complete cooperation. Even if it meant roughing it in a ramshackle cabin for four weeks. Agnes shuddered as she imagined the worst.

But then, as if to remind her of *why* she'd agreed to go in the first place, June mumbled something in her sleep that included the word "Mommy" and huddled closer. Suddenly, Agnes would wade into an active volcano if it would make her little girl happy.

Agnes accepted that a month in a cramped cabin was a small price to pay to give June a stronger, happier start as a Cameron. And that was a truly humbling thought because there wasn't a soul alive who could have talked Agnes into spending *four minutes* in that cabin before she'd fallen hopelessly in love with June.

It was a strange metric and one that most people would never understand, but Agnes was encouraged and hopeful. She was saying yes to things her mother would have run screaming from and it was working! That was probably a dangerous way to go about parenting, but Penny was there to hold up the guardrails and act as a safety net. She knew the good ways to get into trouble and healthy ways to nurture Agnes's and June's curiosity.

Penny was so completely wholesome—when she wasn't being a seductive minx—and entirely dedicated to creating positivity and peace. There wasn't a coy or calculating bone in her body and she wasn't capable of being selfish or malicious. People like that rarely entered Agnes's sphere and she usually sent them fleeing. But for whatever reason, Penny was still willing to give Agnes a chance so she'd do her best to behave.

The thought tickled Agnes and a soft smile tugged at her lips as she grew drowsy. It had taken motherhood and an untamed nanny to get Agnes to settle down and set aside her own needs and desires. She certainly desired Penny in a very potent way, but even that had become secondary to her desire to please June and make her feel safe.

In a way, the cabin would be a test of Agnes's self-control, maturity, and ability to put June's needs first. It all would have been laughable before June, but Agnes had faith in herself and she knew that Penny was there to back her up and guide her.

And Agnes knew exactly where she'd guide Penny if it were up to her...

For the love of—!

Why couldn't Agnes go five minutes without thinking about Penny like that? She gave herself a mental flick on the forehead and refocused. She reviewed the shoes she'd selected and the fun things Melinda had found for the trip. There were travel games to play with June, cute bug-repellent bracelets, shimmering sunscreens, inflatable emojis and glazed donut rafts, sunglasses for just about any occasion or ensemble...

Agnes paused in her inventory. She was asking for trouble, packing her "lucky" red bikini and her sexiest Louboutins. But she felt unstoppable in the ensemble and the extra confidence would come in handy. Unfortunately, Agnes was also irresistible because who didn't appreciate a beautiful woman in a little red bikini and high heels? It never failed and Agnes felt electric as she turned heads. She reasoned that she could tone it down with a sheer black cover-up, an oversized, floppy black hat, and her biggest black sunglasses. If needed.

Agnes might be going into the wild, but she wasn't going unarmed and she'd look like dynamite while she was doing it. Knowing herself as well as she did, Agnes accepted that it was best to follow Penny's lead. That was a little risky because there was no telling where Penny's boundaries were or if she had any. Oddly enough, Agnes still trusted Penny completely. She might be rough around the edges and unpredictable, but Agnes *liked that.* And she respected Penny's distrust of the wealthy and privileged. After a lifetime of having her ass kissed, it was incredibly refreshing to meet someone so frank and authentic.

And if there was one thing that Penny Tucker was, it was authentic. There was no doubt she was only guided by pure love and an innate desire to give June her very best. Penny would *always* put June's welfare first and nurture her confidence and curiosity the way no other nanny in the city could.

And Agnes would consider herself lucky if some of the magic rubbed off on her. She wanted to see where Penny had been made. As scary as the accommodations sounded, they had created the Tuckers. And if Penny believed that June would love it, how could Agnes deny June something so simple and wholesome? Saying no seemed like an act of selfishness, so Agnes ignored the pampered voices in her head and accepted Penny's offer.

Eventually, Agnes drifted off to sleep, only mildly concerned and gently excited. She dreamed of a campfire and making S'mores with June. They laughed and splashed in a crystal-clear lake and Agnes read to June as they relaxed in a hammock. But there were also Penny's wild red tresses and torrid kisses in the dark and Agnes found paradise in a cabin in the Catskills as Fin had promised.

Chapter Eight

It was time to rip off the Band-Aid. Penny had accepted that she had to talk to someone about Agnes, and Dash was the safest and most convenient option, being her roommate in addition to her BFF. She was leaving the city in less than twelve hours and she could trust him not to tell Penn or Reid *if* she made him swear not to tell anyone. He would run straight to Briarwood Terrace to give them the news if she didn't swear him to secrecy. Dash would never break a promise, though, and he always had Penny's back.

She trudged up the front steps of the place she and Penn had inherited from their maternal grandparents. It was a comfort knowing that Dash would keep an eye on it while she was away, but he was going to see right through her as soon as she told him they were leaving. Which made coming clean a matter of practicality, in the end.

Being her BFF, Dash knew exactly how little self-control Penny had, and he could always tell when she was hiding something. She'd managed to change the subject to Gavin and had arts and crafts to keep Dash distracted the night before, but there was no getting around an entire month at the cabin. And he'd know that Penny was just asking for trouble, secluding herself in the country with a sexpot like Agnes Cameron.

"Here we go," Penny said as she unlocked the door and let herself in.

Dash was ready with a mug of wine and a hug. "Hey, Penny Lane, how was your day? Fin sent a text and said you're taking the girls camping?" His head was cocked and he had his usual confused expression. But his lips twitched into a smile and Penny didn't like the twinkle in his eye.

She stared him down, trying to calculate how much he already knew. Dash was a good indicator of how much the others knew because he was always hovering around Briarwood Terrace and she could read him just as well as he could read her. He was pinging with excitement and his curiosity was luminous as he waited, so Penny assumed they hadn't learned anything specific and were still hoping and guessing over at Reid and Gavin's.

"Yup. We're heading to the country," she said, shrugging as she headed to the kitchen. "I'm starving. Is there any pad Thai left from last night?"

"Ooop!" Dash was right on her heels. "Of course, there is. We went overboard and made too much, as usual. But you're running away because something happened."

Penny spun around and grabbed his hands, chewing on her lip as she debated. People had a habit of underestimating Dash because he was so kind and passive, but he watched everyone and paid attention to the little things. "Something...happened and I might be in trouble," she confessed with an awkward cringe.

"What happened? Did you steal something?" Dash asked and Penny gasped.

"What? No! Why would you even think that?"

His nose scrunched. "I know you wouldn't assault anyone, but you'd take something from the government or the cops."

"For sure." Penny squinted over his shoulder and nodded. "But it's nothing that exciting. It's about Agnes Cameron."

"Did she steal something?" Dash whispered.

"I don't know. Probably." It seemed like something Agnes might do for a rush and for the hell of it. She was impulsive like that and it was one of the reasons why she was so hot. There was no telling what Agnes Cameron might do. She was a frequent topic of gossip and her name was often in the news because she wasn't afraid to tell the mayor off or punch a mugger. "We might have..." She widened her eyes at him and cleared her throat.

Dash's brows pulled together as his head tipped in the other direction. "Did you help her steal something?"

"No! Nobody stole anything. We hooked up at Fin and Walker's wedding and then at Penn and Morris's ceremony."

"Oh!" Dash's mouth opened and closed and he pursed his lips again. "Really?" He looked surprised.

"What do you mean, 'Really'?" Penny crossed her arms over her chest and he cringed apologetically.

"Don't get me wrong. Agnes Cameron is a beautiful woman and she seems like she'd be really cool to hang out with. But she's not the type you usually go for. The last girl you were really into was Buddhist and she didn't wear shoes," he explained. Penny groaned and ground the toe of her sneaker into the kitchen rug.

"I know! Jacinda was so hot and the sex was intense. And Agnes is like the total opposite, in every conceivable way, but somehow hotter," Penny puzzled out loud. "I barely knew Agnes when we hooked up. We just had this wild, instant chemistry and I went for it because...*why wouldn't I?* She's hot and it was really hot and a lot of fun because she doesn't give a damn. At least she didn't, then. Now, she's my boss and she's someone's mother."

"She's a MILF now," Dash said solemnly, then smothered a giggle. "Is that why you didn't tell Reid? Are you afraid that he'll tell Penn that you're into MILFs?"

"Yes!" She gave Dash a swat so he'd be serious. "But I also really, really wanted this job. It would have been a dream come true if I hadn't goofed up and banged Agnes."

"Twice!" Dash added.

"Trust me, that's not the kind of thing I'll forget any time soon," Penny said out of the side of her mouth.

"That good?"

"Ha! It might have been the best sex I've ever had."

"Oh, no. You're taking them camping in the country! What are you going to do?" He asked, finally realizing Penny's conundrum.

She held up her hands. "I'm not going to make it weird. Especially if she's cool with it."

"And what about...?" Dash gave her a loaded look. "No offense, but neither of you is very good at following rules."

Penny made a *pffft!* sound. "Some rules are just stupid, but I can behave when I need to. And I am *always* a professional. Nothing comes before my client."

"But what if your client is a MILF?"

"I will still be a professional," Penny vowed with a firm nod, then slid him a sheepish look. "Unless I'm off the clock?"

"This is gonna be so messy," he predicted, but Penny shushed him.

"It won't get messy. I'm just saying that I wouldn't say no."

Because who said no to Agnes Cameron? Not that Agnes had to ask or even needed to. Penny was the one who'd invited Agnes to dance at both weddings and it had been her idea to sneak away and fool around. She couldn't resist the chance to shoot her shot with the legendary temptress. Agnes was stunning and irresistible up close and in person.

"This might get messy," she conceded, making Dash laugh.

"But it'll be the fun kind of messy and there might even be a happy ending," he said while holding up two sets of crossed fingers.

"No way." Penny slapped at them. "We hooked up because we had this amazing chemistry, but we're not that compatible when we're not drunk and at a wedding. This will be different," she predicted. "We can put that behind us and act like competent adults."

Dash made a dubious sound. "You're one of the most competent people I know, but so far you've managed to avoid being an adult."

"I take that as a compliment," she said as she turned on her heel and went to find the pad Thai. "Everything's been totally cool between me and Agnes. In fact, it's almost like *nothing* happened. We're both focused on June and she's not settling in at The Killian House as well as the Camerons had hoped."

"Well..." Dash hissed and shook his head. "I'd be scared and I'm thirty. Imagine being a little kid who's never seen the inside of a house like that or been around maids and butlers."

"Yeah." Penny snorted in disbelief as she recalled how disoriented and out of place *she* felt when she first arrived. "And neither of us is afraid of fitting in or being loved like June is. That's why we're going to the cabin."

He scrubbed the back of his neck and frowned. "Which cabin? The one you and Penn drag me to every time one of you gets sick of the city?"

"Yes!" Penny cheered and Dash burst into laughter.

"No way!"

"Why not?" She asked as she yanked open the fridge. The pad Thai was in her grandmother's antique soup tureen because it was the only thing large enough to hold the gallons of noodles, tofu, and sprouts they had prepared. She was hugging the tureen when she turned and Dash raised a brow at her.

"Think Agnes Cameron's ever seen one of those used for anything other than soup?" He wondered out loud and tapped on his chin.

"What's your point? She's being surprisingly flexible."

"You made an old bathtub into an herb garden and Penn turned a hollowed-out tree trunk into a tub for the bathroom. I don't think those are the kinds of accommodations Agnes Cameron's expecting."

"So? That tub is awesome. Our cabin is awesome," she said defiantly and hefted the tureen onto the counter.

"It is!" Dash agreed. "But my mom would have a heart attack if I took her there and she's not half as rich as Agnes. And it's *really small*. Did you tell her how small it was?"

"I did..." Had Penny been clear enough, though? She hadn't wanted to scare Agnes off so Penny had glossed over a few details. She hadn't mentioned the family of squirrels Silas had recently found in one of the cupboards. Or the opossum living under the front porch who was great at keeping those pesky ticks away.

"June's going to have so much fun!" Penny said, changing the subject. "She's been to the zoo in the park a few times. But aside from that, she's never had a chance to play in the woods or see any real wildlife. We're going to focus on that and helping Agnes and June bond. It's going to be great."

"Totally," Dash said, sighing dreamily. He fell back against the counter and was smiling at the fridge as he pictured it. "You can get ideas for your dream camp while you're up there. And you and Agnes are going to have so much filthy sex and fall deeply in love."

"I don't think so. She isn't interested in me like that anymore and we're both focused on June now," Penny said, feeling oddly smug and virtuous as she used a fork to heap a mound of noodles into a mug. Her plan for Camp Laurel hadn't even occurred to her, she was so caught up in June and Agnes, but Dash was right. It would be a great opportunity to see what kinds of activities a former foster kid from the city enjoyed most while at camp. "Sex is the last thing on our minds," she lied. She could pretend to be a level-headed adult for June's sake if Agnes could.

"I kind of want to come so I can see this blow up first-hand..." He murmured thoughtfully. "But I'm committed to three mornings a week at the library and Reid's got that family coming from Athens next month."

"You can't come because there won't be any place for you to sleep. June's getting the loft because it's the coolest and Agnes will be in the downstairs bedroom so I'll be on the sofa or the hammock," Penny informed him.

"Nice!" He was rubbing his hands together again. "Basically an only-one-bed situation downstairs. There's no way the two of you don't hook up within a week."

"Ye of little faith!" She said and clicked her teeth, then stuffed a forkful of cold noodles into her mouth and chewed. Penny wasn't all that optimistic either. The mattress in the pull-out loveseat was rickety and uncomfortable, and she didn't want to admit that she was an animal. Or try to explain what came over her every time she was in the same room as Agnes. "Why did you have to compare Agnes to your mom?" She gagged because while Dash's mother was a perfectly lovely woman, Penny didn't want to think about Sandy Griffin like that.

"They're around the same age and my parents go to the

89

same club in Connecticut as the Camerons," Dash explained, making Penny groan into her noodles.

Dash's parents were wonderful people and had put up with their antics since Penny and Dash met in preschool and became instant best friends. They'd both been wearing the same "Blues Clues" T-shirt and blue sneakers. Dash had sat next to Penny during story time and put his nap mat next to hers. It turned out that Dash's parents had a townhouse right around the corner from Penny's maternal grandparents' house so they were inseparable for the rest of their elementary school careers and beyond. Dash's parents had eventually retired to Connecticut, leaving him to run amuck with Penny under Penn's supervision.

Penny fell back against the opposite counter. "Your parents are the normal kind of rich. Agnes is the kind of rich person who doesn't know how normal people live. This will be good for Agnes and help her understand where June came from a little better."

And any residual attraction Agnes felt would probably evaporate once she saw just how different she and Penny were. If it hadn't already. In the past couple days, Penny had noticed some lingering looks and Agnes had gotten a bit flustered when they were close. That was probably because Penny was incapable of polite boundaries and had hugged and poked and called her new boss "Aggie." But Penny hadn't sensed that Agnes had minded or wanted strict professional boundaries like Pierce preferred.

"It didn't mean anything before and wouldn't mean anything if it happened again, right?" She risked a look at Dash and he was shaking his head.

"That place is your heart and soul! Like, you'll be letting June and Agnes Cameron live and sleep inside of *you*. There's no way you don't get attached and Agnes doesn't fall in love with you. Especially if you're doing it a lot," he added with a pointed look.

"I'm pretty sure this is guaranteed to kill any lingering desire Agnes might feel toward me," Penny said with a shrug. "I'm willing to sacrifice that for June and the sake of our professional relationship."

"How do you figure?" Dash laughed.

"You just said Agnes would run screaming when she got a look at the inside of the cabin, which you also think is like living inside of *me*." She smiled at him sweetly, letting Dash connect the dots. He didn't, so Penny pushed out a heavy sigh, poking at her noodles like they were her insecurities. "I know what I'm doing and how to impress someone like Jacinda. Agnes is gonna see that I keep my fishing pole next to my bed and that I don't use soup tureens properly and that I *like* taking baths in a tree. Everything about her world is wrong and weird to me, too, and she's going to figure that out pretty quickly when she sees how I live when I'm not in the city."

Dash bit down on his lower lip. "She'd probably think the way you live in the city is pretty weird too," he said gently. "Agnes Cameron doesn't strike me as the sort of woman who's afraid of a little weird, though. She might not be thrilled about roughing it in a cabin, but I think she's a lot like her brother and is ready for something new and fun."

"Ha! We'll see if she's had her fill of new and fun after a month with me. She probably thought I was a lot more civilized and sophisticated when I was dressed up and we were sipping champagne at our brothers' fancy weddings."

Dash held onto his stomach with one hand and the counter with the other as he laughed. "She'd never make the mistake of thinking you were civilized or sophisticated. I might be your closest friend in the whole world, but I am also bisexual so I have a pretty good idea of why Agnes likes you. And I have a feeling certain things are inevitable if we stick the two of you in a secluded cabin."

"That's what I was afraid of..." And why she had confided in him. "How do we make sure that what happens at the cabin, stays at the cabin?"

He burst into laughter again and reached for Penny. "God, I wish I was going. This is going to be *amazing*. Trust me." He pulled her into a hug, crushing the mug between them as he rocked her. "Can I tell them?" He asked, making Penny gasp as she pushed him away.

"No!" She unsheathed the fork from the mug and pointed it at him. "On pain of death!" She said, the tines brushing his jugular.

Dash stretched his neck and licked his lips nervously. "Alright! I won't tell them!"

"I mean it," she whispered lethally, slowly lowering the fork. "I get the feeling they're meddling and I expect that from them, but I don't want to give them any ammunition or false hope. *Nothing* is happening between me and Agnes except a few one-night stands," she said, pausing when Dash raised his hand. "Yes?"

"How many one-night stands with the same person before you're 'a thing'?" He asked, curling his fingers. "Let's say six so we know when you've crossed the liar-liar-pants-on-fire line," he suggested as he made an invisible line between them.

She glared as she stuffed what was left of her noodles into her mouth and chewed petulantly. "We can't be a thing. We have nothing in common and we'll be on each other's last nerve by the end of the first week." She passed him the mug. "Do me a favor and wash that. I have to pack and get up extra early."

"Sure," he said with a chuckle. "It's gonna take you ten minutes to stuff a pair of overalls, your favorite swimsuit, and some extra underwear into your backpack. The only other thing you need is extra shoes and your mom's fishing pole."

"You don't know me." Penny stuck her nose in the air as she strutted out of the kitchen. "I'm taking *two* swimsuits—my red one *and* my blue one—and I found a really nice flannel for Silas at the thrift shop last weekend," she boasted on her way up the stairs.

"You got me there," Dash replied and held the mug up in salute. "I'm sure you won't act like a horny hooligan and Agnes won't fall wildly in love with you."

"That's a terrible thing to say. Goodnight, Dash," Penny said and blew him a kiss because she probably wouldn't see him until they returned from Cherrytown. "Just terrible," she repeated, shaking her head as she continued up the steps.

"I love you and I'm really excited about this!" He called after her, but Penny loudly swung her bedroom door shut.

Just like she'd shut the door on the possibility of "a thing" with Agnes. They had made a pact and were both committed to giving June the best start possible. A few...slips here and there wouldn't be a big deal to a woman like Agnes, and Penny would never be able to hold her interest for more than a few weeks. Or a month if they were in the country and there wasn't anything else to do...

Chapter Nine

Agnes was far less optimistic about the trip the following morning but was once again grateful for the comfort of Walker's wisdom as her nimble Range Rover bounced over roots and rocks. He'd chosen a Range Rover for the times he was in the mood to drive and for transporting the girls to Connecticut or the cottage. Agnes had bought one as well, deciding that if the SUV was good enough for Walker, it would be more than adequate for her since she rarely drove herself anywhere.

There was plenty of room in the back for all of their bags and the basket of snacks Pierce had prepared for the two-and-a-half-hour drive from Manhattan to the Catskills. Of course, most of the bags were Agnes's. As requested, her assistant had packed for anything and everything. And June now had two large duffle bags and a brand-new backpack filled with new books and fun stationery so she could stay in touch with the triplets over the summer.

Agnes repeatedly told herself that she was prepared for

anything and to have faith in Fin's promise. It became her mantra and she was on a mission to prove to June and Penny that she was far more versatile than they were expecting. She'd fumbled at first and acted like a brat when Penny warned her about the cabin, but Agnes was going to be brave and put her years of carefree partying to good use. She was going to show June and Penny that she was anything but a stick in the mud.

There were obvious flaws in Agnes's plan, and her courage had buckled as they turned off the rural highway. They had passed Cherrytown several miles back and the road had narrowed into a bumping, winding trail until branches scraped the sides of the car and smacked against the windshield.

"Are you sure we shouldn't go back and ask for directions? I can barely see where we're going," Agnes said, ducking and squinting as she searched for any hint of civilization.

"Directions?" Penny humphed indignantly and waved for Agnes to keep going. "I was born up here because Mom went into labor two weeks early. Mabel helped with the delivery. And Uncle Silas was teaching me how to climb trees before I could walk. You could blindfold me and leave me back in town and I'd be able to find my way."

"But only on foot," Agnes added, casting Penny a baffled look. She still couldn't believe that neither Penny nor her brother, Penn, could drive. They both despised automobiles and neither had the desire to learn, apparently.

Penny shrugged obliviously, too interested in the foliage outside the vehicle. She had opened her window, and Agnes almost expected Penny to stick her head out. She kept taking deep, loud sniffs of the air. Her arm was extended and she would pluck whichever leaf, flower, or berry that was within reach and share its name and any possible uses with them.

"See these little white flowers?" Penny asked, turning in

her seat to pass a small branch back to June. She in turn was creating a bouquet with a ribbon and the samples from Penny's lesson. Penny was living up to her title as Plant Nerd Supreme and Agnes suspected that she could happily survive in the woods by foraging if she had to. "This is autumn olive and in the fall, there will be little red berries all over the woods! They're one of my favorites because they're so tart and sweet and make the loveliest syrup. Even though most people think of the autumn olive as an invasive species," Penny continued.

"Penny, are you sure—?" Agnes began warily, but Penny shushed as she turned and dropped back into her seat.

"Onward, Aggie! We're nearly there," she said with a wave at the windshield, making June giggle.

Agnes's expression was dubious and she was about to ask again when she spotted a moss-covered A-frame cabin. It was almost hidden beneath ancient oak, elm, and maple trees, and there was an abundance of flowering bushes shrouding the small, and extremely rustic-looking shelter.

"See!" Penny proclaimed, beaming even brighter as Agnes came to a stop and parked.

"It's *amazing*!" June whispered, leaning over the center console to get a better look.

Agnes craned her neck as she searched for the rest of it. As far as she could tell, there was just the one small, slightly lopsided structure. She hadn't seen another house—or any sign of life for that matter—since they had turned off the rural high-way. "Yes. It's..." She swallowed loudly to clear the lump in her throat. "Lovely." Her voice had cracked, but Agnes smiled at June, then at Penny. "Shall we?"

"Don't worry!" Penny gave Agnes's hand a quick squeeze before pushing her door open and hopping out. She grabbed her backpack and fishing pole from the back and bounded up the stone path to the porch while Agnes and June got out of the car and scanned the woods around them. "Mabel and Silas's place is through there." Penny pointed at a gap in the trees and Agnes could almost make out a path and a glimpse of another A-frame cabin if she squinted and leaned just right. "They'll be along soon, now that they know we're here."

Agnes wondered how they'd know, but had her answer when Penny opened the cabin's screen door. A loud creaking shriek echoed through the woods and Penny whistled loudly around two fingers before unlocking the door and heading inside.

"Let's go!" June said, taking Agnes by the hand and towing her around the Range Rover. "It looks like a tree house!"

I was afraid of that.

But Agnes kept a smile stretched across her face as she was pulled up the crooked porch steps and into the cabin. It took her eyes a moment to adjust in the dimness and she continued to blink, confounded and silently overwhelmed.

The inside was much roomier than Agnes expected, but it was still far too small for her liking or comfort. She was already antsy and wanted more air but she remained calm and noted the quaint kitchen with its vintage pink appliances and what appeared to be a bedroom in a small nook. A quilt had been hung and tied back, in lieu of a door.

"The bathroom's over here," Penny called from the other side of the kitchen, throwing back another quilt to reveal a simple pedestal sink and what looked like a large, knotted wooden hull in another nook.

"Nice," Agnes replied weakly. Her cheeks and lips began to ache as her smile grew wider and more brittle. "Is there just the one bed?" She asked, earning an amused chuckle from Penny.

"The loveseat's a sleeper," she said as she pointed behind Agnes. The loveseat was upholstered in an ancient, faded floral print and looked older than Agnes. "And wait until you see

June's room!" Penny made a giddy sound and clapped. "It used to be mine and Penn's. We got rid of the old bunk bed. I usually stay up there and Penn takes the downstairs room when we come up together," she explained as she gestured at the loft and headed for the stairs.

The steps were wide and sturdy, but they let out a terrible groan as Penny climbed them. June scrambled up after her and Agnes assumed she was pleased, given all the excited gasps and squeals. Agnes followed, pausing to peek over the landing, and let out a surprised gasp herself.

A wide, triangular window offered a misty, breathtaking view of the lake and the woods. Crystals had been suspended from a strand of twine strung across the window, casting rainbow halos on the whitewashed timber ceiling. Flowering vines crept overhead and around the loft, giving the space even more of a magical treehouse feel.

"This is my room?" Junes asked, her eyes sparkling as she went to the bed and ducked under the mosquito net canopy. She sat on the edge and gave the mattress a test bounce. It had been stripped, and there were two neatly stacked pillows, and another cheerful floral quilt folded on the foot of the bed.

"Yup!" Penny said as she went to the window and opened it, allowing the breeze to waft through the loft. "You might not be as excited about it tonight. There's no air conditioning because you really don't need it out here. But we'll want to keep this open in the evenings and it'll sound like you're sleeping in the woods," Penny said, warning June.

"I think that sounds awesome. I can't wait!" June said as she joined Penny at the window. Penny laughed softly as she smoothed June's hair and slid Agnes a wink.

There was a lot of promise in that wink and Agnes wasn't sure what to make of it. Her body reacted as if Penny had invited her to sneak away again, though, and Agnes laughed nervously as she tucked a strand of hair behind her ear and blushed.

Get a hold of yourself, Agnes.

This was definitely the wrong place and the wrong time. Wasn't it?

Agnes had assumed that she was done with having a sex life, for the time being. June was supposed to receive her complete and undivided attention until...college, probably, and Agnes had been happy to commit to that. She'd had more than her share of flings and had caused enough havoc so it didn't seem like that much of a sacrifice to put her sex life on hold.

Motherhood was Agnes's final frontier and very serious business. It required sacrifice and a certain amount of piety to be a proper role model and prove one's commitment. At least, that's what Agnes had believed. She'd happily put her playgirl days behind her and was ready to be reformed for June.

"Stop being so damn horny" was probably Step 1 in most parenting handbooks, but Penny hadn't made it easy during their drive to the Catskills. Just when Agnes's nerves stopped fizzing like her cork had just been popped, Penny would shoot her a wink or one of her crooked, teasing grins and the jitters and shy giggles would return with a vengeance. Agnes thought she'd burst into flames, her face got so hot, whenever Penny's hand brushed her thigh or arm.

"I better get unpacked," Agnes said, raising her brows at Penny and silently inquiring about their sleeping arrangements.

Penny answered with an easy shrug. "You're in the downstairs bedroom. I'll crash on the pull-out or set up my hammock on the porch. There are built-in drawers under the bed for all your things."

"Great!" Agnes replied too quickly, then bit into her lip and bowed her head. "Just yell if you need me." She turned, rolling her eyes as she hurried down the stairs. Each step moaned and barked in protest, making her exit even more awkward.

Downstairs, Agnes took a moment to explore and get her bearings. She remembered how brave little June had been, going into The Killian House and meeting its staff and the rest of the Camerons, and Agnes felt foolish for letting a tiny cabin get the better of her. She told herself to stop focusing on the *tiny* part and to start noticing the things she liked about the cabin.

The kitchen was rather charming once she got over how small the space was. She liked its pink appliances and antique porcelain farmhouse sink. The backsplash was a chintz mosaic made of broken plates and saucers and there were shelves lined with handmade pottery pieces glazed in soft greens, blues, beiges, and pinks. Colorful rag rugs were scattered over the fieldstone floor and a rocking chair and pellet stove occupied a cozy corner on the other side of the kitchen table.

Agnes had to duck to avoid the ceiling's wooden beams as she made her way back to the bedroom. She smiled as she pictured Penny's much taller brother bent over as he swept aside the quilt curtain. Inside, the space was only slightly bigger than the bed, with just enough room to pass through to get to the patio.

A set of sliding glass doors offered another enchanting view of the lake. The ceiling was low and lined with clumps of moss and string lights glowed pleasantly overhead. Agnes flipped the switch on the wall, turning on an antique Tiffany lamp. A down comforter, clean white sheets, and a quilt were folded at the foot of the bed and there was a vase of freshly picked wild-flowers on the nightstand. Like the bed upstairs, a mosquito net canopy was draped over the bed, lamp, and end table, adding to the dreamy aura.

Agnes backed out of the little nook and peeked behind a

quilt that had been hung under the stairs, finding shelves stocked with jars of pickles and preserves. There were baskets of potatoes and onions and bags of rice and flour. Agnes suspected that Penny's great-aunt and "uncle" had prepared the cabin for their arrival and she was looking forward to meeting them.

They must have heard her thoughts because there was a brisk tap at the front door before it opened and a very large bald man in a pair of overalls stuck his head inside. "Hello there? Anyone home?" He called, then bowed and smiled at Agnes when he spotted her. He had a long gray beard and soft, pewter eyes that twinkled as he searched the cabin, probably for Penny.

"Heya, Silas!" Penny called back as she skipped down the stairs and leaped into his arms. "I've missed you!" She pretended she was being crushed as he hugged her. Then a petite, elderly woman elbowed Silas out of the way and reached for Penny.

"There's my sweet Penny Lane!" The newcomer said, her voice wavering as she cradled Penny's face. The old woman's hair was swept into a classic bouffant and she was drowning in a floral housecoat, she was so small and frail. But she was energetic and spritely, introducing herself to Agnes before barking orders at Silas and promptly arranging lunch for everyone.

"It's a long drive from the city. I'm sure you're all starving. Get the pan out and I'll fry some tomatoes for sandwiches, the way Penny likes them."

"Yes, ma'am," Silas replied with a salute. He had a large bowl of what appeared to be a pasta salad and a pie under each arm and was on his way to the kitchen, leaving Penny to finish making introductions.

June warmed up to Silas and Mabel immediately. She was

blown away when she learned that they grew "a little bit of everything" and had chickens and two cows on their property.

"It's like a tiny farm, hidden in the woods," Penny said, making June's eyes widen in wonder.

"Can I see it?" She asked, and Silas chuckled.

"See it? I'll be expecting you bright and early tomorrow. We'll have eggs and tomatoes to gather and those cows aren't going to milk themselves," he said, winking at Agnes.

June's arms shot into the air. "Yes! Can I help Silas tomorrow, Mom?" she asked Agnes excitedly.

"Of course," she answered, her voice cracking as she nodded. Her heart felt like it was about to explode. Agnes acted as cool as she could, smiling and shrugging despite her watery eyes and quivering lip. She had told June that she didn't have to call her Mom unless she felt comfortable enough, but hadn't expected it to happen so quickly. "Whatever you want, sweetheart, as long as Silas and Mabel don't mind."

"Mind?" Mabel laughed and waved it off. "Let me tell you about the time Penny decided to help us clean the chicken coop. Had us chasing the girls halfway up the mountain because she'd let them all out," she said, her eyes glowing with fondness as she recounted the episode, which clearly entertained June.

Agnes used the moment to compose herself, but Penny must have noticed and sidled closer. "You're my hero, Agnes Cameron," she whispered out of the side of her mouth. Her shoulder bumped Agnes's and she offered her an encouraging smile.

"Me?" Agnes shook her head. "I would have made a mess of this ten times over if it hadn't been for you."

"No, you wouldn't have." Penny shook her head. "I can already tell that you mean it when you say you'll do whatever it takes and I can see how much you already love that little girl."

"It takes a lot more than a willing heart. I'm so glad Walker had the good sense to hire you."

Penny gasped, crossing her arms over her chest as she turned to Agnes. They had been forgotten as Mabel taught June how to bread and fry thick slices of ripe red and purple tomatoes while Silas set the small round table. "I'd argue that *all* it takes is a willing heart. I can't help a parent who doesn't care. And I can feel that you're scared. You're *way* outside of your comfort zone, but you're grinning and bearing it for June's sake."

"I wouldn't say I'm—"

"I can *feel* it, Aggie." Penny widened her eyes at Agnes, daring her to deny it. "And you've got the look of a cat that's been shoved in a cage that's way too small."

"Maybe a little and just at first," Agnes conceded. "But it's actually rather lovely here and it's...growing on me."

Penny's green eyes glowed and there was a taunting quirk at the corner of her lips as she rocked closer and smiled up at Agnes. *"Good."* She said, her voice lower and huskier. "I'm going to get unpacked and put up the hammock on the porch in case you and June need a little extra space tonight."

"I'm sure that won't be necessary," Agnes said quickly. "I mean, it's your cabin," she explained as she edged a little closer. She examined one of one of the buckles on Penny's overalls. It was attached to what had been a pair of men's suspenders and the stretchy nylon straps were yellow and marked like a ruler. The garment was both disorienting with its homey floral pockets and gingham patches and utterly enchanting: just what a punky nanny would wear while adventuring.

"We'll see! June can also curl up with a book or take an epic nap in it in the afternoons. There's no better spot once the sun's over the trees. There's so much shade and the breeze is always just right."

"That does sound nice," Agnes agreed, then excused herself so Penny could "unpack."

She had turned up at The Killian House at 6:45 that morning, munching on an apple, with nothing but her "lucky" fishing pole, a backpack, and her everyday bag slung across her chest. Penny needed only a few minutes to dump half a dozen tank tops, a few pairs of jean shorts, a backup pair of overalls, several wads of socks and panties, two swimsuits, and a couple of oversized t-shirts into a basket she had pulled out from under the bottom step.

Penny gave the whole pile a few shoves to get it all to fit then rolled up her backpack and stuffed it into another basket alongside her extra Converse and a pair of flip-flops. Penny deposited her toothbrush and a curious-looking bar of soap on the wooden ledge next to the bathroom sink, then fell back on the loveseat and put her feet up on the coffee table.

"I'm all set," she declared as she dusted off her hands. "Let me know if you want some help getting settled," she told Agnes, folding her arms behind her head.

"No. I can manage," Agnes said, sidestepping around Mabel, Silas, and June as they chopped, fried, and chatted in the tight galley kitchen between the bedroom nook and the small living/dining area.

She didn't want Penny there when she unzipped her rolling suitcases and hanging bags. Agnes felt ridiculous and her face was hot when she saw her Louis Vuitton luggage neatly arranged around the bed. Silas must have brought everything in while Agnes was distracted and had done his best to leave her a path around the bed.

Step 2 of any parenting guide would probably be "Stop being a high-maintenance pain in the ass" and Agnes had certainly bungled that. But Agnes couldn't stay mad at herself for long before her nose tickled and her mouth watered as the smell of fried tomatoes and freshly squeezed lemons filled the cabin. The small table was covered in a red gingham cloth and set for five by the time she was done cramming the contents of her luggage into the drawers under the bed. Silas helpfully stowed Agnes's suitcases back in the Range Rover and then they all gathered to eat, sitting practically shoulder-to-shoulder around the table.

The simple meal was delicious and the afternoon was one of the most enjoyable experiences of Agnes's life. The fried tomatoes were served on thick slices of freshly-baked bread along with an herby pasta salad, a crisp cucumber salad, home-made bread-and-butter pickles, and a pitcher of freshly-squeezed lemonade. Mabel sent Penny over the moon with a vegan strawberry shortcake. It was one of her all-time favorite desserts, apparently, and Agnes couldn't blame her. She helped herself to a second serving of the fluffy biscuits with fresh strawberries and heartily agreed when June declared that the whipped coconut cream was heavenly. June was adorably surprised when Penny pointed out that they'd all just enjoyed an entirely vegan-friendly meal.

"Mabel gave coconuts and almond milk a chance and started making these just for me," Penny boasted around a mouthful of strawberries and cream.

"I couldn't let my girl starve," Mabel grumbled from the sink, making Penny roll her eyes.

"As if I could around here. And I can always find some-thing to eat. There's food all over the woods and the city if you know where to look."

"Really?" June asked, her whole focus once again locked on Penny. Agnes was paying attention as well, but she was wary as Penny talked about foraging for edible berries and mushrooms and wild herbs.

"Nature provides!" Penny proclaimed and Mabel and Silas

chuckled in agreement. "But don't eat anything unless you're sure it's safe because nature can also kill you," she qualified as she held up a finger. "The city provides too if you know where to look and what to look out for," she continued, but Silas's lip curled and he shook his head as he gathered the last of their plates.

"I don't know about any of that and that's fine with me," he grumbled.

Penny waved him off as she turned back to June and Agnes. The three of them had squeezed onto the loveseat together so Silas could have the stool while Mabel sat on the cabin's only regular chair. "You wouldn't believe how much food restaurants and food trucks throw away every day," she said excitedly.

"I think I'll help clean up," Agnes decided, easing herself up and over the armrest. She shook her head as she picked up a hand towel and began drying dishes.

Mabel laughed and nodded at Agnes. "You'll do," she said, smiling as she studied Agnes over the top of her glasses. "I believe you'll do rather nicely. But I get a little deja vu," she said quietly, more to herself. She let out a thoughtful "Huh" and her eyes clouded. "I have a feeling everything will work out this time, though," she said, giving Agnes's arm a reassuring pat.

"This time?" Agnes asked, but Mabel waved a gnarled, shaking hand, dismissing her question.

"This is different. *You're* different and so is she," she explained with a jab of her finger at Penny.

"What's that?" Penny asked as she popped up.

"You mind your own business, Penny Lane, and help Agnes dry the dishes," Mabel barked, sharing a brief half-smile with Agnes before telling Silas it was time to go.

They left Penny, June, and Agnes with full bellies and drowsy smiles. Agnes was no longer concerned that the trip would be her first big blunder as June's new mom. In fact,

Agnes was half-convinced that she could keep her head out of Penny's pants and survive a summer in the Catskills without her assistant and the comforts of civilization.

At least she was until Penny found a tick on June's scalp while checking her over before her bath.

Chapter Ten

"You can be totally honest and it's okay if you don't like it here," Agnes said quietly, just so that June could hear. But the little girl shook her head quickly as she set *The Lightning Thief* on the bedside table and tugged the quilt up to her chin. She wiggled her shoulders, getting more comfortable.

"I love it here!" She whispered. "Uncle Walker's house is the most beautiful house I've ever seen, but it's really big and I'm afraid I'm going to touch something I'm not supposed to and get in trouble."

Agnes hushed her softly and bent so she could kiss June's forehead. "You have my permission to touch whatever you want when we're there. If something breaks and someone says something—not that anyone would—you tell them to take it up with me. But I promise, Walker cares more about you than some dusty old vase, and he will always understand."

She stifled a giggle and waved a hand in front of her face, recalling the sight of an entire Meissen dinner service obliterated after a ten-year-old Walker attempted to swing from the dining room chandelier like a buccaneer. He crashed onto the table and careened through approximately $300,000 worth of priceless porcelain. Walker still held the record for the most expensive "natural disaster" in the Cameron Estate's history.

"You could do your worst and you still wouldn't shock Walker. But I encourage you to try," Agnes said, making June laugh.

"I won't! Uncle Walker is really nice and I like him."

"Good. Sometimes, he acts stuffy and serious, but he's the best brother in the world and he's my best friend. I *think* he might turn out to be the world's best uncle after you've whipped him into shape." She gave June's nose a soft flick. "And do you still feel comfortable with Penny?"

"I love Penny! She's the best!"

"Good," Agnes said evenly. She'd had her moments of doubt throughout the day and had feared that she'd fallen under Penny's spell, but she no longer worried about what she'd gotten them into. But Agnes had another reason for asking about Penny, and her nerves bubbled as she smoothed June's hair. "You know how Penny is a nanny and she was sent by my friend, Reid Marshall? He runs a very special agency," she said, and waited for June to nod before continuing. "Fin is Reid's brother and he was sent to The Killian House because Walker and the triplets needed help. Walker and Fin fell in love and got married so Fin lives with them and he's the girls' daddy now too. Reid started that agency because sometimes, it's hard for families like Fin and Walker's to find a nanny. And sometimes, it's hard for nannies like Penny and Fin to find work because people can be really mean when you're different. But being different is great, right?" June nodded quickly. "Penny might want to marry a woman someday and Fin fell in love with your Uncle Walker and married him," Agnes concluded. She'd been worried about how June would react when she found out that Walker was gay and married to Fin, but so far the little girl didn't seem too concerned.

"Fin's awesome! I really like him, and Penny said that we can go skating in the park with Fin, and Riley, and Penn, and Morris! I don't know how to roller-skate and I've never tried skateboarding, but Penny said they could teach me."

"How fun! I always wanted to try roller-skating myself," Agnes said. "I'll get us some skates and boards and we can learn together."

June's whole face lit up. "Really?" She asked and Agnes shrugged.

"There will come a time when I won't be able to, so it's better to learn as much as I can now. And take my word for it, you rarely regret the times you stumbled when you look back. It's all the times that you *didn't* go for it or try something new that will haunt you."

June nodded solemnly. "Carpe diem. It's Latin for 'seize the day.'"

Agnes's jaw hung for a moment. "Yes, it is!" She laughed. "Where did you learn that?"

"A lot of the really old books are in Latin and I want to be able to read them so I'm teaching myself."

"Unum un carissimi." *My beloved one.* Agnes shook her head, awed again at how perfect June was and how perfect she was for Agnes. "You are so, so brilliant and it feels like I've been waiting for you my whole life."

"Me too," June said and sniffled softly. She chewed on her lip and fidgeted with the edge of the quilt. "Anthony said that sometimes, it was better to have no parents than really bad parents. But I didn't care. I would have settled for any kind of mom or dad. I never thought that there were mommies like you or that places like this really existed. It still feels like I'm dreaming."

"You're not dreaming, sweetheart. But, you should be. Get some sleep and be ready for another big day. I have a feeling Penny has an adventure planned for us," Agnes said as she kissed June.

June yawned and tucked her hands under her cheek as Agnes rose to leave. "Are you going to marry Penny?"

Agnes jerked to a halt. "Eh? Why—?"

"Fin married Uncle Walker after he was sent to work at The Killian House. I thought that you might marry Penny because she's a nanny too and she wants to marry a woman one day."

"What?" It came out as a nervous burst. Agnes covered her cheeks so June wouldn't see them turning red. "That's not how that usually works and it was different with them."

"How?"

"How? Well..." Agnes squinted down at June as she tried to remember how, exactly. She never approved of lying to children and hiding difficult truths. "Walker liked being married and he's very good at being a husband. I was almost married once and it didn't go well. And I don't think I'd make a very good wife."

This time, June's jaw fell and she let out a disgruntled gasp. "Yes, you would! I already know you're the world's best mom and you just started."

"I don't know... I might have to share you and you're so little!" Agnes tickled June's ribs, making her squeal and changing the subject. It was a relief to know that June understood and accepted that love, marriage, and parenthood came in different shapes and sizes. And that a family could be two dads and three identical girls, or just a mom and one brilliant little girl. "Right now, I just want to learn everything I can about you and survive this place," Agnes added in a conspiratorial whisper.

"It's not that bad, and I'll help you." June hooked her pinkie around Agnes's. "Us city girls have to stick together."

"We sure do. But you're right, it's not that bad. It was really nice of Penny to share her cabin with us so I'll do my best to be a good sport."

"Do you think we'll see a bear?"

June sounded excited, but Agnes shook her head. "I hope not, and we are out of here if we do. I wouldn't mind seeing some deer or rabbits," she said, suddenly concerned because she'd never asked Penny about bears or larger cats.

She kept June chatting about the forest's less frightening inhabitants and the two of them came up with a checklist of fauna they hoped to see while they were at the cabin. Birds were at the top of their list and Agnes was glad that she had spotted an old Audubon Society field guide among the books tucked under the steps.

Eventually, June nodded off, so Agnes whispered one last goodnight and backed away on tiptoes. She winced at the loud creaking of the steps as she descended, glancing back at the bed, but June was sleeping peacefully. Agnes sighed at the soft smile spread across her little face and said one more silent "goodnight." The change in June was immediate and so obvious, compared to the tentative, anxious child Agnes had witnessed at The Killian House.

Instead of kicking herself for being so wrong and bemoaning her terrible parenting instincts, Agnes was even more grateful to Penny for giving her a chance and a safe space to learn and grow. That's why they were there, Agnes reminded herself as she crept down what must have been the world's loudest set of stairs. She and Walker knew how warped and broken *they* were so they had hired better people to mold them into competent parents.

Downstairs, the front door was open to pull the breeze through the cabin. Penny was on the porch, leaning against the post with a Mason jar in her hand as she studied the night sky. A hammock had been strung on the other side of the porch between two posts. Like many of Penny's possessions, it was patched and ratty, but still inviting, and it made Agnes smile. Her anxiety did spike as she thought of Penny sleeping alone, out in the open, though.

"June's out cold," Agnes informed her, then raised a brow when Penny offered her the jar.

"Silas's wine. Mostly elderberry but he'll toss in whatever's in season and growing within a day's walk from here."

Agnes took a cautious sip and grunted in delight. The wine was light for a red: nicely balanced and not at all tart or bitter. "That's lovely." She swallowed a larger gulp before passing it back.

"And really strong. It likes to sneak up on you," Penny warned out of the side of her mouth. "Silas always leaves a case of it in the pantry for us when he knows we're coming."

"Good man," Agnes said, eyeing the quaint floral curtain hiding the small pantry under the steps. Agnes laughed softly as she admired the cramped yet cozy cabin from her vantage point on the patio. "This place is just as...rustic and isolated as I was dreading, but it's *lovely* and soothing. It's like we've escaped into a fairytale forest," she decided, thanking Penny when it was her turn to take a few sips from the jar.

A faint chuckle of agreement wafted from Penny. She slid her hand around Agnes's side, pulling her closer. "I've always felt safe and freer out here and was never bored when I was a kid. I still find something I've never seen when I go exploring."

"I can see why," Agnes said, recovering and relaxing against Penny. "Thank you for bringing us here and sharing this with us." She handed Penny the jar and watched as she drank. The moon and stars filled up the sky and reflected off the lake, casting Penny's face in a soft glow.

Agnes was enchanted by the twinkle in Penny's eyes and the mischievous tilt of her lips as she licked them and smiled. It was easy to imagine they were in a midsummer dream and Penny was a puckish nymph of the forest with her messy pigtails and the flowers and bees tattooed around her shoulders and along her collarbone.

"I thought you and June would love it here. And I'm hoping it'll be easier for the two of you to connect without the city and *life* getting in the way. She'll settle in better once she knows we're a team and that we're up here for her."

"I was skeptical before, but I get it now that we're here and I see how much June's come out of her shell," Agnes admitted, earning a chuckle from Penny.

"I can't tell you how many times I've wished I could bring my city kids out here. I've always believed that there's no better place to learn than out in nature and no better medicine than some fresh air and sunshine. But I wasn't with the right agency before and the parents were never invested enough."

"That's such a pity," Agnes said sincerely.

Penny hummed, then became alert and pointed across the lake. "See that spot where the trees dip?" She asked, her face brightening when Agnes nodded. "One day, that's gonna be Camp Laurel!"

"Camp Laurel?"

"Yup!" Penny punctuated the P with a firm nod. "Silas showed me the spot a few years ago and so far, I've saved up $40,000. I'm going to start a camp for foster kids like June.

Dash is already in, of course, and my brother and the guys are going to help me build all the cabins."

"Wait a moment!" Agnes stared down at Penny, touched and impressed. Forty thousand dollars was *nothing* to Agnes, but she understood that it was a tremendous amount for Penny to have saved. "I would *love* to help you. I could talk to Melinda tomorr—" She began and stopped when Penny shook her head.

"We're here for you and June right now. And I want to buy that land by myself. I don't want to feel like I owe anyone anything and I want to name it after my mom. We can talk about scholarships once it's done because the kids are staying for free and I only want to hire former foster kids to be the counselors."

"*I'm in.* Just let me know when you're ready, Penny. You clearly understand kids and have a passion for sharing nature with them."

"Thanks, Aggie! But this is just how I was raised and I feel closest to my mom when I'm up here with my fishing pole. I want my mom's legacy and love for nature to live on and I want kids like June to have as much fun and feel as safe and free as I did as a kid."

Agnes turned to Penny, even more grateful. "I keep thinking about how overwhelming the past few days must have been for June. I would have missed it and totally botched this with her. She never would have trusted me if you and Fin hadn't stepped in."

"Nonsense," Penny said, draping her other arm loosely around Agnes's neck like they were slow dancing. "You wouldn't have botched it. June just would have taken a little longer to adjust and feel accepted. But she would have been fine because she's a fighter and you're already a way better parent than most of the people I've worked for."

"No. I—" Agnes started, but Penny pressed a finger against

her lips. Whatever argument Agnes was going to make was completely swept away, leaving her hot and breathless.

Penny's eyes sparkled as she tucked a curl behind Agnes's ear and traced the curve of her neck, making her shiver. "I've seen you with the triplets. You love them unconditionally and, more importantly, they love and trust *you*. You've already got the right instincts and your heart is in the right place." She rested her hand on Agnes's sternum and her heart galloped despite Penny's easy, encouraging smile. "You've just got to learn what June's needs are and how to tune into her the way you do with the triplets. That's why we're here. And to relax and have some fun."

"Okay," Agnes mouthed, incapable of much more as she swayed closer. Her chin dipped and her eyelids sank. "I'm glad we're here," she murmured and angled her chin.

"Me too!" Penny replied brightly, bouncing onto her tiptoes so she could kiss Agnes's cheek. "I'm gonna take a shower and then I'll crash on the pull-out tonight. June said she'd feel better if I was inside and closer."

"I would too," Agnes admitted, wrinkling her nose at the patched-up hammock at the other end of the porch. "I am looking forward to trying it out with June tomorrow," she said as she held up a hand apologetically.

Penny laughed it off. "It takes me longer to recover from a night in the hammock these days. See you inside," she said, leaving Agnes with the jar and a dreamy smile on her face.

She finished the wine and went inside and saw a pillow and a quilt on the loveseat. A warm glow seeped from around the faded pastel quilt in the corner. It had been clothes-pinned to a length of twine, dividing the kitchen from the bathroom, and Agnes could hear Penny singing softly to herself behind it. Agnes had braved the shower while Penny was tucking June in and it was actually rather neat, standing in what had once been the trunk of a massive tree. The tree had split during a storm and Penn had joined and sanded the large sections so the tub looked like brown marble.

Water pitter-pattered against the wooden tub in the bathroom, not quite muffled by the threadbare quilt. Agnes glanced up at the loft and then back at the quilt, truly torn. She wanted to invite Penny to share the much more comfortable bed in the back nook. They could *sleep* in the same bed without anything inappropriate happening. Agnes would explain and was sure June would agree that Penny didn't need to suffer on that sinking, lopsided loveseat when there was plenty of room in the back.

She took a few steps toward the bathroom quilt and opened her mouth to ask Penny, but chickened out. The words glued themselves together, sticking to her tongue.

Oh, this is bad!

Agnes backed away and hurried around the kitchen and the pantry into the safety of her bedroom nook and pulled down the other quilt. She rushed around the bed and cracked the back door as she pulled her nightshirt away from her body, unsticking it. A swing swayed and creaked softly in the smaller back porch's shadows and Agnes wondered how many memories had been made there. Her instincts told her that that swing had been treasured, but that there was a reason one of the chains was broken and the slats had warped and rotted.

It was so at odds with the rest of the cabin. The wooden tub, quilt doors, and chintz backsplash had been lovingly repurposed and came together to create a wonky, cozy haven for the Tuckers. The only reason Penn would have left the swing in that state was if it was attached to a broken heart. Agnes was saddened, but she understood that some things were better left alone or until old wounds had healed. And it seemed that Penn saw the wisdom in holding on while time fixed the things he couldn't.

"This place is full of magic and mysteries," Agnes noted, feeling more somber as she went to turn in for the night, regretting the vacant stretch of bed and the empty pillow next to hers.

Chapter Eleven

Thank goodness June and Agnes weren't early risers. After waking up at dawn, Penny pulled on a pair of rain boots and skipped and slid on the dewy grass down the hill to the lake in a hoodie and her pajamas. She ran to the end of the dock and checked the signal, cheering when she saw a single solid bar.

Her father answered after just two rings. "Hey, kiddo! Did you get settled in? Get any fishing done yet?" Gus sounded good, like he was smiling.

"Not yet, Pops!" Penny laughed. "We got in early yesterday afternoon and hung out with Silas and Mabel for most of the day while we unpacked."

"Everything still in good shape up there?"

"Yup! You know how Silas is and Penn and Morris were up here earlier in the spring." Morris's parents, Evelyn and Morris Sr., kept Cadence for a long weekend so her dads could relax, and Penn had made some repairs and upgrades to the cabin.

"Good. So, you'll be fishing this morning?" He asked, his voice rising hopefully.

"Yes! We're going fishing this morning." She shook her head and rolled her eyes. Like he had to ask. "Got the poles out and a bag of bread from the Cherry Mart for squishin'. Picked it up yesterday on the way in."

"That's my girl! Think June will like being on the boat?"

"Shoot, yeah! She can't wait for her first fishing lesson," Penny said with a whoop and twirled, but her heart sank a little as she thought back to the last time she went out on the lake with her father. They often went to Weehawken Cove to fish since it was closer to Gus's place in Hoboken. It had been several years since Gus had come up to Cherrytown. He all but stopped coming after her mother, Laurel, died. They had been able to get him to come up for a few of Silas's and Mabel's birthdays, but he rarely stayed more than a day and he avoided their swing on the back porch. Then, Gus's cancer diagnosis and the grueling months of treatment and recovery made it impossible for him to make the trip. "I always miss you when I'm fishin'," she said shakily. She wiped her cheek with the sleeve of her hoodie.

"I miss you too, Penny Lane. But I'll always be right there with you."

"I know, Pops. How are you feeling? You sound good."

"I feel good today. The boys are coming over with my Cadie Rose for lunch and then we're taking my scooter down to Pier C Park so I can watch her play." He chuckled fondly and Penny smiled at the way Gus's voice rose whenever he used his nickname for Cadence. Gus was smitten with his granddaughter. Heperked up and had more energy whenever she was around.

"That sounds like a blast!"

"We'll go with June when you guys get back."

"It's a date!" Penny was already looking forward to it.

"How's it goin' with the boss?" Gus asked, catching Penny off guard.

"Who? Agnes?" She asked cluelessly and Gus snorted.

"Who else? You up there with Bruce Springsteen?"

Penny cackled and clapped a hand over her mouth. "That was *awful*."

"Yeah. Almost as weak as that attempt to dodge the question. Your brother says she's a looker and she's got a wild streak of her own."

"He knows better than to gossip," she grumbled, rushing up the dock. She smiled when the signal began to fade and the line crackled. "Oh, no. I'm losing you," she said flatly and hung up the phone.

As far as she was concerned, she had gotten what she wanted out of the call: Gus was feeling good and Penn and Morris were keeping a closer eye on him while she was out of town. The rest was just gossip and nonsense, and she didn't want Gus to get his hopes up. He was living his best life, spoiling Cadence and teasing Penn and Morris about being lovesick nerds. He wanted that for Penny, too, but her thing with Agnes was purely physical and totally different than her brothers.

For one, Penn was worried about how much his heart could hold and if loving Morris would change him. Penny wasn't worried about her heart or changing. She knew she would never run out of love or the capacity to care for others. But love wasn't on Agnes's radar. They both had other priorities.

Neither wanted the messy, inevitable complications that often occurred when two totally unsuitable people confused lust for compatibility. Sex did not automatically equal romance, especially in Penny and Agnes's minds, but Penn and Gus would jump to all the romantic conclusions. Then, they'd be disappointed and for the rest of their lives, Agnes Cameron would be the one that got away.

Penny didn't want to spend eternity explaining that Agnes was never "the one" and that they had done it on a lark and just for fun. Especially to her father. She gave her head a firm shake, resolute in her decision to avoid the topic at all costs in the future.

Agnes was awake, bleary-eyed and pawing at the jars in the pantry when Penny returned. "Please. Where is the coffee?"

"Coming right up!" Penny promised as she took Agnes by the wrist and led her around the kitchen to the bathroom. "Why don't you finish waking up while I get breakfast started?" She suggested, receiving an appreciative grunt from Agnes before she yanked the quilt closed across the clothesline.

Silas knocked on the screen door before letting himself in a few minutes later. "Heard you were up and about," he said as he dropped a pail of wild blueberries on the counter, then went to the table and sat with a weary groan. Penny raised a brow at him, concerned. He'd never been one to sit still or complain about an ache. It was easy to forget that he was almost seventy, but his long, bushy beard was completely gray and he wasn't as wide and solid as he used to be. He was getting leaner and less steady, but Penn had warned that Silas would die before he slowed down, and asking him to try would just offend him.

"How about some blueberry pancakes?" She asked him.

"You make them for you and your ladies," he said as he stretched and crossed his ankles. "Had a bowl of oatmeal with Mom. Just wanted to drop those off and see what the three of you were up to."

"Probably a little fishing and maybe some exploring." She poured him a cup of coffee and had Agnes's mug ready when she reappeared, looking more coherent and composed.

"You're an angel," Agnes sighed before taking a deep whiff.

"Good morning, Silas," she said, offering him a nod on the way to the sugar dish.

"Ma'am," he said, raising his coffee. "And will you be joining the fishing expedition?" He asked her.

Agnes nodded slowly as she stirred. "I'm not sure if I'll be much help, but I'm game."

"Don't listen to him," Penny said, rolling her eyes. "It's just a walk down the hill to the dock and I don't like going too far out. It's a pain coming back when you've really gotta pee," she informed Agnes.

"I see," she said, and risked a glance at Silas.

He was pinching the bridge of his nose and his chest shook with laughter. "She's always had a bladder the size of a blueberry and she refused to pee in the lake."

"Not with you all *right there*," Penny shot back. "I'm not an actual animal." Agnes coughed and coffee sprayed from her mouth as she giggled. Silas was in tears and wheezing loudly. "Would you two—!" Penny hissed at them and waved, afraid they'd woken June.

"What was that about blueberries?" June called from the loft. She appeared at the top of the stairs, scrubbing her disheveled bob. Agnes had given June one of her college T-shirts to sleep in and she looked precious in the oversized shirt, rubbing sleep from her eyes.

"I'm making blueberry pancakes!" Penny said cheerfully.

June became alert. "Yes!" She was an unstoppable force after that, zipping back and forth and up and down the stairs, preparing for their day while Penny prepared breakfast. They ate while Silas answered all of June's questions about the chickens and cows. He promised to give her a tour after she and Penny caught him a trout, then left them to get ready for the lake.

Just a little over an hour later, Penny was tying the laces on her Converse when Agnes threw back the bathroom curtain and strutted past the kitchen sink. It was a good thing Penny was sitting on the floor because her jaw fell open in shock as she stared at Agnes.

"You look..." Penny didn't know a fancy enough word to describe how Agnes looked, but she was too beautiful for a rickety old dock in the Catskills. Agnes was wearing a sexy red bikini and matching high heels. Her massive, wide-brimmed black sunhat, oversized black sunglasses, and flowing sheer black cover-up were perfect for a *Vogue* cover or Saint-Tropez.

"You look like a model!" June breathed as she watched Agnes turn and pose elegantly by a table.

"You really do," Penny agreed, then scrunched her nose. "But are you sure you want to go down to the dock in that? Not that you don't look *perfect*," she added quickly.

Agnes shrugged off the compliment with a flip of her perfectly curled hair. She'd spent most of the hour in the bath-room spraying and whispering curses at herself to get it all just right. Penny didn't know why Agnes had gone to the trouble. She didn't have the nerve to ask, though, so she and June had spent the time making tick repellant and wadding slices of cheap white bread into globs for fishing bait.

"These old things?" Agnes asked, gesturing at her ensem-ble. "I practically live in this when I'm at the cottage."

"Okay..." Penny couldn't recall an inch of the place in Sagaponack that hadn't been perfectly landscaped and main-tained by professional gardeners. Here, it was a downhill walk to the dock and there was no telling what type of mole hole or rabbit's den they'd encounter along the way. Not to mention the multitude of roots, rocks, and slippery spots. "There isn't a decent footpath so you might have a little trouble," she warned, but Agnes just shrugged again.

"I've been wearing heels for longer than you've—" Agnes

started, then cleared her throat. "It doesn't matter. I'll be fine," she said with an airy wave.

"If you're sure. Let's get you sprayed down." Penny jumped up and got a bottle off the table. She aimed it and was ready to spray when Agnes held out her hands, blocking Penny.

"What's in that and are you sure I need it?"

Penny frowned at the refillable glass spray bottle. "It's... apple cider vinegar and a bunch of oils that critters don't like. Like citronella and peppermint."

"I think I'll pass. My assistant got us these," Agnes said, holding out her wrist so Penny and June could inspect her red floral bracelet. "The package says they protect against mosquitos and most biting insects. I have plenty if you and June would like one." She opened her black woven tote bag and removed a handful of individually wrapped bracelets.

"Ooh!" June selected one immediately but Penny shook her head as she looked down at her own ensemble. She kept one of her dad's old bowling shirts on the hook by the door to wear over her swimsuit and jean shorts. Her cotton socks were pulled up to her calves and she was wearing her Chucks. June had been loaned a pair of tall socks and an old bowling shirt and was holding Penny's lucky pole.

Penny gave up on the spray and shrugged. "I'm good. We sprayed our shoes and socks and clothes and we're gonna stay out of the brush." She wasn't sure Agnes had on enough clothing to spray, aside from her gauzy black cover-up. Penny glanced at Agnes's long, toned, bare legs and envied New York's mosquitos and the Catskill's flea and tick population. She was in the mood to do a little biting herself... "We already put on sunscreen, but I can give you a hand when we get down to the dock if you need one."

"I just might." Agnes murmured absently as she returned

the rest of the bracelets to her bag, then blushed and risked a glance at Penny. "I mean... I can't reach my back and—"

"Right! That's what I meant too!" Penny nodded quickly and opened the door before the conversation got weirder. "Here we go!" She waved them through. Penny thanked June for handing her her lucky fishing pole, then jogged down the steps so she could lead the way to the dock.

"I thought we'd see if we could catch a trout for Silas and Mabel before we jumped in and got to splashing around," she explained. "I won't eat it, but I like to catch dinner for them. It gives Silas one less thing to do and Mabel always cooks twice as much when we're here. And her cornbread, hot and covered in maple syrup or strawberry jam, is *amazing*. Mabel makes it with almond milk when I'm here and it might be my favorite dessert in the whole world." Penny's lips twisted as she reconsidered. "Unless it's her cornbread with apple butter. And then there's her strawberry shortcake..."

"Can I help you catch the fish?" June asked and hopped over a large rock.

"You betcha!" Penny said, checking behind them to make sure Agnes was alright. Agnes was slowly picking her way down the hill, her long legs bending and stretching awkwardly with each careful step. Penny shrugged and explained to June that the first half hour or so was usually spent getting unpacked and quietly situated on the boat. It was hard to catch anything once you raised a ruckus and started splashing. Penny and Penn usually sipped on jars of Silas's wine while they waited for the trout to bite, then progressed to cannonballs off the dock and synchronized swimming once Mabel and Silas's dinner was caught. "You will have to settle for some fresh mountain berry lemonade. But your mom and I will be puttin' up our feet and sipping on some wine while you watch the fishing line."

June cheered when Penny handed her the rod. "Okay! If you think I'll be ready."

"You'll be a pro in no time! I can tell you're a natural." Penny was about to share her best fishing advice but was interrupted by a startled "Ack!" She and June spun around, only to discover that the toe of Agnes's shoe had sunk into a mole hole. Her arms windmilled at her sides and she toppled forward.

"Oh, no!" Penny yelled and reached to catch her, but had to dive out of the way as Agnes tumbled over her tote bag, spilling bracelets, magazines, and various makeup tubes and compacts. A bottle of sunscreen and one of Silas's wine bottles rolled and bounced over roots as Agnes skidded and toppled down the hill past them. "Hold on!" Penny called, stopping to pick up a magazine and Agnes's sunglasses as she hurried to catch up.

Agnes had rolled and slid until a bush and a mulberry tree broke her fall. "I'll wait right here," Agnes said in a strained whimper while getting onto her hands and knees. The palms of her hands were scraped up and smeared with dirt, and one of her bikini's shoulder straps had ripped. Her sheer black cover-up hadn't done much to protect her and was tattered and shredded from catching on twigs and thorns. And, to add insult to injury, Penny suspected that the bush that had broken Agnes's fall was actually overgrown poison ivy.

"Let's carefully ease you out of there," Penny advised as she lifted Agnes up by her armpits, careful not to touch more than necessary or disturb any of the foliage around her. She flicked a tick off Agnes's thigh before she noticed it and thanked June when she arrived with Agnes's other high heel and her hat.

"Are you okay, Mom?"

"I'm fine!" Agnes said cheerfully, but she grabbed onto Penny's wrist when she almost fell into the bush again.

"Let's get away from here!" Penny said cheerfully, not wanting to alarm Agnes or June. "We're going to have to adjust our plans for the afternoon. June, you might have to hang out with Silas while I help Agnes." She kept her voice light and calm while easing her wrist out of Agnes's grip. There was no telling what parts of Agnes had come into contact with the poison ivy and the plant's oils would irritate any skin it touched.

"Help me?" Agnes asked, then swore when she tried to stand up straighter. "My ankle!" She grabbed her right ankle gingerly and hopped on the other foot.

"I had a feeling you might have sprained something and

you're going to want to take a bath and soak in some baking soda and oatmeal."

"I will?" Agnes asked, sounding scared as she reached for Penny again.

"Easy!" Penny swayed back and offered her a sheepish wince. "You *might* have fallen into poison ivy so we're going to take some extra precautions, okay?"

"What do you mean by *'might'?*" Agnes countered, her voice rising with alarm. "You're the Plant Nerd Supreme and you said you know this mountain like the back of your hand."

"Let's not get hung up on the details," Penny said dismissively. She squinted and gazed up toward the top of the hill. "I'd give you a piggyback ride if I could, but we're going to have to get creative..." She planted her hands on her hips as she considered their options, then smiled when she recalled her favorite winter ritual. "June bug, run on over to Mabel and Silas's and tell them we need a sled, some Crisco, and a rope."

"On it!" June shouted as she raced up the hill, leaving Penny with Agnes.

"This will be fun," Penny assured her, but Agnes's lip wobbled as she took in her scuffed-up knees and elbows, ripped bikini strap, and the broken heel in her hand.

"Fun?" She croaked, breaking Penny's heart. Agnes was trying so hard to be a good sport and not cry. But she'd taken a nasty tumble and Penny could already see a rash spreading down Agnes's right thigh.

"I promise I know the best way to treat poison ivy and we're all going to laugh about this later."

"I'm sure *you* will." Agnes muttered. She clutched her shoe and her hat against her chest and took a few hops on her left foot. "That's not so bad. I should be able to make it back up to the cabin by...tomorrow afternoon." She hopped a few more inches up the hill.

Penny would have tackled Agnes and kissed her senseless if she could. She looked so bedraggled, but still somehow ethereal. And instead of having a tantrum and whining about her heels or the poison ivy, Agnes was bravely hopping on one foot and doing her best to smile when she clearly wanted to cry.

"Once, when I was...eight or nine, I decided to go swimming in the rain. But instead of listening to Penn and waiting for the worst of the storm to pass, I ran out while it was pouring and slid all the way down the hill in the mud on my belly."

Agnes laughed and looked at the hill as she pictured it. "Oh, no!"

"And I slid *all* the way down," Penny said as she pointed at the dock. "I crashed just about there, but my shorts stayed at the top of the hill," she added. Her finger swung around and Agnes groaned when Penny aimed it up at the cabin. "Thank goodness Dash wasn't here or there would be pictures."

"Next time, I will defer to your experience," Agnes vowed, earning a chuckle from Penny.

"Believe me, if there's a way to injure yourself on this mountain, I've done it and I've got the scars to prove it." She folded her arms and swung her elbow toward Agnes. "See that?" She said, gesturing at a thick, but short scar. "Mom had to give me stitches after I climbed that tree over there. I wasn't *totally vegan* then. There was a huge beehive and I thought I could sneak up there by myself and steal some honeycomb."

"Penny!" Agnes complained. "What if you'd been seriously hurt? You could have been stung."

"I was! That's how I fell out of the tree. I'd been stung plenty of times and figured it was worth the risk for the comb, but it's hard to be a honey thief and protect your face *and* hold on so evolution and gravity taught me a swift lesson that day." Penny flashed her a cocky grin. "Not that I paid much attention. I fell out of that tree two more times that summer, trying to mess with those bees and their honey. Dad says it's a miracle I survived this place."

"Truly," Agnes said, shaking her head at Penny.

June and Silas arrived a few minutes later with the items Penny had requested. It didn't take long for Silas to pull Agnes up the hill with Penny pushing the sled from the bottom. Penny nicknamed Agnes "Cleopatra of the Catskills" and June used a magazine to fan their lounging queen as they made their way up the hill.

"Thank you," Agnes said with a graceful bow once they reached the porch steps. "That was far less humiliating than I deserved."

"I'm having fun!" June announced, and began winding the rope around her forearm.

"Want to learn how to throw a lasso while they get Agnes patched up?" Silas offered, effectively stealing June's attention. The two wandered over to the far corner of the porch for their lesson, leaving Penny to help Agnes into the cabin.

Agnes took a quick shower to wash away the poison ivy and any loose ticks, then soaked in oatmeal and baking soda for twenty minutes. Penny steeled herself when it was time to see to the many scratches and blisters scattered all over Agnes's body.

"How's your ankle?" Penny asked when Agnes limped out of the bathroom, leaning on the counter and table for support. She was able to dress herself in a pair of pajama shorts and a camisole that Penny had retrieved from Agnes's room.

Agnes made a dismissive sound, still determined to be a trooper. "It's not happy when I put weight on it, but I'll manage," she said, and Penny shushed Agnes as she helped her turn around.

"We'll get it elevated and iced as soon as we get your...um... backside treated. This is gonna itch and burn like mad, but you'll be right as rain in a few days. My mom had plenty of opportunities to perfect her remedy for poison ivy because we managed to roll into it at least once a summer," Penny said, glad that Agnes was turned. Her face was burning as she reached for the bottle of witch hazel and the baking soda paste she'd prepared.

"Thank you, Penny," Agnes said quietly. Then she gathered her hair and pulled it over her shoulder so it was out of the way, and Penny immediately noticed the patch of red creeping up Agnes's neck. But it wasn't a rash picked up from a bug or a bush. Agnes was blushing. Penny blew softly and delighted at Agnes's stifled gasp and faint shiver.

"It's no trouble at all." Penny dipped the end of a clean tea towel in the baking soda paste and dabbed at Agnes's skin while checking the window. Silas had taken June down the hill so they could practice lassoing a tree trunk by the dock. They were having far too much fun to worry about them so Penny cleared her throat as she raised the back of Agnes's cami. She knew that she was playing with fire, but Penny couldn't resist and reasoned that a little bit of flirting wouldn't hurt. "I'd even say it's a pleasure if it weren't for your poor ankle and all this road rash and poison ivy."

"You mean hill rash. No roads were involved in this collision. I'm just a clumsy oaf who lost her step," Agnes said with a shaky laugh but Penny shushed her again.

"I told you, I nearly kill myself here at least once every summer. If I don't, I know I'm not having enough fun."

"We have very different definitions of the word fun, then," Agnes murmured and gasped when Penny's lips trailed over her shoulder blade. Penny couldn't help it. Agnes's skin was *so soft* and she smelled like heaven. And witch hazel.

"Oh, I'm pretty sure we don't."

"Penny!" It came out as a nervous laugh, and Agnes was

now blushing deeply as she looked over her shoulder. "I didn't think you'd be interested anymo—"

"Interested?" Penny countered loudly and rolled her eyes. "I'd have to be dead to be *un*interested in you, Aggie. Lordy, all you have to do is breathe and look at me and my brain and my body turn to goo."

"Really?" Agnes appeared flustered as she brushed at her side ponytail with her fingers and squirmed. "I was so afraid I'd say or do something inappropriate, but I wasn't sure how I was supposed to act. I've never hired anyone I've..." She gave Penny a suggestive look, making her grin.

"This is a first for me too. I've never hooked up with anyone I work for or with, but it seems like a big waste of time and energy for us to keep pretending it didn't happen."

"Pretending? I can't seem to forget but it seems like I should try at least," Agnes scolded herself with a wistful sigh.

"I know what you mean," Penny said as she traded the paste for the witch hazel and cleaned a scratch on Agnes's hip. It required Penny to lower the waistband of Agnes's shorts, and she used the opportunity to caress the soft curve of her ass, earning a strained groan.

"This could be trouble. Neither of us has much in the way of impulse control," Agnes noted.

Penny wasn't sure what she wanted, but she knew they couldn't get into too much trouble while they were at the cabin. They'd be too busy with June and had Silas and Mabel as chaperones during the day. The nights were an entirely different matter...

"I told you, we're just here to have fun and get to know each other better. It's up to you, how much fun *we* have when we're alone and I'm off the clock."

"I see." Agnes humphed and arched her back, offering Penny a tempting view of her bottom as she worked. It was hard to tell if Penny had pushed too far and she worried that Agnes's humph had been one of displeasure.

"Unless you'd rather put it all behind us and start with a clean slate. I can totally do that too," Penny said with a breezy laugh. "It's not like we can't go a few weeks without having sex and I'm sure you have...someone," she added, wincing awkwardly.

Agnes snorted as she pushed the back of her shorts lower and leaned over the table. "I'll think about it. We both know I don't have...*someone.*"

"Isn't that interesting?" Penny's teeth dug into her lip as she considered biting one of Agnes's asscheeks. "Neither do I," she supplied absently, her head tilting as she fantasized about replacing the towel with her tongue.

"Interesting, indeed."

Chapter Twelve

Interesting was an understatement.

Thanks to Agnes's tumble and her swollen ankle, she found herself with very little to do *but* ponder Penny's comments. Had she made an actual offer and was Agnes brave/foolish enough to accept it?

June followed Silas around most of the afternoon, blowing into the cabin to show Agnes a bug she'd caught, a rock she'd found, or the bouquet of wild flowers she'd picked. They were in a Mason jar on the coffee table, meant to cheer Agnes up while she was recovering. But Agnes wasn't feeling all that down and like her mother, was beginning to suspect that she was safest indoors with a cocktail in her hand.

"Stop it. I'm nothing like her and I can do this," she told herself. While taking another gulp of Silas's bathtub berry wine. Agnes noted that the cabin and the pace of life on the mountain in Cherrytown was a lot like Silas's wine. It wasn't complex or elegant, by any means, just simple, sweet, and more than adequate if you were willing to give it a chance. The wine was made by whatever rough and wild magic Silas had conjured in the basement or bathroom of their even more ramshackle cabin and was just one of the many wonderful surprises awaiting Agnes if she'd give Penny and her Catskills getaway a chance.

She'd gotten off to a rocky start, and was kicking herself for thinking she could be hot *and* outdoorsy in a classic Louboutin sandal with a 120mm heel. Agnes would mourn her "lucky" red heels, but she would always smile when she looked back on her afternoon as Cleopatra of the Catskills.

Instead of mocking Agnes or calling her shallow or pampered, Penny comforted her and made her laugh. Agnes was getting a little antsy, though. She hadn't been allowed to leave the loveseat unless she was being helped into the bathroom. Despite that, and even with an itching, burning, splotchy rash covering most of her right leg and torso, Agnes was having a relaxed and rather pleasant evening. They ate dinner—Mabel sent over fried fish for June and Agnes along with a fresh corn salad—and played Scrabble. June had cuddled up next to Agnes while they played and she had trounced the adults, winning both games handily.

Agnes was so proud, and took pleasure in how the day had been all the more successful for them as a team because she'd taken a tumble. She could hear June recounting her favorite moments from the day as she brushed her teeth and prepared for bed. Penny was humming along from her perch on the kitchen counter, flipping through an old almanac as she listened.

According to June, Agnes was indestructible because a normal mortal wouldn't have walked away with just a few scratches and a sprained ankle. And June *liked* being able to care for Agnes and enjoyed her crash course in mountain medicine from Penny and Silas. Agnes was learning a lot as well and it was just their first full day at the cabin. She hadn't even missed the use of her smartphone or worried about checking in with Melinda.

"Goodnight, Mom!" June raced to the sofa to hug and kiss Agnes. Her arms wound Agnes's neck easily and she quickly kissed her cheek before hugging Penny and bounding up the stairs. Agnes had nodded along and squeezed June back, but she'd been delightfully stunned again at how *natural* those hugs already felt. Unlike the nervous, overly obedient girl from a few nights earlier, June was already more confident, outgoing, and affectionate with Agnes and Penny. Agnes noted that she'd *earned* that hug and June's trust and affection by being herself and being present. And as Penny had predicted, that was all that June needed or truly cared about.

It was dawning on Agnes that she could never truly be herself or leave her upbringing behind at The Killian House or even at the cottage in Sagaponack. She could count on one hand the number of times she'd visited the cottage with her parents as a child. But their expectations and indifference—and her bitterness—would always follow her there. As much as Agnes loved Camilla, an old nanny's affections would never replace or heal the wounds created by parental neglect.

Agnes refused to be like her mother, and had set out to create the family she'd always craved. But she could see that she was holding on to a lot of negative baggage that June didn't need. She would have held on to that longer at The Killian House or the cottage and it would have been another wall for her and June to have to climb, another barrier between them. Instead, they were both starting fresh at the cabin in Cherrytown and Agnes was so glad that June *wanted* her as captain of their team.

"Are you alright?" Penny asked as she lowered onto the loveseat next to Agnes, passing her a jar of wine.

"I'm fine! My ankle is hardly swollen and it barely twinges

when I move it now." She was sitting upright again and no longer lounging on her back with her leg elevated. Agnes wasn't sure what it said about her, but being incapacitated like that for an afternoon had bothered her more than her achy ankle.

"I can see that," Penny said, her eyes twinkling as she turned towards Agnes, crossed her legs and leaned closer. "But I can also see that something heavy is going on in there," she whispered, tapping Agnes on the nose.

Agnes laughed softly and rocked toward Penny so she could knock their foreheads together gently. "You've helped me escape my terrible childhood and given me a salve for my mother's rejection, if that's what you call heavy," she said, earning a low whistle from Penny.

"That's a lot, Aggie." She swept the hair away from Agnes's face and made a soft, soothing sound as she scooted in closer until their knees bumped. "Talking about it might help." Penny's voice rose hopefully; there was so much pure kindness and generosity in her offer. Yet if the tables were turned, the very last thing Agnes would have wanted was to know more. *Everyone* had problems, and the problems of a spoiled socialite were the least interesting and the least worthy of sympathy.

"I pay my therapists to listen to me bitch about my mother never loving me and being unwanted because I wasn't born a boy to carry on the Cameron name and legacy."

"Therapists?" Penny asked, sounding a touch concerned, and Agnes snorted.

"As if one would be enough. I have far too many things that need fixing, and Dr. Altovar kept going on and on about having other patients and sticking to regular hours and scheduled visits."

"Oh, Aggie."

"I know, but that's the gist of it, really. I'm high-maintenance because I only respect the boundaries of people I don't want to lose. I wasn't important to my parents because I didn't have value like Walker. I've always been lonely and looking for love because I've learned to commodify most interactions and relationships. I don't respect people like Dr. Altovar because I pay him to make time for me and I can pay him more than his other clients, therefore I am more important. But none of that matters here and you and June seem to like me despite all my awful baggage. It feels *nice* to be able to leave it behind—or attempt to—and it's nice being...*real*."

Penny purred as she wound her arms around Agnes's neck. "Listen, lady. You keep opening up and growing like this and you're going to have to beat me off with a stick. I was hoping you'd relax and have a little fun. I thought that might be hard for you, but you came with an open mind and an open heart. I think you deserve something...*extra* fun and relaxing."

"And by fun and relaxing, you mean..." Agnes nipped at Penny's lower lip and gave it a firm tug, making her groan.

"That's entirely up to you," she whispered. "Have you given any thought to what I said earlier?"

"Just a little," Agnes replied facetiously, then leaned back and cringed up at the loft. "That's all I've been able to think about since we arrived. When I'm not worrying about June," she admitted as her hand skated up Penny's thigh.

"I kind of assumed," Penny said in a low murmur, capturing Agnes's lips for a slow, drugging kiss. "I don't see any point in pretending it didn't happen or pretending we don't want it to happen again, as long as it doesn't interfere with June's care."

"Really?" Agnes's brow hitched because this seemed too good to be true. She was more than willing to be whipped into shape and turned into a decent parent. She was looking forward to it, actually. But she had assumed that exploring and enjoying Penny's body was no longer an option. "You know I would *never* expect anything or pressure you to—"

Penny shut her up with a kiss. "You're even hotter out here than at our brothers' weddings. And you make me feel like I just ran up the hill and spun around and around in circles. I could waste a lot of time and energy pretending my tummy doesn't tickle and my mouth doesn't water when I remember how good you taste. Or..." She bit into her lip as she breathed Agnes in.

"Or?" Agnes asked, dizzy and desperate to know what Penny had in mind.

Penny's eyes were heavy and clung to Agnes's as she stole another kiss. "I'm going to take a quick shower. You can leave the curtain open if you'd like me to join you afterward." She swung her head toward the quilt dividing the bedroom nook from the kitchen.

"I would, but—" Agnes agreed too readily and her face got hot. She was sure she was blushing and her camisole was sticking to her back. "What if June hears us or comes downstairs?"

Penny tapped her lips, signaling for Agnes to listen. The song of the forest swelled around the cabin once Agnes actually *listened*. She'd already tuned it out because she was so used to the constant chatter of the city. It was a very different type of loud, but the forest was just as lively as the city at night. Chirps, hoots, snaps, and various cries carried on the breeze and mingled with the rustling leaves.

"It's like sleeping in a treehouse up there. And trust me—I know from experience because my parents had a very healthy appreciation for each other—you can't hear what's going on downstairs. All June can hear are the katydids, crickets, peepers, owls, and mourning doves," Penny said quietly. They heard a haunting scream and Penny smiled. "And the occasional fox.

June won't hear us as long as *you* don't start screaming," she challenged with a wink.

"Are you sure we'll hear her if she comes down?" Agnes asked, earning a snort from Penny.

"It's impossible to sneak down those stairs. They're as solid and sturdy as stone, but Silas and Mabel can probably hear us going up and down them from their place."

"True," Agnes conceded. "And you're sure this won't be... weird for you?"

Penny snorted again. "It would be even weirder if we pretended we weren't attracted to each other. And it would be weird, worrying about whether I'm sending the wrong signals or reading stuff into everything you say and do. I'd prefer to just be myself and for us to be honest with each other."

"That's shockingly simple and mature," Agnes complained. There was a pleasant tingling in Agnes's fingers and toes from Silas's wine, and she was warm, despite the chilly, breezy evening. "And I just leave the curtain open if I'm in the mood for company?"

"Yup. I like simple and uncomplicated." Penny pressed her lips to Agnes's, then slipped away. "See you in a bit," she whispered and winked before leaving Agnes to collect her scattered wits.

"Well." She gave her head a shake, still delightfully stunned. Agnes was counting her blessings as she reflected on her day as Cleopatra of the Catskills. Now, her evening had been transformed into a fantasy.

The sound of water pelting the wooden tub as Penny showered had Agnes's nerves fizzing. She'd reached the bottom of her jar of wine so she shuffled into the kitchen in search of a refill. A naked glass bottle with a stopper had been left on the counter, and Agnes gave it another appreciative sniff before pouring.

She was truly getting warm so she limped into the bedroom nook at the back of the cabin and cracked the sliding door, enjoying the slight chill and the goosebumps that spread down her arms and chest. Agnes lowered onto the bed, wincing at the soft creaking of the old metal frame as she scooted to the middle. The mattress was newish and firm, but the rest of the space felt ancient and tranquil as Agnes's eyes scanned the timber planks and beams. Vines curled and spread around the room and bits of moss clung to the walls and the ceiling.

The hodgepodge of mismatched antique furniture, vintage floral prints combined with dangling crystals, and colorful pottery made the space and the mood even more whimsical. Agnes could easily imagine she'd stumbled upon a forest fairy's chamber. And she was under a lovely spell as she leaned back on one hand and sipped Silas's mountain berry wine, waiting for her sexy nymph.

Try as she might, Agnes couldn't remember feeling more aroused and enamored. She'd been wooed by actual princes and had a torrid affair with a Saudi princess, once. But none of her past lovers had enthralled Agnes or made her feel the same rush as one of Penny's smiles. They'd showered her with gifts, hoping to win her heart, and all Penny had to do was wink at Agnes and it was over.

Her lips twitched into a smile as she recalled the wild spark in Penny's green eyes that promised mischief and pleasure. Sex was never serious with Penny, and she didn't worry about impressing Agnes or sweeping her away. Instead, Penny played and explored, teasing and learning Agnes's sensual secrets until they were both frantic and demanding.

Penny shut the water off in the bathroom and Agnes's heart raced as she waited. She was able to track Penny's movements in the bathroom and the kitchen by her humming. She held her breath when Penny came around the corner, but Agnes still lost it.

"You sure you don't want more ice for that ankle?" Penny asked as she let the quilt curtain fall behind her.

"It's fine," Agnes mouthed, too struck by the sight of Penny in nothing but a plain white tank top and a white cotton bikini to speak above a whisper. Her wet hair hung over one shoulder, leaving patches of wet, transparent fabric. A dusky pink nipple peeked between the damp tresses, drawing Agnes's eyes and her attention. "You'd think I'd be used to these feet by now," she added distantly, giving her head a shake. "We must never speak of this when we get back or my brother will never stop teasing me about my clumsiness."

"Stop!" Penny laughed as she set a knee on the bed. "I've never seen anyone move the way you do. You glide like you're floating. Like you don't have feet or walk like the rest of us," Penny said, lowering so she could lick the arch of Agnes's foot and her tender ankle.

"I had size nine feet when I was fourteen. Learning to walk gracefully was a matter of survival," Agnes informed her, making Penny click her teeth as her lips skated higher. She was avoiding the poison ivy blisters, but Agnes frowned in concern. "Isn't it contagious?"

"It's just the plant's oils we have to worry about and you've washed it all off. You have beautiful feet and they're proportional to the rest of you." She moaned appreciatively as she licked Agnes's knee and dragged her tongue up her inner thigh, causing it to tremble. "I never thought of anyone as a tall drink of water or thought that expression made much sense until I met you. You make me so thirsty, Aggie, and I want to lap up every luscious drop until I'm drunk on you."

She eased Agnes's shorts down, kissing, nibbling, and licking her legs and feet with greedy abandon. "I feel like I'll scream if you don't come here." Agnes reached for Penny, hungry for the taste of her lips and to feel their bodies naked and intertwined. "Take this off," she pleaded, drawing Penny's top up and over her head. Agnes whipped off her camisole and shifted their positions so she could push Penny's panties down. "Finally." Agnes curled a leg around Penny's hip and tangled her fingers in her hair till the damp strands were twisted around Agnes's fist. Both women were starving as they writhed and wiggled until Penny was on top.

"Finally," she panted, sliding a leg between Agnes's thighs before angling and rocking her hips. They were both gloriously slick and hot, pressed against each other. Penny made a low growling sound as her pussy glided over Agnes's, her hips swiveling in a lazy figure-eight.

"Dear God, that's so good, Penny." Agnes grabbed Penny's ass so she could help her grind harder.

They were both so wet. Penny's hand snaked between their bodies, her fingers swirling around Agnes's clit, slowly stoking their passion until they were both burning and drenched.

"Please!"

Penny took Agnes just to the brink, but stopped and withdrew her hand, raising it to her lips. She sucked on her fingers, moaning euphorically as she writhed and bucked faster. The tension in Agnes's core tightened, heat and need coiling and becoming excruciating. Penny pinched one of Agnes's nipples and she *snapped*. Every nerve burst into bright, flickering heat and warm, honey-like pleasure radiated from her center.

"Sweet Jesus, Penny," Agnes slurred as she held onto Penny's hips, encouraging her to keep doing exactly *that*.

"Sweet, indeed," Penny drawled and slid down Agnes's body.

Agnes protested and reached for her, only to hiss ecstatically when Penny's mouth latched onto her cunt. She sucked and licked, making the softest, happiest sounds as she feasted on Agnes. "My, you're thorough," Agnes said, sighing as she sank into the mattress. There was an answering moan from Penny before her tongue curled and thrust into Agnes's core. She split into a million smoldering pieces again, biting her tongue as Penny sucked on her clit.

"You. Up here. Now." Agnes flapped a hand in the direction of her face, incapable of much more, but desperate to taste Penny and hear her come.

"Yes, ma'am," Penny said, scooting up the bed on her knees. She swung one leg over Agnes's face without any hesitation.

"I think I might love you, Penny," Agnes said, the words muffled against soft, succulent flesh. Of course, Penny laughed as she held onto the curved iron headboard and squirmed against Agnes's tongue. She thought it was a joke, but there were tears in Agnes's eyes and she had a very different kind of orgasm as she held onto Penny's ass and helped her rock harder and faster. It was a hot, emotional burst of joy and devotion in the center of her being that Agnes had never experienced before. She wanted to pull Penny into it and touch that part of her too.

"Agnes! Oh, gosh!" Penny jerked hard and her back arched. "Aggie, Aggie, Aggie!" She panted as a rush of slick sweetness coated Agnes's lips.

"Mmmm..." Agnes chuckled lazily as her tongue washed over Penny's trembling folds, gathering every last trace. Penny shivered and giggled, her fingers brushing Agnes's scalp playfully as she lingered there, shamelessly enjoying another mild tremor.

"I feel like I've turned into stars!" Penny made a dreamy sound as she dismounted and landed in a heap next to Agnes. Her hand curled around Agnes's and she shut her eyes as her lips curved into a drowsy, contented smile.

"Me too," Agnes murmured, staring at their entwined hands. It was her habit to kick her partners out of her bed once the fun was over, but Agnes recalled how lonely she'd felt the night before. "You can stay if you want," she said casually, as if it wasn't a big deal and she was just letting Penny know. At least she'd asked and wouldn't spend the rest of the night kicking herself, Agnes reasoned.

Penny's smile widened and the mischievous glint was back when her eyes opened and flicked to Agnes's. "Don't worry, I'll be up way before June comes down. But I'm not done with you yet, Ms. Cameron."

Chapter Thirteen

The problem with finding Nirvana was that you couldn't stay there forever. Penny reminded herself of that every time she wondered if life could get any better than the lazy days she shared with June and Agnes at the cabin.

Every morning started with a taste of Agnes. Penny would wake with their naked bodies tangled and she'd lick and nibble as she extricated herself and made her way down her sleeping goddess's body. She'd get her tongue so deep into Agnes's pussy, where she was sweetest and wettest, and Penny would make her quiver. Agnes's strained swears and whimpers were an early morning aria just for Penny.

It was impossible to keep her hands to herself. Thankfully, Penny had been given permission to do her worst—as long as she was careful and discreet—and the secret goal every day was to see how many times Agnes could get off. Penny's hands went right into Agnes's shorts or up her shirt as soon as they were alone. And it only took Penny a few moments to get Agnes to shatter so it was possible to get her off two or three times while

June popped over to Silas and Mabel's for a cup of sugar or to return a dish.

But Penny hadn't lost complete touch with the world. She missed her brothers, her niece, and her father when she wasn't wrapped up in Nirvana with Agnes and June. She was also acutely aware of the time and how fast the days were slipping through their fingers, especially this afternoon when she lowered onto the end of the dock and called Gus. While Penny would have loved to freeze time and make their summer at the cabin last forever, she also missed Gus and regretted that she couldn't be back in Hoboken with him.

Her time with Gus was slipping away, too, and Penny's heart broke whenever she worried about how much was left. But she'd promised her father that she would give each day 100%. Even if that 100% was just enough to fill a thimble, she had to give it her all and hold nothing back because the rest would go to waste. Chances didn't roll over to the next day and you never got do-overs in life. They had hard talks about cancer and Gus's remaining days and he was adamant that he didn't want to spend what was left watching his kids grieve. He wanted to see them *living* and to know that their futures were full of beautiful, happy things.

Gus's days were full and beautiful now as well and Penny was mindful of that while she waited for him to answer his phone. When he did, he was laughing, and Penny heard Penn and Morris laughing, too, a basketball game in the background. "Hey, kiddo! How's life at the lake?"

"Brilliant," she said, plunging her heels into the water with a satisfying *thunk-thunk*. She kicked her feet, making a small splash while Gus updated her on Cadence's latest words. Her niece was learning so many so fast, Penny was worried Cadence would be in kindergarten by the time they returned to the city. "Gosh, I miss her so much," Penny said. "And I miss you too. I was talking to Penn about getting rid of the loveseat and bringing a decent daybed up here so you can join us." Gus couldn't climb the stairs into the loft or make it down to the dock without being carried, but they agreed that a few weeks at the lake would be good for him. Plus, Mabel's birthday was just around the corner. Penny could come up with them and stay in the loft and Penn and Morris could have the downstairs bed. The pull-out bed wasn't suitable for Gus, but he would be comfortable on a daybed. The three of them could help him get around pretty easily with a few modifications to the cabin.

"I wouldn't mind that," Gus said and that pretty much made Penny's day. "What about you and your girls? Where are they going to stay?"

"My—?" Penny snorted. "What are you talking about?"

"You and June and Agnes," he explained, making her laugh.

"I don't know. I'll probably take a few days off and leave them in the city. It's not like that with Agnes, I swear."

"That's not what I'm hearing," Gus mused, then clicked his teeth. "Not what I'm hearing at all."

"Slow down!" Penny pulled her feet up and spun on her bottom so she could lean and look up the hill at the cabin. "What have you been hearing? Agnes and I are just..." She wasn't going to admit that they'd been licking each other raw for the last two weeks because he'd get the wrong idea. "I think we're becoming very good friends." *With very, very good benefits,* she noted as a calculating smile spread across her face.

She had left Agnes and June on the front porch, set up for an afternoon of painting. Silas had pulled out an easel and an old box of painting supplies and June had begged Agnes for an art lesson. If Penny timed it right, they would be packing up by the end of her call home. Penny would send June along with Silas to help Mabel snap beans and peel hard-boiled eggs for their dinner. Mabel was making deviled eggs at Silas and June's request, and Agnes was excited to try them for the first time. Penny was hoping to get Agnes off while June was helping Mabel.

"*Very* good friends from what I've heard," Gus said accusatively.

Penny growled and got to her feet. "Who have you been gossiping with and what did they say?" She had a feeling Silas had been clucking like an old hen to her brother.

"You know I won't give up my sources. But the two of you are gettin' real friendly up there and you're having a blast with that little one." He gave her a moment to deny it, then made a knowing sound. "And I can't see why that would be a bad thing or why you'd need to hide it."

"It's not like that and we're not hiding all that much," Penny argued. They were having *a lot* of sex, but it was just a wonderful benefit. Nothing else was going on between her and Agnes. There weren't any expectations or feelings attached. As soon as their bodies cooled they teased each other and whispered about everything *but* sex, sharing their weirdest and most embarrassing memories and occasionally their deepest, secret fears.

Not like lovers, of course. Just friends who liked to kiss and hold hands while they were whispering in the dark.

The anxious tickle in Penny's tummy was totally normal and there was nothing remarkable about the way it would turn into a swarm of butterflies when Agnes walked into the room.

"You got any oceanfront property in Arizona you wanna sell me?" Gus asked gruffly, giving Penny a mental shake. "So what if there's something going on with the three of you? You'd be good for them, Penny Lane, and it's time you settled down."

"How dare you?" She gasped, making Gus wheeze with laughter.

"Not too much, mind you. But this doesn't have to be all fun and games, girl. You should give it a chance."

"I need to get goin'," she blurted, cringing at the phone.

"Hold on now!"

"Not because of this," Penny fibbed. She gave herself a hard flick on the nose. "I need to help them gather up all the art supplies, and Mabel's gonna need a hand with dinner."

"I guess you're technically on the clock," he conceded, and let Penny go after she promised to call again on Sunday.

Her feet were heavy as she trudged up the hill and joined everyone on the porch. The easel had been wide enough for the two smaller canvases Silas had found in the box of supplies. Agnes and June had worked side-by-side and Penny was blown away by both pieces.

"Oh, my word!" She held onto her pigtails as she bent to get a closer look. "You're both geniuses," she declared.

June had painted a landscape featuring the view of the lake, complete with *three* tiny fisherwomen sitting on the end of the dock. Her brushwork was obviously more simplistic because it was one of the artist's earlier attempts, but Penny could clearly make out their lake and she had to sniff back a tear at the tiny figure with long red pigtails.

"I can't believe it. It's like you looked inside my brain and you painted my very favorite day," she said in sincere disbelief.

"Thanks, Penny!" June blushed and hugged Penny tight around the middle.

The canvas next to June's was an explosion of color— mostly pinks and greens. Agnes had created a crackled chintz mandala wrapped in flowering vines that sucked Penny right into the cabin's kitchen as she stared at the various patterns.

"Holy moly. That's incredible, Agnes," Penny whispered, unable to pull her eyes from it. "How did you do this in..." She reached down into the pocket of her overalls and checked her phone. "Three hours. You created an intricate geometric masterpiece in three hours," she said, shaking her head. "You're both so, so clever!"

Silas was nodding as he joined them and pointed at the landscape. "Hate to start an argument, but June's already promised me that one. She's gonna sign it so it can go over our hearth," he boasted.

Penny opened her mouth to complain, then remembered that she would get to see June and Agnes just about every day when they returned to the city and that Silas and Mabel would get so much joy every time they looked at it.

"Fine. We'll just have to find more canvases so June can create more masterpieces," she decided. "This one has to go in the cabin," Penny said as she claimed the mandala and Agnes shrugged.

"Sure. I've painted about a hundred of these. I'll turn just about anything or any place that inspires me into one."

"No way!" Penny was in awe at how perfectly symmetrical the design was. But within all that symmetry Agnes had imitated—down to the crackled glaze—were the broken floral patterns on the bits of china Penn had used to make the kitchen's backsplash. She had also mimicked Penny's mother's handmade pottery in the milky green and pink swirls within the patterns and there were flowers with mug handles for leaves. Rusted forks and spoons were crisscrossed and hidden in the pattern as well and the background looked like warped wood. "It's *beautiful*."

"Look at the time!" Silas said as he gave June a nudge and swung his head toward his and Mabel's place. "We better get over there or she'll sneak raisins in the eggs."

"Ew! Let's go!" June said, and followed Silas as he jogged down the steps, leaving Agnes and Penny to clean up after the art lesson.

"Raisins?" Agnes asked, making Penny gag.

"Mabel can be a bit of a trickster if you leave her to her own devices. That's how she'd keep us in the kitchen when she needed a hand. We'd help out so she couldn't sneak any raisins into anything they didn't belong in."

Agnes laughed. "That's diabolical! I love it."

"*That's* Mabel," Penny said with a soft laugh, grinning in the direction of the other cabin. "Silas has two boys, Sam and Walt. They live in Syracuse and out by Watertown. They come out here as often as they can, but Sam's health hasn't been great and Walt's a pediatrician with a busy practice."

"What about the boys' mom?" Agnes asked quietly, causing Penny to wince.

"Aunt Jean passed away about eighteen years ago. Silas went into town more when she was alive and they used to visit the boys pretty regularly, but he rarely comes off the mountain anymore. Not since she passed. He just hides up here with Mabel and keeps this place from falling apart," she explained.

"I'm so sorry." Agnes caught Penny's hand and gave it a squeeze.

"Thank you." Penny had fewer memories of her Aunt Jean because she died just a few years after her mother. "It's sad. We don't talk about her as much as my mom because it's so hard for Silas, so I don't really know what Jean was like. I know she was tall like Silas and she could get him to dance after dinner. Dad would play his guitar and Mom would sing and Aunt Jean loved to dance."

"Sounds like a wonderful time," Agnes said.

"There's always been lots of magic up here." Penny checked to make sure no one was watching then towed Agnes around the corner of the porch. She backed her against the wall and planted a hand next to Agnes's head. "Wanna take a bath?" She asked as she swooped in for a kiss.

"Right now?"

Penny giggled and shook her head faintly, giving Agnes's lip a playful tug. "Tonight," she whispered, plucking the button on Agnes's fly open.

"I'm listening," Agnes said, angling her hips so Penny could pull the zipper down and slide her hand inside. Penny's fingers slipped beneath the fine cotton thong and found silken heat. There was a burst of slickness as Penny parted Agnes's soft flesh and pressed two fingers into her core. "Fuck!" Agnes held on tight to Penny's shoulders.

"Mm-hmm... In the tub. Tonight," Penny promised as she pulled her hand free and raised it to her lips. She moaned at the clean and softly sweet taste of Agnes as she sucked on her fingers. She got them wet with spit and slid them back into Agnes's thong and reached lower. Penny hooked and curled her fingers deep, grinding with her palm and lifting Agnes onto her toes.

"*Penny—!*" Agnes whimpered through clenched teeth as Penny pushed her up to the peak. "I'm...! Oh fuck, oh fuck, *oh fuck!*" Agnes's shoulders came off the wall and her head rolled back. She was radiant as she came apart, gasping and chanting Penny's name.

Penny's hand was drenched when she withdrew it, and she purred in delight as she licked her palm and fingers clean. "Very good benefits," she said with a pleased hum.

"What are you talking about?" Agnes asked in a daze. She fumbled with her fly and her shirt, then patted at her hair with limp hands. "Reid better be offering you good benefits. That was incredible."

"Thanks!" Penny allowed Agnes to capture her cheeks and kiss her. "Just one more kiss. We should pack everything up and get to Mabel's."

Agnes pouted and chased Penny's lips when she pulled away. "But I *have* to touch you!"

"Tonight," Penny reminded her. "I'll get the bath and the wine ready while you tuck our girl in."

"I can't wait." Agnes held onto Penny's hand and followed her around the corner of the cabin. "What if I want to do something for you?"

Penny pointed at the mandala and raised a brow at her. "How much would one of these go for?" She had seen Agnes's art in galleries and public spaces around the city.

Agnes held up her hands. "I don't sell a lot of those. I usually gift them to friends because they're...specific to a moment or a place. That's made to go in there," she said simply, nodding at the cabin's open front door.

"That's really hot and I'd want to *go in there* if I thought we could trust Mabel," Penny said, glaring petulantly at the woods and the other cabin.

"I'm being serious." Agnes turned Penny's cheek and found her eyes. "I made that just to show June and because it was something fun to do. You get a little help with the cooking from Silas and Mabel, but you do almost everything for us. You even make my coffee every morning and you don't even drink it." She checked behind her before she stole a quick kiss and nipped Penny's earlobe. "And I lose track of how many times you make me come each day. Why do you always make me wait until bedtime to taste you?" She whispered, her lips, tongue, and the hot huff of her breath tickling Penny's ear. Agnes's lips traced the column of Penny's neck and she blew softly, causing a cascade of goosebumps down her arms and back.

Heat unfurled in Penny's core, making her restless and achy. She cherished it and bit her lip at the spike of wild lust pounding in her veins, making her feel more alive and ready to be reckless. It was a rush and would keep her on edge and idling throughout the day. Penny sighed as she leaned into Agnes and teased her lips. "I would ride your face right now and until my knees were bleeding if I could." She said it as if she was singing Agnes to sleep. "And I like imagining all the dirty things I'll do when we're alone because it makes me feel like I'm about to explode when I finally let you touch me."

"Good God, Penny," Agnes murmured, then reared back and gave her head a shake. "How on earth do you function like that? I don't know how you manage to be so competent because I'm going to be a mess for the rest of the afternoon."

"Lovely!" Penny said as she popped up onto her tiptoes and kissed Agnes.

"I'm being serious. How do you take such good care of us and keep June engaged and entertained with all...that?" She gestured vaguely at Penny, making her giggle.

"I don't know. I've always got one eye on June. That little girl is always on my mind." She smiled just thinking about June snapping green beans at the kitchen table with Silas. Penny decided it was worth the raisins, and her smile curved crookedly as she towed Agnes into the cabin. "And you just have to breathe and I get dizzy."

Agnes pushed out a weary breath as she followed. "You're going to do it again, aren't you? And you're still going to make me wait."

"Mm-hmm."

"Fine. Just hurry, Penny. I don't like raisins."

Neither did Penny. And that was when she first suspected that she was in a heck of a lot of denial and that life wouldn't be so simple once they left Nirvana and returned to the city.

Chapter Fourteen

Whoever said that life comes at you fast must have had children. Because despite the standstill her life had taken up at the cabin, Agnes could feel her priorities and motivations shifting and rushing like currents in a stream. Every day, some new revelation about June or herself redefined huge elements of Agnes's psyche and eroded old concepts and beliefs.

Like when June explained that she had recycled aluminum cans to save up the money to complete her beloved *Percy Jackson* collection. Agnes was aware that soda cans *could be* recycled for money but had never given the matter much thought. She rarely encountered them in the course of her daily life. Most of Agnes's beverages sparkled and were served on a tray by Melinda or a server.

Of course, the value of a can was very little so June had collected thousands of them and had saved for months. That alone was humbling because Agnes had never waited and saved money for anything. And she realized that was why so few things in her life had value. In fact, few things in her world—

including the priceless gems and masterpieces in the Cameron Estate's vaults—would ever be as valuable as June's *Percy Jackson* collection.

As the days crept past, Agnes learned that in *many* ways June had lived and learned a hell of a lot more than Agnes in her short eight years on Earth. She obviously had a far better understanding of the value of money, budgeting, and the meaning of hard work. And she was far more streetwise because the world didn't coddle or make excuses for her.

At least, it hadn't. All of that would change now that June was a Cameron. Agnes wanted all that adoration and easiness for June after a life in the foster care system. But the child would always be more grounded than her mother and her cousins. Even with Fin's down-to-earth, laid-back influence, the triplets would lack June's experience with the harsher realities of a life that didn't come with wealth and privilege.

Agnes's upbringing had lacked any grounding, and she had been oblivious to her privilege until she'd met Connor at Tisch. He was the very first person to tell her to get over herself and that she wasn't *that* special. It was what had made her fall in platonic love with him and why she knew he was perfect for Walker. But thanks to Connor, Agnes learned that she couldn't trust people's opinions because they'd always be corrupted by her status. That was why she could never trust anyone when they said her artwork was good. She had no idea what it was truly worth because her name and notoriety would always matter more than what was on the canvas or the pedestal.

June was wiser in ways that Agnes was only now beginning to grasp. And just when she thought she was catching up, June would transform and blow her away again. In the weeks since they arrived at the cabin, June had bloomed into an active, adventurous, and affectionate child brimming with confidence.

Agnes liked to think that she'd rubbed off on June in that respect and couldn't wait for Walker to see her again.

They texted regularly throughout the day and talked on the phone a few times a week, but Agnes couldn't convey to Walker just how much June had changed. Each morning June was a brighter, warmer, livelier girl when she came down for breakfast.

Well. Figuratively, and maybe not first thing. It did take a little while for their June bug to get warmed up, and Agnes smiled into her coffee cup as she heard her daughter stomp down the steps. She was only half-awake, with bed-rumpled hair, and she stretched and yawned loudly before crashing into Agnes for a hug.

"Morning, Mom," she mumbled and offered her forehead for a kiss. Agnes chuckled a good morning as she kissed June, then traded amused grins with Penny when it was her turn. "What's for breakfast?"

"Mabel sent over muffins and strawberries," Penny told her.

"Yes!" June pumped a fist, becoming awake and alert as she spun and ran to the bathroom to brush her teeth and wash her face. She left the curtain open and Agnes was entertained as June studiously brushed, flossed, and scrubbed her face with a washcloth. Agnes noted that June's sharp little bob had grown out and that her hair was wavier where it brushed her shoulders.

"You're going to need a haircut when we get back," Agnes said when June returned and scooted onto the loveseat next to her. She swept the hair out of June's face and behind her ear, and the child nodded.

"Can you braid it into pigtails like Penny's?" She asked, looking up at Agnes.

Agnes's lips pulled tight with regret and a little embarrassment as she shook her head. "I'm afraid I never learned," she admitted, looking to Penny for help.

But Penny didn't miss a beat. She clapped and squeezed in next to Agnes so she could give her a lesson, never once teasing her for not knowing how to do something as basic as braiding hair.

"Like that?" Agnes asked, holding the short pigtail in her palm for Penny to inspect.

"You got it!" Penny gave her an encouraging nudge with her elbow. "Told you you'd get it in a snap."

"My Mom's really smart!" June agreed with a quick nod, making Agnes and Penny laugh as they lost their braids and watched them unravel.

"She is, but hold still!" Penny ordered, placing a hand on top of June's head. They took turns, re-braiding and tying bows, then sent June up to get dressed while they tidied after breakfast.

Agnes and Penny were pondering various activities like rock hunting and forest foraging when June skipped back down the stairs, buzzing with energy and much more alert this time.

"Alright, sweetheart," Agnes said, opening her arms. "What are you in the mood to do today?" But June didn't slow down, swiping her lips against Agnes's cheek as she passed on the way out.

"I'm gonna go help Uncle Silas with the chickens!" June called just before the screen door slammed shut behind her.

"Well!" Agnes laughed. "I'll see you later... I guess."

"What's wrong?" Penny wrapped her arms around Agnes's waist.

Agnes turned and shook her head. "Nothing!" She kneaded Penny's arms absently as she tried to pin down her feelings. They were pinging all over the place and it felt like life was spinning faster and faster around her, despite the cabin's lazy calm. "I was expecting the transition to be a bit...bumpier and take a little longer. And I thought she'd need me more."

"She does need you and you're both doing great!" Penny pressed a kiss to Agnes's lips and rubbed the tips of their noses together. "June feels secure and comfortable enough with you—with us—that she's ready to explore and make new friends. Remember how she was at The Killian House? She felt like an alien. Like she had no place to hide and no one she could trust. Now, our little bug can spread her wings because she knows she has a safe place to land."

"When you put it like that..." Agnes was beaming as she glanced at the door. "She does seem truly *happy,* doesn't she?"

"So happy!" Penny angled her head and her teeth grazed Agnes's neck. "And I bet I know what would make *you* happy." Her hands slipped beneath Agnes's blouse. The pads of Penny's thumbs grazed her nipples, making them pucker and creating sparks of heat and longing in Agnes's core.

"What are we doing?" She whispered shakily. With past lovers, the rules of engagement had always been simple: Agnes called the shots and always got exactly what she wanted. Now, Agnes craved Penny and thrilled at her touch like it was her first crush.

"That's entirely up to you, madam," Penny purred, her thumbs wreaking havoc on Agnes's focus and her self-control. She had so little as it was, but Penny made Agnes want to be even more reckless. "I can use my fingers, but I'd love to get my tongue all the way—"

"Not like that!" Agnes said, then paused and reconsidered as the tingling throb between her legs intensified. Penny was making Agnes so wet, and she had an extra mischievous tilt to her lips. "Maybe like that, but in a minute. What are *we* doing? What is this? Are we...dating?"

Penny's eyes widened in surprise a split second before she

burst into giggles. "No way!" She kissed Agnes, laughing against her lips as she pinched Agnes's nipples and rolled them between her fingers. "Don't worry! We're just having fun and taking advantage of our obvious chemistry."

"Worry?" Agnes leaned back and frowned as she searched Penny's face. "Why would I be worried?"

"I won't let this get out of hand and I have just as much of a reason to keep this quiet," she crooned, craning her neck for a kiss. But Agnes pulled away.

"Get out of hand?"

"Shhh! Calm down!" Penny backed Agnes into the nook and let the quilt curtain fall behind her. She was soothing and gentle, placating Agnes as she guided them toward the bed. "There won't be a scandal and it won't be weird when we go back to the city."

"Now, hold on!" Agnes gripped Penny's wrists, not liking the direction they were headed at all. Figuratively, obviously. She was rather pleased to be in the bedroom. "Do you truly think I'd care if people found out we were dating?"

Penny burst into genuine laughter. "But they won't! Because we aren't!"

"We *could be*," Agnes countered, and raised a brow at Penny as she crossed her arms over her chest, blocking access to her nipples. She needed her wits for this because Penny was winding her in knots.

"That's ridiculous!" Penny waved a hand in front of her face. "Could you imagine? *Us*?"

"I'm trying to."

"Oh." All traces of humor vanished and Penny made a serious sound as she rubbed her lips together. "I don't think we'd fit very well." Her brow furrowed and Penny shook her head slowly. "Do you?" She asked, sounding extremely skeptical and sending Agnes's heart crashing to her feet. It was a thoroughly disorienting sensation after years of believing it had gone cold and shriveled.

"We did last night." She hadn't meant to snap, but Agnes didn't enjoy feeling so foolish and naive.

"We did!" Penny agreed, shushing Agnes as she rose on her tiptoes and pecked at her lips. "And we'll fit together again and again, whenever we want until this season passes and we move onto something else."

"Something else?" Agnes looked around suspiciously. There had to be cameras because this couldn't be happening to *her*. "I'm being serious, Penny. What is it about me—about us—that's so...funny?"

"I'm so, so sorry!" Penny grabbed Agnes's hands and shook her head quickly. "You're the loveliest creature I've ever seen and the sex is *phenomenal*."

"But?"

Penny gave another one of her thoughtful hums and her head tipped to the side as she considered. "You're very cynical, Agnes, and you're awfully jaded," she stated simply. She shrugged casually but the words still stung like a slap. "I have done my best to see and touch all the pretty flowers in the garden, but I still believe in magic and I'd like to fall in love one day. Maybe soon..." Her voice trailed off as if Penny had already left Agnes behind.

"You think I don't?" Agnes asked.

Penny began to laugh again and clapped a hand over her mouth. "I'm sorry! It's just that I *never* imagined, Agnes."

"Imagined what?" Agnes demanded.

"That you would even consider it. You're *Agnes Cameron*!" Penny's voice lowered and Agnes sensed a touch of awe, but she had a feeling it wasn't working in her favor.

"So?"

That made Penny snort and she rolled her eyes. "One of

the King of England's cousins proposed and you turned him down! They call you a billion-dollar wrecking ball because you almost started a war within the Saudi Royal family. Everyone knows you take whatever you want and nothing ever touches you. Which is totally cool with me!" Penny reassured her. "You're a legend and you know I'm all about sowing some wild oats!"

"I'm a legend?" Agnes asked flatly, earning an enthusiastic nod from Penny.

"You're like one of the rarest Pokémon in the city! We're all hoping for a chance to catch Agnes Cameron." She grinned cheekily, but Agnes wasn't pleased. And she knew the news was about to get worse when Penny tapped her chin. "You know, you've hooked up with two of my friends."

"Oh, God."

"No!" Penny waved her hands. "Three! You slept with my friend Emily *and* her husband! They were dating at the time, but they just celebrated their first anniversary a few months ago," she said with a delighted cheer.

Agnes blinked back at her, not knowing who Penny was talking about. *Walker was right. I really am an animal.*

"They're the best! They own a gallery in Chelsea," Penny offered helpfully and Agnes's eyes watered because that hadn't narrowed things down at all. "He's really tall, has a lot of tattoos, and a dark, mysterious aura. She's wee with silver hair and the prettiest green eyes. *Lots* of piercings," she added. Bells were beginning to ring for Agnes... Penny took pity on her: "His name is Jed Keller. He owns the Keller Gallery and he's a sculptor. He works mostly with salvaged metal and car parts. Jed and Emily Keller."

"Yes!" Agnes gasped in relief. "I remember them. Lovely couple." She supposed. She did remember the gallery and the piece she purchased. It was a mobile made of working tail lights and rearview mirrors called *Running from the past and just before the crash*. She recalled staying after the opening for a few drinks and that they had been really hot in bed, but Agnes couldn't remember anything specific about *them*.

"See? You're a legend!"

"That's a terrible thing to say," Agnes sniffed, indignant and rather ashamed. But Penny groaned apologetically.

"I didn't mean it in a bad way."

"I'm not sure there's anything good about being a legendary slu—"

"Whoa!" Penny pointed at Agnes sternly. "We do not shame each other for pasts or our predilections as long as we're all consenting adults," she scolded, reminding Agnes of Penny's *only* rule. There were no rules as long as they weren't on June's time. There was never any judgment, just vibes.

The irony was, that used to be Agnes's motto as well.

Somehow, this is Walker's fault.

She narrowed her eyes at Penny since he wasn't there. "Of course, we don't. But it does seem like you're holding my past against me."

Penny's jaw fell. "I promise, I'm not!"

"Then why do you assume I don't want to fall in love? I might have a...reputation," Agnes confessed with a dismissive wave. "But it appears that I also have a heart."

"I know you do!" Penny threw her arms around Agnes's neck and kissed her. "And I don't blame you for guarding it so fiercely. I've seen and felt how people change when you walk into a room. Their entire auras burn with jealousy while they smile in your face and laugh at your jokes. Everyone looks at you like you're the golden ticket and they think you're too selfish and self-absorbed to care."

"I am the last person anyone should feel sorry for," Agnes said. "I've done exactly what I've wanted for over fifty years."

"But have you ever been in love?" Penny asked gently.

Damn it! Agnes squirmed and wondered how she'd backed herself into this particular corner. "I have." She rubbed her ear against her shoulder as she experienced a very different kind of chill—and incredible shame. She felt like a fool, disgusted with herself and repulsed by *him*.

Penny's arms tightened around Agnes protectively. "Oh, Agnes. What happened?"

"Pretty much what you'd expect. I fell madly in love and was engaged to the perfect man."

"Did he die?" Penny whispered, and Agnes nodded solemnly.

"Yes. I murdered him after he got one of the maids pregnant."

"Fair enough!"

They laughed and Agnes sighed wistfully. "He's somewhere in Florida, the last I heard." She shuddered again at the thought. "I got over it a long time ago and it's just embarrassing now. I should have known better when I caught him with his hand up the wedding planner's skirt."

"I don't think it's embarrassing at all," Penny argued, her frown deepening as she backed Agnes onto the bed. "I think it's terribly sad, and I understand why you've kept all those barriers up."

"I don't have any barriers with you," Agnes pointed out.

Penny nodded and pecked at her lips. "We're different because we're both sharing everything with June and for June. It would be selfish of me to take advantage of all this beautiful communication and sharing just so I could shoot my shot with you."

"You'd never do anything like that, but what if I wanted you to?" Agnes challenged. She captured Penny's face and kissed her deeply. "What if I want to fall in love with you?"

Agnes released Penny's lips and waited for her eyes to open, searching for any hint of her intentions.

They were soft and clear as they held Agnes's. "I fall in love with you every day, Agnes, and a little more every time we touch."

She didn't offer any other clues, though. No sign that this was a permanent condition or something she'd shake off eventually. Instead, Penny pushed Agnes's tank top up and eased aside her shorts and the gusset of her thong. Her lips tugged at Agnes's nipple as her fingers plunged and twisted, conjuring sweet heat and muddling Agnes's thoughts.

Penny also stirred a different kind of longing, and Agnes's spoiled Cameron soul stomped its foot. She wanted *all* of Penny and she didn't want to share or have to let her go. *Ever.* A season wouldn't be enough.

It didn't make sense, how Penny could think it would be. But yet again Agnes unraveled beneath Penny's lips and her fingers, too lost in the vibrant pleasure and joy of the moment. She had hoped that at some point she'd get a handle on whatever was happening between her and Penny. That minuscule kernel of common sense that Agnes possessed warned that much like June, matters between herself and Penny were swiftly shifting and swirling around her.

Chapter Fifteen

hat if I want to fall in love with you?

If anyone had asked Penny that question a week or a month ago, she would have said they were confused or joking. But there she was, hook firmly pinched between her fingers and her hands wound together in fishing line, contemplating the impossible with Agnes.

Penny was helping June wad up a piece of cheap sliced bread and load it onto a hook for bait. Agnes was looking on from the middle seat of the boat, bemused and dubious. They'd set out bright and early for a morning on the lake and the trio had successfully marched down the hill to the dock without any mishaps.

She often joined them and reclined like a siren while Penny taught June the basics. Their first morning on the water had been a pleasant surprise. Instead of turning her nose up at the simple aluminum fishing boat, Agnes quickly stepped down onto the bench and reminded Penny and June that she'd grown up on the water. Agnes had babbled about owning boats of all sorts, rowing on crews, sailing in regattas, and her two-summer stint as a country club lifeguard. Apparently, Agnes was half-fish and happiest when she was around water.

Today, Agnes looked happy, and June was clipped into her life vest and absorbed by their lesson, leaving Penny's mind free to ponder the puzzle she had created. It was a bit like the cat's cradle that had twisted around her and June's fingers while they baited their hooks.

Penny was using Penn's pole because she'd loaned hers to June. But secretly, Penny missed her lucky fishing pole and felt a tug of guilt because she wished she was alone on the lake this morning. The time spent meditating on her mother's memory and Gus might have brought Penny some much-needed clarity.

Penny had crept onto the porch at sunrise with her yoga mat and had even meditated after several poses. She'd also tried her most reliable five-card tarot spread for clarity before breakfast—pulling most notably the Five of Wands. It was very apropos because she *was* experiencing much conflict and transformation and feeling some tension, like she was being pulled in opposite directions. The Five of Wands also said it was time to gather up her feelings and doubts and be more open-minded about the possibilities. Chunks of clear quartz and amethyst were tucked in each half of her swimsuit's top for extra clarifying oomph, but Penny still felt muddled and tangled.

Mostly because she *wanted* Agnes to fall in love with her. Penny was beginning to accept that she was in serious denial and already thoroughly and completely in love with Agnes. She had meant to soothe and placate Agnes when she said she fell in love with her a little more each day. But it was true, and

Penny didn't understand how it was possible because Agnes was the last person Penny *should* have fallen in love with.

That *should* was the reason Penny thought they were safe. A few fast bangs at a wedding *should* have been safe because Agnes and Penny would never move in the same circles. Penny *should* have been safely off Agnes's radar, the last person she'd ever *want* to date because 1. Agnes did not date, and 2. Penny was entirely unsuitable for many obvious reasons. And vice versa! Agnes *should* have been the last woman Penny would want as well. If Penny had seen Agnes on a dating app, she would have swiped and laughed at how very wrong Agnes was for her.

Penny stole a glance at Agnes and snorted inwardly. She didn't understand how they were still getting along, let alone so wildly attracted to each other. Instead of growing bored and losing interest, they were fusing and becoming one. They were reading each other's thoughts, and Penny felt better and more like herself the closer she got to Agnes. Their connection wasn't just intellectual and emotional, either. Their hands brushed and linked without their bidding and they made each other laugh and blush with just a glance. Penny's body hummed with anticipation and she could *feel* it when she and Agnes found the same frequency.

There was a very good chance June had noticed and was playing matchmaker as well. She was always the first to grab a seat at the table, on the loveseat, or in the boat so Agnes and Penny had to sit next to each other and as close as possible. June found any excuse to leave them alone and lingered longer with Silas and Mabel. She had even informed Agnes that there was a fancy restaurant over in Marbleville, and that Silas and Mabel could babysit if she wanted to try it with Penny.

Of course, Penny had laughed the suggestion off, saying that she was too punk for a place like that and they'd probably throw her out. But Penny was a great big fraud because secretly, she wished she could dress up in something pretty for Agnes again and wine and dine her like an adult.

What could be more absurd than that, though? Penny had unhappily put on dresses for Fin's and Penn's weddings because she was over the moon, she was so excited for them. And Penn had made those dresses from thrift shop finds—just for Penny. She had always been proud to model her brother's brilliant creations, whether it was a pair of overalls or an exquisite flapper dress. But even when she was wearing her dream dress, Penny felt like a fish out of water.

Agnes swam in a very different sea than Penny did when they were back in Manhattan. It wouldn't take long for it to become obvious once they left the cabin and Cherrytown. Their differences would be all that people would see or care about. They didn't know that Agnes was actually warm and full of wonderful surprises, nothing like the spoiled, rampaging playgirl she was reputed to be.

And everyone would think that Penny was a sell-out, that her punk, witchy, vegan lifestyle was all an act. They'd think that she'd tossed aside all of her principles and seduced her über-wealthy boss because she'd found her meal ticket. Penny didn't even want to think about all the icky gossip that would spread about Agnes because of their age difference.

Penny winced just as a dragonfly buzzed around Agnes's oversized hat. It landed on the brim and she jumped. "Shoo!" Agnes ordered and waved, but it dodged her hand and settled on the other side. "No!" Agnes batted it away, then spluttered when it dove at her nose. "For the love of..."

Penny had to give Agnes credit for keeping her cool because the dragonfly was not taking rejection easily. It zipped around her head, hopping on her shoulder before beating against her ear. Agnes cursed while she swatted, then yelped when it got caught in the hair at the base of her neck under the brim.

"Easy!" Penny warned when Agnes popped up and whipped off her hat.

Agnes growled and waved wildly. "Go awaaaay! *Ohhh!*" She cried, just before she tipped backward and over the side of the boat, plunging into the lake with a loud *Splash!*

"Mom!" June yelled and scrambled to the other side, dragging Penny and their poles with her.

Penny let go of the hook and shook her hands frantically, trying to extricate them. "Aggie!" She watched the water for Agnes or a burst of bubbles, but she was gone. The water was dark and murky and quickly settling.

"Mom?"

"Agnes?" Penny called, her voice rising in concern. She'd gotten her hands free and was searching the water, about to dive in.

"Boo!" Agnes said from behind them. Penny and June spun around as water splashed over the other side of the boat, hitting their faces.

"Mom!" June laughed, but Penny had reared back and yelled as she went over the side and crashed into the lake. Penny knew it would be ice cold, and it sucked the breath right out of her. She flailed and bit back a string of curses as she doggie paddled.

"I've got you!" Agnes said before taking a deep breath and ducking beneath the surface. She swam around the front of the boat before disappearing again. Penny felt Agnes's hands gliding up her legs and around her body. Her head broke the water, just behind Penny, before she was pulled against Agnes's body. "Just relax," she murmured, gentling Penny as if she hadn't learned to swim in that very lake.

Agnes's arm looped around Penny and her hand spread

across her abdomen, protectively and possessively. Penny shivered but it wasn't due to the icy lake. She bit down on her lip to hold back a tortured whimper as Agnes's long, strong thighs rubbed and slid around hers. It was a good thing Agnes was competently pumping with her other arm and pulling them toward the boat. Penny's brain had turned to horny goo and all she could do was hang on and pray she didn't cause the lake to start boiling, because she had to be radiating that much heat from her loins.

Which was ridiculous because Penny didn't think that loins existed outside of a romance novel or a supermarket. But there she was, *burning* for Agnes's touch and ready to beg for relief. She would have done a lot more than beg if they had been alone when Agnes held onto the side of the boat and wedged a knee between Penny's thighs. Agnes easily boosted Penny up and out of the water so she could pull herself into the boat.

"That was so awesome!" June proclaimed while Penny went to the other side and leaned, keeping the boat balanced as Agnes pulled herself over the side.

"I can't tell you how many times my brother's thrown me overboard," Agnes murmured as she wrung out her hair. "Or how many times I've pantsed him or snapped his Speedo... It's a wonder he never drowned me." She shrugged dismissively and reached over the side of the boat when she spotted her hat floating nearby.

She wasn't the least bit bothered after her spill into the lake and was relaxed as she reclined along the middle bench on her elbows. Agnes let her legs dangle off the side of the boat and shut her eyes, basking in the sun. *Nothing*—not even Megan Fox, sweaty and holding up the hood of a Camaro—would ever come close to Agnes Cameron on Cherry Lake in Penny's mind. Nothing could be hotter, and Penny's mouth watered as she imagined licking every inch of those legs, starting at the arch of Agnes's foot.

"Sorry about the interruption. Go back to your lesson and don't mind me," Agnes said with an imperious wave. "In fact, I might just take a nap," she informed them.

As if.

Penny blamed it on the dragonfly and her own out-of-control hormones, but it was impossible to concentrate and calmly hold her fishing pole while Agnes lounged just a few feet away like a temptress. She used her towel as a pillow, letting her arm stretch along the side of the boat and her fingers trail in the water, claiming the lake along with Penny's heart.

Oh, how she wanted Agnes. And Penny was beginning to suspect that she wanted more than an afternoon or a few lust-filled summer months. In fact, Penny wanted to keep the three of them there at the cabin forever, away from all the gossip and the consequences. She couldn't do that, though. Penny would have to give them back and reality would pull them apart when they returned to the city.

Because it would be a very big deal, and people would have a lot to say about a woman like Agnes Cameron taking up with her feral nanny. It wouldn't matter that Agnes's brother had done something similar just a few years prior. He was a wealthy, well-respected widower. And he was a man. People had rolled their eyes and snickered a little at first, but it eventually blew over and opinions softened because that was the way the world worked for rich and powerful *men*.

Penny wasn't sure if people would be as forgiving with Agnes. She expected them to be crueler, actually. Because while Agnes hadn't gone a lot farther beyond the pale than her male counterparts, the consequences were always worse and the nicknames were always uglier when a woman had the nerve to flout the rules.

But this time, Agnes wouldn't be flouting the rules by being too promiscuous, too avid of a sportswoman, or by partying too hard. She'd be flouting society's expectations of her as a mother, and June would get caught in the middle. People would doubt her commitment to June and lump Agnes in with all the other wealthy, careless parents who had affairs with their employees. That wasn't accurate or fair to Agnes, and Penny didn't want June to hear those things whispered about her mother.

They'd assume terrible things about Penny as well. But in her case, Penny was afraid that those things would be true. Had she abandoned her principles? Had she sold her soul without realizing it? It didn't feel like it. But surely she must have if she could forget how many people had to be exploited for a billionaire to exist or overlook all the tax loopholes that had been created to protect the wealth of people like the Camerons.

The carbon footprint of a person like Agnes had to be astronomical—as much as a small town if Penny had to guess—but somehow, none of that mattered. All Penny saw was Agnes's radiance and her wild, willful spirit. Instead of being her own weird but savvy and wildly independent self, Penny went gaga and forgot who *she* was. She didn't worry about manifesting loving support for her friends and family or saving the planet, she hung on Agnes's every word and tried to guess what she'd do next.

Her life had been so simple before. Penny had lived to take care of her dad, Penn, Dash, and their close network of friends and family. She had a job she adored and a warm, happy home. All that Penny had lacked was a long-term position with a family. Or so she had thought.

She'd waited so long for Reid to find "her family" and for a chance to make a real difference in a child's life. Penny had that now with Agnes and June. But it wasn't enough anymore, and as much as she had tried to maintain a professional barrier between them, Penny knew she had fallen in love with June, too, and was thinking of her as her own.

Now, there was so much more at stake if Penny lost her head and her heart to Agnes. She'd be losing a lot more than an insanely hot girlfriend if things fell apart after they returned to the city and to reality. Penny could lose Agnes and June, her job, her reputation, her identity, and her self-respect.

Penny felt like she was sinking and grimaced at the reel in June's hands. "Hey, would you mind switching poles for a little while?" She whispered to June. "I'm missing my mom and I need all the luck I can get right now."

"Okay." June was intently focused, and her lips twisted adorably as they carefully exchanged poles. "Is something wrong?" She asked once they were settled and watching the surface of the water again.

"Nope!" Penny said, checking over her shoulder to see if Agnes was paying attention. A faint snore fluttered from Agnes's softly curved lips, distracting Penny for a moment while her thumb rubbed absently over the duct tape around the handle. It was almost dawn by the time they had drifted off to sleep this morning so it wasn't any wonder that Agnes would be tired. Penny *should* have been too, but she was always too giddy and flustered around Agnes. And Penny had never been good at naps. "I just have a lot on my mind and I have a feeling I'm worrying about the wrong things. Channeling my mom usually helps and nothing makes me feel like I'm closer to her than this," Penny explained as she cast the rod and let the line go. But her attention settled on the duct-taped grip in her hands instead of the water.

"Hmmm..." June frowned thoughtfully. "You should talk to Agnes. She's really good at being a mom and she makes me feel safe and happy." Her trust and certainty melted Penny's heart and only made Agnes all the more appealing. Which caused

Penny to feel even more conflicted as Agnes's potency as a MILF intensified and collided with her admiration and respect.

But June wasn't wrong. Penny needed to talk to Agnes. She couldn't keep changing the subject or playing confused every time Agnes hinted about her feelings or their intentions. The situation required honesty, and Penny would have to admit that she was scared and confused. She thought about calling Dash or Penn and finally asking for their help, but she knew the signal would be choppy and that they'd tell her to grow up and go for it.

Penny had already texted Dash and vaguely implied that she and Agnes were hooking up again. He'd responded with rows of laughing and celebratory emojis and that was about as helpful as tits on a turtle. She was on her own at the cabin, Penny had decided, and the only way to make heads or tails of the mess they'd made was to talk to Agnes.

That was easier said than done because...sex was just easier. Penny knew how to *show* Agnes how she felt and they made so much more sense together when they were alone and touching. She understood herself better and she knew who Agnes was when reality and the outside world weren't there to distract them.

"I'll talk to Agnes about it later," Penny murmured, mostly to herself, but June nodded in agreement.

"I bet she can help. I bet she'd be a good wife, too," June said, and smiled knowingly up at Penny.

"What do you know?" Penny asked, narrowing her eyes at June suspiciously.

The little girl's smile grew into a wide smirk and Penny braced herself. "You and Mom are in love!" She whispered excitedly. June grabbed onto Penny's wrist, possibly to stop her from jumping into the lake. "I think I saw you two kissing on the porch the other day!"

Penny shook her head. "No." But her voice was gone and she was sweating profusely. "We just..." Her voice cracked and she didn't know what to say. Lying wasn't cool, but she didn't want to put June in an awkward position later or ask her to keep their secret.

"It's okay! I think it's the best thing ever, actually," June said, sounding a touch pleased with herself.

"I know it sounds like fun, me and Agnes dating. But it would be..." She bit her lip pensively and considered. Penny didn't think it was her place to explain certain aspects of Agnes's past—or her own—or how society would view their relationship given their age and socioeconomic differences. "It would be tricky because I work for her and because the rest of the world will want to put their noses in our business and make everything weird and even more complicated."

"You should just marry Mom and skip dating," June stated simply. "Then it will be too late for them to say anything and we can all be happy together."

"Oh, my little June bug." Penny kissed her hair and cherished the moment with June. She'd truly become Penny's little girl, too. "I love you and we'll always be family no matter what happens between me and Agnes. I'll always want to take care of you and keep you safe. Even when you're forty or fifty, okay?" She promised, earning a tearful nod from June before she dropped her pole and hugged Penny around the middle.

"You're the best, Penny!" She said shakily. "I love you too."

"See? We're a family. No matter what happens or what anyone says."

June leaned back, wiping her cheeks and gathering up her pole and line. "But you and Agnes could get married and then we'd be that kind of family too."

"I don't know. Anyway, we have more pressing concerns right now. Let's try to catch two fish today. Silas can fry them up for you and Aggie for dinner tonight," Penny said, changing the subject. The thought made Penny feel like she'd swallowed the sun, but it was all too much. She hadn't even worked up the nerve to admit that they were dating or that she had serious feelings for Agnes.

Chapter Sixteen

What were the rules of courtship in the Catskills? Were they vastly different than the rest of New York and the United States? Not that Agnes had particularly cared about the rules before, but if she were anywhere else and if anyone had asked her, she would say that she and Penny Lane Tucker were definitely an item.

But all signs from Penny indicated that nothing of significance had occurred between them. She behaved as if she was unaware and unaffected as she led them on hikes and hunts. There were no bows or bullets on their expeditions, though. They set out with a bird guide or in search of rocks and flowers. Penny would grab Agnes's ass or put her hands under her shirt the minute June was distracted, then go right back to extolling the wonders of nature as if it had never happened.

Agnes had never enjoyed the outdoors more or found hikes as invigorating. But afterward and when they were alone, Agnes would search Penny's face for hints and listen for clues as to what was in her wayward heart. Her frisky nymph remained evasive, though, scattering Agnes's wits with kisses and illicit touches and leaving her delightfully disoriented after each encounter. She was often left wondering if there was some mountain ritual she had yet to perform or some hillbilly riddle she had yet to solve before Penny's heart was finally hers.

Of course, the physical act of going on a date hadn't occurred for practical reasons: it was not an easy trek down the mountain and there were few places within an hour's drive that were worth the effort. At least, that was the impression Agnes had been given. She heard some whispers about "a fancy place" a few towns over, but Penny had scoffed and insisted it wasn't as nice as folks claimed and that they probably wouldn't let her in.

That had rankled because why would Penny think that Agnes would allow that? And Agnes wouldn't stand for Penny putting herself down and suggesting that she wasn't good enough for any establishment. Agnes would like to think that they *could* go on a date if they had better and more convenient options, but Penny had acted like the whole idea was preposterous.

And it did seem likely that they were dating as far as June, Silas, and Mabel were concerned. Penny could tiptoe around and whisper like it was a secret all she wanted. They were onto her and Agnes, and they all approved from the looks of things.

Which made it all the more confounding to Agnes, the way Penny hemmed and hawed whenever the topic came up. Agnes had mentioned "them" and where they were headed a few more times, but Penny got flustered and flighty or she got horny and quickly changed the subject to sex. So Agnes had to wonder if there was some signal that Penny was waiting for before they were officially a couple.

Not because Agnes wanted to claim Penny as hers—she did —or was afraid that someone else might catch Penny's eye while they were in the Catskills. But because Agnes wanted to openly woo Penny and hold her hand or kiss her cheek when she was being silly.

She was being particularly silly at the moment, and Agnes was getting tired of pretending she wasn't completely smitten with Penny. Unfortunately, there was no getting the upper hand. Penny was the master of confusion, so all Agnes could do was follow and trust her chaotic minx to show her the way.

That's why Agnes now found herself acting as a lookout for Penny while Silas taught June how to clean the fish they'd caught earlier. A wooden plank had been mounted on the trunk of a tree just off the porch and Agnes gagged as he flicked a glob of guts and scales at a pail by his feet to be used as fertilizer later. Thankfully, a waft of cinnamon-scented fumes from the kitchen tickled Agnes's nose and made her mouth water. Mabel was baking a peach and berry cobbler to go with their dinner, much to Agnes's delight.

There was a loud *Psst!* sound from the other side of the porch. Agnes checked to make sure Silas wasn't looking and held up a thumb, signaling that the coast was clear. Penny ruined the effect by giggling as she dashed through the woods to their cabin with a crate of stolen mountain berry wine. She hopped over a root, creating a soft clanking sound, and Agnes rolled her eyes when she heard another giggle. Silas chuckled from the cleaning station and shook his head.

"So much for subterfuge," Agnes said wryly, propping her shoulder against a post. They'd finished their last bottle the night before and Penny had come up with a plan for "the perfect wine heist" while fishing with June. The plan included fried fish and dessert at Silas and Mabel's so Agnes was willing to assist. June was an unwitting accomplice, all too happy to help cook and learn how to clean fish.

It had been fun, whispering and giggling with Penny as they went over their plan, and Agnes was looking forward to celebrating the success of their mission. But Agnes couldn't help wondering if she'd missed something. Penny was still her flirty yet evasive self whenever they were alone. But June would beam at Agnes like she had ridden into the room on a unicorn, only to insist that she was not smiling and that *nothing* was going on. Then Penny would turn as red as a beet.

Which meant that something had to be going on, Agnes reasoned. Both of her girls were acting strange, and there had been knowing grins and some soft teasing from Mabel and Silas. The jokes had started a few days after their arrival on Cherry Mountain and had become more frequent as Silas and Mabel's suspicions were confirmed. But Agnes didn't mind and was warmed by the approval she sensed. Neither Mabel nor Silas were the sort to hold onto their opinions and would have spoken their minds if they didn't like what they saw.

"Why don't you come in here and make yourself useful, Agnes," Mabel called from the kitchen. Agnes pushed away from the post, smiling as she reached for the screen door. It shrieked, making her jump and curse, and Mabel chuckled. "I told you, it won't bite. Check that pot of jam on the stove for me." She pointed from her seat at the kitchen table. She had a bowl of boiled potatoes in front of her and was peeling the skins off with a knife. There was an ancient cast iron stove and a small fireplace with a hearth on the other side of the kitchen, but Penny explained that those were only used in the winter.

Agnes's nose wrinkled as she went to the narrow electric stove and peered into a dented pot. A dark gel bubbled softly and she groaned as she sniffed. "I haven't a clue what I'm looking for, but it smells lovely," she informed Mabel.

"There's a plate in the freezer. Use that," she told Agnes, her thumb hitching at a small enamel refrigerator in the corner. It looked like it was older than Mabel, but Agnes found a frozen saucer on top of the ice trays.

Agnes went to the stove and frowned at the pot, then at Mabel. "Do I just give it a dunk?" She asked, earning a cackle from Mabel as she pulled herself up from her seat at the table.

"It's about time you learned how to make jam, young lady."

"About time? Why would I?" Agnes snorted. "And who are you calling 'young lady'?"

"You know, there was a time when this was a prized skill. You learned how to cook down all your extra berries so they'd keep and you could have something sweet and full of those sunshine vitamins in the winter," Mabel explained while she stirred the pot with a wooden spoon. "It was something special if your neighbor came over with a jar of jam for Christmas because it had been made in the summer when berries were at their sweetest, and put away for the darker months."

"I see," Agnes said, nodding raptly as she watched as Mabel dropped a dollop of jam on the plate.

"Now, run your finger through that and see what it does," Mabel ordered, tapping the edge of the saucer with a bent, wagging finger. Agnes dragged her fingertip through the small puddle and was surprised at how much thicker the liquid had become. It parted into two separate globs, instead of bleeding together, and Agnes moaned as she licked her finger clean.

"It's perfect. It tastes like sunshine and summer."

Mabel grunted in approval as she went back to stirring. "I don't like a full sugar jam because you can't taste the fruit, but blackberries and blueberries have their own pectin so they'll thicken up enough on their own with some slow cooking."

"Berries, sugar, and...?"

"A little lemon juice to brighten them up a bit more and that's it," Mabel said, gesturing for Agnes to take the plate to the sink. "That won't wash itself."

Agnes shrugged and shamelessly licked the plate clean on the way. "And you know it's done when it sticks to a frozen plate?" She asked, earning a hum from Mabel as she returned to her seat at the table.

"How long it takes will depend on how much fruit you use, what type of fruit, and the amount of sugar. You can use equal parts fruit and sugar and it'll thicken up real fast and make you a heap of jam, but it'll taste like candy. You can go the other way and only use a little sugar. You'll just be hovering and stirring longer and that's fine, too."

"Huh. Maybe I'll try making jam at home with June," she mused.

"You should. There's all kinds of good kitchen science that goes into making jams and jellies and we don't pass those skills onto our kids anymore. You can use your smartphone to find exact measurements when you know what kind of fruit you're using. Or, you can call me," she said and nodded at the old rotary phone on the wall.

"Thanks, Mabel. I'll definitely call you." Agnes smiled over her shoulder as she washed the plate, once again touched by Mabel's generosity and acceptance.

"I'd like that. Those city kids of ours stay so busy, they don't get to call as often. You seem like you've got a little more time on your hands so you can keep an eye on Penny and Penn for us and let us know what June and them are up to."

"Yes, ma'am!" Agnes laughed and saluted her. She thought it would be nice to have someone to share their news with. Aside from Walker, Agnes didn't really have anyone she could call if she wanted to brag about June or Penny or laugh about their adventures. Her parents wouldn't care and they didn't answer phones or take calls. Their nurses handled those duties and relayed messages if the need to communicate arose.

"About Penny..." She said a silent prayer as she dried the dish and turned back to Mabel. She was taking a chance and returning the older woman's trust and generosity. "Let's say I wanted to impress her and get her to take me seriously," she said, blushing at the waver in her voice.

So much for playing it cool.

Agnes rolled her eyes. Her hands were shaking, and she felt like a complete fool asking this elderly woman how to impress her grandniece. It was so absurdly old-fashioned—no, just plain absurd, because Agnes had never cared about impressing anyone before in her life. Even though for Agnes, it had always been a given. Everyone was impressed and adored her.

"You're already goin' about it the right way as far as I can tell," Mabel said, as she headed back to her seat and the bowl of potatoes.

"The thing is, Mabel, I'm actually trying. But I've never done anything like this before so I can't tell if it's working," she confided as she took the seat across from Mabel.

"I could tell. And that's what I meant, Agnes. You're *trying.* We could tell as soon as we laid eyes on you that none of this was your cup of tea." Mabel snickered as she leaned in toward Agnes. "You were scared shitless, actually, but you didn't let that stop you. You *tried,* and you tried your best, and Penny's noticed. And I honestly don't think you could have done more to impress her."

"Oh." Agnes's head pulled back and she let out a surprised huff. "I wasn't doing that to impress her. I didn't want either of them to think I was a stick in the mud, but I wanted to prove to June that I would do whatever it takes. Even put up with...this," she said as she gestured around them. "But this has all been heavenly so it wasn't really a sacrifice."

Mabel laughed as she reached across the table and patted Agnes's hand. "You have been drinking a lot of Silas's wine. You can admit you wanted to run. It just proves you're the right kind of stubborn because you stayed and you kept on being brave until you turned into one of us."

"Am I one of you now?" Agnes asked and was pleased when Mabel nodded.

"You were baptized when you rolled down the hill and into that poison ivy."

They burst into laughter, and it was several moments before they had recovered. Mabel slid the bowl of potatoes over to Agnes and told her to take over peeling while she made the cornbread and got the pan ready for the fish. "Penny's got a stubborn streak herself and it can take her a while to see the light, especially if she's being willfully obtuse."

"But what's she being obtuse about?"

Mabel planted one hand on the edge of the stove and the other on her hip. She looked weary as she shook her head. "There's no telling with that child, once she gets an idea in her head. You just have to give her time and let her go, even if it means letting her find out the hard way. She's always learned best by scuffing her knees and busting up her palms. But she always figures it out in the end and she always does the right thing."

That felt oddly familiar, and Agnes found it comforting, because like Penny, she'd always gone her own way and learned the most from her mistakes. They were similar in that respect, but Agnes lacked Penny's patience or ability to see where life took her. Agnes was used to acting and taking once she decided on a course and found something she wanted.

"Don't you go pushing her, now," Mabel warned, reading Agnes's thoughts and waving a wooden spoon at her. "If there's one thing that'll get Penny to dig in and hunker down, it's backing her into a corner or putting her on the spot. Just give that girl time and she'll do the right thing."

"Okay. I can do that," Agnes said, then smiled because she *could*. Maybe she *had* become one of them. Agnes shrugged, relaxed as she picked up a potato and the knife, deciding she'd let time and the mountain work their magic on Penny.

As if they'd heard their cue, Silas and June clamored into the cabin with the cleaned fish. Penny arrived a few minutes later and the five of them told jokes and old stories while they prepared dinner. The cabin was cramped and primitive and the food was rustic and simply prepared, but Agnes had a lovely evening and the meal was delicious. She predicted that it would be an evening she'd look back on often and with great fondness. And Agnes was truly grateful as she laughed with June at one of Silas's jokes because this would be just one of many magical evenings she'd bring back with her when they returned to the city.

Aunt Mabel's Mountain Berry Jam

- 4 cups fresh blueberries
- 1 cup white sugar
- 1 tablespoon fresh lemon juice

You might be lucky enough to come across a heap of wild blueberries or huckleberries. If not, blackberries or just about any berry will do! You may need to adjust cooking time because some berries have less pectin and may need longer to thicken.

Mix blueberries, sugar, and lemon juice in a saucepan. Cook, stirring constantly, over medium heat until thickened, about 30 minutes.

Chapter Seventeen

Penny was about to pop, she was so full. Mabel had made a big plate of vegan-friendly hushpuppies before she fried the fish. They were heaven, along with garlicky, herb-flecked potatoes, sautéed green beans, and tomato and cucumber salad. A big bowl of peach and berry cobbler had nearly killed her, and Penny was reeling as she turned and stretched her legs under the table. She hooked her high top around Agnes's ankle and shot her a wink when she blushed.

"Hey, Silas," Penny said, nudging him gently with her elbow. His chin was dipping as he nodded off and he jumped and gave his beard a few tugs.

"What's that?" He asked as they all laughed.

"You didn't happen to see that old croquet set when you found that box of art supplies, did you?"

"Nah," he said as he shook his head and snorted. "I imagine half of the balls are in the lake. Don't know what Penn was thinking, bringing it out here."

"Anyone can play croquet on a flat lawn," Penny said and

rolled her eyes. "Make it an uphill battle with booby traps and then you've got yourself a real game!"

"I want to play!" June declared.

"I do not, but I do want to watch," Agnes chimed in, making the cabin erupt in more laughter.

Mabel gave one of Silas's sleeves a firm tug. "Why don't you fetch that box of photos you found while you were looking for the easel," she told Silas, then turned to Penny as he got up to retrieve it. "I bet you haven't seen some of these since you were an itty bitty thing."

"I'd wondered where they all went," Silas said as he got up and returned a few minutes later with an old hat box. "Lots of old pics of your mama in here," he told Penny as he set it on the table and gave the lid a thump.

Penny cheered as she opened it and felt a flutter as soon as she spotted all the sepia tones and old Polaroids. "I remember this!" She said, pulling out a picture of Penn pushing her in a wheelbarrow. "I must have been...four or five," she told June. "Look at him! Fifteen and already a string bean." She tapped on the photo and giggled at Penn's gangly legs and the size of his feet and hands.

There was an amused snort from Agnes as she peeked over June's shoulder. "And look at who never grew out of her pigtails."

Mabel hummed in agreement and picked up a larger photo. "Here's Laurel's first car." She handed it to Penny and she gasped in shock.

"Mom had a Beemer?" Her face twisted in disapproval but Mabel clicked her teeth at Penny.

"She saved up for two years to buy something decent and then she won that photo contest. She used the prize money to buy the car and spent her savings on a new camera."

"Huh. I can't believe she'd go for something that flashy," Penny murmured, passing the photo to June and Agnes.

"Your mama wasn't opposed to a little flashy now and then," Mabel said as she flipped through photos, then snorted. "Check this out!"

"Oh! Pretty!" June declared when Mabel held up a photo of Laurel in a shimmery teal gown. It had a plunging neckline and was slit all the way up the side to her hip.

"What?" Penny's eyes bulged as she stared at a complete stranger. Her mother's hair was *huge* and she was wearing stilettos. "Who is that?"

"She sure could clean up when she had somewhere to go," Silas said. Penny was appalled as she turned in her seat to face him.

"You take it back! Mom didn't need all of that to look beautiful."

"Settle down, turnip," he chuckled. "Laurel could look good in a paper sack, but sometimes she'd get fancy for a date or for work."

Penny knew that her mother had studied photography in school and had worked for a newspaper for a few years after college. "You think you know someone..." She mused and shrugged it off. "This is more like it!" She declared when she came across a picture of her parents. They were on the porch swing and laughing. Penn was still an infant and was sitting on their father's lap.

"I think Penn was only two there," Mabel said. But Penny noticed that she'd flipped through several pictures quickly.

"What are those?" Penny asked, standing up so she could reach for them.

"They're nothing, dear," Mabel replied. She attempted to slide them to the side, but Penny snorted.

"Hand them over."

"I'm not sure..." Mabel said, but Silas groaned in warning at her.

"Let her look, Mom."

Mabel made a concerned sound and her hand hovered over the pile. "She won't appreciate these if the sight of Laurel in a dress upset her."

"I'll be fine," Penny scolded, and gestured for Mabel to hand the photos over. But Penny's stomach crashed through her ass as she stared at the first picture. "What...?"

Her mother was in a frilly white dress, kissing a handsome young man in a tuxedo. They were standing next to a six-tiered cake and Penny recognized her Aunt Jean in the background. Penny refused to believe it. But when she flipped to the next picture the room began to spin around her. Laurel was sunbathing on a yacht and wearing a skimpy black bikini while the young man from the wedding photo reclined next to her with a glass of champagne.

Penny slapped the photo onto the table, face down, hoping to make it disappear, but the next picture was just as bad. Her mother and the other man had gone skiing, apparently, and had stopped to kiss in front of a chalet.

"Who the hell is that and *what is going on?*" Penny demanded, looking to Silas and Mabel for an explanation.

"Well..." Mabel stalled and threw a nervous glance at Silas. "That's Patrick Monahan, dear. I'm sure you knew that he and your mama—"

"I did not!" Penny said, shaking her head.

Mabel sighed as she reached for Penny's hand. "Laurel didn't like to talk about him and the baby and I can't imagine your daddy or Penn would have said much either."

Penny felt dizzy and nauseous and held onto the table for support. "The baby?" Her voice cracked and Mabel's eyes glittered as she nodded.

"They were on their way back from the Hamptons. They'd spent the weekend with his family and we're not sure what happened, but Patrick crashed the car. He died and Laurel lost the baby."

"Mom was married and was going to have a baby?" Penny said woodenly. She frowned at the picture of them on the yacht. She felt like she was miles away and seeing everything through a telescope while her ears popped and voices grew muffled around her. Penny had never fainted before and wondered if she was about to. "Why do I know him?"

"Patrick?" Mabel asked. "His father and his grandfather were senators. The whole family's been in politics for ages."

"Oh my God." Penny dragged her gaze to Agnes, who looked just as surprised.

She held up a hand. "We've known the Monahans for years, but I didn't know Patrick very well. I was probably off with Walker and Connor when he was seeing your mother."

The thought of Laurel living *like that* with a man other than her father hit Penny like a bucket of cold water and immediately set her teeth on edge. She shook her head as she pushed away from the table. "I need some air."

They let her go. Penny was glad it was raining when she slipped out the front door and went to the end of the porch. The raindrops on the lake made it look like it was coming up to a boil, which matched her mood as the shock wore off. She braced her hands on the rail and forced out a slow breath, attempting to center herself.

The door opened and Agnes peeked around it. "Alright if I join you?"

Even though Penny wanted to be alone, being alone with Agnes seemed like it might be a little easier. She nodded and went back to watching the lake simmer. "Ever find out your life is a lie?"

"I spent the first thirty years of my life hoping it was," Agnes said. She leaned back against the rail so she could see Penny's face and offered her a wry smirk. "When I was little, I'd imagine my real family finding us and the police taking my parents away in handcuffs because they had stolen me and Walker."

"I know, it's silly because I had the best parents in the world," Penny admitted. "But I thought I *knew* who my mom was and I've spent my whole life trying to be just like her."

Agnes made a thoughtful sound. "Which version of her? You're not the same person you were when you were twenty-four or twenty-five, are you? That wasn't even all that long ago, but you've changed. Your mother would have lived a few lives by the time you came along and they all made her the person you remember."

"But she was—" Penny waved wildly. "Nothing like that! My mom couldn't stand rich people and she hated yachts. She thought cars were a waste of money and killing the planet."

"Want to know what I was like in my twenties before I grew up?" Agnes offered. "I have a feeling that her time with the Monahans is why she couldn't stand rich people and hated yachts. I'm sure Patrick was a prince. The Monahan men can be very charming. But the family—as a whole—is an entirely different matter and they've never been kind to outsiders."

"Of course, not." Everyone knew about the Monahans. They were almost as famous and as influential as the Kennedys. "I can't believe Mom would even be involved with them," Penny said and Agnes sighed.

"She was probably in love, and Patrick couldn't help who he was, could he? Sometimes, you have to make sacrifices for the sake of love," she said as she held up her hands. "It sounds like Laurel was willing to settle for yachts and weekends in the Hamptons."

"I guess. But it's so..." Penny rolled her eyes and had to blink back bitter tears. "Typical, right? I thought she went to a fancy college because she wanted to do something big and save the world. But she went so she could meet a rich guy from a 'good' family and live in the Hamptons."

Agnes cleared her throat scoldingly and crossed her arms over her chest. "That's very harsh, Penny. And not fair at all. Rich people can be decent and some of us even have feelings. From everything I've heard, Laurel was a brilliant and generous person. Loving Patrick didn't change that and there's an outside chance that he was worthy of her love."

"I know," Penny said, and gave Agnes's arm a squeeze. "And I'm sorry. Some of the loveliest people I know are rich," she whispered, checking the window and the door before she stole a quick kiss. "I'm definitely upset and jealous because he wasn't my dad. And it's hard, finding out my mom was kind of a fraud."

"I think you're still being harsh."

"How can you say that?" Penny asked. "I can understand *how* and why she'd fall in love with someone like Patrick. Mom and Dad were total opposites too. But the Monahans and that whole lifestyle were the antithesis of *everything* Mom stood for. They're everything she told me not to be. She warned me about trusting the government and rich people, but she was one of them for a little while."

It was Agnes's turn to roll her eyes. "I'm not so sure that this is about her."

Penny leaned back and gasped incredulously. "What does that mean?"

"You think you'll have to come off that pedestal if she does," Agnes said, making Penny gasp even louder.

"How can you say that?" Penny knew good and well, though.

Agnes laughed and shook her head at Penny. "You said I was too cynical and jaded—*too rich*—but you still believe in magic and you want to fall in love."

"I never meant—" Penny started, then stopped before she told an obvious lie.

Agnes raised her brows and pointed hard because Penny might as well have said it. "Laurel was better than all the Monahans put together because she saw past the yachts and the weekends in the Hamptons. She loved Patrick *despite* his flaws and his rich family because *that's* the sort of person your mother was, from all I've heard." Agnes closed the lesson with a firm nod before leaving Penny. "I'll get June. It's almost her bedtime."

"I can be a real jerk," Penny noted.

Penny toed off her sneakers, leaving them by the door so they wouldn't get soaked. Then she headed downhill, enjoying the cool squishiness of the wet grass and soggy earth beneath her feet and between her toes. She sat at the end of the dock, letting her legs dangle and her feet skim the water. It wasn't long before rain dripped from the end of her pigtails and the tip of her nose.

Penny cried, her tears mingling with the rain and leaving her drenched in remorse and confusion. Was she projecting her own insecurities and misgivings about Agnes onto her mother? She couldn't deny that she felt like a hypocrite whenever she imagined what a relationship with Agnes would look like.

That wasn't fair to Agnes because she was so much more than her money and her family's influence. Like Agnes, Patrick had to have been a wonderful person if her mother had loved him. Penny cried even harder as she imagined how much his loss must have hurt Laurel. And Penny's heart broke as she considered the aftermath and trauma from the wreck itself and losing a baby.

Her mother had *several* scars, and had told Penny they were from running amuck in the woods and getting into trouble all over the city. But now, in hindsight, Penny knew some of them had been more than basic cuts and scrapes. Penny had been a tomboy her whole life so she knew the difference, and Laurel had needed a lot of stitches on her abdomen and legs.

But Penny had never asked about them after her mother died. And she had put Laurel up on a pedestal. What else could Penny do? She had been there during the best years of Laurel's life. And all anyone had ever shared was their favorite memories. Why hadn't they told Penny about Laurel's first marriage or the accident?

She had a feeling she wouldn't understand or feel better until she talked to Penn. But it wasn't the kind of conversation she wanted to have on a noisy, glitchy phone call at the end of the dock so it would have to wait until they returned to the city.

The lights were off when Penny climbed back up the hill and snuck into the cabin. June was already in bed and Agnes was in bed with a book and a jar of Silas's wine. Penny took a quick shower and pulled on an oversized T-shirt.

"I'm sorry, Aggie. I have no right looking down on you or Patrick," Penny said as she set her knee on the bed and crawled to Agnes.

"That was a lot to learn and you were in shock," Agnes said, and raised the quilt so Penny could snuggle up against her side. But Agnes's eyes stayed on her page and she was distant.

"And I'm sorry about how childish I've been about us," Penny added, gently sliding the book from Agnes's hands and setting it on the table. That got a raised brow from Agnes.

"We've achieved 'us' status, have we?"

"Stop it. *We've* been on my mind since Reid sent me to The Killian House to take care of you and June," Penny admitted quietly. She was still scared of what *us* meant and what it said about her own principles. But Penny knew she owed Agnes a lot more than an apology and hoped that maybe they might find a little clarity together if she finally owned up to her side of things. "At first, I didn't think you'd ever take this seriously and I told myself that we were more of a cozy friends-with-benefits situation. I thought we were safe from developing feelings for each other because why would you be into me? I'm not polished or powerful enough to impress you and you *should be* the last person I'd ever date."

"'Should be?'" Agnes's eyes narrowed, making Penny laugh. She kissed Agnes and rubbed their noses together.

"It's absolutely unethical how much money your family has and your carbon footprint is a nightmare. You're an unrepentant snob with too many homes and too many cars. You have an asinine amount of shoes and I can't even begin to fathom the number of atrocities in your jewelry box and fur collection. I feel a little like a sellout because none of that matters to me when we're together."

"I don't know why it should. I wasn't planning to share any of it with you," Agnes murmured dryly, but her lips spread into a wide grin as they pecked at Penny's. "That's why I know this is real and that I can trust you. I'll be the first to admit that I'm a monster and—"

"You are not," Penny stated, sliding over Agnes and straddling her.

"Fine. I'm difficult," Agnes amended, and waited for Penny's approval before continuing. "Most people tolerate me because of who I am and how much I'm worth, but you want me despite loathing almost everything about me."

"I do not! I could list ten things I love about you that have nothing to do with your body or how much I want you."

Agnes grunted dubiously while her hand glided up Penny's thigh and under the hem of her T-shirt. "I'm almost tempted to make you do it, but that could take hours and I have a better idea."

"Nope." Penny grabbed Agnes's wrist and held onto it so they could focus. "One: You are a brilliant artist and it breaks my heart that you can't see how good you are. Two: The way you love June makes me *weak*. Three: Don't get me started with how much you adore your brother and the triplets." She had to stop and fan herself. "This list wasn't supposed to be sexy, yet here we are. Four: You know exactly who you are and you never dim your shine or dilute your potency to please other people. You are always *the* Agnes Cameron and nothing gets in your way. Five: You aren't just smart, you're cunning. I've never met anyone whose brain works like yours. You would make an amazing detective."

"Probably because I've always had to stay one step ahead of Walker. And I had a lot of time on my hands as a child. All we had were books to entertain us, back before television got interesting and Al Gore invented the internet."

"Six: Unlike *many* of the rich people I've worked for, you are aware of how privileged you are and you genuinely appreciate the people who tend to your needs and help you care for June," Penny continued, but Agnes shushed and tried to kiss her.

"I think that's enough for now."

"I don't," Penny replied and pulled away from the kiss. "I should have picked a much higher number. I could go on all night. Seven: You are *funny*. You might be one of the funniest people I've ever met and I love how easy it is to make you laugh. Eight: You are fearless and you are always up for shenanigans. Sometimes, you pretend to be snooty and uptight, but you're so much fun. Nine: You're incredibly generous and you look out for everyone around you. I thought you'd be more selfish. Instead, you're compassionate and you sincerely care about making a positive impact in real, useful ways. And Ten..." Penny tapped her chin. "If I had to pick just one more thing, it would be..." She smiled and sighed dreamily. "You believe in me and you trusted me with the most important thing in your entire world. Like, right away. You never doubted my competency or my judgment. I've never felt like I had to prove myself and you've never treated me like a child because of my age. Everyone else still treats me like their little sister and like I need someone to look out for me."

"Ridiculous. You're one of the wisest people I know," Agnes said, brushing the hair away from Penny's face. "And there's nothing you can't do. By the way, I inherited all the furs and most of the jewelry, if it makes it any better. I never wear fur and I'll never sell any of it, but I take good care of the pieces that were left to me because...they're already there and it would be an even bigger crime not to. And I only make and buy sustainable jewelry."

"See? Not a monster," Penny said as she swung forward and captured Agnes's lips for a slow, clinging kiss. "But, sometimes, I am," she whispered. "I worry that I'm not enough like my mom and that I'm letting her down. And I was afraid that I was changing and losing the pieces of me that made me just like her."

Agnes sighed heavily, but her fingers were light as they swirled around Penny's ribs, tickling and leaving goosebumps in their wake. The pad of her thumb grazed Penny's nipple, making it pucker and causing her to shiver. "Having been a mother for almost a month, I can safely say that all your mother would want is for you to be happy, Penny."

Penny purred and guided Agnes's other hand to her breast. "I know, and I think she'd love you," she panted. She reached between them and teased Agnes through the whisper-thin panel of her silk panties, getting her good and wet.

"She would probably be...concerned about my age, but I'd bring her around and she'd love me because I take good care of you and I think you're utterly perfect."

"You're perfect," Penny countered, then bit and sucked on Agnes's chin. "Want me to show you ten things about your body that drive me wild?" She said silkily, tilting her head and dragging her tongue up Agnes's neck. "This is so long and so elegant. You're so graceful, like a goddess."

"Please," Agnes said, attempting an eye roll. But her jaw fell and she stifled a moan when Penny swooped lower and caught a nipple between her teeth. She flicked at it with her tongue, making Agnes buck and whimper.

Penny groaned as she sucked. "The way you walk... I'd have sex with *that* if I could."

"Penny!" Agnes pouted. She wiggled and shifted her hips, spreading her thighs and allowing Penny more access. Penny hummed in approval as her thumb kneaded Agnes's clit through her panties.

"Gosh, I love how wet you get," Penny breathed, then blew on Agnes's nipple, making it pucker tighter.

"Only for you! You're the only one who makes me feel like I'll fall apart if you don't touch me." Agnes bit back a curse as Penny tugged with the tips of her teeth.

"Your tits are heavenly," she whispered. Her lips spread around the tip and Penny ached at Agnes's throaty swear as she sucked.

"Please!" Agnes clutched at the quilt, radiating impatience and frustration. Penny could practically taste it as she lapped at the underside of Agnes's breast and slowly slid lower. Agnes's need was heady, and Penny had never had that kind of power over anyone before. And she knew that Agnes had never tolerated that kind of impertinence from her other lovers.

"Like this?" Penny asked as her hand pushed down the

front of Agnes's panties and reached low to cup her. There was a slick burst against Penny's palm as Agnes nodded frantically. She stroked and slid two fingers into Agnes's core.

"That's it!"

"I promise, it's not."

Penny stripped away Agnes's panties and her T-shirt and sank into the lush sweetness between her thighs. She gorged herself, suckling and fucking Agnes with her tongue and fingers until they were both delirious. Agnes's hands and lips found their way to Penny's pussy as well. She was breathless and giggling after her fourth orgasm when she crashed into the pillows next to Agnes.

Their fingers tangled and Agnes's chest heaved as she pulled Penny's hand to her lips. "Please say you're mine."

"Is there any doubting it after that?" Penny's chuckle was an exhausted wheeze as she rolled toward Agnes and kissed her shoulder. "I've never felt like this before and I don't want it to stop. Ever."

A relieved breath whooshed from Agnes as she rolled toward Penny for a drowsy, heavy-limbed kiss. "So... Are we...?" She asked and a hard snorting giggle burst from Penny.

"You're asking a lot after the day I've had, lady. I have no idea what we are, but it feels really good and I don't want to mess it up."

"Neither do I," Agnes agreed softly, holding onto Penny's hand as they scooted closer until their noses and foreheads touched. "I know it sounds banal, but I really like *you* and who I am when we're together. I feel all the other romantic bells and whistles—some of them I've felt before—but I've never *liked* anyone as much as I like you. And for the first time in my life, I feel good about myself, where I'm at, and what I'm doing when I'm with you. I think..." Agnes paused and wrinkled her nose suspiciously. "I think that this is what it feels like when you're falling in love."

"I think so!" Penny agreed shakily as she kissed Agnes. "It's new for me too, but I'm excited to see where this takes us."

They kissed and shared groggy, yawning confessions until Penny fell asleep with the biggest, goofiest grin on her face.

Chapter Eighteen

Agnes was sad when Penny announced that they only had a week left. Their days at the cabin were officially numbered. Penny had created two lists: one to keep track of all the fun things they had to do and see before they left, and one a combination checklist and timeline of what needed to be collected and packed before they made the trip back.

There was much to do to get the cabin ready to be closed up until the next visit. And there were plants and flowers to be pressed, critters to photograph, and recipes to be transcribed. June was determined to master the lasso and catch and clean a trout all by herself before they left.

She was currently by the lake with Silas while Penny reorganized the jars in the pantry, pulling the ones that needed to be eaten soon to be packed and loaded into the Range Rover. Agnes missed her brother terribly, and she was desperate to hold the triplets again. But she was tempted to throw the Range Rover's keys into the lake every time they talked about loading something else into it.

Unlike when they first arrived, Agnes was tuned into June's and Penny's frequencies now and could feel their ambivalence as they made plans for the rest of their stay. They were no longer magical mysteries, and Agnes was afraid she'd lose those precious connections when they left the mountain and Cherry Lake and returned to Manhattan.

What if Agnes went back to being impatient and pampered and June and Penny no longer liked her? She wanted to be as open and flexible as she had been on the mountain, but Agnes wondered how much of her entitlement and unawareness was a product of her upbringing, her environment, and the people around her. There wasn't much Agnes could do about that unless she changed her name and started over from scratch. She wasn't going to do that, but she would ask Penny and Dr. Altovar to tell her when she was slipping back into old, unbearable habits.

Agnes didn't sense any hesitation or concern from June when they discussed their return to the city, the triplets, or visiting The Killian House again. In fact, June chattered almost nonstop about everything she wanted to show and tell them. Her focus had pivoted and June wanted to bring as much of the mountain back to Manhattan with her to share with the rest of the Camerons.

But Agnes also felt June's sadness when she said goodnight to Silas and Mabel at the end of the day. Now, she lingered because she knew they'd have to leave soon and she'd miss them. Agnes shared June's sadness and would miss them too, but she had yet another reason to be grateful to Penny for bringing them to the cabin. June's new family had grown even bigger and she'd gained a great-aunt and granduncle who absolutely adored her.

Penny's moods were heavier and the frequency got choppier when they were alone and the subject of the trip home was broached. It was still impossible to define what was going on between them and what Penny's feelings were, but Agnes could tell that Penny was casting about and clueless as well. She wasn't being vague and flighty because she was avoiding the topic. Penny just didn't know. Agnes could certainly relate and it was easier now that they were fumbling along together.

There was an itch or an inkling, now and then, and Agnes sensed that Penny was getting anxious about their return. She wondered if Penny had the same concerns about Agnes sliding back into her old self and the walls that would create between them. Instead of promising she wouldn't change, Agnes silently vowed that she would prove how serious and important this—Penny—was by continuing to grow and adapt after they returned.

She'd done it on the mountain when she was terrified of ticks and covered in a burning rash. So why couldn't Agnes learn to cope on her home turf in Manhattan? If anything, emotional clarity and maturity should be easier to acquire once she was back in the bosom of civilization.

Suddenly, Agnes was intrigued by the idea of wooing Penny in the city. She would have made a mess of it before, and Agnes wanted to laugh every time she recalled inviting Penny to the Baccarat. Now, Agnes understood how much of a turn-off that would have been for Penny, and what sorts of places would be inside her forest fairy's comfort zone.

Agnes knew the perfect Indian restaurant with the most amazing vegan dishes and she couldn't wait to take Penny to a vegan Soul Food restaurant for "chicken" and waffles. An evening walk in the Shakespeare Garden or the Met Cloisters would dazzle Penny far more than limo rides and champagne. She pictured them shopping for tofu and art supplies, and Agnes looked forward to all the new places Penny could show her.

Who knew monogamous dating could be so exciting?

She had always craved the chase and the thrill of the conquest, losing interest as soon as she had what she wanted. But not with Penny. Every new facet of Penny's personality drew Agnes in deeper and made her want to know more. And it was impossible not to be captivated by Penny's bright vitality and open curiosity. Everyone had their own life and their own story, but Penny *lived* every moment. Her every molecule radiated energy and grew, a wild sprout reaching for the sun's rays, every moment of the day. The only time Penny ever rested was when she was asleep, but even then her eyelids and her lips flickered as if she was exploring and scheming in her dreams.

Pondering date ideas for the city reminded Agnes of something she'd spotted earlier in the morning while hiking with June and Penny. She'd glimpsed it out of the corner of her eye and would have told Penny to pause so they could take a look, but June was in the middle of a story about Anthony and the neighborhood bully. And Agnes thought it might be fun to surprise Penny later...

"Hey. Wanna go for a walk?"

Penny's pigtails tilted and her brow furrowed as she turned from the pantry. "Sure... Why?" She asked suspiciously, sniffing at the air.

"What are you doing?" Agnes laughed as she uncurled her legs and rose from the loveseat.

"We already went on a big walk this morning and we just..." Penny cleared her throat and wiggled her brows suggestively because she had gone down on Agnes as soon as Silas and June were headed down the hill. Agnes had held onto the window, keeping an eye out, while Penny sat on the floor between her legs.

"Just a walk. There's something I want to show you."

"Okay..." Penny was still wary as she set a jar of wild grape jam in the box.

They waved at Silas and June as they set out, heading up the mountain and west like they had earlier in the day. Agnes waited until they were out of sight, then slipped her hand around Penny's and kept them tethered as they walked.

"I'll miss this," Agnes said, and pointed at a large oak up ahead.

"Really?" Penny asked, sounding surprised. "We can come back whenever you want. I mean, June has school in two weeks. But we could come up whenever she's got a long weekend. I'm not sure how much you'd enjoy this place when it's cold and rainy, but foraging in the fall is lots of fun and it's so gorgeous up here when the leaves are changing. And there's winter and all the snow and tapping trees for syrup..." She was rambling again, but Agnes hummed and nodded along, just as excited at the idea of autumn and winter in the Catskills with Penny and June.

"Of course, I'd want to. I love it here. I thought you could tell," Agnes teased as she pulled Penny away from the crude trail and aimed her at the large oak at the top of the rise.

"I thought you might, but I also thought you'd be so glad to be back home that we'd never get you out of the city again."

"Nonsense. I love it up here and Mabel says I'm one of you now."

"Yup," Penny agreed with a knowing smirk.

"What?" Agnes asked as she cut her eyes at Penny.

"Remember how you wandered off up here and almost got lost because there was a beetle in your hair?"

Agnes huffed indignantly. She'd got to swatting and panicking and wasn't watching where Penny was leading them. "I'm not afraid of *anything*. Unless it gets in my hair," she added with a grimace, making Penny giggle.

"I love that about you," Penny said, and halted them so she could pull Agnes down for a kiss.

"I love how you're not afraid of anything, too," Agnes murmured as she nibbled and swept her tongue along Penny's lips. They tasted like wild grape jam. She wanted to stay right there on that mountain, kissing Penny's tart, smirking lips. And Agnes wanted to say I love you, full stop, but neither of them was ready for that. "And I think you're going to love this."

Agnes guided Penny up the rise and around the oak tree, then pointed at the base. Weeds, wild grasses, and flowers had flourished in the shade there, but Penny let out a loud, long gasp at the big, bright yellow and orange ruffle curling over a root and a large branch that had fallen and rotted.

"Oh, Agnes!" Penny's hands clapped against her cheeks and her voice carried through the forest like she was having an unrestrained orgasm. "I've never seen one so…" Her eyes grew wider and she shook her head as she carefully sidestepped around the tree. "It's so…" Penny looked drunk and aroused as her gaze swung to Agnes's. "It's *beautiful!*" Her voice trembled as if Agnes had handed Penny a large diamond. There were tears in her eyes.

"I wasn't even sure if that was what I thought it was." This was when Agnes played it cool and leaned to brace her hand on a tree trunk.

"Not there!" Penny said, and waved frantically before Agnes planted her palm on a poison ivy vine. "But that is definitely chicken of the woods!" She said with a giddy squeal as she danced over on her tiptoes and kissed Agnes hard.

"Good," Agnes replied dazedly while Penny went to get a closer look. She pulled back a cluster of soggy leaves and let out another squeal.

"Black trumpets! Agnes, you found the mother lode! We'll never be able to eat all of these before we leave. I'll have Silas vacuum seal and freeze most of these chicken of the woods for us. We'll dry the black trumpets in the sun and they'll keep for weeks." She was giddy and rambling again and had pulled a pocket knife out of her sneaker. Agnes got out of the way and found a safe tree to lean against while Penny began cutting off sections of mushroom. It wasn't long before the ground was littered with the large, foam-like orange discs and piles of shiny gray curls.

"How are we going to get all of this to the cabin? I would have gone back for a basket if I'd known there was going to be *this much*," Penny said, looking slightly dismayed as she surveyed her fungal haul.

Agnes's lips twisted thoughtfully. Neither had come prepared for more than a short walk. But she had on an extra shirt over her camisole so she began unbuttoning it. "This is pretty big once it's opened up. Could you make some sort of sling out of it?"

"Probably," Penny said weakly. She was staring at Agnes with an odd expression.

"What's wrong?" Agnes looked down at herself. She wasn't standing in anything poisonous—that she was aware of—and there was nothing but a few smudges of dirt on her shorts and legs.

"You look *really* hot, and you're like, really smart, and this is one of the most exciting things that's ever happened up here," Penny explained as she leaned into Agnes and offered her lips in a kiss.

"It was nothing," Agnes murmured, lowering so she could brush her lips along Penny's. "You told me what to look for and I guess I picked up some of your mountain ingenuity."

"Whoa," Penny panted and held onto Agnes as she swayed. "Now I know you're trying to get into my pants."

"I'm *always* trying to get into your pants."

"I love that about you, too."

"You seem to love a lot of things about me," Agnes noted.

"I do," Penny purred softly, and Agnes felt herself smile. "It might be time for another list."

"Stop it. Let's get your mushrooms and go home," Agnes said as she spun Penny back around and gave her a shove to get going.

Penny clapped as she skipped back to her piles and loaded up Agnes's shirt. "I love the sound of that! And just wait until tonight. This deserves something *extra* special." She hummed to herself as she worked. Agnes helped by finding two long sticks and Penny tied a corner of the shirt and a sleeve to each stick, creating a crude hammock for her mushrooms. Agnes helped carry it down and Penny strutted back into camp like she was carrying a stag or a moose. "Look at what Agnes found!" She boasted when June and Silas ran up the hill to greet them.

"What's all of that?" June asked excitedly.

Silas looked and nodded but was only mildly enthusiastic. "Mushrooms, kiddo."

"Oh." Her tone had dropped considerably and her nose wrinkled.

He grunted in agreement. "I don't mind 'em, but I don't get rhapsodic like this nerd does when she finds 'em." He said as he pointed at Penny and she slapped at his hand.

"Do you have any idea how much these go for in the city? Like twenty-five dollars a pound! This is the score of the century and we are eatin' good tonight!" She announced so that Mabel could hear from her cabin. "I'm gonna fry these up like chicken fried steak and I'll make a gravy with the black trumpets."

"Now, that does sound good," Silas conceded.

"Ha!" Penny tipped her chin back. "You're a lot more excited about my mushrooms now, aren't you?"

"I'm excited about a lot of things once they're fried," he said flatly.

Silas had a point but later that night, Penny's fried mushrooms with vegan mushroom gravy were phenomenal. She had dredged five large mushroom steaks in various flours and spices and deep-fried them in a cast iron skillet. She'd soaked and processed cashews over at Mabel's using her blender to create a creamy sauce that was divine with the fried mushrooms, and prepared a side of garlicky mashed potatoes.

"That was almost as good as Mabel's fried chicken. You might even be able to convince me to give up regular fried chicken for that," Agnes said as they finished the meal, earning a disgruntled humph from Mabel.

"You'll never get me to say a fried mushroom is better than fried chicken. This was close, though," the older woman said in a muffled mumble, earning shocked looks from Penny and Silas. "You won't convert me. I don't mind cooking with some almond milk every once in a while for my Penny Lane, but I won't give up fried chicken and I like bacon." Mabel shook her head as she got up to gather their plates but everyone complained until she sat back down. They then made quick work of the dishes.

"I didn't think I liked a lot of vegetables before," June said as she dried a plate. "But now I eat all kinds of stuff since we've been up here."

"Yes, you do!" Penny caught June's nose between her knuckles and gave it a playful shake before kissing her forehead. "So proud of my little June bug."

"Thanks, Penny!" June was glowing as she kissed Penny's cheek. "Can I take my bath now? I wanna draw some pictures of Penny's mushrooms in my journal before story time."

"Okay! I'll help you get it started," Penny said, and they excused themselves while Silas and Agnes finished the dishes.

"Looks like you figured out how to impress her after all," Mabel said to Agnes, making her blush.

"It's amazing what can happen when you *try*," she said warmly. "I was thinking about the possibilities in Manhattan and realized that I didn't have to wait to make her day, that there were lots of beautiful surprises around here once I gave it a little thought."

Silas looked impressed and raised his brows at Mabel. "I think she'll do. We better get out of their hair," he said with a toss of his chin at the door.

"I have a feeling we're about to wear out our welcome," Mabel agreed, easing herself up. They waited until June raced through in her pajamas to say goodnight, then left.

All the lights were turned off and candles glowed from the bathroom when Agnes came down from tucking June in and reading her to sleep. Penny had filled the tub and was waiting in one of Agnes's silk robes with a jar of berry wine. Petals floated on the milky surface and lavender and rose-scented steam wafted from the tub.

"For my lady," Penny said as she let the quilt fall behind them.

Agnes felt like a lady in an ancient woodland realm as she was stripped of her camisole and shorts and helped into the tub. She lowered herself in the water and watched, enchanted as Penny let the robe fall. She'd pulled the braids out and her hair hung down in shivering spirals as she approached the wooden tub and stepped over the side. Penny sank and let out a low, sultry moan as she reached for Agnes.

Penny pulled her onto her lap, and Agnes adjusted herself so her legs were on the outside. It was cramped, but they both fit and the water felt heavenly.

"My beautiful, clever lady of the mountain," Penny crooned as she kneaded Agnes's shoulders and the long muscles of her back, turning them to jelly. She took her time, sucking on Agnes's chin and pecking at her lips as her fingers gripped and squeezed soothingly. The water was softened with oats and oils and clung to Agnes's skin.

Agnes was drowsy and limp in Penny's arms when she felt wicked lips pluck and suck on her nipple. "Yes," she groaned as her head fell back. Penny supported her with one arm while the other hand dipped below the water. She strummed Agnes's pussy with her fingers before parting her folds and pressing deep. Penny twisted and sawed in and out as she flicked her tongue against the nipple she had between her lips, making Agnes gasp and writhe.

The pressure in her core swelled until Agnes came apart in Penny's arms. Penny drank Agnes's ecstatic sob and her hands became soothing again as they slid apart. Penny was massaging Agnes's foot when she recovered and raised her head off the lip of the tub.

"I've changed my mind: we're staying here forever."

Penny shushed as she kissed the arch of Agnes's foot, then

lowered it and sat up. "Nothing has to change between us and I'll always want to take a bath with you—here, or in Manhattan, or Narnia."

"Narnia?" Agnes chuckled as they kissed, then obediently turned when Penny twirled her finger. She washed Agnes's hair, pulling the last of the tension from her muscles and making her eyelids too heavy. By the time they finished bathing, Agnes was boneless and already drifting off. She dried herself, then stumbled around the kitchen and into her cozy bedroom nook. Penny held back the mosquito net and raised the quilt so Agnes could crawl to her pillow. She got on her back and Agnes gestured languidly with her hand. "Up you go."

"Yes, ma'am!" Penny bounced onto the bed after Agnes and scooted to the headboard on her knees. No dream could be sweeter than Penny holding onto Agnes's head and using her face with spritely abandon. She came, whimpering Agnes's name as she shivered and glowed like a candle flame. Then, Penny followed Agnes into her dreams, radiantly joyful and brimming with delightful mischief.

Chapter Nineteen

Penny was sad to say goodbye to her cabin when they rolled out of Cherrytown late Friday morning, but their return to the city felt like a major victory for their little team. June was a whole new child, bouncing excitedly in the backseat as she babbled about all the things she wanted to show and tell the triplets about their summer in the woods. June was particularly excited about the scrapbook and the dozens of rocks she'd collected, and looked forward to polishing them into crystals with her cousins.

She talked almost nonstop during the drive, but grew quiet when Agnes parked in front of a stately townhouse on East 63rd Street. Penny had grown quiet too and gulped as she looked up at the elegant limestone and red brick facade. Agnes turned off the car and smiled brightly at June in the rearview mirror, then at Penny.

"Ready to see our new place?" She asked them, giving her shoulders an excited shimmy.

"I'm ready," June gave a decisive nod and unbuckled her seatbelt.

"That's my girl!" Agnes cheered as she got out and one of the doormen hurried around to get June's door.

Penny offered Agnes a thumbs-up when she knocked on the passenger window. "Here we go," she whispered to herself before getting out.

Agnes warned June about the staff and not to run anyone over. "She looks really excited, doesn't she?" Agnes slid an arm through Penny's and squeezed it excitedly. "Thank you for helping me get this right!"

"You did all the hard work, Aggie," Penny said, bumping against Agnes's side and hugging her arm back. "I had to kidnap you and hold you hostage in my cabin first, but you were so awesome," she said with a cheeky grin, making Agnes laugh.

"I was a very willing captive," she reminded Penny while June ran to the door and pushed it open before the other doorman could get it for her.

Penny gave Agnes a pointed look as she unlinked their arms. "Careful, Ms. Cameron," she said under her breath. "Someone might think you were flirting."

"What if I was?" Agnes challenged haughtily.

It was not the time or place to have *that* discussion so Penny thanked the doorman and skipped through the arched entryway. June whistled appreciatively as she turned in the middle of the soothing, pale green gallery and looked up the winding marble staircase. It was one of Penny's favorite shades of green and made the space feel less harsh than the city outside. More airy and natural.

"This is all for us?" June asked. They heard a soft laugh as an older woman in a simple black dress came to greet them.

"Welcome home, Ms. Cameron, June, and Miss Penny," she said, smiling as she dried her hands on a tea towel. "My name's Glenda and I'm the housekeeper," she informed them.

"Please let me know if there's anything I can do for you." She turned to Agnes to discuss a delivery and their plans for the evening, giving Penny and June a chance to sneak away and do some snooping.

There was a large open living room and dining room on the first floor and Penny and June waved at a pair of maids when they peeked into the bright, cheerful eat-in kitchen. There was also a library and June was crying as she climbed the ladder and Penny pushed her toward the atlases.

"I always wanted to live in a house with a library, but I never thought I'd actually get to!" She exclaimed, making Penny's heart melt. The library wasn't as imposing as the one in The Killian House but it had two oversized gray velvet sofas and large pillows scattered on the overlapping Persian rugs, inviting guests to read and nap.

"It's not too bad," Agnes agreed as she strolled into the room. Her hands were clasped behind her back. Classic Agnes, cool and composed. "But you should check out the library upstairs on your floor."

"I have my own floor and my own library," June said dazedly and looked at Penny. "Can you pinch me?"

"Okay." Penny gave her arm a playful pinch. "Let's go check it out!" She winked at Agnes, silently promising to catch up with her later.

"Let's go!" June ran for the door, hauling Penny with her.

"You're on the fourth floor. I'll be right up," Agnes called after them. "I need to check in with Melinda and let her know we're back."

The second floor appeared to be a large formal sitting room and an office for Agnes and her assistant with a reception area for visitors. The third floor was Agnes's. Penny and June oohed and ahhed at all the pale gray marble and the decadently soft gray carpet. Their feet sank as they padded through the dressing room and bedroom, admiring the lush velvet uphol-stery. Everything was sleek, cool, and soft like Agnes.

The massive stone soaking tub stopped Penny in her tracks when she passed the bathroom. It had an elaborate chrome faucet with porcelain levers and *two* handshowers. Her face got hot when she imagined using one of the handshowers to rinse Agnes's long legs.

"Swanky!" Penny declared abruptly, giving June's elbow a tug. "But let's check out your floor!"

They bolted and raced up the stairs, their socks skidding on the same pale gray marble when they reached the fourth land-ing. "Whoa..." June breathed and Penny nodded in agreement.

The entire ceiling had been painted to look like the sky and the walls were in soft blues. Light, white cloud-like curtains swayed with the breeze and the balcony doors were opened, granting them a stunning view of the park. The furniture in the sitting room was low and upholstered in soft white velvet. There was a huge TV and Penny spotted *three* gaming consoles.

June was speechless as she tiptoed across the sitting room so she could peek into her bedroom. Her startled gasp would stay with Penny forever. "Oh, my goodness!" She squeaked out. "Penny!"

Penny jogged over to her, taking a moment to check out June's bathroom as she passed. It wasn't as big or as decadent as Agnes's, but it was bigger than Penny's bedroom at her apart-ment. It had a giant built-in tub and a massive mirrored vanity that any teenager would kill for. It was a suite that any child could grow into and it was ready for June to make her own, but there was no doubt that the bedroom had been designed with *only* June in mind.

June didn't just have her own library: her bedroom was a bibliophile's fantasy, too. The walls were lined to the ceiling with books. A four-poster bed with more billowy curtains and fairy lights glowed in the corner and there was a reading tent fit for a princess filled with pillows and stuffed animals.

June was a weepy, spluttering mess as she turned in the middle of the large room.

"I had a feeling you'd like this better," Agnes said, leaning against the doorframe. She sniffled discreetly, but Penny could see that Agnes was crying as well.

"This is the most amazing thing *ever!*" June cried, running to Agnes. She threw her arms around Agnes's waist and hugged her tight. "I already thought I was the luckiest girl in the world because I got *the best* mom. Now it feels like a dream and like this can't be real."

"I promise this is real and I'm the one who got lucky because I got you," Agnes told her, tracing June's cheek reverently. "I love you, June Cameron."

"I love you too!" June was crying as she buried her face in Agnes's chest. Penny had to look away and dab at her eyes with a knuckle. She busied herself with lugging June's bags to the closet when they were delivered by a doorman. It was that or make a scene by throwing herself at Agnes and June and professing her love and devotion.

They were chatting about dinner when Penny joined them in June's foyer.

"Glenda says we can make our own pizzas and salads and she said the crust is vegan-friendly," Agnes informed them with a thumbs-up for Penny.

Penny held up her thumb and smiled, despite the knot in her stomach. "Sounds perfect. Glenda's a genius."

She truly was. A great big salad and a personal pizza would always hit the spot. And it was nice to have someone else handle the details and manage the kitchen after weeks of preparing most of their meals from scratch herself.

Not that Penny minded doing it or needed anyone to feed or clean up after her. And she was not at all envious of how perfectly the house suited all three of them or confused by how soothing and tranquil each space felt as she explored with June.

Not at all. *Nope.*

"Can we invite the triplets over so I can show them my new room?" June asked, changing the subject and making Agnes laugh.

"Of course, but not tonight, alright? The girls have soccer practice this evening, I believe. And we need to unpack and catch our breath. I'm sure we'll see them sometime this week-end," she explained while stroking June's hair. She was such a natural now and the two were so at ease with each other, Penny wondered how long it would take Glenda and the rest of the staff to realize that Agnes didn't need a nanny, that she and June were just fine on their own now. Instead of being sad, Penny was so proud of Agnes and the little family she'd helped build.

"Yes!" June pumped her fists. "I'm going to take a shower in my new bathroom and pick out something to wear!" She turned and made a happy whooping sound as she raced back to her room. "Thanks, Mom!"

"Oh!" Agnes whispered, clutching her chest as she watched June go, then spun back to Penny. "Did you see that? She's so much more confident now, and she's so excited to see the triplets!"

Penny nodded and did a quick scan to make sure they were alone. She thought it was too sweet, the way Agnes still got emotional when June called her Mom. It was also really sexy. "She feels more secure now and she understands that she's part of the family, that she and the triplets are equals. Thanks to you," Penny added, pulling Agnes with her around the stairs. "I saw a nice corner on the second floor we can make out in before I have to go."

"Go?" Agnes groaned and stretched toward Penny for a kiss.

"Wait!" Penny giggled, checking to make sure no one had seen.

"Why? And why do you have to go?"

"Because I technically haven't had a day off in a month," Penny said carefully, possibly to remind herself as well as she scrambled for more reasons. The more she found herself liking East 63rd Street, the more she wanted to escape and touch down in the real world. "And I have to unpack. I know Dash hasn't given me all the deets about him and Gavin and I've missed my bed." Now, *that* was a lie, so Penny stomped and ground a heel hard on her toe in penance while offering up her lips.

"But my bed is nice too. And I was looking forward to showing you the bathtub after June went to bed," Agnes pouted.

"I had a peek, and *wow!*" Penny gasped appreciatively. "It might be the bathtub of my dreams. You can show me when I come back on Monday," she suggested.

"Monday?" Agnes asked loudly and leaned back. "You're not coming back until Monday?"

"Well... I'm normally off on Saturdays and Sundays."

"Right, but..." Agnes's mouth opened and closed several times and she looked around the foyer as if she was confused. "Couldn't you...stay here? With us?" She tugged at Penny's pigtail, silently pleading. It would be so easy to give in and stay *for Agnes*, not because East 63rd was exactly what Penny's dream house would look like if she didn't give a damn about the housing crisis or despised conspicuous consumption.

She had that sinking feeling again and knew that

everyone would see through her. "But you don't need a live-in nanny. June's almost nine and she's starting school in two weeks."

"Not like that, silly!" Agnes said, waving a hand at Penny. "No one would believe it anyways. Why don't you just move in?" She suggested airily.

She tried to kiss Penny but she pulled away. "What do you mean and *what do you mean?* No one will think anything's going on if we're careful. Lots of women have nannies, even if they don't *need* them. But I can't live here. That would be bonkers." Penny widened her eyes at Agnes, expecting her to agree, then became concerned when she didn't. "It would be bonkers, Aggie," she repeated, but Agnes bit into her lip and squirmed.

"Would it really be all that strange? Everyone's going to know soon enough," she added, making Penny see stars as her ears popped.

"What...? Why...why would everyone need to know?"

Agnes's neck craned warily. "Is there a reason we'd want to hide this?"

"Well..." Penny stalled. "I assumed we would because..." She held up her hands, completely baffled because why wouldn't Agnes want to hide that she was having an affair with her nanny?

"This isn't a cheap fling, Penny. I'm in love with you and I wasn't planning on sneaking around and pulling you into corners like I'm cheating on my husband," Agnes said sharply, stunning Penny.

"I didn't mean it like that."

"But that's how it would feel and how it will look if we're caught sneaking around. That's definitely not what I want. We were happy at the cabin and I want us to be just as happy here." Agnes licked her lips nervously and her hands were shaking as they held Penny's. "This feels like it's meant to be and I want to see where it goes."

"Oh." Penny's skin felt prickly and the stars in her eyes had turned into floating blotches. She leaned into Agnes because she was dizzy, but she also needed to kiss her. "That's so lovely." Their lips brushed and Penny felt less confused as she took a deep breath and filled her lungs with Agnes. "So lovely. And I'm so wildly in love with you too."

"Then say you'll stay with us!" Agnes whispered as she backed Penny into a wall. Her hands spread down Penny's back and kneaded her ass. "I've been looking forward to taking a proper bath with you for weeks."

"Have you?" Penny murmured as her spine turned to jelly and heat coiled in her lower belly. "I'd love that, but..." She didn't know what she'd say to Dash or her brother and Reid. Penny could see their shocked faces and hear their cackles when they found out, and she was mortified. "Can I get back to you about that?" She asked, gently setting Agnes away from her.

"Um?" Agnes blinked at Penny.

"I'm sorry! I am in love with you, too, and I do want to stay with you—I think—it's just *a lot* to absorb, Aggie." She batted her lashes and gave Agnes her biggest puppy dog eyes. "And everyone's going to think I've sold out."

"What?" Agnes laughed and shook her head. "No one's going to think that. But you're right, this is a lot to absorb and we both need to get our bearings. You've been away from home and your friends for weeks and June and I have a new home to get acquainted with."

"Thank you!" Penny gasped, winding her arms around Agnes's neck. She kissed her loudly and guided her around the corner so they weren't out in the open. There was an elevator and Agnes swatted at the button blindly until she found and pressed it. Penny purred as she plucked open the buttons on Agnes's shirt. "Let's get our bearings and we'll decide how we want to handle this on Monday."

"I'm going to miss you so much, though."

"Me too, but I'm sure you and June are ready. You don't need me here to be your training wheels anymore. I'm just your backup now," Penny said, feeling so proud she could burst. "It's bittersweet because I'll always want to take care of you two, but I know you can do this without me."

"Okay." Agnes nodded jerkily. "I can do this!"

"You've got Glenda here to handle your meals and the cleaning and I'm just a phone call away if there's an emergency," Penny reminded Agnes. There was a catch in Penny's voice, but she coughed to cover it and flashed Agnes a cocky grin. "And I'll make sure you're...taken care of before I go."

"That's very considerate of you. Why don't we stop by my suite instead? There's something I'd like to show you," Agnes murmured distractedly, towing Penny with her as she backed into the elevator.

The doors closed and Penny purred as she unzipped the fly of Agnes's jeans. She intended to leave Agnes sated and smiling, but Penny wanted one last taste to hold her over until Monday. "Where are we going?" She asked when the doors opened and Agnes hurried them past the bedroom.

"In here." Agnes pushed Penny into one of the large walk-in closets and locked the door behind them. There was a mischievous tilt to Agnes's lips as she guided Penny to a seating area and a wide ottoman. "Sit and close your eyes," she said.

Penny dropped onto the soft gray velvet and scanned the shelves around them. *This* closet was dedicated to Agnes's shoes, bags, jewelry, and perfume. There was a whole wall of high heels in just about every color and heel height conceivable.

Penny didn't know a thing about designer shoes, but even she was turned on by the endless rows of stilettos.

"This is gonna be naughty, isn't it?" Penny covered her eyes, but she peeked between her fingers for a second and saw Agnes stand on her toes and take a white box off a high shelf. Penny closed her eyes, then bit back an excited yelp when the box was placed on her lap.

"You can look now."

Penny snatched the lid off the box and gasped loudly at the collection of toys, lubricants, and restraints. "Ms. Cameron!" She whistled as she held up a large hot pink vibrator. It had nubs in the middle and chunky rabbit ears. There were also two glass dildos, a set of nipple clamps, padded handcuffs, a flogger, and a harness.

"I have two more boxes," Agnes said as she pointed over her shoulder. "Are you *sure* you don't want to stay the night?" She batted her eyelashes and pushed out a lip.

"I'm sure," Penny said weakly. She swallowed loudly, staring into the box. Penny's brain was bombarded by a rush of filthy ideas and her heart pleaded with her to reconsider. But those pesky doubts piped up as well. She worried she'd only wind up more confused and that it would just get harder to leave the longer she lingered. "Let's see what this can do." She pressed the button on the base of the vibrator and tested a few of the settings. Penny raised a brow at Agnes, daring her.

"We have to hurry." Agnes shoved her jeans and thong down and kicked them away. "June's going to take a while and she can call me on the intercom system if she needs me, but I want to surprise her with ice cream when she's done."

"Yes, ma'am." Penny raised Agnes's leg so she could rest a foot on the ottoman. Penny licked her fingers, getting them wet before parting the soft folds of Agnes's pussy and finding her clit. There was a low buzz from the vibrator as Penny slid it into Agnes's core, turned it so the ears weren't in the way, and slowly filled her with deep thrusts. Penny watched Agnes's eyes, waiting until they rolled and the lids fluttered to rub and thrust faster and harder.

Agnes's hands clutched at Penny's shoulder and cradled the back of her head. "I'm so close!" She muffled a loud moan when Penny bent and angled her head so she could taste Agnes.

Her tongue swept over Agnes's clit, lashing at the tight nub and making her moan louder. Penny sucked hard and Agnes's body bucked and writhed. The hand holding the vibrator became hot and slick, but Penny didn't stop until Agnes's legs began to shake and nearly gave out.

After the box was neatly packed and back on its shelf, Penny left Agnes lounging on one of the sofas, giggling and disheveled. Penny was glad for the long walk and the two trains to get across Manhattan to her place. She needed the time and fresh air to clear her head and cool down before she returned home and faced Dash. It had been weeks since she'd climbed her stoop but the flowers in the window boxes were thriving and the ivy crawling up the exterior of the brownstone had exploded over the summer.

She unlocked the door, letting herself in, and dropped her bags and fishing pole. She ducked and braced herself when Dash leaped over the coffee table and ran at her. "Hey, Penny Lane! *You're back!*" He pulled her into a tight hug and cradled her head. "You haven't checked your phone since you've been back or talked to anyone, have you?"

"No... You know how bad the signal is up at the cabin and June and I had some serious planning to do while Agnes drove. Why...?" She didn't like the way Dash's teeth dug into his lip as he passed her his phone. He leaned away like it was going to explode.

"I have everything ready for margaritas," he said soothingly and took a step back.

"Okay..." Penny tapped the screen and her eyes widened as she stared at an Instagram post. It was a picture of herself and Agnes outside the new place on East 63rd. They had their heads together. Penny recalled that Agnes had been thanking her for helping her get their homecoming right. It had been a special moment and Agnes had flirted a little, but the angle and the timing of the shot made it look like... They looked like they were staring longingly into each other's eyes and were about to kiss. Which was true. The only reason they hadn't was because Penny had gotten self-conscious and pulled away.

"Say something," Dash begged.

"Right." It had been several moments since she'd moved or even blinked. "That was fast," she said, because what else could she say? They couldn't keep their hands off each other *before* they spent a month at the cabin exploring each other's orifices. Penny realized she had been deluding herself thinking they could hide it. She'd never been capable of maintaining professional boundaries before but she couldn't look at Agnes now without drooling. Penny *had to* touch her. And Agnes didn't do anything halfway; she never tempered her affections with those she loved.

Something in Penny's heart or her head—or maybe both—clicked and she had the mother of all epiphanies. It was incredibly silly to think they could fly under the social radar because Agnes would never hide her love for Penny. She wasn't capable of pretending to be aloof and unaffected or that Penny was just another employee. Nor would Agnes want to. Knowing Agnes as well as she did now, Penny suspected she'd be *offended* if she was asked to hide it.

She loves me?

They'd talked about falling "in love" but Penny could see

from the photo that they were well beyond that and that Agnes *loved* Penny. And, from the looks of things, Penny loved Agnes to the moon and back. Penny would have laughed in anyone's face and said it wasn't possible before. Now, Penny knew without a shadow of a doubt that that's what she saw as she stared at the picture of them following June into the mansion on East 63rd. And Penny didn't care who knew.

"Are you okay?" Dash said softly.

"Yeah." Penny nodded and fought back a sniffle. "How, though?" She checked the account that had posted the picture and frowned. "Who the heck is @JonaThorne?" There was a pained hiss from Dash as he tried to retrieve the phone, but Penny snatched it back when she read the caption.

jonathorne Agnes Cameron's playing Mommy Dearest and surprise, surprise, she's hired a "nanny!" Caught them outside their new luxury love nest!

"Motherf—!" Penny started, but Dash's hand covered her mouth.

He lowered it, rolling his eyes as he took back his phone and tossed it on the sofa. "JonaThorne is Jonathon Hawthorne. He's Muriel Hormsby's nephew."

"Motherfu—" She said but Dash's hand slapped over her mouth again.

He gave her a disapproving look. Neither of them liked to use profanity unless it was in an emergency or during sex. But this was kind of an emergency... Dash cleared his throat and removed his hand. "His aunt's had a grudge against Reid since

Fin stole Walker from Jonathorn. I mean, Jonathon." He paused so they could laugh because there was no way Walker would have dated the wannabe "influencer."

"I had a better chance than Jonathong." Penny said and they had to hold each other up, they laughed so hard.

"Apparently, his aunt heard," he said once they had caught their breath. "She found out that Agnes Cameron had adopted a child and hired one of Reid's nannies. She also found out about the house so she's had Jonatron staking it out like the paparazzi."

"You're too cheap to hire a private detective, but minding your own business is free, Muriel," Penny said, clicking her teeth.

"Are you okay?" Dash asked gently and Penny nodded as she wiped the tears from her eyes. She thought she'd want to move to the cabin and change her name when everyone found out about her and Agnes. But instead, she'd laughed harder than she had in ages. And the accusations in the caption were so obvious and cheap.

"Yeah." She thought about her friends' and family's reaction and how they'd know better to believe anything like that about her or Agnes, and another laugh bubbled in her chest. "It's so, so...stupid, isn't it?" She said, shaking her head. "I've been *dreading* this, Dash. You have no idea! But now that it's happened, I'm kind of glad we can get it out of the way and move on with our lives. And it's just so stupid, isn't it?" She wasn't going to care if Agnes didn't and Penny already knew she wouldn't. "What else did I miss?" Penny asked as she wound her arm through Dash's. They headed into the kitchen and she nodded when he pointed at the tequila. "This definitely calls for margaritas. What's been going on with you and Gavin?"

"Well!" Dash whispered, giving her a loaded look. "Gavin

still won't go out with me, but I realized he goes to my library and I think he's hiding something!"

Penny looked around, not sure why he was whispering because they weren't in the library and they were alone. "What's he hiding?"

Dash's lips pulled tight and he shook his head. "I don't know and I don't want to say anything to anyone else in case he has a good reason for keeping it a secret."

"But how do you know it's a secret?" Penny asked.

His face scrunched. "I stopped by Briarwood Terrace last Wednesday morning to drop off a bag of Demerara sugar for Gavin's tea and he was just leaving. He was dressed for work and Reid said Gavin was headed to the office. But he was at the library, reading in the periodicals section when I got there, and he stayed all morning."

"What?" Penny went ahead and scratched her head because that was very strange. "Good call, though. Let's keep an eye on this and see what Gavin's up to before we say anything to Reid or Penn. He doesn't keep secrets from them so he must have a reason."

Dash nodded quickly. "That's what I thought! I've been waiting for you to get back so we could investigate."

"We're on it," she said, and offered her fist so he could bump it.

"We're going to save Gavin and then he'll have to get coffee with me."

"What makes you so sure he needs saving?" Penny asked as Dash produced a jug of their top-secret margarita mix and she went to check the freezer for ice cubes.

"I may have checked the trash after he left..." Dash hugged the jug and cringed at Penny. "There was a letter from one of *his* accountants and he said that Gavin wouldn't be able to recover from...something if he didn't consider liquidating more of…whatever." He waved and shook his head. "I'm not an accountant but it didn't sound good and it sounded like he had asked Gavin about this before or a lot."

"Oh. He *is* in trouble," she agreed. They filled large jars with ice, mix, and tequila and sat cross-legged at the coffee table with a bag of chips and fresh salsa.

"He is, but I don't think it's like super urgent." Dash snorted before loading a chip with salsa and dumping it into his mouth. He chewed, then took a long sip from his metal straw. "I caught him napping in periodicals a few days later so he can't be in *that* much trouble. What about you and Agnes? Your texts have been unusually brief and vague."

"They have been." She stirred her drink as she stalled, then began reasoning and rambling out loud. "I guess the cat's out of the bag… But I'm kind of glad, honestly, because I love Agnes and I don't think I can live without her. She's the best thing that's ever happened to me and June's my life now. I don't think I can keep something like that to myself for long and we were definitely going to get caught again because I can't keep my hands off Agnes," she continued, ignoring Dash's slack jaw and unblinking eyes. "Gavin's not the only one who's in trouble. I've been having an identity crisis since I found out my mom was *married to a Monahan* and was pregnant with his baby." She ended with an awkward shrug.

"Oh, boy!" Dash laughed as he got to his feet. "I'm gonna find that other bottle of tequila and make more ice. We've got *a lot* of catching up to do."

The Emergency Margarita Mix

- 1 (6 oz) can frozen limeade concentrate
- 2/3 cup orange juice (about 2 large oranges)
- 1 teaspoon orange zest

Combine and store in the fridge until ready to serve.
For a whole pitcher: add 2 cups of white or gold tequila. Mix can also be frozen in cubes and blended for frozen margaritas!
To serve: mix equal parts sugar and salt in a saucer or a wide, shallow bowl. Rim glasses with a lime wedge and dip in salt/sugar blend before filling with ice and equal parts tequila and mix.

Chapter Twenty

Saturday morning was a rude awakening for Agnes and June. The night before, they had both been exhausted and crashed into their beds after a chapter of *The Lightning Thief* and goodnight hugs and kisses. But they awoke groggy and confused by the lack of Penny and finding themselves in a big new house. They stuck their heads out of their bedroom doors and peeked down the staircase at the same time.

"What are we supposed to do?" June whispered down at Agnes.

Glenda's head appeared from the main floor's foyer below. "Would the two of you like breakfast?"

"That would be lovely, thank you," Agnes said, then looked at June. "Wash up and meet me in the kitchen?" She suggested and June gave a thumbs-up before she disappeared.

They met in the kitchen about a quarter of an hour later, and Glenda had a breakfast of French toast, scrambled eggs, bacon, and a fruit salad waiting.

"Any plans today, ladies?" Glenda asked once they were

finished and she was gathering their dishes. June's and the older woman's gazes settled on Agnes expectantly.

"Um..." She wasn't sure why they assumed *she* would have a plan. "I was hoping that we might..." She stalled again because she only had one idea and she wasn't sure if June would be up to it yet. "I thought we could stop by The Killian House and tell Walker, Fin, and the girls about our trip," she said hesitantly, then said a silent prayer.

"Can I bring my scrapbook?" June asked excitedly as she slid off her stool. "And I have to give them all the rocks I collected so we can put them in the tumbler."

"Of course!" Agnes said, nodding quickly. She hopped off her seat and quietly thanked Glenda for breakfast while June continued rattling off a list of treasures she wanted to share and stories she wanted to tell them.

June talked all the way to The Killian House, entertaining their driver with stories about the cabin. When they got to their destination, she raced up the front steps and shook Pierce's hand when he answered the door. She surprised Walker with a warm hug, bringing tears to his eyes, and she had a high-five ready for Fin. But the biggest change—and Agnes's best reward —was seeing June happily embracing the triplets and answering their rapid-fire questions with confidence and enthusiasm. She was holding her own and no longer looked to Agnes for support and security.

"She is a totally different child. You and Penny did an amazing job," Walker said as he put an arm around Agnes. A Twister mat had been laid out on the grass in the backyard and Fin, June, and the triplets were giggling and contorting themselves into pretzels.

"She really is," Agnes said with a satisfied sigh. Instead of claiming that it had all been Penny, Agnes was proud of the hard work *she* had done as well and knew that her presence had made all the difference for June. None of Penny's magic or mountain ingenuity could have saved them if Agnes hadn't been willing to show up and make an honest effort.

"Can you hold my headband, Mom?" June called, waving it over her head as she balanced on one foot and her other hand.

"Be right there!" Agnes happily sprang into action and raced over to the mat to get it. She felt silly, but she was proud and rather nervous, letting Walker see *her* in parenting action for once.

"Thanks, Mom." June was intently focused and didn't notice Agnes's shimmering eyes as she backed away, hugging the headband.

"You're doing great, sweetheart!"

Walker hummed in agreement and laughed softly as he handed her a glass of lemonade. "Bourbon," he supplied before she could ask him what had been added to the adults' glasses.

"Perfect," she said, and took a long sip.

"I can't say that I'm surprised, but motherhood suits you," he said as he raised his glass to Agnes. "You look relaxed and refreshed and most importantly, you both look *happy*."

"We are," Agnes confirmed. "We had a wonderful summer. Probably the best summer of my life," she added with a chuckle before taking another sip.

Walker smirked at her over the rim of his glass. "Were you enamored with the bucolic delights of the Catskills or was it the company you found so wondrous?"

Agnes hummed loudly in agreement. "It was definitely the company. You absolutely must meet Penny's great-aunt Mabel. She's a treasure, and her son, Uncle Silas, is a saint," she said sincerely, earning a weary eye roll from Walker.

"I'm sure they are if they put up with you. What about Penny?"

"Definitely a treasure and a saint as well," Agnes said, and laughed when Walker stuck his tongue out at her. "She is a godsend, a pistol, an enchantress, a menace, and the prettiest girl I've ever seen. I could go on and on." She stuck her tongue out at him, enjoying his disgruntled glare.

"*And?*"

"And she's extremely knowledgeable about plants?" Agnes attempted.

"Out with it, Aggie," he growled. "Are you seeing her or not? Penn's sources say that the two of you were definitely fooling around up there."

"Penn's sources?" She snorted. "You mean Silas and Mabel."

"They're considered reliable. Are you or aren't you?" Walker raised a brow, challenging her.

"We are. I think," Agnes dug her teeth into her lip as she hesitated.

Walker sighed heavily at her, as was his habit. "I hope this isn't about your age," he said, winding up for a lecture.

Agnes pulled a face. "I assure you it *is not* about my age. Look at me. I'm exquisite and I'm a delight to be around. Who wouldn't want to date me?" She asked without a hint of doubt, making him smile.

"My thoughts exactly."

"And it would make me a terrible hypocrite after I pushed you into giving Fin a chance, wouldn't it?" She asked and he chuckled as he nodded.

"It would and that's not at all like you. So why are you being so evasive about dating Penny?"

Agnes tapped her thumb against the glass and grimaced uncertainly. "Because it isn't me that's being evasive, it's Penny. I'd shout it from the rooftops and tattoo her name across my chest, but I'm not sure if she's...there yet."

"I see..." Walker replied, his frown returning. "Please don't get any tattoos."

"You mean, aside from the one I already—"

Walker raised a hand and shook his head. "Let me live in ignorance, Aggie. I've gone this long without knowing."

"Very well." She shrugged. "I'm taking my cues from Penny for now. She learned some things about her mother while we were at the cabin and she had a minor existential crisis. And she was in an odd mood when she left us yesterday."

Walker's expression grew thoughtful. "I'm sure she'll land on her feet and all will turn out well if she's anything like her older brother."

Agnes laughed. "She *is* her brother, just more of...whatever it is that makes them so wild and wonderfully weird." After a month at the cabin with Mabel and Silas, Agnes felt like an expert on the subject of the Tucker siblings.

"I rather like that about them," Walker confided. "Penn is a little touchy-feely for my comfort, but he's the kindest, purest person I've ever met."

"Penny is even more so and I love that about her." Agnes sucked in a breath when she realized that that might be what she loved *the most* about Penny. "She's not like anyone or anything we knew when we were little. There are times when I think that it might have been worth it, never being hugged or cherished before. Because, somehow, Penny finds all that love I missed as a child and she smothers me with it." She laughed but it wavered, and tears blurred her vision. "She's so *good* and she makes me want to be a better person so that I can deserve her. But the pampered, privileged Cameron in me wants to take her and claim her *now*. And you know how good I am at waiting."

Walker made a knowing sound and put an arm around her. "Patience has never been one of your virtues."

"No. And I've never had any patience for the virtuous, so this is extra confusing for me," she said, making Walker laugh out loud.

"Good lord, I'm enjoying this." He gave her shoulders a squeeze. "I couldn't be happier for you and I have a feeling that everything's going to work out."

"I think so too," Agnes said slowly. There was no telling what Penny would do because you never knew what wild leap her mind would take from one moment to the next. But Agnes did know that Penny wouldn't let her and June down. She wouldn't leave them hanging because they were a team. "I learned to have faith and wait while I was at the cabin. I just have to remember all the things I learned so I can be the same person here."

"How interesting. Did you learn to hunt and cook over a fire while you were up there?" Walker asked, making her laugh.

"We hunted mushrooms and rocks and June learned how to lasso."

"Valuable life skills, I'm sure," he replied with a befuddled frown. "I...didn't realize it was so difficult to catch a mushroom."

"Mmm..." Agnes hummed into her glass. "They're quite elusive."

"Fascinating." He gave his head a shake and cleared his throat. "Summer is almost over and June will be starting school soon. Have you given any thought to what's next for the two of you?"

"The three of us," she corrected and earned a pleased rumble from Walker. "I know it's going to be a challenge, domesticating Penny Tucker, but I can't picture a future here for me and June without her."

He raised his glass and tapped it against Agnes's. "If there's anyone that can do it, it's you. Assuming *you're* domesticated, and that's a whopper of an assumption."

"It is, but I'll behave for Penny and June."

Agnes tapped into the insight and intuition she'd gained on the mountain and listened to her instincts. They told her that Penny would find her way home, and then, she'd show Agnes and June the way. That didn't mean that Agnes couldn't find Penny a mother lode of mushrooms in the city if she put her mind to it.

Metaphorically speaking, of course. Agnes wasn't sure if she trusted something that had grown in an alley or had been touched by the waters of the Hudson. Instead, Agnes turned her thoughts to fields that played more to her own natural strengths.

How could Agnes impress Penny and win her heart in the city? She had to think bigger than vegan dinner dates and enchanting evening walks. This was a far more serious challenge than she had faced at the cabin because Agnes had to prove that she was worthy of *Penny*. The stakes were so much higher than setting out to prove she wasn't a stick in the mud and that she was willing to do anything.

What did Penny truly desire? What would it take to steal her wild, wonderful heart? She couldn't turn Penny's head with extravagant gifts or luxurious getaways. Money would never impress Penny like a handful of mushrooms or wild berries could. She would always love fields full of flowers and bees over the structure and routine of the civilized world.

How could Agnes use her money, influence, and privilege to make Penny's wildest dreams come true? That was the rub because Penny's dreams were the antithesis of Agnes's existence. And Agnes would be asking Penny to sacrifice far more than her principles as an environmentalist and an activist.

Their relationship and June would require all of Penny's

focus and devotion. Because she was only capable of giving 100% of herself and she held nothing in reserve. Agnes knew Penny well enough by now to know that she wouldn't be able to work as a nanny for another family until she was absolutely sure that June didn't need her anymore. She also wouldn't work as a nanny elsewhere if Agnes asked Penny to marry her and they became a family in every sense of the word.

Agnes would be taking Penny away from a calling she felt passionate about and was profoundly gifted at. That was something she couldn't take lightly, and Agnes vowed she'd make it up to Penny. She'd help her find a new passion and Agnes would use her privilege and influence to empower Penny.

And just like that, a rather clever idea came to Agnes. She squinted thoughtfully at Walker and nibbled on her lip. "You know, there's nothing we can do about this getting out. If it hasn't already."

He bowed his head and groaned sympathetically as he drained his glass. "It will get out, but if there's anyone that can withstand the gossip or use it to her advantage, it's you," he said, gesturing for her to follow as he went to refill his glass from the pitcher on the terrace.

"Exactly," Agnes said and thanked him when he topped off her drink. "I was thinking that it might be fun to beat the gossips at their own game."

Walker's brows jumped and he grinned. "I'm listening..."

"How much do you think *Vogue* or *Shout* would pay for access to the season's most exciting engagement announcement and an inside look at one of the most exclusive and expensive weddings in New York history?" She wiggled her brows, daring Walker to join her as she prepared to make a tremendous splash.

His eyes sparkled as he tapped his glass against hers. "I'm in. Let's shout it from the rooftops," he said, then hissed warily.

"I'm not so sure that Penny's going to be as excited about a fancy, exclusive wedding..."

"Oh, not at all!" Agnes predicted, but she was so certain and delighted at how *good* her plan was. "She'd hate everything about it and will run if she finds out she'll have to wear a dress. Until I tell her how much money we're going to raise for her dream camp for foster kids and that the Cameron Foundation is going to match all the funds for scholarships as a wedding gift. I'm going to put a big fat bag of cash in her hands so Penny can build the biggest, wildest summer camp of her dreams."

"Now *that* sounds like something that would please a Tucker. And you could be creating an animal, once you teach a Tucker how to forage in rich people's pockets..." Walker warned with a teasing wink. But Agnes adored the idea of using the public's interest in their relationship to make Penny's dream come true and give more kids like June a place to run wild.

"I already know *exactly* what everyone's going to say about us. But we're going to rub our beautiful, blissfully happy family in their faces and make them sick with jealousy." Agnes sighed.

"The havoc the three of you will wreak around this city..." Walker whistled and shook his head, but his chest shook with laughter as he pulled her close.

"I know," she said with a smirk as she sipped and watched June with Fin and the girls. They had collapsed onto the Twister mat in a tired, sweaty, giggling heap. "They're going to whisper about us like we're common and tawdry. But we'll rub their faces in it by becoming *the* power couple and by the time I'm done, everyone will know that Penny's a force of nature."

"They won't know what hit them," Walker said, looking pleased as he enjoyed his drink.

Both siblings were deeply content. They continued to watch Fin and the girls while the sun set, filling the New York skyline with bright pinks, oranges, and purples. "I love every-thing about this," Walker said distantly.

Agnes wasn't sure if he was referring to their plan or the heartwarming tableau in front of them, but she agreed. "So do I," she said, resting her head on his shoulder.

Chapter Twenty-One

It was time for answers.

Penny stood in front of her brother's place in Lenox Hill, working up her courage before she rang the buzzer. The secret was out and the news was spreading through Manhattan via social media, but Penny couldn't make sense of what was going on between her and Agnes or what she wanted until she understood her mother better.

Her hands were sweaty and her stomach was queasy because Penny didn't want to lose what was left of her mother if there was more to the truth. And she didn't want to lose even more of herself. She thought she'd known who she was before she learned about Patrick and fell in love with Agnes. Now, she was questioning everything, and wasn't sure who that was having a severe attack of bathroom envy back at Agnes's. It couldn't have been Penny Lane Tucker, could it? She *did not* lose her head over soaking tubs and high-end plumbing fixtures.

She had, though, and Penny had spent the last two nights tossing and turning, wishing she was at Agnes's. Her perfectly adequate queen-size bed was suddenly lumpy and loud, and every creak of the springs made her eye twitch as she flopped back and forth like a trout on a dock. Eventually, Penny would pass out, waking just before the sun with a stiff neck and an aching back.

Her tarot deck affirmed that Penny was out of sorts because she was carrying strange baggage and that some tidying was in order. She couldn't ask Gus about it, obviously, so she'd set out for Penn and Morris's, hoping to finally get a grasp on her mother's past.

Penny knew that Gus would tell her the truth. But he couldn't talk about Laurel without sinking into sorrow and Penny didn't want the days she had left with him to be heavy. While she could trust Penn to tell her the truth, it bothered Penny that he hadn't told her yet. He'd never hidden *anything* from her so it was both disappointing and concerning.

Penny hadn't taken it well when she saw pictures of Laurel in a dress and on a yacht. What if there was more that Mabel and Silas hadn't told her? But she thought of Agnes and June. She didn't want to blow it with them because she'd lost her own way. She had to make peace with her mother and herself before she could dedicate herself to them. Because she had no idea who or what she had to offer anymore.

Was she still her mother's daughter? And what did that mean?

"Here we go," she whispered and pressed the buzzer.

The door opened a moment later and Morris laughed as he reached for her. "God, I've missed you!" He wrapped her in the tightest hug and Penny sighed in delight as her feet came off the ground.

"I've missed you too!" She leaned back and searched his face and his aura. Both were glowing and he seemed deeply content.

"I was about to drive up there and drag you back, I missed

you so much," he said with a tweak of her nose. "But you look good! And I heard the *big* news! Is it okay to congratulate you?" He asked, hugging his chest and tilting toward her expectantly.

"Maybe," she said as she scanned for Penn, but she couldn't feel or see him. She did hear a soft coo from the other side of the sofa and made a beeline for the play yard. "My sweet Cadie!"

"Penny!" Cadence dropped her stuffy and held out her arms.

Penny scooped her up and was treated to the best tiny hugs and kisses. "Please grow slower," she whispered to Cadence before looking around. "Where did my brother go?" She asked Morris while rocking Cadence.

"Briarwood Terrace, I think. He was supposed to help Reid and Gavin replace the garbage disposal."

"Ugh." Penny smooshed her face against Cadence's cheek and blew loudly, making the toddler squeal and giggle. That helped a lot; Penny felt happier and stronger as she kissed Cadence's pillowy soft cheek. "I didn't want to have to do this in the lion's den, but I think I can face them now."

"What are you talking about?" Morris asked as he yanked on Penny's pigtail.

"Me and Agnes. Does Penn know about the Instagram post yet?"

That got a loud laugh out of Morris. "Barely and only because I explained it to him. You know he doesn't have a clue about what's happening on social media or care what the gossips are gonna say. He wants to have a talk with this Jona-Thorne, though."

Penny rolled her eyes. "I thought we'd have to hide and that it was going to be a nightmare when it got out. Now, it's out and I...don't care. Last night, I realized that it's only going to be a big deal until someone does something more interesting."

"There you go!" Morris said, winding an arm around her. "You know that people have really short memories, especially on social media. This is *your* fairytale, Penny Lane. You really gonna let them stop you from saving the day and getting the girl?"

"*Pfft!* As if!" She hugged him and Cadence tight, the three of them giggling as they kissed each other's cheeks. "I'm gonna get the *girls*," she corrected, then groaned as she handed Cadence to Morris. "After I work some things out with Penn. I have some questions about Mom," Penny explained and loaded up on more hugs from Cadence and Morris before heading around the corner to Briarwood Terrace.

"Penn's not here but he should be back soon," Gavin informed her as he buzzed Penny into the lobby.

"Hello, handsome!" Penny called and ran around the desk to give the doorman a hug.

"There's my sunshine! How was the cabin?"

"Wonderful as always, Norman! How are you feeling today?" She kissed his cheek and smiled because she could *feel* that he was well and in a happy mood.

"Can't complain, can't complain."

"When did Penn leave?" she asked as she dug in her bag and found a jar of Norman's salve. She made it out of olive oil, beeswax, cayenne, ginger, turmeric, and arnica to help with his arthritis, and always had a jar with her in case she stopped by Briarwood Terrace.

"He took off with Reid about an hour ago. Oh, thank you!" he said when she passed it to him. "This stuff works wonders. Especially when it rains." He handed her an empty jar from behind his desk and she gave him another kiss before heading around the corner and letting herself into Reid and Gavin's unit.

"Penny," Gavin said distractedly. She found him in the

kitchen, frowning out the window. "It took Penn about ten minutes to switch out the old disposal for a new one so they've moved onto the back terrace. They think it needs a raised bed for lettuces and peas. Penn knows a guy who's setting up a greenhouse so they went to talk to him about scraps."

"Nice!" She replied. He wasn't as enthusiastic as he studied the view behind the thick leaded panes.

"It seems like a lot of work for some lettuce and peas and I'm not particularly fond of either."

Penny's brow jumped and she squinted at him, confounded. "Lettuce? How can you *not* be fond of lettuce?"

"The same way I'm not fond of pencils and have no interest in growing them. I like the backyard the way it is."

"I see," she said quietly, and peered out the window with Gavin, trying to see what he saw. The little patch off the terrace had been paved, and aside from a bistro table and two chairs, the area was bare. Penny wanted to fill every space with growing things and couldn't understand why he'd prefer the empty solitude.

It was just the two of them so Penny edged a little closer and gave Gavin a nudge with her elbow. "Can I ask you something?" She whispered, searching for that spark of secret wildness that Dash had glimpsed. But all she saw was the same stoic and sedate Gavin as he patiently blinked down at her through his spectacles.

"Of course," he murmured before his gaze returned to the window.

"What are you doing with Dash?"

Gavin jumped as his attention swung back to Penny and his gaze sharpened. "Dash?" He croaked, and Penny felt a glimmer of hope as Gavin turned a telling shade of red. "What do you mean? I'm not doing anything with Dash."

"I know and that's why I'm so confused. It's not like you to be vague or indirect, but you have to know that he's *deeply* in love with you," she said gently, careful not to sound like she was scolding him.

He nodded and his eyes darted around Penny's head anxiously. "I do know and I've done my best to discourage him."

"But you haven't!" She turned Gavin to fully face her and gripped his arms. "You could let him down easy and tell him to move on, but you've allowed him to follow you around this apartment and woo you with cups of tea for over a year."

"I've tried to. I just—" Gavin shut his eyes and pushed out a hard breath. "He's...*wonderful*, Penny, and I wish I could. But I can't date Dash and I don't know how to tell him—"

"Sure, you can!" Penny said, giving him a shake. "He already knows what you're like and he's shy too!"

Gavin's hand shot up and his eyes were hard, pinning hers. He wasn't blushing anymore and was suddenly serious. "This isn't about my nerves or his. I'm telling you, I *can't* date Dash. Regardless of how I may feel or what I might want, *I can't*."

"What do you mean you *can't*? Dash is thirty and you're almost forty and neither of you is seeing anyone..." She frowned in confusion and gave her head a stubborn shake. "This doesn't make any sense. You're both free, consenting adults, and you obviously like Dash and wa—"

"Please, Penny." Gavin held onto her, silently pleading with her to let it rest. "I can't," he said simply, then nodded at the front door when it opened and Reid and Penn spilled through it. They were slapping at each other's hands and trying to hit the other in the face. "What is it this time?" Gavin asked them with an eye roll for Penny, attempting to clear the air and put the discussion behind them.

"He started it," Reid said, earning a belligerent snort from Penn.

"We stopped to talk to Omar on the way back and Reid tried to take the last falafel sample."

"They're for *everyone*," Reid argued, glaring at Penn. "He thinks that just because he's vegetarian that he gets dibs."

Penn sneered at Reid and waved dismissively. "You've got *thousands* of hot dog stands and pizza places to choose from. It's a carnivore's paradise out there. I get first dibs on free falafel."

They both looked at Gavin, waiting for his verdict. He stared at them for a long moment. "I don't like falafel," he said, then ducked his head and excused himself so he could return to the window.

The falafel was forgotten as Penn and Reid took turns hugging Penny and calling her kiddo. They were thrilled to have her home again and she was glad to be back in their brotherly embrace.

"But why are you here, instead of enjoying your first weekend off in a month? Did you need to see me about a work matter?" Reid coughed, gently prodding.

Penn wasn't in the mood to be subtle. "My sister has a girlfriend and I learned about it from Morris because he read about it on Instabook." He shook his head and gave her a disappointed look that lasted for half a heartbeat. "Come here!" He spun her around and Penny allowed Penn and Reid to get all the rib poking and hair mussing out of their systems. "When were you going to tell me?" Penn asked.

She pulled a face and held up her phone. "When would I have had the chance? You know how bad the reception is at the cabin and you *never* have your phone on you. And I knew you'd all be dorks about it."

"Definitely," Penn confirmed as Reid held up his hands.

"We'd be miserable excuses for brothers if we didn't," he

said, earning a grunt of agreement from Gavin as he went to his seat at the table.

"And you wouldn't want to deprive them of weeks and weeks of meddling and scheming, would you?"

Penny snorted. "We couldn't have that," she said, and nudged Penn with her elbow. "I went by your place because I needed to talk to you about something."

"Something other than *this*?" Penn asked as he threw an arm around her neck and kissed her hair. "I've missed you so much. I'm heading home. Wanna walk with me?"

"Sure!" Penny said, and they were on their way after saying goodbye to Reid and Gavin.

"So... Tell me all about your summer at the cabin with Agnes and June!" Penn said as soon as they were outside. He poked Penny in the ribs again and gave her braid a yank.

"It was great," she said, shrugging a shoulder. "I texted you just about every day. You should check your phone more often."

Penn gave her another poke. "Come on! I want to hear about everything—the fishing, the wine, the heated looks... We had a feeling that nature would take its course if we just got the two of you together." He wiggled his brows at Penny and she laughed as she pushed him away.

"What do you mean you had a feeling?" She narrowed her eyes at him.

He stopped and crossed his arms over his chest. "I didn't ask before because I knew you didn't want to lie to me. But I *knew*."

Penny kicked at the pavement and debated. She had blamed it on the weak signal and not wanting to get into it over the phone, but Penny didn't know how to explain without feeling like a fraud. And like *she* was the one being shallow because she couldn't look past Agnes's reputation and her wealth.

"It wasn't supposed to be serious. I didn't think there was any way she'd ever take this seriously," she explained.

Penn cocked his head and his brow furrowed. "Why wouldn't she take this seriously? Agnes is a lot of things, but she isn't cruel or selfish. She'd never hurt her friends."

"We weren't friends," Penny argued, but Penn widened his eyes at her pointedly.

"Reid is her friend and she respects him. I'd like to think that she considers me a friend as well and would be careful not to lead my sister on..." He mused with a thoughtful hum. "Now, would my sister be as careful if she thought she was getting away with something and no one was going to get hurt?"

"No one's been hurt," Penny grumbled and turned on her heel. "Are you coming or are you gonna set up camp there?" She asked over her shoulder and heard him chuckle as he jogged to catch up.

"Why don't you want to talk about Agnes?"

Penny threw him a scowl. "Who said I didn't want to talk about Agnes? Agnes is amazing and we had an amazing time at the cabin."

"I can see that," Penn said, wincing. "Why don't you seem happy about it?"

"I am."

"Are you sure?" Penn's eyes were soft and seeking as they touched Penny's. His shoulder bumped against hers. "You don't *feel* happy. You feel... muddled. And that's not like you at all. You're always so clear and strong."

Penny's cheeks puffed out as she decided it was finally time to come clean. Penn was going to tell her she was being a ninny, but that was probably just what she needed to hear. "I thought it was safe to fool around with Agnes because I didn't think feelings would be an issue. I couldn't see any way that we would fit, aside from the obvious."

"You didn't think Agnes would fall madly in love with you?" Penn asked, looking both shocked and offended. "You're...the most beautiful girl in the whole world, Penny."

"Ha!" She let out an inelegant snort, then clapped a hand over her mouth, smothering it. "You're just saying that and she's in a way different league."

A hard, weary groan rolled from Penn. "No, she's not, and I have a feeling Agnes doesn't think so either."

"No, she doesn't," Penny confirmed.

"So, it's you," he reasoned and waited for her nod. "I can tell that you're in love with her. You glow and get warmer every time you think about her or hear her name."

"I am. It's just—" She stopped and shook her head at her own pettiness. "Why didn't anyone tell me about Mom and Patrick Monahan?" She blurted out and Penn tripped.

"What? Where did you...?" He turned and walked backward, looking perplexed. "I just forgot," he said, holding up his hands. "And it wasn't a big deal by the time you were born."

"A big deal?" Penny asked loudly. "Mom was married to another man and she was going to have his baby!"

Penn's lips pursed and his eyelids fluttered. "Wow. I guess I can see how that might seem like a bombshell to you..."

"Really?" Penny was mystified because she couldn't see how it wouldn't be. "Our *mother* had a whole other life that no one thought I needed to know about."

"We weren't hiding it from you, we just..." Penn's lips pursed and he made an exploding sound. "Mom said it was like something that had happened in another lifetime and she'd get so *sad* whenever she talked about them. It was the only time I can ever remember Mom being sad. Mom said that she and Dad were both really lost when they met and that they found a way to start over together. And I think that by the time you were old enough to understand, it had become something that had happened to Mom in another life. It had to be so she could move on."

"I get that..." Penny said, her lips twisting as she tried to pinpoint *why* it still bothered her. "But doesn't it make her seem kind of like a fraud?" She asked in a hushed whisper.

Penn reared back and shook his head. "No. How?"

"Because she was supposed to be...this super eco-warrior who hated the wealthy, the government, and the military-industrial complex. Her and Dad didn't make any sense because he'd been a soldier, but a man like Patrick Monahan? Come on!"

"I see." Penn laughed as he hooked an arm around Penny's neck and steered them around the corner. "You don't think you knew who Mom really was because she fell in love with a Monahan. And you think you're letting us down if you fall for someone rich and powerful like him."

This time, Penny tripped, and Penn had to catch her before she wiped out on the sidewalk. She barely understood why she'd been so out of sorts, yet he had managed to diagnose all of Penny's problems before they had reached their destination.

"How did you know?"

He chuckled as he kissed her temple. "All your life you've wanted to be just like Mom and follow in her footsteps. We let you grow wild because you're her spitting image and it's like getting her back, but there was more to Mom than being vegan and an eco-warrior. We might have done you a disservice by letting the hardest parts go by the wayside."

"Did she love him?" Penny asked, almost afraid to hear the truth because it hurt to imagine her mother loving anyone other than Gus.

Penn gasped and nodded. "She loved him so much!" His eyes shimmered and he had to look away for a moment. "She said he wasn't at all what she had expected and that he wanted to do something *good* with his family's power and influence."

"Oh my God."

"Sound familiar?" He asked with a knowing grin, and Penny nodded.

"I wasn't expecting Agnes to be so lovely. Physically—yes, obviously—but I didn't think I'd actually *like* her so much. She's such a kind and warm person and she's so funny. And, boy, is she smart!"

"I know," Penn said simply, his large smile telegraphing his satisfaction. "That's why I thought you'd be perfect together."

"*Pfftt!*" Penny rolled her eyes. "You did not. No one would ever think that me and Agnes Cameron would work."

"You can ask Walker and Reid if you don't believe me."

"Hold on!" Penny said when the metaphorical penny finally dropped. "The *three of you* planned this?" She accused and Penn's smile spread, becoming beatific.

"It was Walker's idea. But Reid and I were onboard right away because we think the world of Agnes and we knew you two would go together like peanut butter and jelly."

"How?" Penny laughed, earning another eye roll from Penn.

"Aside from the fact that you're *both* kind, warm, funny, and smart?" He began with a hard look at Penny. "You're both horny, chaotic hooligans who can't keep your hands off each other."

"There is that," Penny said, rubbing her chin thoughtfully. "I was afraid that I was selling out and falling for someone Mom would be ashamed of. Then, I found out about Patrick and I've been wondering if I ever really knew her."

"Stop!" Penn gave her shoulders a squeeze as they walked. "You're taking this personally because you think Mom had a secret life and that we hid it from you. But she didn't and we didn't tell you because...it was in the past and it had nothing to do with you." Penn shrugged. "Mom was a complicated woman and some parts of her life weren't any of your business or mine," he added, shushing Penny when she tried to argue. "I'm not telling Cadence about everyone I dated before Morris. And he's not getting into his romantic past with her either, I'll bet."

"You're being really generous because you weren't *dating* any of the men you hooked up with in the 'before Morris' times."

"Not the point," Penn said, holding up a finger. "There's no reason for Cadence to know all the gory details about what happened before I fell in love with Morris. I'm not ashamed because I've always been honest with my partners, but it just isn't relevant."

"You didn't think it was relevant that Mom was married and pregnant with another man's baby." Penny raised her brows expectantly, but Penn shook his head.

"I just forgot. It was a weird and really sad part of Mom's past that was water under the bridge by the time you were old enough. And then Mom died and there were so many other things that were too hard to talk about."

"Right...but when said man was supposed to be the next JFK?" She challenged, making Penn grimace.

"More like the next JFK Jr. That family has been cursed like the Kennedys, and Patrick was a serious catch, from what I've heard. None of that mattered to Mom, though, and I got the sense that she saw him very differently than the rest of society."

"The yacht and the place in the Hamptons probably helped," Penny said out of the side of her mouth.

"Hey!" Penn gave the back of her head a swat. "Mom accepted Patrick for who he was and she didn't make him choose between his family and her. She was able to compromise. Did you know that he spent weekends with Mom up at the cabin, too?"

Penny shook her head, a wave of guilt rolling over her. "I saw a picture of them on the dock, but I didn't want to ask Mabel or Silas. I didn't want to talk about it."

"Why?" He asked softly.

Penny swallowed hard, feeling bitter. "Because I felt like I was losing *my* mom and that I wasn't as much like her as I thought I was. Or, that I was just like this *other* version of her and we were both big frauds."

"For falling in love with two people who happen to be rich and powerful?" Penn clarified, and she nodded. "That's silly. I think you're *amazing* and you're more like Mom every day. And I know she'd be proud of you."

"Do you really?" Penny asked shakily. Her eyes stung with tears and her nose started running. She sniffed hard and scrubbed at her cheek with the back of her hand. "Because sometimes, it feels like I made her up—like I imagined her. How could anyone be that perfect?"

"She was real." Penn pulled Penny into his arms and rocked her the way he always did when she cried. "She was real and I wish you had more time with her so you'd understand. Mom wasn't perfect—no one is—and she had her flaws and her wounds. She never would have hidden them from you. That's just something that *we* did because...that's what you do when you lose someone you love. You keep the version of them that gives you the most peace and you allow others to do the same."

"Yeah..." Penny nodded, rubbing her soggy cheek against his shoulder. "I think I wanted both of us to live up to every-one's rose-tinted version of Mom. I want to be just like her, but I'm not sure if I'll ever be as good as the Mom we remember."

"You're wrong, Penny Lane. You're the best parts of Mom and she'd think you're perfect because you're also the best parts of Dad. I've managed to rub off on you too. Falling in love with someone who happens to be extremely wealthy doesn't make you a sellout. Look at Fin and Riley. They've managed to pass themselves off as mature, respectable people, despite being married to obscenely wealthy men. Morris has a lot of money, but I don't hold it against him," Penn added with a smirk.

"Mm-hmm... And you're almost mature and respectable," she noted, then laughed when he went for her ribs and tickled her.

Penn tortured Penny until she was out of breath and begging for mercy, then turned serious. "You'll never be mature or respectable, but Agnes is a lovely woman and I couldn't be happier for you. We're all so happy for you." He stopped and pointed at his and Morris's place. "We'd only think you were a sellout if you turned up in a limo wearing furs and diamonds."

"Ew. Never." Penny's tongue pushed out as she gagged, making him laugh.

"See? Still my Penny Lane. Where you live and who you live with isn't going to change how we feel about you. I promise, you ninny." Penny threw her arms around his neck, too overcome to speak. She knew he'd say that because he always did and she hadn't really changed that much after all. "Feel better?" He asked and she nodded.

"Lots! And I think I'm gonna need a hand getting packed. Agnes wants me to live with her and June. Wanna help me move?"

"I'm glad I could help and I'd love to," Penn said with a sly smile. "And once we've got you and Agnes settled, let's see what we can do to help Dash move things along with Gavin."

She grinned and held up a hand so he could slap it. "Now, we're talkin'. Dash has made some progress, but he's gonna need our help because I think Gavin might be in trouble."

Chapter Twenty-Two

After weeks of fantasizing about returning to the cool, clean bosom of civilization, Agnes's first weekend back in the city was a bit of a letdown. June was happy and thriving, but Agnes's bed was too big, the sheets too smooth, and the room was too bright and bare. She tossed and turned, reaching for Penny throughout the night. Then, the sun would brazenly light up the room as it rose, reminding Agnes just how big, bright, and empty the place was.

A faint knock on the door saved Agnes from texting Penny first thing Monday morning. She was moments away from begging her to rescue them and take them back to the cabin.

"Agnes?" June leaned around the door and offered a shy wave when she spotted Agnes.

"Come in, sweetheart!" Agnes sat up and patted the bed next to her. "I was just missing you and wondering if you were up yet." That wasn't exactly true, but Agnes was lonely and she would have gone after June once she stopped feeling sorry for herself. Agnes immediately forgot about her boring, oversized bedroom as June raced to the bed. She scrambled on and cuddled up against Agnes's side, making everything instantly better. "Did you sleep well?"

June nodded as Agnes kissed her hair. "I slept like a princess! But then I woke up and I didn't know what to do because Penny's not here and there aren't any eggs to collect or berries to pick."

"I miss Penny too, but she'll be here soon."

They had managed to scrape along well enough on Sunday without Penny, but neither Agnes nor June could go more than two minutes without mentioning her. "It'll take a little getting used to, but we'll have lots of fun things to do here too. And we'll figure out how to give Penny a day or two off without going feral," she said, wrinkling her nose at June. "Although, I am actively plotting because I'd like her to move in with us as soon as possible," she confided and June giggled.

"Everything would be perfect if Penny lived with us!" June's eyes narrowed as if she were plotting as well, so Agnes cleared her throat. She *wanted* to confide in June and include her in the plans she'd hatched with Walker. It didn't seem right to keep something so wonderful from June, especially when Agnes knew that she loved Penny and wanted her to be a part of their lives as well.

"I think so too. Would it be alright if I asked Penny to marry me? After you and I have had some time to get settled and things have quieted down," she clarified, but June was excited and nodded quickly as she rose on her knees.

"Could we have a big wedding and wear fancy gowns and have lots and lots of flowers? Penny's favorite thing in the world is flowers!"

"An explosion of flowers!" Agnes promised as she reached for June, pulling her into a hug. "And the fanciest gowns you've ever seen."

"Unless Penny doesn't want to wear a dress. You know how she doesn't like dresses," June said seriously.

Agnes hummed and nodded. "She's not very fond of dresses. But she's breathtaking when she gets dressed up, June!" Agnes whispered, a loopy grin curving her lips as she recalled Penny at Penn and Morris's commitment ceremony. "She looks like an angel and I can't take my eyes off of her."

"Penny's always pretty. Even when she helped Uncle Silas clean the chicken coop and muck out the barn."

"This is true."

"So are you, Mommy!" June said as she kissed Agnes's cheek.

"Thank you!" Agnes booped her nose before brushing the hair away from June's eyes. "But I think you could be the most beautiful thing I've ever seen and I'm so lucky because I get to keep you." She tapped her forehead against June's and kissed her. "Wanna see what we can find for breakfast while we wait for Penny?"

"Yes!" June cheered and bounced across the bed as Agnes swung her feet over the side. They marched down the spiral staircase in their pajamas and Glenda was waiting in the kitchen with pancakes, bacon, and smoothies.

"Foraging for eggs and berries is fun, but this isn't bad either," Agnes pointed out as June munched on a piece of bacon while perched on a stool at the counter. Glenda had prepared blueberry pancakes for Agnes, and June had blueberry *and* chocolate chip pancakes with whipped cream on top.

"I could get used to this," June decided, making Agnes and Glenda laugh.

There was a soft chime and Glenda gave the counter a brisk pat. "That was the front door. I'll bet that's Miss Penny!" She said as she hurried from the kitchen.

Agnes and June exchanged excited looks before they

hopped off their stools and raced into the first floor's gallery. They skidded to a halt, both confused as Penny backed through the front door with her fishing pole and a stack of milk crates. One appeared to be filled with sneakers and the other two contained books, records, trophies...

"You can leave that wherever," Penny told Dash as he wheeled a dolly in. It was loaded with a tote bin and cardboard boxes.

"No, you cannot!" Glenda said, pressing a hand to her cheek as she looked at Agnes in distress. "Ma'am?"

Agnes looked behind Penny and Dash and saw a van parked on the curb. Fin and Riley were quickly unloading it. Fin offered Agnes a jaunty salute as he dropped a green military duffle bag inside the door and ran back to the van.

"What's going on?" Agnes asked Penny.

"I missed my girls too much this weekend so I'm moving in," she announced with a resolute nod, causing Agnes's tummy to flip.

"Oh. Are you?" She glanced at June and the little girl was turning purple. She was so thrilled she was about to burst with glee.

"Yes, yes, yes!" June's fists shot into the air as she hopped up and down. "We missed you too and Mommy said she was going to ask you to move in and—"

Agnes covered June's mouth before she could give anything else away. "And you beat us to it. How wonderful!" She said, widening her eyes at June so she understood that they still had some planning to do before Agnes could propose. Agnes cleared her throat as she lowered her hand and winced at the boxes, bins, crates, and bags filling the small entryway and gallery. "But we will need to find a place for all of this quickly or Glenda might resign."

"I wouldn't, ma'am," the older woman said, shaking her

head. "But I might push the whole lot onto the curb if I find any of it here when I'm done preparing lunch," she warned before returning to the kitchen.

"You heard the woman," Agnes said, looking around the gallery and through to the van. "We've got until lunchtime to get her moved in."

June ran upstairs to change into "work clothes" while Fin and Riley finished unloading the van. "There better be an elevator," Riley said as he dragged the last duffle bag through the front door. He panted as he rested against the jamb and brightened when Glenda appeared with juice and cookies. "Thank goodness. I'm starving!"

"How?" Fin asked everyone with a snort. "He ate two breakfast burritos on the way over."

Riley shrugged and bit into a cookie. "I'm still growing and I've got hollow legs, I guess."

Penny sidled up to Agnes and flashed her a sheepish smile. "You probably heard about the Instagram post."

"Melinda mentioned it and I wasn't the least bit surprised. I'll be having a word with Muriel, though," Agnes said with a hard eye roll. She knew the old menace had a grudge against Reid, she just wasn't expecting herself or Penny to get caught in the crossfire. "I'd rather get it over and done with, personally. Everyone will find something better to talk about in a week."

"That's what Morris and I decided too," Penny said, then gestured at the bodies rushing around them. "I hope you don't mind, but I brought everything. I figured I wasn't going back and told Dash we'd find someone cool to rent my old room out to."

"I think we can find a way to make this work," Agnes murmured as she hooked a finger under Penny's chin. Their lips brushed and Agnes's eyes widened in surprise when

263

K. Sterling

Penny's arms wound around her neck and she kissed her soundly. Right in front of everyone.

"We both know this works. Really, really well."

"Nice!" Riley declared, then pouted when Glenda turned him around and pushed him toward the kitchen.

"Give them some privacy. And I just took a pan of peanut butter cookies out of the oven if you're still hungry," she said, clicking her teeth as she scanned him from head to toe. "Why, you're just a wisp of a thing. You need to eat more," she scolded.

Riley nodded as he followed. "That's what I keep telling them," he said, making Fin laugh and shake his head as they watched them go.

"I give it a week before he's banned from her kitchen. Riley's a locust. Where's all this going?" Fin asked Agnes as he pulled a baseball cap from his back pocket and put it on backward.

"Take it all up to my suite and we'll figure it out from there," Agnes said, her heart fluttering at the thought of Penny's things filling the shelves of her closet. She suddenly felt covetous and greedy and anxious to take everything out of the duffle bags and bins. Not because she wanted Penny's repurposed hand-me-down overalls and dirty Converse for herself. Agnes inwardly shuddered because she would *never*, even though they were perfection on Penny. But she wanted to claim Penny's things and for Penny to lay claim to anything of Agnes's she pleased because that meant that Penny finally belonged to Agnes and Agnes belonged to her.

It was childish and too silly for Agnes to put into words so she played it cool again while everyone lugged the bigger items into the elevator and hurried up the stairs with armfuls of odds and ends. An hour and a half later, all of Penny's things had been moved upstairs and most of her clothes had been put

264

away. There were boxes containing tarot decks and photo albums, *crates* of her mother's pottery, and candles of every color—many already partially melted and some in shapes like mushrooms and gnomes. What couldn't go in their closets was stacked in one of the guest rooms until they could designate which corner of the house would become Penny's domain. But Agnes was impressed with how quickly and painlessly Penny's move across Manhattan had been accomplished. Both literally and emotionally.

Fin and Riley stayed for lunch, then took off in the van, leaving Agnes, Penny, and June to cope with yet another dramatic upheaval. But June handled it in stride, making plans for the upcoming week and offering to show Penny all the cool hiding places she'd found over the weekend.

They spent most of the afternoon exploring the house and getting Penny settled until June ran out of steam and passed out in the living room with a book. Agnes found Penny watching June from the gallery and eased up behind her.

"It's been a big day," she said quietly as she rested her chin on Penny's shoulder and held her. Penny's soft laugh was distracted but content as she leaned back against Agnes.

"It's been a big summer. For all of us," Penny sighed and turned in Agnes's arms.

"Are you alright?" Agnes asked, searching Penny's face. "You seemed like you were...freaking out a little when you left us Friday evening and I didn't hear much out of you this weekend." They'd exchanged a few texts and had talked briefly, but Agnes hadn't been able to gauge Penny's moods.

Penny pulled in a clarifying breath and rolled her eyes as she let it out. "I had this...*silly* vision of who I was supposed to be and who I was supposed to fall in love with. I thought I had to be *just like* Mom and that I had to find someone *just like her* or I'd be letting her and Penn and Dad down. And I thought that I'd... I don't know..." A blush spread up Penny's neck and her ears turned red. "I kind of felt like I was going over to the Dark Side when we came back and you started talking about me staying here."

"Why?" Agnes asked in disbelief. She couldn't see how it made all that much of a difference. Penny and Dash's place wasn't exactly on the other side of the tracks.

"Because I *wanted* to stay with you and June and I could see myself living here and being happy."

Agnes stared back at Penny, growing more mystified. "And that's a bad thing?"

"It felt like it at the time," Penny confessed, then bit her lip apologetically. "I felt like a sellout because I was falling in love with this house right along with you and June, and I'm not supposed to like all of this," she said, flailing her arm at the luxury around them. "I thought I was going to marry an aid worker or a biologist and we'd spend our lives backpacking through jungles, delivering medicine or building wells or finding new species of plants. I wasn't supposed to fall in love with a snobby socialite," she teased and rolled her eyes. "And I wasn't supposed to wind up in a posh mansion with a house-keeper and maids."

"Want me to get rid of them?" Agnes said, completely serious. She'd hate to let Glenda go because she had come *highly* recommended and hiring her had been a coup, but Agnes would do whatever it took to make Penny feel comfortable.

"No! I'm not going to be responsible for putting people out of work!"

"It's not like they wouldn't get snatched up. I'd make sure of it. Besides, I stole half the household from The Killian House," Agnes said with a shrug. "I don't know the first thing about vacuuming and dusting, but I suppose I could learn."

"Oh, Aggie!" Penny threw her arms around Agnes, crying

as she kissed her. "I can't imagine anything you'd like less. But it means the world, knowing you'd be willing to do that for me."

"There's nothing I wouldn't do for you and June," Agnes said. She rubbed her nose against Penny's and breathed her in. Now, everything felt right and like they were home. "The two of you are all I need to be happy. I learned that while we were up at the cabin."

"This is considerably bigger than my cabin, though, and you'd be cursing me by the end of the week if we had to clean this place on our own."

Agnes looked around them and cringed at Penny. "I don't think I'd last a day. What was I thinking, buying a place this big and with this many floors?" She asked, making Penny laugh.

"At the time, you were thinking about finding the best home possible for your child. You never do anything halfway and you're never subtle. I love that about you," Penny said firmly. "And I love that you *never* hesitate to do what's best for the people you love. Even if it's something bonkers like getting rid of your staff and learning how to vacuum."

"That is pretty bonkers," Agnes agreed, and wondered what the hell she'd been thinking. "Love really does make you say and do the strangest things..."

"It really does, and I forgot about that when I learned about Mom and Patrick. I felt like I didn't know who my mom was, and I made that about me and us. Then we came back and I freaked out because I was afraid that I didn't know who *I* was because I was ready to go all in with you here."

"That's rather understandable," Agnes said slowly, then snorted. "Except that you're Penny Lane Tucker and you're not capable of being shallow or selfish."

"But I am!" Penny stopped Agnes and gathered her face in her hands. "I am *really, really* sorry for being so stubborn about *you*. I could see you growing and changing for us, but I was still worried about the Agnes Cameron with the reputation for being a billion-dollar wrecking ball when that's not you at all."

Agnes sucked in a hiss and her head tilted from side to side. "That's not so unreasonable. We're still going to be the butt of jokes and gossip. I made peace with that ages ago, but I can't expect it to be as easy for you to ignore."

"Nope." Penny shook her head. "I'm proud of you and I didn't fall in love with a wrecking ball. I fell in love with a warm, intelligent, and magnetic woman who gives 100% of herself to the people she cares about. I love *you* because I'm the most *me* when we're together. And I can't wait to show the world that *I* tamed and claimed the unstoppable Agnes Cameron."

"You certainly did. I love you, Penny Lane, and I can't picture my life without you now. Want to sneak away and play while June's asleep?" She suggested, but Penny shook her head as she tugged Agnes toward the stairs.

"How about a nap? I think we beat a record for crosstown moves."

"A nap? Since when do you take naps?" Agnes asked suspiciously, earning a drowsy smirk from Penny as she glanced over her shoulder.

"Since we came back from the cabin. I've barely caught a wink at night because I can't sleep without you."

"Isn't that interesting?" Agnes noted as she followed Penny up the stairs. But it wasn't interesting. It was actually rather lovely.

Chapter Twenty-Three

This was what she was afraid of? Penny wanted to give herself a swift kick in the backside as she watched June and Agnes laughing over milkshakes in the kitchen. A perfect vegan strawberry milkshake was melting in front of Penny because she was busy swooning like a nerd. Her chin was resting in her palm as she stared dreamily at *her girls*.

Glenda had made a gorgeous mushroom risotto and Agnes and June ate theirs with roasted chicken. Dinner in the new kitchen had been just as cozy and enjoyable as at the cabin, minus Silas and Mabel for entertainment. Penny missed them dreadfully, but she was relieved at how quickly June, Agnes and she were connecting and finding their own rhythm in the city.

Dinner had been a different type of comforting than at the cabin, but Penny adored Glenda and eating as a family in the kitchen. She almost asked June to pinch *her* as they played a dancing game on one of the consoles until it was time for bed. June showered and changed into her pajamas while Agnes and Penny tidied up the controls and turned down the lights. Then the three of them piled into June's bed and they finished *The Lightning Thief*.

"I *loved* that and I can't wait to start *The Sea of Monsters* tomorrow!" Agnes declared with a soft clap.

"I knew you'd love it, Mom." June's eyes were large glowing pools, brimming with love and adoration, as she stared up at Agnes.

Agnes leaned over and kissed her cheek. "You were so right, sweetheart. I love it *almost* as much as I love you," she sang softly, making June sigh as she hugged Agnes's neck.

Nothing could have been more beautiful, and in that moment, Penny had never wanted anything as badly as she wanted June and Agnes to be *hers* forever and ever. And they were hers for the taking, Penny finally realized. She resolved to do whatever it took, to give 100%, to win them.

Penny and Agnes held hands as they left June's suite and headed downstairs, passing a young maid along the way. Agnes was oblivious to the young woman's smile and quickly averted eyes. She hadn't noticed Penny's blush either and sang something softly to herself as they strolled.

Or perhaps Agnes had noticed that Penny was blushing. There was a knowing gleam in her eyes and a wicked tilt to her lips as she led Penny through the bedroom and past the bed. "Right this way," she said as she held the bathroom door for Penny.

"Oh my!" Penny's blush deepened until her cheeks burned.

Someone had prepared a bath while they were reading with June. Steam and an intoxicating aroma wafted from the tub as rose petals floated on the surface. There were *two* champagne flutes next to a bottle chilling in the ice bucket and *two* fluffy white robes on the long ottoman in the center of the room.

Agnes shut the door behind her and sauntered toward

Penny. "I don't know if anything will be as magical as our baths at the cabin, but I think we can find a little magic in here if we try."

"That's all it takes!" Penny planted a kiss on Agnes's lips, then yanked her to the ottoman so they could undress. She picked at the laces of her Chucks, then pushed her overall straps down, letting the garment drop to the floor. Penny had whipped off her T-shirt and shimmied out of her panties before Agnes had even unbuttoned her blouse. "Hurry up, slowpoke!"

"You should have told me we were racing," Agnes chuckled.

"Come on!" Penny hopped into the tub, moaning appreciatively as she lowered herself into it. The water was just right. Hot enough to make her skin sting and tingle, but not too hot that she couldn't stand it. "It's longer than me!" She declared as she stretched her arm and reached for the other end.

"I'm a tall woman and I like to fit in a bath while I'm soaking my cares away. It's not much fun if your knees are smooshed against your chest and you're shivering," Agnes explained with a haughty shrug. Penny's eyes were glued to Agnes's leg as she stepped over the side, her long foot pointing gracefully as it dipped below the surface of the water.

"I love every sexy inch of my goddess," she said, sliding closer and smiling shamelessly as her hands glided up Agnes's leg. "In fact..." Penny's jaw fell and her tongue extended as she craned her neck and licked up the inside of Agnes's thigh.

"Hold on!" Agnes planted a hand on Penny's head, halting her. "I'm in charge of bath time tonight."

That made Penny's heart skip a beat and her nerves flicker with anticipation. "Oh! Yes, ma'am!" She scooted back and pulled up her knees, holding onto her ankles obediently while Agnes leaned back against the cool stone of the tub.

"Come here," Agnes held out a hand. Penny went to her

and turned so her back was to Agnes. She eased back and rested her head on Agnes's shoulder. "Just like this," Agnes whispered, her breath mimicking the steam from the bath as it huffed against Penny's ear. "I've fantasized about having you just like this for days." Her fingers trailed up Penny's ribs and over her breast to circle her nipple, causing it to pucker and pebble. The other hand parted Penny's thighs and raised her leg, so her ankle was resting on the edge of the tub.

"Aggie!" Penny had to gulp for air when Agnes pinched her other nipple, rolling both between her fingers.

"You might be too young to remember, but there's an old song called 'Second Hand Rose' that reminds me of you..." Agnes's voice was a soft, silky purr that would have made Penny *wet* if she wasn't already up to her neck in rose-scented water. "But you're never pouty, you're my priceless, precious Penny Lane."

Penny knew the old Ziegfeld Follies song and tried to hum the chorus, but it wavered and became a long, strained gasp when Agnes's hand drifted between her legs and lazily strummed a thigh. Agnes took over, singing softly about a piano in the parlor and secondhand curls as she made Penny's toes curl. Her wicked fingers parted Penny's folds and twisted and stretched as they slid in and out of her pussy, winding her tighter and tighter.

"But my love makes secondhand magic," Agnes crooned at Penny's temple. She pulled her fingers from Penny and lifted one of the handshowers off its cradle. It plunged into the water between Penny's legs and there was a faint *whoosh* and a wave as Agnes turned it on. The warm current swirled against Penny's cunt and she moaned in delight when Agnes aimed it at her clit. There was a rush of pleasure and Penny floated up, up, up, spiraling toward a glowing peak, then burst into shimmering bits when Agnes tweaked her nipple hard and sucked on the corner of Penny's neck.

She held Penny there, trembling and floating in ecstasy until her legs began to shake. Her foot cramped as it extended in the air and curled. "Okay! Enough!" Penny laughed, sweat beading on her forehead and upper lip as she held onto the side of the tub and hunted in the water for Agnes's wrist.

Agnes answered with another one of her sexy, silky chuckles as she replaced the handshower. "Are you sure? I could listen to you come and watch this all night." She nibbled on Penny's ear and held her as she floated back to earth and Agnes's arms.

"We'll turn to prunes," Penny said, checking her hand. The pads of her fingers were already wrinkling. She slid around and onto her knees. "Up you go! It's your turn." She coaxed Agnes out of the water and onto the wide lip of the tub. Her hands spread possessively over Agnes's legs as she opened them and slid forward, angling her shoulders so she could rest her head at the apex of Agnes's thighs. "Right where I belong," she sighed happily, nuzzling her face against Agnes's petal-soft folds.

"Right where you belong." Agnes's hand curved around the back of Penny's head, lovingly guiding her home. Penny licked, savoring Agnes's soft gasp and the delicate tremor that passed through her. She found Agnes's slick, hot center and drilled with her tongue, coating it in sweetness. Once Agnes was squirming and her chest heaving, Penny moved higher. She replaced her tongue with her fingers as she sucked on Agnes's clit. "Yes!" Agnes urged, holding Penny's head there.

Penny moaned appreciatively, winding her tongue around and around and around the tight nub until Agnes jumped and bucked against her face. She swore and chanted Penny's name as she jerked and swayed until she went limp and sank back into the tub.

Penny wrapped her arms and legs around Agnes and they were content to hold each other in quiet peace, stroking each other's backs and running their fingers through damp strands of hair.

Right where I belong.

Penny was herself again, complete and content because she was with Agnes. They fit together perfectly, their limbs curling around each other like the petals of a sleeping flower as their bodies cooled and they became drowsier.

Eventually, Agnes roused Penny and helped her out of the tub. They dried each other off before stumbling into bed together. Their limbs tangled like vines as they whispered and made each other giggle under the duvet.

"This is so much better," Agnes said as her arms and legs tightened around Penny possessively. "And this is all that matters now. You and June. That's it, and the rest of the city can kiss my difficult ass if anyone has a problem with us."

She was so completely unbothered, so supremely confident as she closed her eyes and held Penny tighter. Her certainty was contagious, and Penny's heart swelled with pride and joy as she imagined the future with *this* woman and her extraordinary child.

Agnes had been clear, and Penny suspected that a proposal was imminent. She hadn't let herself take it seriously before or considered how she'd respond. But now that Penny had come to terms with loving Agnes Cameron and what that meant, she truly *wanted* to say yes.

Not just yes, Penny wanted to shout it from the rooftop and tell all of Times Square. Instead of feeling embarrassed or like a sellout, Penny couldn't wait for the world to see how exquisitely beautiful *her* woman was. And Penny was proud of Agnes because she was so much more than her big, bold reputation made her out to be. She was fearless and generous and everyone who truly knew Agnes adored her unstoppable energy and independence.

So much was right, and Penny's world was warm and bright, as she nestled beneath the duvet with Agnes. She tried to decide if she should act surprised when Agnes proposed and wondered if she'd cry. Would she even have a choice? It was still possible for Agnes to surprise Penny and tears seemed likely no matter what.

Visions of picnics in the park, beaches at sunset, and rings in fizzy glasses of champagne swirled around Penny's brain as she drifted off. They were also in the boat on the lake and in The Killian House. There were so many possibilities and Penny thought that *any* of them would do as long as Agnes asked and Penny got to say yes. Then, just as Penny was letting go, a magical and truly unexpected idea came to her.

What if I asked Agnes to marry me?

All of a sudden it hit her.

Her eyes snapped open on a startled gasp, making Agnes mumble in her sleep as she snuggled against Penny's side. The certainty and finality that Penny had always hoped she'd feel when she found "the one" bloomed within her. And she felt her mother's presence—a tide of love and pure happiness. *This is it. You're home now, Penny Lane,* a voice said from deep within, and she felt so safe and satisfied.

"That's one problem solved. But how in the heck do I...?" She whispered, cutting her eyes at Agnes as she calculated.

Penny would have to act fast because Agnes didn't drag her feet when she saw something she wanted. That presented Penny with a whole new challenge because she had never given a single thought to how she'd propose to anyone. She was so sure monogamy and marriage were a distant prospect, but now she was in a race.

Her eyes widened, and Penny was even more excited. And

she was far too awake to go to sleep. "I have to find my fishing pole!"

Agnes raised her head and blinked at Penny in the dark. "Huh? Now?"

"Yes! But you go back to sleep," Penny whispered, carefully extricating herself from Agnes and sliding out of the bed.

"Good luck and don't stay out too late," Agnes said, drowsily slurring and flapping a hand before she rolled over and hugged her pillow.

Penny stifled a laugh as she kissed the arch of Agnes's foot. "I don't need luck. I've got you!" She backed away from the bed silently, then danced a little jig as she set out to find her lucky fishing pole.

Chapter Twenty-Four

"This is a disaster. It's the end of the world." Penny stormed out of the closet dragging an empty duffle bag behind her and dragging Agnes from a dream about Penny's lips and her...lips.

Agnes scrubbed an eye with the palm of her hand and struggled to make out the digits on the clock on her nightstand. "Dear lord, it's only four-thirty. The world had better be ending." She glanced at Penny, who was bleary-eyed and wild-haired, her lips trembling as she shuffled closer to the bed.

"I. Can't. Find. My. *Fishing pole.*" Penny's fists curled at her sides and her nostrils flared as she fought to maintain her composure.

"Okay..." Agnes held out a hand, attempting to calm Penny as she sat up and threw back the duvet. "I'm sure it's here somewhere."

"I've looked *everywhere*, Aggie. It's not in this house," Penny said, her voice rising.

Agnes pushed out a slow breath and gestured for Penny to

do the same. "Just take a deep breath. It has to be here. I saw you carry it in," she said as calmly as she could.

Penny nodded. "I know you saw me carry it in because I remember," she said in the same cadence and tone, then smiled sweetly at Agnes before her face fell. "But it's not here anymore. I have searched this entire house and *it's not here.*"

"No. It has to be here," Agnes stated as she headed into the closet to put on clothes since it appeared that a search was underway. "Where could it have possibly gone?" She mused, swiping a T-shirt and a pair of shorts off a shelf.

"That is the billion-dollar question, isn't it?" Penny asked with a disgruntled grunt. She crossed her arms over her chest and stared at the wall behind Agnes. "Where in this billion-dollar dream house is my mother's fishing pole?"

"I'm sure the house didn't hide your fishing pole or eat it."

"No, but it's been a nightmare since you fell asleep and I—" Penny's mouth snapped shut.

"You—?" Agnes waited but Penny just blinked back at her.

"I just wanted my fishing pole. What's so strange about that?" She shrugged and hurried out of the closet. Agnes quickly dressed and Penny had her arms jammed between the mattresses when she walked back into the bedroom.

"It isn't there," Agnes promised as she leaned against the door, growing even more confused as Penny sat on her heels and pushed out a hard, defeated breath.

"I didn't think it would be, but it's the only place I hadn't checked. I didn't want to wake you up before."

"May I ask...why?" Agnes attempted gently. "I've heard of sleepwalking, but a middle-of-the-night fishing expedition?" She teased, earning an eye roll from Penny. She was smiling, though, as she got up and came around the bed.

"It'll all make sense after I find it. I just have to find it. It's my mom's fishing pole and it's never been out of my sight."

Penny's voice wavered and her eyes glittered as she reached for Agnes.

"We'll find it." Agnes hushed her when Penny tried to argue. "I don't care if I have to hire every last detective in the city to dive in every last dumpster—"

"Why would it be in a dumpster?" Penny asked loudly, and Agnes grabbed her so she wouldn't run for the door.

"It isn't! I should not have said that. I was just saying that we won't leave a single stone unturned," she clarified.

"Okay, because if it was, I would *die*, Aggie," Penny said heavily.

Agnes thought Penny was being a touch dramatic. But she knew better than to say so because she understood how much that pole meant to Penny. "We will find it," she repeated, putting an arm around Penny and giving her an encouraging hug as they headed for the hall.

Two hours later, Agnes was afraid they'd never find it. They'd gone room-by-room, searching everywhere including the places it couldn't possibly fit. They even tiptoed around June's room, checking under her bed and under cabinets with their phones' flashlights. June eventually woke up and joined the hunt.

"Maybe we can get you a new pole that looks just like your old one," June suggested when she dropped onto the stairs next to Penny in the first floor's foyer. She wound her arms around Penny's middle, attempting to comfort her.

"Maybe," Penny said, but her voice broke and she was crying as she kissed June's hair. "That pole was really, really special, though." She sniffled and cast her red, watery eyes up at Agnes and shattered her heart.

"Oh, Penny." Agnes ducked in front of her and cupped Penny's chin. "We're not giving up. I'll get a crowbar and we'll start pulling up the floors."

"They're marble, silly," Penny said, but she let out a teary laugh as she rubbed her cheek against Agnes's palm.

"What is going on in here?" Glenda asked as a doorman let her in and she took off her hat and scarf.

"Penny's fishing pole is missing. We've been searching the whole house for hours," Agnes explained.

Glenda's face pinched. "That old thing? I found it in the closet there," she said as she waved at the door across the foyer by the elevator. "But I moved it because it didn't belong in the house."

"You *moved it*?" Penny shot to her feet. "Where, where, where?" She demanded and Glenda pointed.

"I sent it out to the shed in the backyard."

"No, no, no, no, no!" Penny bolted, skidding and crashing into the kitchen door. They heard it slam shut behind her.

Glenda laughed and shook her head. "All that over a rusty old fishing pole? I could barely tell what it was beneath all that duct tape."

"You don't understand, but *thank goodness*," Agnes said, exchanging relieved looks with June as she nodded.

"It's Penny's most prized possession! It's like my *Percy Jackson* books."

"I see," Glenda said and shrugged. "I'll leave it in the closet, then."

"*I found it!*" Penny exclaimed when she returned a few minutes later with her pole firmly clasped between both hands and extended in front of her. She looked like she was leading a parade as she marched into the foyer, then returned to her seat on the stairs.

"Whew!" June scooted closer to Penny. "Are we going fishing?"

"Nope." Penny shook her head and was focused as she

carefully angled it and began picking at the tape around the handle. "Not today, June bug."

"Then, why'd you need your pole so bad?"

"You'll see in just a minute," Penny told her, then chewed on her lip while slowly turning the pole and peeling away the tape.

"Do I need to be present or can I get started on breakfast?" Glenda asked, earning a snort from Penny.

"You don't have to stay, but do we have any champagne?"

That sounded like just the thing. Agnes clapped her hands together and opened her mouth to tell Glenda that she could use a glass to celebrate the recovery of Penny's pole when she saw something shiny beneath the duct tape.

"Penny..." Agnes shook her head and blinked hard because she absolutely refused to believe her eyes. They were misting over as Agnes's legs began to shake. "Penny, please tell me you *didn't*..."

But Penny continued to tear away the tape until Glenda and June let out loud gasps when she pried a ring off the pole's handle. "Ew. It's kind of gunked up..." Penny murmured as she let the pole clatter to the floor and held the ring up to the light so she could inspect it. She picked at the adhesive caked around the simple gold band and solitary stone, her nose wrinkling as she worked.

All the while, Agnes silently sobbed.

"It was there the whole time?" June asked incredulously and Penny's shoulder bounced.

"Where else would I keep it?"

Agnes and Glenda exchanged baffled looks. "A safety deposit box?" The housekeeper guessed.

"A safe?" Agnes chimed in shakily, but Penny's lips fluttered.

"Nah. When would I go to the bank? And I don't have a

safe, but I *usually* know exactly where my lucky fishing pole is and that's where Mom's ring has always been. It used to be my Nana Tucker's ring and she passed it on to Dad to give to Mom. It came to me because Penn wasn't ever going to propose to a woman. He told me to save it for someone special. It's part of the reason my pole was so lucky."

"Oh, Penny." Agnes pressed her hand against her chest to stop her heart from bursting through it.

"We're probably going to want to clean this up, first, but will you marry me?" Penny asked, holding up the ring. "I don't have a lot of money or a fancy family pedigree like you do. But I have a really swell cabin up in the Catskills and I think you're the most amazing woman in the whole world. I'll always love you, Aggie, and I'll always want to get into trouble with you and make you laugh."

Agnes nodded frantically and spluttered, her nose running as she began to cry harder. "Yes!" Agnes pulled Penny to her feet and gathered her in her arms. "Yes! Of course, I'll marry you, Penny!"

Agnes felt like she truly had everything and was on top of the world for the first time in her life. She was ecstatic as she held Penny and reached for June, pulling her into their tearful embrace. So much had changed in just one summer. Agnes had a family of her own and she had *two* amazingly good people who loved her for exactly who she was.

"I'd better get that champagne," Glenda had pulled a handkerchief from her sleeve and was dabbing her eyes as she hurried into the kitchen.

A few hours later after breakfast—with champagne for the adults—June and Agnes pushed Penny upstairs and into bed. She tried to fight them off, swearing that she was fine and that she *never* took naps. But Penny was out almost as soon as her head touched the pillow.

June's cheeks puffed and her bangs fluttered as she pushed out a relieved breath. "What a morning."

Agnes nodded in agreement. "What a morning," she said, smiling as Penny grumbled something about her lucky pole before letting out a loud snore.

"You know," June began thoughtfully. Agnes braced herself because she had a feeling this would be a doozy and either bring her to tears or break her heart when she shared it with Penny later. "Anthony said that no mommy was better than having a bad mommy, but I don't think he ever thought about having *two* mommies."

"No. I don't think he did," Agnes agreed weakly.

"But I think that two mommies might be the luckiest thing in the world."

Agnes was touched and could only nod for a moment. "I think you might be right, sweetheart." Although, Agnes imagined having two like her mother and suppressed a shudder. "But I think Anthony might be partially correct and that it could depend greatly on the mother. Or mothers."

"Maybe." June shrugged. "But I got the best moms."

Agnes gathered June's hand in hers and gave it a squeeze. "And we're so lucky because we get to keep you."

June bounced happily at Agnes's side. "What happens next? You don't have to ask Penny to marry you anymore. She beat you to it."

"Well... Want to help me give Penny the wedding of her dreams?"

Chapter Twenty-Five

"I wasn't expecting to be so nervous!" Penny confided to Agnes and June, her voice wavering as she covered her eyes and peered through the bakery's window and hunted for Evelyn Mosby.

Inside, the kitchen and dining area were bright and inviting. Slice Of Evelyn felt more like her Nana Tucker's kitchen in Hoboken with its bright white counters and cheerful floral valances. The appliances were mint green and only looked vintage. The mixers, scales, and ovens were all modern and the bakery's employees were sharply dressed in pink polos, jeans, and crisp white sneakers.

The bakery was run like a well-oiled machine by a savvy, no-nonsense businesswoman. But Slice of Evelyn had become a second home to Penny, and Evelyn a second mother, since Penn married Morris.

"You're nervous because this is so special!" June reminded her, and Penny felt an answering burst of fireworks in her chest.

"It really is!" She agreed. Penny felt like she was going to explode every time she thought about marrying Agnes and all the adventures the three of them would have together. "Like, how could anything ever be better than this?" She shook her head and Penny's eyes teared up because she couldn't imagine wanting anything more or anything that could make her happier than Agnes and June.

"Come on!" Agnes said, nudging Penny with her elbow, then waved at Evelyn through the window. "There's no going back now, she's seen us. Let's get in there and make this official!"

"That's the scary part!" Penny whispered at them as she went to the door and pushed it open. They had shared the news with Walker and Penn earlier in the afternoon and it was slowly spreading through their friend group, but it would be official and *everyone* would know once they told Evelyn and commissioned a cake from the celebrity baker.

"Well, hello ladies! Get in here and give me a hug," Evelyn ordered, gesturing impatiently as she hurried around the counter. "And welcome, June! It's wonderful to finally meet you in person. I've heard so much about you from Penn, it feels like I already know you." She scooped June into a warm hug and rocked her. "Get suited up and make yourself any kind of cupcake you want!" She said, releasing June so she could put on gloves and a hairnet and play behind the counter.

"Yes!" June cheered but halted and looked at Agnes and Penny. "Can we tell her our big news first?"

"What big news?" Evelyn asked, leaning back. Her eyes narrowed and settled on Penny.

"Well..." Penny stalled, wrinkling her nose at Evelyn when her nerves fizzed and her knees knocked. "I asked Aggie to marry me and she said yes."

"Oh!" Evelyn gasped and covered her mouth. "Oh, baby! That's *wonderful* news!" She threw her arms around Penny and reached for Agnes. "Congratulations! I'm so happy for the two of you!" She said, then turned to June. "What do you think? Are you as excited about this as I am?"

"I can't wait!" June hopped excitedly. "I'm gonna be in the wedding and I get to pick my own dress and help with the rings! Can I go make a cupcake now?" She asked, making everyone laugh at the quick shift in her priorities.

"Go!" Evelyn said, wiping her eyes as she regarded Penny and Agnes. "And I think it goes without saying that we'll be making your dream cake here at Slice of Evelyn."

"We're looking at next summer and starting here with the cake and planning everything else around it," Agnes stated, earning a pleased nod from Evelyn.

"Good. What did we have in mind? Will this be a vegan cake?" She asked, all business again as she reached over the counter for a clipboard.

"It doesn't have to be—" Penny started, but Agnes cut her off.

"It has to be vegan. And I know you make the best vegan cakes in the city, Evelyn," she said, effectively putting an end to the discussion.

Evelyn agreed that vegan was the only option, and Penny was delighted as the three of them designed her dream cake. She had never given much thought to her dream wedding cake, but six tiers of white sponge, fresh strawberry filling, and vegan whipped cream sounded like her idea of heaven and perfect for a summer wedding.

"Have you given any thought to the venue?" Evelyn asked. "We can keep the decorations simple or rustic for a country wedding or we can do something more elegant."

"Elegant, I'd think," Agnes replied with a hesitant glance at Penny. "We're only inviting close friends and family and we're having it in the city so their children can attend. But it's going to be extravagant. Walker's already promised something over-the-top and obnoxious because he's so relieved to see me settling down."

"Ha!" Penny said. "We'll show him."

Agnes held up her hand so Penny could slap it. "That's my girl. But I want all the pomp and drama, even if it's just us and our nearest and dearest. They're already being tacky and making us sound like a tired cliche on social media so we're going to have a big, glamorous, *private* wedding and rub their judgmental noses in it."

"Then, eight tiers it is!" Evelyn said as she crossed something out on her clipboard. "We're going to need a lot of whipped coconut cream. I'll also be preparing hundreds of dark chocolate-dipped strawberries for the cake and to serve with champagne," she noted.

Agnes groaned in approval. "I knew we could trust you."

Evelyn winked as she put an arm around Penny and gave her a tight hug. "Only the best for my little girl," she said firmly, but she coughed and her eyes watered as she studied her clipboard.

Penny felt Evelyn's mood dip and sensed a hard ache in her center. "I love you so much, Evie!" She knew Evelyn missed her daughter, Michelle. Penny had never met Morris's twin sister before her death, but her loss still hurt. It was impossible not to fall in love with Michelle as Penny got to know Morris and the Mosbys better. She pulled Evelyn close and held her tight. "I'm so, so sorry!" Penny whispered.

"There isn't a day that goes by that I don't miss her, but God sent you and Penn so we could help each other heal and be strong again together." Evelyn took a deep breath and gave Penny's nose a gentle flick. "And you're just going to have to put up with me. Your mother isn't here to look after you, so it's my job to make sure my sweet girl gets the wedding of her dreams."

"Thank you so much." Penny didn't have the heart to tell Evelyn that she didn't care as long as she didn't have to wear a big, silly dress and stand still for a long ceremony in a stuffy old church. Agnes wasn't pushing for a traditional ceremony either, so Penny was willing to compromise and put up with some pomp and drama if it made her happy.

And who knows? A little glamor and extravagance might be fun for a day.

Penny shrugged, then wondered who she was or what had gotten into her.

Love. Love had gotten into her, and Penny was realizing that love had the power to make people change and do the strangest things. Like, offer to get rid of your housekeeping staff or get excited about a fancy, expensive wedding.

"I want lots of strawberries and lots and lots of flowers," Penny declared, fully embracing her inner bridezilla.

"I think we can manage that," Evelyn said, nodding at Agnes.

"Oh, you'll get your flowers," Agnes vowed. "I won't rest until it looks like Monet threw up in Manhattan."

That earned another pleased nod from Evelyn. "Perfect."

No one had ever made such a big deal about dinky old Penny Lane Tucker before. And while she didn't think she'd ever wanted that kind of attention or special treatment, she felt precious and truly cherished as she listened to Agnes and Evelyn plan a fairytale wedding.

She excused herself, saying she'd be better at helping June pick frosting flavors and sprinkles for her cupcake. Penny was happy to entrust Agnes and Evelyn with all the big decisions, but she needed a moment to pinch herself and take it all in.

This wasn't the life she'd expected, and Agnes wasn't the partner Penny had envisioned. She certainly hadn't imagined she'd walk into Slice Of Evelyn and order an eight-tier wedding cake *and be excited about it*. But there Penny was about to jump out of her skin at the thought of chocolate-covered strawberries and wedding venues.

She was also tickled that Agnes's intimidating brother had been the ringleader of the matchmaking cabal that had brought Penny to The Killian House. He was delighted when he learned that Penny had proposed and warned that he was going to make a *very* big deal about their engagement and wedding.

Penny found June in the midst of an eight-year-old's wildest dream, decorating her ultimate cupcake with an entire bakery's kitchen and staff at her beck and call. Frosting, sprinkles, edible flower petals, and filling samples were spread on the worktable around her. She was deeply absorbed as she tasted different combinations of flavors and scribbled on a clipboard.

"Need any help?" Penny asked, but June shook her head.

"I think I've narrowed it down. I just need to choose between custard filling or coconut cream."

"That's a big decision," Penny said heavily, holding up her hands as she backed away and went to see how Agnes and Evelyn were doing. "How's it going, ladies?" They turned to her with wide smiles. Evelyn whispered a quick prayer as she grabbed Penny's hand. "What happened?" Penny asked warily.

Evelyn gave her hand a reassuring squeeze. "Agnes told me what she's got in mind and I...*love this*, but you should brace yourself."

"Brace myself?" Penny looked at Agnes and then at Evelyn.

Agnes grabbed Penny's other hand. "I'd like to invite *Shout* magazine to follow us as we plan the rest of the wedding and to document our big day."

"What?" Penny laughed, her neck craning suspiciously. "Why on dogs' green earth would we want to do that?" It sounded like her worst nightmare.

Agnes and Evelyn took turns nudging each other forcefully before Agnes threw her hands up.

"Because I want to give you lots and lots of money, like *a million dollars*, for your dream camp. I know you won't take my money because you want to do this on your own. But what if we could make good use of all the unwanted attention? People like Muriel and her nephew are going to make a lot of noise and spill as much gossip as they can so they can steal a little attention for themselves. Melinda's made a few calls and *Shout* magazine would pay good money for exclusive access. Think about how much free publicity this could be for Camp Laurel. I bet we could fund *hundreds* of scholarships off of this."

"Hold on." Penny's left eye squeezed shut and she checked her conscience. Could she really sell access to something as sacred as her wedding to raise a million dollars for Camp Laurel and fund *hundreds* of scholarships? "I'm in. We're just talking about photographers and a few journalists, right?"

"Let's not get hung up on details," Agnes said, waving dismissively as Evelyn offered Penny a chocolate-covered strawberry.

"It's vegan! I was thinking we could have a cascade of them like a croquembouche with threads of spun *dark chocolate*," she said with a loaded look at Agnes.

"That's genius!" Agnes declared enthusiastically and Penny nodded as she took a bite and chewed. Because it was, and it *would* be a waste if the world didn't get to witness Evelyn's brilliance in pictures, at least.

"What about a whole piece about the cake and how Evie came up with it for us? It would be a great way to include the bakery in the coverage," Penny said, earning a groan of approval from Agnes.

"I knew you'd get it and be ready to run with this once we explained. Just think of what *we* could do together if we harnessed all the goodwill and asskissing that's about to come our way."

Penny's heart felt like it would burst as she imagined the rows of cabins and all the bunk beds. She could see the canoes, fishing poles, and all the little life jackets. And she could already hear the silly camp songs and smell the bonfire by the lake at night. "That's going to take months of planning and I'll have to be away all summer," she warned, glancing at Agnes. "You'd be okay with that?"

"Okay?" Agnes caught Penny's hand again and reeled her in. "Absolutely. We'll be depriving the city of its most enchanting nanny but this way, you can carry on your mother's memory and share your love of nature with hundreds of foster kids. I'm more than *okay* with that, Penny Lane. And June and I will be coming with you. We can't wait to make *your* dream our family's next big adventure." Her thumb swiped Penny's cheek and she realized she was crying. Agnes shushed softly and winced. "We might have to talk to Penn about another room and a few more upgrades to the cabin since we'll be spending more time there."

"I'm willing to compromise since I get my girls and my dream camp. I really love you, Agnes Cameron," Penny sighed as she offered her lips.

"I love you, too. And we won't change too much. There's a lot of magic in that cabin."

The End

Epilogue

O*ne year later...*

The media and the internet had declared it New York City's "royal wedding" after Agnes and Penny were married at The Killian House. Walker had set out to make a statement and had wanted the world to know how happy and proud he was to see his big sister finally find her soulmates. The three of them, along with Walker, Fin, and the triplets, were the Cameron family's present and represented its beautiful future.

An army consisting of two wedding planners and their assistants, a catering team, and a landscaping crew had transformed the back garden into an extravagant fairytale, but the guest list had been very short. Only close friends and family had been invited to experience the magic and celebrate with the brides and June.

There were plenty of photographers and videographers,

though. Dash had been their communications director and the editorial team at *Shout* had run everything through him. As Penny's best man and a social media savant, he was in charge of supervising all filming. He had enlisted June as his "assistant" so she could be "behind the camera" and choose when and where her likeness was used. The two had done a brilliant job and the photos and videos had made Agnes and Penny's wedding the most exclusive event of the season that almost no one had the good fortune of attending.

Agnes had been true to her word and The Killian House's back garden was filled with flowers. But, instead of a Parisian garden, Walker had spent a small fortune turning the back lawn into a field of wildflowers that must have attracted every butterfly in the state, there were so many. There were also massive wildflower arrangements spilling from rustic barrels, and Penn had built a beautiful arbor that had been draped with even more flowers. He also built long benches for the guests and a swing for the brides to sit on during the reception. The swing had been a wedding gift and went with them to the cabin when they returned there for their honeymoon.

The wedding itself had been short on ceremony but big on romance. Agnes wore a vintage Dior sage green silk and lace gown that made her look like fairytale royalty, according to Penny and the girls.

Walker escorted Agnes down the aisle as a string quartet from the New York Philharmonic played "I'll Stand By You." Agnes's waterproof mascara was put to the test when he had cried and hugged her tight. "I've wanted this for you as much as I wanted it for myself. Live *happily* ever after, Aggie. You deserve it."

"I will," she vowed.

Then, Agnes turned into a sniffling mess when Penny appeared on the terrace with Gus and the quartet played

"Penny Lane." Penn had taken one of their grandmother's floral dresses and turned it into a striking pant and halter ensemble with a long scarf train for Penny. Everyone was moved as the Tucker siblings walked down the aisle with Gus. Penny carried her mother's fishing pole instead of a traditional bouquet, but flowers and ribbons had been wound around the handle. She had never looked more radiant as she passed it to Gus, who was sobbing ecstatically as he kissed her and Agnes's cheeks before Penn helped him into a waiting wheelchair.

They exchanged their vows as June looked on and cried from her spot next to Walker. She had the rings and was ready to help Agnes and Penny when it was time. All three were crying tears of utter joy when Agnes and Penny were declared married and were immediately surrounded by tearful well-wishers.

Walker and Agnes's parents clapped sedately in their chairs before being wheeled away and transported back to Connecticut. Agnes was pleased that they could come, but it meant the world to her that Walker had arranged for Camilla to attend. And he'd surprised everyone, including the Tuckers, by arranging for Mabel and Silas to come down from Cherrytown for the wedding. Penn and Penny were convinced they'd never come to the city and had been overjoyed.

Of course, Reid Marshall was there, along with the agency's other nannies. Fin, Riley *and* Giles Ashby came, and the reclusive billionaire even danced with his husband. Morris Mosby was at the wedding with his parents, but the highlight for the group seemed to be when Dash talked Gavin into "just one dance" toward the end of the evening that had turned into two.

But it was the photoshoot and the resulting spread that had occurred a week later in *Shout* magazine that Agnes was most proud of. The headline said it all:

New York's new royal family: the next queens of Manhattan

June looked like a fierce little queen in a purple velvet jumpsuit and matching cape. She was wearing a crown and standing on one of the ladders in The Killian House's grand library. Agnes and Penny were posed next to the ladder, projecting grace and elegance. Agnes wore a matching purple jumpsuit and cape, but her jumpsuit had a plunging neckline that went all the way to her navel and hugged her willowy curves.

Once again, Penn had created a whimsical purple and teal off-the-shoulder gown for Penny from vintage treasures. She looked like a wild but fearsome fairy princess with deep purple roses braided into her hair. An antique scepter completed the look and Agnes got chills whenever she beheld Penny's direct, unapologetic gaze as she stared down the camera.

Penny no longer harbored any fears of being a sellout. She used the accompanying interview to raise awareness of Camp

Laurel and the number of children in the foster care system. There were many more children like June in homes like Mary Wilson's in Harlem who dreamed of being adopted and living happily ever after. Penny was building them a camp on Cherry Lake where they could escape the city for a few weeks of exploring and fishing in the Catskills.

Their family was also thriving as they settled into their new life together at East 63rd. June loved her new school and had started The Young Librarians Club with help from Dash. Her young librarians were partnering with local libraries to inspire kids to read more with fun extracurricular programs and reading challenges. She had a tight circle of friends, including the triplets and Milo Ashby, Riley's stepson. June was well-liked by her peers and teachers because she was warm, kind, and outgoing.

There was much for Agnes to be grateful for and she had a feeling she owed Reid Marshall. That was why Agnes was now standing outside of Briarwood Terrace on a sunny afternoon in early September, pondering how she could ever repay him. She had eventually ferreted out all the details about how Walker and Pennsylvania were the main culprits behind hers and Penny's "downfall." But Reid had been the one to set the wheels in motion and had sacrificed yet another one of his superb nannies to matrimony.

She had requested an appointment, and could tell Reid was still wary when he buzzed her into the lobby. Agnes had visited once before with Walker so she knew the general layout. She offered the drowsy doorman a quick wave as she passed, taking a left at the grand staircase to the converted conservatory apartment. It was a charming place and Agnes was truly glad to be there.

She found Reid waiting, leaning against his door with his arms folded and his brow arched.

"Mrs. Cameron." He gave her a deferential nod and kissed her cheek, waving her in. "To what do I owe the pleasure? You were rather vague when you called earlier."

"Because I've come to apologize and I knew you'd tell me there was no need and not to waste my time." She strolled past the leather sofa and armchairs and into the kitchen with Reid on her heels.

"But there isn't any need and it *is* a waste of your time as far as I can tell..." He was scratching his head, an irritated look on his face. "We talked at your wedding a few weeks ago and I told you it was cool, that I was happy for you and Penny and June."

"And I told you that we weren't finished discussing this," she countered, earning a grumble from Reid as he went to the refrigerator.

"Champagne?" He asked and she hummed in confirmation as she sat on the window seat next to the little round table. "What else?" He said with a chuckle.

Agnes shrugged and thanked him when he handed her a flute and took the seat across from hers. "I have so much to celebrate these days, thanks to you," she said, holding her glass out.

He frowned as he tapped his glass against hers. "That was all Walker and Penn. I wasn't sure if it would even work and I did not want to be on your shit list when you came looking for revenge."

"At least you had the good sense to see that this had the potential to be a disaster," she said, but he wagged a finger at her.

"I never doubted that you and Penny *could* work or that you were exactly what Penny deserved. I just didn't know if you were ready to settle down or if you really wanted to."

"No. I don't think I did..." Agnes conceded. "I wanted to be a mother, but I wanted to do *everything* on my own terms." A mature relationship or monogamy hadn't been part of the equation when Agnes set out to create her own family. If she was being truthful, she wasn't sure if she was even capable before, and had just assumed that she'd put her roaming on hold until June was in college. "Now, I can't imagine my life without Penny and I know that June and I wouldn't be as happy or as close as we are now if it weren't for her."

"Maybe," Reid said with a shrug. "You have the right instincts when it comes to parenting, you just needed someone to hone those and help you make the most of them."

"Thank you," Agnes said, then took a long sip, using the time to recover. That was very high praise, coming from Reid Marshall. He was an expert in families and children, with degrees in psychology and education and extensive experience as an educator and a nanny. And his and Fin's parents were celebrity psychologists. Reid had seen every type of parent and cared for families of all sorts so he was much more than a casual observer. "I know you don't like me enough to blow smoke up my ass," she added.

"What are you talking about?" He asked as he reared back. "I adore you, Agnes, and I wouldn't have trusted you with Penny's heart if I didn't think you had a decent one of your own. I love that girl like she's my sister," he said and looked around before leaning across the table. "But I never envied Penn because..." Reid whistled loudly. "I can't tell you how many times she's almost made me faint by pulling something living out of her pocket or eating something dubious she found in a dumpster or—"

"*What?*" Agnes interrupted.

Reid nodded and widened his eyes. "*I know.* She truly is a wild child. And while I wasn't sure if you were ready to settle down or would appreciate Penn and Walker's meddling, I knew you were one of the few people in the city who could keep up with her."

"I didn't know about her eating out of dumpsters," Agnes said, grimacing into her champagne. "This is nearly empty. Please tell me there was more than one bottle."

"Coming right up!" Reid said, hopping to his feet to get her a refill. "Everything's going to be fine because she's got you and June now to direct all her wild, creative energy toward. Your family is her new adventure and Penny knows she has responsibilities now. She can't take risks like she used to and June needs a stable routine," he explained as he poured.

That all made sense and sounded like Penny as well. "Thank goodness," Agnes whispered before taking a sip.

"People change. Look at you," he said as he returned to his seat and reclined.

"Indeed. It took me fifty-three years, but I think I've finally grown up."

"Not too much, I hope," Reid said with a wink, making Agnes laugh.

"Not too much! I've never feared aging, I just didn't want to turn into my parents. Especially my mother," she added, wincing at how ridiculous she'd been. "I thought that the only way I could prevent that was by acting like a perpetual child and turning my nose up at them every chance I could. But I've realized that I'll never be my mother because I care enough to...care."

"You care a lot, Agnes. The whole city knows you're a pill, but everyone also knows you're devoted to your family and you'll fight anyone who says a bad word about your brother. I've always respected that about you. That's why I was so pleased when I heard you were adopting. I knew you'd be a great mom and that some lucky kiddo was getting a hell of a family."

"We are such a *good* family now," Agnes said, her voice catching with emotion. Reid reached across the table and grabbed her hand. She held onto it and squeezed his hand back affectionately. "Walker has always taken good care of us and tried his best, but calling you was *the best* thing he's ever done. You saved us when you sent Fin to The Killian House and then you saved me when you sent Penny Lane."

Reid made a dismissive sound as he leaned over the table. "I don't believe in destiny or divine intervention, but I believe that Fin was meant to go there. He was made for Walker and the girls. And I wouldn't have this agency if it hadn't been for Walker. He gave me that final nudge and he was the one who set everything in motion by hiring professionals to help me get this thing off the ground."

"But it can't help that we keep stealing your best nannies," Agnes argued with a sheepish smile, but he laughed and waved it off.

"I haven't had a hard time recruiting nannies. You'd be surprised at how rampant discrimination is in this city," he said sarcastically and rolled his eyes. "And it turns out there are *a lot* of good caregivers who want to feel safe and respected in the work environment. But that's neither here nor there because Fin and Penny aren't employees to me. They're my family and so are you, Walker, and your girls. You're my family and I'd never put business before your happiness," he added simply, touching Agnes.

"I'm so glad and truly grateful," she said, then took a mental step back and paused. Reid was family now and Agnes wondered what or *who* he was waiting for. She sensed that like she had before Penny, he was feeling less needed as his brothers and sisters found love and moved on with their lives. "What about you?" She asked, keeping her tone just curious and only mildly concerned. He didn't need to know that Agnes already had a few candidates in mind.

He gave her a hard look and pointed. "Don't even think

about it. I like my life just the way it is. Men are messy and distracting and I have a good system. Everything has a place and everything stays neatly separated," he explained, using his hands to create imaginary boxes, then pushing them apart and away from him. "Simple and tidy. That's how I like it." He punctuated the declaration with a satisfied nod.

Agnes hummed along and raised her glass in salute, but she was looking forward to upending Reid's well-organized life. She was already calculating and rejecting possible contenders for Reid's affections. Only a man of the highest quality would do. Agnes inwardly cringed because while she knew a lot of wealthy, eligible men, most of them had rather dark and dubious reputations.

"To simple and tidy," Agnes said as she raised her glass. She'd see Reid tied up and simply happy within a year or her name wasn't Agnes Eleanor Fuller Tucker-Cameron.

"Amen," Reid agreed as his glass tapped Agnes's, oblivious that the clock was ticking.

Welcome to Camp Laurel!

Chapter 1

nother year later...

Agnes Cameron had so many *good* things these days it was getting hard for her to count all of her blessings. She had an amazing little girl and a wife she adored. Their home was filled with love and laughter and was often the loudest on East 63rd Street. Especially when one of their many brothers—biological, through marriage, or honorary—dropped by with their children. Agnes was now an aunt to several girls and boys and she took every opportunity she could to spoil them.

But it was the twelve brand new cabins, arranged in a horseshoe and facing Cherry Lake, that Agnes was particularly proud of at the moment. There were eight cabins with three sets of bunk beds in each and there were four cabins for the twelve counselors. They were scheduled to arrive early the next morning on two school buses that had been refurbished and painted in bright, rainbow colors.

There was a larger cabin for the camp's office and the nurse's station and a dining hall with indoor and outdoor dining areas. In addition to two swimming pools and tennis and basketball courts, there was a little amphitheater with a stage for talent shows, singalongs, magic acts, and award ceremonies. Four pavilions had been built for classes and activities like crafts and games and there was a clubhouse with arcade games and foosball tables as well as a small theater for movie nights when the weather turned inclement.

And campers could go to the June Cameron Library & Resource Center to check out books, relax, and talk to a counselor if they had any questions or needed someone to talk to. The staff, including two therapists, a librarian, and two teachers operated June's library and resource center as a dedicated safe place for campers to learn about anything and get help with *any* problem. And they'd get confidentiality, if needed. The entire staff, with the exception of Penny and Dash, were former foster kids and all were committed to providing a fun, loving, safe, and healthy environment for Camp Laurel's guests.

Penn, Gus, and Silas had acted as advisors, but a professional architect and a construction company had been hired to build the state-of-the art facility. Penny wanted only the best for her campers and this was a massive job. It had taken almost a year to plan and complete, and Penny and Agnes had invited *everyone* to celebrate the camp's grand opening with a barbecue and a bonfire the night before the first campers arrived.

Agnes couldn't contain her pride as Walker and Fin arrived with the triplets in their Range Rover. Riley and Milo Ashby—Giles stayed behind at the Olympia with Milos's little sister, Luna—rode along with Penn, Morris, and Cadence. Agnes boasted about the cheerful and airy cabins and the "meditation" huts Penny had designed with the architect. And you would have thought Agnes was showing off her collection of Louboutins, she was so excited as she led Walker and the girls down to the dock to see all the canoes, paddle boats, and the rows and rows of brightly-colored life jackets in the boathouse.

Her pride and excitement was all for Penny. She had put every single penny she had received from *Shout* and the resulting donations to fund her dream camp and tuition for *ten* summer seasons! Penny was already thinking about opening another camp because there had been so much enthusiastic support from donors. And there had been more demand than they were anticipating. They received applications from all over the city and Penny's new goal was to have enough bunk beds to never turn away a camper.

Even with all the planning meetings, counselor interviews, and checks to sign, Penny made time to clear several trails with Penn, Dash, and a team of engineers, a conservationist, and a universal design expert so they were safe and free of dangerous obstacles and poison ivy. Signs had been posted throughout the camp and along the trails describing local plants and their uses. There were also little decks with recommended yoga poses, benches with Laurel's favorite poems carved into them, and climbing stations with zip lines all around the camp's eight acres.

Penny had asked for June's input and the two of them had built a bright, peaceful oasis for foster kids ranging from age eight to eighteen to play and explore in the country. The accommodations were just as comfortable as the state's best summer camps, but the campers never paid a cent of tuition and all of their meals and boarding costs were completely covered. She had to sacrifice her trademark retro/punk/recycled aesthetic for safety, but Camp Laurel was still bursting with Penny's bright, happy wholesomeness.

It felt like the quiet before a beautiful storm as Agnes checked June's sleeping bag and pillow. She was staying the night in one of the camp's new counselors' cabins along with Walker, Fin, and the triplets. Penn, Morris, Cadence, Riley, Milo, and Dash were in the cabins next door.

The weekend was also a celebration of Agnes and Penny's anniversary. They would be leaving June with her uncles and taking the boat across the lake for a quiet evening alone in the Tucker Family cabin. It was the first time Agnes was leaving June for a night and she was nervous, but it felt like another important milestone for them. June was excited about a sleepover with her cousins and she felt safe enough with her squad of uncles to spend a night without Agnes. There was a walkietalkie tucked into June's sleeping bag and Agnes had its partner by her pillow, in case of a bedtime emergency. Penny had predicted that June would be fine, but was expecting that Agnes would need to check in frequently. Agnes would show them, she vowed.

The old cabin had undergone a few upgrades but Penn and Silas handled those under Gus's supervision. Another room had been attached off the kitchen and the downstairs bedrooms and the bathroom now had doors since they were all spending more time there together. They had brought a daybed up for Gus and the old swing on the back porch had been repaired and was seeing use again. There was a real footpath down to the dock and Penn had added a lounge chair and shade for Agnes. It had a plaque that read "Cleopatra of the Catskills" and it was Agnes's favorite spot to sunbathe while Penny was on the lake with June.

Other than that, very little had changed up at the family cabin in Cherrytown. Agnes, Penny, and June went up there for long weekends, but still visited the Camerons' "cottage" in Sagaponack and spent most of the holidays with Camilla. After they did their duty at the family estate in Connecticut, of course.

Agnes often called Mabel to keep her and Silas posted on Penny, Penn, and June's adventures in the city. The three stayed busy so Agnes had plenty of excuses to call and enjoyed her chats with Mabel. She taught Agnes how to make several different types of jams and fruit butters and Penny's favorite vegan biscuits and cornbread.

Her world had gotten smaller in that Agnes rarely moved in the same circles as Muriel Hormsby and her ilk these days. She rarely went to parties or attended fundraisers unless they were for Camp Laurel. But her world was so much bigger now because Agnes had a large extended family and a wider circle of *real* friends who kept her busy and often took her from the city. And she lived for her weekends in the country with Penny and June.

They were her world but they were currently giving Fin and the triplets a tour of the hiking trails with Penn, Morris, Cadence, and Dash. Walker opted out of the hike and was on the porch admiring the view of the lake. He was also enjoying Silas's wine and raised his Mason jar in salute when Agnes joined him.

"I can see why you've grown so attached to this place," he said, nodding toward the lake. He'd traded his usual suit and tie for a red flannel shirt, jeans, and boots, and Agnes thought he looked dashing and somewhat outdoorsy. "It doesn't get more beautiful than that."

Agnes made a knowing sound as she leaned against him and stole a sip of his wine. "Wait until tonight and all the stars come out. The lake will be full of them."

A bonfire and s'mores were planned before Agnes and Penny took off for the other side of the lake. They'd enjoy a peaceful night and breakfast in bed, then take the boat back to prepare for the arrival of their first campers. The buses were due at 10:00 so everyone could get settled into their cabins before lunch and opening activities.

"I'd *love* to help Penny build more of these camps," he said and Agnes nodded and wound her arm around his.

"She's already planning the next one and thinking about how to raise the money."

"Will we be having another wedding or can I just write her a check this time?" He asked, making Agnes laugh as she led him down the steps and turned him toward a hammock that had been hung between two trees.

"You know, I think I could talk *Shout* into covering the city's most romantic and expensive vow renewal, but it would probably be the end of my marriage," Agnes mused.

Walker chuckled but frowned when she halted them in front of the hammock. "I don't know, Aggie... Are you certain it's safe?"

"Of course!" Agnes snorted and looked around for help but everyone was off hiking with Penny and Penn. Agnes had *almost* gotten the hang of getting in and out of the hammock by herself... "Children and hippies can operate these. I'm sure we can figure it out," she said, turning and using one arm to hold the hammock open.

He took a long sip from his jar, grimacing as he watched Agnes awkwardly lower herself and recline on the hammock with her feet still in contact with the ground. She got into a somewhat comfortable position and raised a brow, daring Walker to join her.

He shook his head. "You look like you've got that all worked out and I'm not sure if there's enough room," he said, stepping back and shaking his head again. "I'll just hang out here where it's safe."

"Don't be a chicken! It's perfectly safe," she said and patted the hammock next to her. "And it's three feet off the ground. What's the worst that could happen?"

"How many times have I heard that?" He muttered into his wine before turning and cautiously backing up. Walker reached back and held onto the hammock as he sat.

"Ouch!" Agnes complained when he grabbed her hair instead of the edge of the fabric.

"Just a moment! Why does it have to move?"

"It's not that complicated. Just sit down!" She gave his arm a yank but her foot slipped and the hammock swung forward and clipped the back of his knees, toppling him. Walker fell back, taking Agnes and the hammock with them. They were swiftly rolled and dumped onto the ground on the other side.

Walker immediately popped up and brushed the dirt off his hands and knees. His shirt was soaked in wine but he was still holding the jar. He gave Agnes's elbow a tug, hauling her up and onto her feet.

"Thank you," she said as she quickly dusted off her backside and knees. Both looked around to make sure they hadn't been seen.

"We speak of this to no one," Walker said out of the side of his mouth. Agnes nodded and held up her pinkie.

"This goes with us to the grave," she agreed.

They locked pinkies before they burst into laughter. "At least my shirt is red and I can blame it on you if anyone notices," he murmured as he turned back toward the cabin. "I think we need to try that again, but I'll get more wine first," he said and Agnes nodded.

"That should help," she said dubiously but was willing to give it another go if he was.

Half an hour later, they were safely swinging in the hammock and enjoying their wine and a cool breeze. "And you say Penny's uncle Silas makes this in that wonky little cabin across the lake?" He asked as he held up the jar, sounding impressed.

"I told you, this place is magic, and Silas and Mabel are lovely people."

Walker sighed happily as he put an arm around her. "To the Tuckers," he said, and Agnes hummed in agreement as she tapped her jar against his.

"To our wild and wonderful Tuckers."

Walker chuckled and it turned into genuine laughter. "Penn told me we'd be family one day when we first met. He said he had a premonition and at the time, I was inclined to believe he was high."

"He probably was," Agnes noted and Walker nodded.

"Probably, but I knew he was right the moment I laid eyes on his sister."

"You did not!"

"I did," Walker insisted. "I saw that wild, beautiful girl and I thought 'Now, there's someone who could catch *my* wild, beautiful girl's eye and tame her heart.' And I could tell she'd caught your interest by the way you stared and stumbled. I just had to make sure you two met a few more times before it stuck because you're both hedonists," he said with a pointed look at Agnes. "I swear, it would have been easier to herd kittens or the triplets."

"But not as much fun," Agnes observed, smiling as she recalled all the fun she'd had with Penny before they stopped pretending they weren't head over heels. Then, Agnes remembered going literally head over heels and tumbling down the hill because she'd tried to impress Penny. "And I wouldn't have learned as much about myself or life, I suspect."

"You have... I wouldn't say that you've calmed down because you're just as difficult as ever," he began, and a warm smile stretched across his face. "But you do seem to know yourself so much better and you don't seem as lost as you used to. I used to worry that you'd never forgive yourself for your mistakes and that you were too afraid of turning into our mother to take a chance. You always thrilled at being reckless because it made our parents and their friends uncomfortable, but you'd never risk your heart. That stayed safely tucked away and I never sensed any joy until the triplets came along," he said softly.

Agnes nodded and wiped a stray tear from her cheek. "You were the only bright spots in my world and I was afraid of turning into a fifth wheel as you and Fin and the girls became more of a happy family and they got older."

"I understand why you'd feel that way but you know that we love you, Aggie, and I wouldn't have survived without you."

"I know." She hugged his middle and rested her head on his chest. "How long has it been since it was just the two of us like this?"

"I don't know...a few years," Walker guessed, then kissed her hair. "Too long. I'm so happy for you, but I've missed you since you went and got yourself a big, beautiful life."

"I've missed you too," she said, and laughed softly. "It really is a big, beautiful life."

"It is. We're both very lucky."

As if on cue, Penny and Fin skipped into camp, arm-in-arm and singing about worms and butterflies. June and the triplets were giggling and skipping along with them as Penn, Morris, and Dash brought up the rear. An even bigger smile spread across Walker's face and he pushed out a deeply satisfied breath. His arm tightened around Agnes as he watched their spouses and their children singing, laughing, and teasing each other.

"Look at our family!" Agnes whispered, her eyes filling with tears.

"It's amazing and I'm so grateful," Walker said sincerely. His voice had crumbled into a ragged mumble.

Agnes knew that he was thinking of Connor and gave him a moment. She felt him push out a slow breath and took time to ride her own wave of grief. There wasn't a day that went by that she didn't miss her best friend and she missed him most at times like these. She would get so *angry* because June and Penny would never know how brilliant and magical *he* was, and she couldn't tell Connor all the things she loved about them. Agnes's heart broke all over again because she couldn't imagine how much worse it was for Walker.

But, then she'd remember that Connor was watching and she knew that he was so happy and so proud of how much she and Walker had grown. She'd think about all the wonderful memories and how lucky they were that Connor was theirs. Amelia, Beatrice, and Charlotte were his "terrible" triplets after all. They were his idea, and Agnes and Walker never would have gotten into any of this if Connor hadn't been so adamant that the three of them were ready to have kids.

"I didn't think life could be this good," she said, feeling incredibly lucky as they attempted to extricate themselves from the hammock. But it turned out that they were only lucky in love, not hammock navigation. Agnes leaned forward at the same time as Walker, rolling them face-first onto the grass, causing an explosion of laughter and officially immortalizing the two of them as the camp's biggest klutzes.

Chapter 2

"June, this is Team Captain, over," Agnes said as she held the walkie-talkie to her ear like a phone.

"This is June, Team Captain! Hi, Mom!" June laughed through the little speaker, making Agnes smile. "We just finished telling stories and Dash and Penn put out the bonfire. We're all in our sleeping bags now."

"Okay. I love you and I'll see you in the morning."

"I love you too, Mommy!"

"Goodnight, sweetheart, over."

"Goodnight! This is June, out!"

Agnes laughed softly as she set the walkie-talkie on the bedside table. She started to reach for it again, then shook her head and turned back to Penny. "She's having such a good time! And the triplets love it here."

"I knew they would!" Penny swung her wet hair over her shoulder and laid on her side, propping her head up on her palm. "I'm so glad they could come and test everything out for us before the campers get here tomorrow. I could tell they were having fun and I know if they're impressed, we're in really good shape."

"Oh, they were! And Walker's so impressed too!" Agnes said excitedly as she pushed Penny onto her back. She threw a leg over Penny's hips, straddling her, then ducked and kissed Penny slowly and thoroughly, sucking on her lip as their hands wandered. "I know how much you like doing things on your own, but I think you should let him help you with the next camp."

"Hmm... You might be able to convince me." Penny had already made her point with Camp Laurel and was assured that her mother's legacy would live on. Penny was beyond proud and satisfied with her efforts, but it had been *a lot* of work. Now, she was on a mission to expand and build more camps because it hurt her heart knowing they'd turned away so many campers. She hadn't expected so many city kids would be excited about leaving the internet and air conditioning behind for the country. But the response had been incredible and there was no getting around the fact that she'd need more money and a lot of it. Penny had planned to ask Walker if he could help her once they had their first season under their belt and had all the operational bugs worked out.

"Walker's ready to write you a check right now," Agnes whispered against Penny's lips, making them curve into a smile.

"He really is a lovely person and a truly excellent brother-in-law."

"Trust me, people pester him all the time for money and it's rarely for anything as worthwhile as this."

"Thank you for believing in me," Penny said, sliding her hands under Agnes's camisole. She was still in awe of how soft Agnes's skin was and still got high on the way she smelled and the sounds she made when she was turned on. "But I don't want to think about anything but you right now. It's our anniversary," she noted and Penny was just as proud that she'd convinced someone as ethereal as Agnes to be hers as she was of Camp Laurel. Holding her on the eve of the camp's grand opening was like winning two gold medals at the life Olympics.

Penny wasn't even thirty-five and yet, she'd made her dream camp a reality. *And* she was married to the fearless goddess of her dreams. She had achieved her professional goals and knew that brighter things were in Camp Laurel's future. *And* she had an incredible family with Agnes and June. She had it all, but Penny wanted to pinch herself every time she touched Agnes because it was hard to believe she was real and that their beautiful life wasn't a dream.

They were planning a big snowboarding trip to Lake Placid with Penn and Morris in the winter and they were taking a road trip to the Grand Canyon for spring break. Agnes wanted to take a private jet, but Penny wanted to drive and camp along the way so June could see more of the country. Compromise came in the form of a swanky RV that belonged to a friend of Agnes's who owned a NASCAR team. He was glad to loan it to them as it had only been used for a handful of hours and was going to waste in a hangar.

But those were the sorts of compromises Penny and Agnes had learned to make and there was no telling what their next adventure would be. Penny loved that about being married to Agnes. Anything was possible because like Penny, Agnes wasn't afraid to stumble and she was always ready to learn and grow. She wasn't afraid to put on a helmet and some elbow pads and learn how to skate with Morris and June. And there was the time she'd burned the bejeezus out of herself making jam over the phone with Mabel.

Agnes was truly fearless and she was never what was expected of her. That was why she made Penny tremble and why Penny felt like she was ten feet tall when they were out.

She was so proud of *her* woman and there was no doubting that Agnes was Penny's. She doted on Penny and stole her away for romantic walks. Agnes had to have listened and been taking notes whenever Penny described an exciting plant or one of her favorite crystals. Penny would find a rare plant cutting or a stunning crystal on her pillow a few evenings later. Penny had no clue where Agnes found them. But they always left her touched and teary-eyed because Agnes had listened and truly understood Penny.

And, boy, was she pretty. Penny still felt like she'd drunk a whole jug of Silas's wine and rolled down the hill when she stared at Agnes.

"I can't believe you're mine," she said, her thumbs brushing over Agnes's nipples. They pebbled and Agnes panted against Penny's lips and nodded.

"From the moment I first laid eyes on you, I've never wanted anyone like that." Her hand slipped between them and into Penny's panties. She parted Penny's folds, getting her fingers slick and stroking her clit. There was a frustrated grunt from Agnes as she withdrew her hand and quickly tugged the garment down Penny's legs and cast it aside. "That's better."

"So much better," Penny said. She gasped in delight as Agnes's head dipped and she sucked on Penny's nipple. Long, graceful fingers filled Penny's pussy, stretching and winding her tighter and tighter. They were hot and wet as she teased Penny's ass, tracing the tight pucker and making her whimper and swear.

"Like this?" Agnes asked as she slowly and gently fingered Penny.

Penny shook her head frantically, wet strands of hair sticking to her cheeks. "More! Fuck my ass harder, Aggie!" She begged. Penny couldn't help it, she swore *a lot* when Aggie played with her ass and the longer they were together, the more comfortable they got with ass play. That was another reason why Penny *liked* being married. There wasn't a part of Agnes's body that Penny hadn't cherished and memorized. She knew exactly what buttons to push to drive Agnes wild, and she knew how to make Penny howl.

And howl was just what Penny did because there was no one but Silas and Mabel on that side of the lake to hear them and they went down before the sun and slept like rocks. Agnes's tongue beat against Penny's clit as her fingers thrust, twisting and stoking until they were both alight and sweating.

"Come with me!" Penny reached for Agnes, craving her lips and her breasts as heat and need threatened to overwhelm them. "I'm so close but I need you."

Agnes rose on her hands and knees, licking and kissing her way to Penny's lips. "I always need you."

They kissed as Agnes's legs slid around Penny's and their hips angled, seeking relief. Agnes's pussy was wet and soft as it slid against Penny's, her hands wicked as they pinched and strummed. Penny wiggled until she could lap and suck on one of Agnes's nipples and found heaven.

"I love you so much!" Agnes's voice wavered as one of her hands curved around Penny's head and the other gripped her ass tight, locking their pelvises together as she bucked faster.

Penny could only nod and push out a breathless squeak. Her mouth was full of Agnes's luscious breast and the pressure swelling in her core, and the hot flickering of her nerves was intense and consuming. Penny felt like she was being pulled into it as Agnes panted her name and chanted the F-word.

"Oh... *Penny.* Fuck!" Agnes's head snapped back and Penny forced her eyes open so she could watch. She was usually too lost in the moment and caught up in her own body and missed it, but Agnes was exquisite when she came. Her lips and thighs quivered and goosebumps spilled down her breasts and her willowy limbs. And Agnes's pale skin was dewy, almost pearlescent in the warm glow of the lamp and string lights.

"Mine." The word floated from Penny's lips just as she ignited, bursting into bright, hot pleasure and crying at the rush of love and joy. Her body throbbed with it and Penny captured Agnes's lips for a deep, clinging kiss as the last tremors of her orgasm made her shiver and jump. "*My* Agnes," she whispered reverently.

This Agnes was Penny's alone and was truly treasured. Penny adored every facet and was treated to sides of Agnes's personality that even Walker or June never got to see. There was Agnes's "secret" soft side and her fierce loyalty that only her friends and family got to see. Although, word had gotten out and tales of Agnes's devotion to June, Penny, and her many nieces and nephews were beginning to spread, intermingling with her reputation for being a wrecking ball.

But Penny was privy to Agnes's deepest thoughts and insecurities and her wildest wishes. They shared their fears and fondest memories and knew the other as well as they knew themselves. Both were intensely competitive and admitted to having the same "newlywed game show" fantasy after their wedding. Neither could stomach the thought of losing or being the one to fumble a question so they delighted in sharing even the most trivial fact or favorite thing.

As a result, Penny knew that Agnes's first crushes were John Travolta *and* Olivia Newton-John and that she didn't like green olives and despised canned mushrooms. And Agnes *loved* peanut butter cups. They were her secret weakness and Melinda kept a mini fridge stocked with them in Agnes's office. Agnes admitted that she rarely had use for an actual office since she had a smartphone and Melinda handled so many of her affairs. But that was where Agnes took the occasional business call and when she was done, she threw her feet up on her desk and enjoyed her peanut butter cups.

Who wouldn't love a woman like that? Penny felt so extraordinarily lucky to be the one to kiss Agnes's perfect feet. And her perfect...

She purred as she rolled them over and slid down Agnes's body. "You're my world, Mrs. Cameron-Tucker." Penny got chills every time she said or heard it. Agnes had insisted on hyphenating her last name and made sure *everyone* addressed her properly because she believed it was an honor to be married to Penny and be a Tucker.

"Thank you, Mrs. Tucker-Cameron!" Agnes giggled as Penny bit into her side. Then, she gasped and groaned when Penny's lips cruised over her mound.

Penny had hyphenated her last name because she wanted the world to know that she belonged to Agnes and June. She was proud of who the Camerons had become and what their name had come to mean in Manhattan. Agnes and Walker were no longer feared or the subjects of salacious gossip. Instead, they were described as devoted and doting parents, siblings, and spouses who were loyal friends and thoughtful philanthropists.

"And I love the way we taste together," Penny whispered, dragging her tongue over Agnes's petal-soft flesh. She lapped and sucked, greedily seeking every drop of their bliss.

There was no telling what tomorrow would bring. Camp Laurel's grand opening could go just as smoothly as Penny had planned. Or it could be one catastrophe after another. The only thing that Penny was assured of was that she was about to make Agnes come again. And tomorrow, after they rode the boat back across the lake to their cabin—regardless of how opening day went—Penny would bury her face in Agnes's pussy and make her come again and again.

Nothing could be better than that and Penny couldn't have manifested a more beautiful happily ever after if she'd swallowed a handful of crystals, bathed herself in moon water, or tattooed a sigil on her forehead.

The End

A letter from K. Sterling

Dear Reader,

Thank you so much for your time and for reading *The Enchanting Nanny*. I hope you had fun falling in love with Penny, Agnes, and June! Before you go, I'd appreciate it if you'd consider leaving a review. Your review would really help me and help other readers find their way to us. And I promise, I read and appreciate every single one of them. Even the negative reviews. I want your honest feedback so I know how to steal your heart.

Please help me out by leaving a review!

Once again, thank you from the very bottom of my heart. I love you for sharing your time with us and hope we'll see you again soon.

Love and happy reading,
K.

About the Author

K. Sterling writes like a demon and is mother to Alex, Zoe, Stella, and numerous gay superheroes. She's also a history nerd, a *Lord of the Rings* fan, and a former counterintelligence agent. She has self-published dozens of M/M romance novels including the popular *Boys of Lake Cliff* series and *Beautiful Animal*. K. Sterling is known for fast-paced romantic thrillers and touching gay romcoms. There might be goosebumps and some gore but there's always true love and lots of laughter.

Made in the USA
Middletown, DE
04 September 2023

37552369R00188